Praise for Mary Gentle

"A rare narrative talent."
C.J. Cherryh

"A fine writer."
Marion Zimmer Bradley

"A major talent at work."
Interzone

"Colorful and inventive . . .
Gentle writes with considerable energy and vividness."
New York Newsday

"She is a writer who knows politics and human nature and gives the reader an exciting romp to boot."
Julian May

"My profoundest gratitude to Mary Gentle for creating such a marvelous world and all the myriad wonders."
Anne McCaffrey

Other Books by
Mary Gentle
in "The Book of Ash" series

A SECRET HISTORY
CARTHAGE ASCENDANT

Coming Soon in Hardcover

LOST BURGUNDY

Other Books by the Author

A HAWK IN SILVER
SCHOLARS AND SOLDIERS
RATS AND GARGOYLES
THE ARCHITECTURE OF DESIRE
LEFT TO HIS OWN DEVICES
GRUNTS!
GOLDEN WITCHBREED
ANCIENT LIGHT

MARY GENTLE

THE WILD MACHINES

THE BOOK OF ASH, #3

An Imprint of HarperCollins*Publishers*

This is a work of fiction. Names, characters, places, and incidents are products of the author's imagination or are used fictitiously and are not to be construed as real. Any resemblance to actual events, locales, organizations, or persons, living or dead, is entirely coincidental.

EOS
An Imprint of HarperCollins*Publishers*
10 East 53rd Street
New York, New York 10022-5299

Cover art by Donato Giancola
Library of Congress Catalog Card Number: 00-132294
ISBN: 0-380-81113-8
www.eosbooks.com

First Eos paperback printing: August 2000

Printed in the U.S.A.

WCD 10 9 8 7 6 5 4 3 2 1

Note to the Reader

Since both political and historical considerations have led to separate publication of the four Books of ASH, this note is intended to bring the reader up to date with the two previous volumes: *A Secret History* and *Carthage Ascendant.*

The fifteenth-century mercenary captain, Ash, has discovered that the North African Visigoth invasion of Europe is being led by a slave general who is her twin. Ash also learns that her "saint's voice" guiding her in battle is, in fact, the voice of the Visigothic *machina rei militaris* (Latin translation: "tactical computer"), transmitted overseas from Carthage. The Faris, her twin, is using the same voice to advise her in the invasion. Ash determines to take her mercenary company from Burgundy to Carthage and destroy the machine.

Charles, Duke of Burgundy, first insists on giving battle to the invading Visigoth army. At Auxonne, the Visigoths field golem and Greek Fire weapons; Duke Charles is injured; and during the confusion Ash is separated from the company, captured, and sent as a prisoner to the capital of the Visigoth Empire, Carthage.

During the coronation of the new Visigoth King-Caliph, Gelimer, Ash attempts to "download" knowledge from the *machina rei militaris*, to find out whether her company was massacred on the battlefield of Auxonne. She finds herself making contact with new voices that are not her *machina* at all—they call themselves the Wild Machines.

Ash, having failed to destroy the *machina*, and on the run escaping from the Visigoth forces in Carthage, witnesses an aurora over the southern pyramids outside the city. She realizes that these structures are the Wild Machines. Taking them by surprise, she downloads the information that they have been feeding their own strategic goals into the *machina rei militaris* for centuries, unknown to the Visigoth King-Caliph and his commanders. The Wild Machines desire the invasion and complete eradication of the kingdom of Burgundy. Ash cannot gain an answer to her question: *why is Burgundy so important?*

Ash finally discovers that, other than herself and the Faris, the Wild Machines' only channel of communication with the world of men is via the *machina rei militaris*. To have destroyed it would have been to destroy their influence on mankind. Leaving it intact means the Wild Machines' war will be pursued with ever-increasing ferocity and efficiency, to the point of the total devastation of Europe.

This third volume contains the remainder of the English translation of the "Fraxinus" manuscript, together with copies of the original publishers' correspondence.

[Original e-mail documents found inserted, folded, in British Library copy of 3rd Edition, Ash: The Lost History of Burgundy, (2001) — possibly in chronological order of editing original typescript?]

Message: #139 (Pierce Ratcliff)
Subject: Ash
Date: 02/12/00 at 12.09 p.m.
From: Longman@

format address deleted
other details encrypted and
non-recoverably deleted

Pierce--

There isn't an easy way to say this. The editorial decision is that we are going to have to suspend publication of your work.

I'm going to do what I can. Maybe I can find another publishing firm for you, one that would be interested in a book of mediaeval myths and legends?

I know that wouldn't be much consolation. You've spent so many years editing the 'Ash' texts under the impression that they were genuine historical documents. But it's all I can think of, right now.

When you do fly back to the UK, let's meet. Have lunch. Something. Yes?

Love, Anna

Message: #204 (Anna Longman)
Subject: Ash Project
Date: 02/12/00 at 4.28 p.m.
From: Ngrant@

format address deleted
other details encrypted by
non-discoverable personal key

Anna, please--

Anna, you have got to let me publish. I know that we're close to deadline for spring publication. Don't call a halt now. Please.

—but why *should* you let me carry on? The Tunisian archaeological evidence has collapsed completely!

Anna, I am pleading with Isobel to have the radio-carbon dating tests on the metal joints of the 'messenger-golem' repeated. The results we had through could be WRONG. I don't believe these 'golem' are merely modern fakes that the expedition has dug out of the silt outside Tunis. I just don't believe it. They are genuine remains from the period of the Visigoth settlement of Carthage: I *know* they are!!

And yet how can I _not_ believe they're fakes, when scientific evidence says the bronze metalwork was cast post-1945?

Schliemann discovered Troy in 1871 by searching where Homer sited it in the ILIAD—but he didn't discover, when he excavated it, that the Bronze Age city of Troy had been constructed in the 1870s! That is the equivalent of what we are facing here.

I know what you'll say. How could we ever have thought this was _history_? The texts I'm using seem to have been re-classified from 'Mediaeval History' to 'Fiction'. And my 'Fraxinus' document, my one great discovery, telling us about the woman Ash 'hearing voices' from a fifteenth century 'Stone Golem computer'? Legends and fabrications! Unbelievable lies and myth!

I'm going to fly out with Isobel to the expedition's ship, now that we FINALLY have official permission. Ironic. I suppose I have very little justification for doing so, but what *else* can I do? I feel bereaved. I know that Isobel is too tactful to point out that I should just fly back to the UK now. I suppose a few days watching the undersea cameras give us images of the seabed north of Tunis will at least take my mind off all this. We might even find a Roman shipwreck or two.

I haven't slept.

Anna, I have finished translating the penultimate section of 'Fraxinus me fecit'. I had an explanatory note that I intended to put with this part of the 'Ash' manuscript

But it's all irrelevant now. The golem are fakes: the 'Angelotti' manuscript is a mere fiction. The ambiguities of the 'Fraxinus' text are irrelevant.

--Pierce

- -

Message: #140 (Pierce Ratcliff)
Subject: Ash
Date: 02/12/00 at 11.01 p.m.
From: Longman@

format address deleted
other details encrypted
and non-recoverably deleted

Pierce–

I'm not even sure you have a 'Visigothic Carthage' land site there now. What is Isobel Napier-Grant saying?

What you've told me so far is that you expected the 'Fraxinus' text to prove the existence of a 15c Visigoth settlement in the area of Arab Carthage, powerful enough to mount a crusade into southern Europe. I could have swallowed this (assuming that things like the burning of Venice are chronicler's poetic licence), and I guess I could have believed that these Visigoths failed, went back to Carthage, and interest in them was lost when Burgundy collapsed later that year.

I guess it's even reasonable to think your 'Visigothic' Carthage was probably so weakened by this expedition that they were overrun by Moors fairly shortly afterwards and wiped out. Or maybe they returned to Spain and were lost in the confusion of the Reconquista. And any evidence has been ignored here on the grounds of race and class.

But I don't see _now_—if your texts are Romances, and the 'messenger-golem' a modern fake based on the texts—what *possible* reason you have for thinking your Doctor Isobel's site is anything to do with any Visigoths!

Pierce, it's *over*. I know it's not nice, but face it. There is no book. Ash isn't history, she's Robin Hood, Arthur, Lancelot—_legend_.

We might still get a programme out of Dr Napier-Grant's dig and her problems with the Tunisian authorities; and I don't see why you shouldn't be a script adviser if that does come off.

Give it a few days, then start thinking about it.

Love,
Anna

Message: #205 (Anna Longman)
Subject: Ash/Carthage
Date: 03/12/00 at 11.42 p.m.
From: Ngrant@

Previous message missing?
format address deleted
other details encrypted by non-discoverable personal key

Anna--

Your last came through scrambled—machine code: did you attach a .jpg? It's hopelessly corrupted! Try again, I'll reply later, much later—Isobel needs this link for the next few hours at least.

I'm no longer at the land site, I'm on the ship; that's one reason the transmission might have failed. We flew out by helicopter this morning to the expedition's ship, the HANNIBAL; we're at sea five miles off the North African coast.

You must not pass this on, any of it, not to Jonathan whatsisname, your MD, to nobody, don't even talk about it in your sleep

Isobel just said get off the machine so here it is:

She and her team have been out here since September primarily because of the discoveries made by the team from the Institute for Exploration, Connecticut, in July and August of 1997. If you remember it from the media coverage, that expedition found—among other things—five Roman shipwrecks, below the 1000 metre mark, in an area of the sea about twenty miles off Tunis. (They had a US Navy nuclear submarine helping them out with sonar. We are using low-frequency search equipment, the same as that used in oil-exploration.)

The wrecks indicate that, far from skulking along the coastline to Sicily, merchant ships since 200 BC have been sailing *deep-water* routes across the Mediterranean. What they found was one of the reasons Isobel could get funding to come and investigate the land site here, and get local government permission to do coastal exploration.

Now OUR ROVs have been sending pictures back, also from below the 1000 metre mark. We thought this had to be a mis-reading, they're going down in shallow coastal seas. But it isn't an instrument malfunction, they ARE sending back from that depth—too deep for human divers, with the limited equipment here. What the ROVs have found is a marine trench in the shallow water, about 60 kilometres north-west of the ruins of old Carthage—I almost wrote, from the ruins of OUR Carthage. And it's what I've hoped and prayed for, since the disastrous carbon-dating report.

We have found a harbour with five headlands. It's all there, under the silt, you can see the outlines clearly. I have been watching green night-vision-enhanced pictures, from bulky machines diving in unclear waters, but I can tell you, it's there

Later—

Anna, it's unbelievable. Isobel is shaken. We have found Carthage, yes, I always thought we might find my 'Visigoth settlement' on this coast; and it's the way it's described in the 'Ash' manuscript, in 'Fraxinus'. Oh Anna. I've found her. I've found the IMPOSSIBLE.

Isobel had me there to direct the ROV technicians. There I was in front of these banks of machines, slightly queasy (I don't like the sea) and a rough pencil sketch of what I'd worked out from the manuscripts MUST be the geography of Ash's Carthage. Great moments always happen when you're wet, or hot, or slightly queasy; when you're looking the other way, as it were. I was trying to pick out the inner wall, the 'Citadel' wall that the manuscripts mention.

We found the wall, on one of the headlands, and we found what was plainly a structure. This IS Gothic Carthage, below the waves, this IS what the manuscripts describe, I have to keep reminding myself of this, because what happened next is so impossible, so shattering in its implications, that I feel I will never sleep again—I feel that my life from here is downhill, THIS is my discovery, THIS is what will get my (and Isobel's) names into the history books, nothing will ever be quite this much of a pinnacle again.

I had the ROV down in the broken walls, sending back pictures from its cameras of silt-covered roofs and rooms, all in a state that would accord very much with earthquake damage. And I turned the ROV to the right—what would have happened if I hadn't? I suppose the same discovery, but later; people are going to be picking over these ruins for the next forty years: this is Howard Carter, this is Tutankhamen all over again.

I turned the ROV to the right and it went into a building that still had some of its roof. This is something the technicians hate. There are all sorts of dangers of losing the ROV, I suppose. Into a building, and there it was: a courtyard, and a broken wall—a broken wall ABOVE WHAT WOULD HAVE BEEN THE HARBOUR.

Even Isobel agreed then, better to lose the ROV in the attempt than not make the attempt. I can see it all, in my mind, from the 'Fraxinus' manuscript, and there it was, Anna, there were the walls of the room, and the stairwell going down, and the great carved stone slabs that would have closed these rooms off from each other.

I suppose it took six or eight hours, I know we had two shift changes of technicians, Isobel was with me all the time, I didn't see her eat, I didn't eat. You see, I knew where it had to be. It must have taken us four hours just to get orientated—among lumps of mud-covered, mud-coloured rocks, in nothing that looks ANYTHING like a city, trying to discover which direction might have been north-east, before the quake, and where, down in that sightless, electrically-illuminated depths it might be. 'House Leofric', I mean. What the manuscript calls 'House Leofric'—and its 'north-east quadrant'.

No, I am not mad. I know I am not quite sane at the moment, but not mad.

We have two ROVs, I was prepared to sacrifice this one. The technicians teased it down, in, under; all the time at the mercy of currents, thermals. I am dumb-founded by their expertise, now, at the time I didn't even notice. The screens kept bringing us lurching pictures of steps, inside a stairwell. I think the moment that Isobel wept was when the stone steps stopped, and the well became just a smooth-sided masonry tube going down into darkness, and we managed to get a close-up of one wall. It had a socket in it, for taking a framework of wooden steps.

All this time I wasn't sure which floor of the House the ROV was exploring, there's enough damage to make it uncertain—the upper floors are barely a house! And it powered infinitely slowly and cautiously through room after room—up a floor, down a floor, through a gap—the silt covers bones, and amphorae, and coins; woodbores have eaten all the furniture. Down, down, room on room, and no way to know where we were, in the pressure and the cold and the depth.

When It came, it was just another broken room, quite suddenly, but Isobel swore out loud: she recognised the silhouette instantly from the description. It was a minute before I knew what it must be. The techs couldn't understand Isobel's excitement, one of them said 'It's just a fucking statue, for Christ's sake,' and then it came into focus for me.

Read the translation, Anna! See what 'Fraxinus' says. The second golem, the Stone Golem, is 'the shape of a man above, and beneath, nothing but a dais on which the games of war may be played'.

What I didn't really appreciate was how BIG the Stone Golem is.

The torso and head and arms are gargantuan, three times the size of a man. Twelve or fifteen feet high. It sits there, blindly, in the seas off Africa, and it gazes into the darkness with sightless, stone eyes. The features are Northern European, not Berber, or sub-Saharan

African; and every muscle, every ligament, every hair is defined in stone.

I think that the Rabbi had a mordant sense of humour. I suspect that, whereas 'Fraxinus' tells us that the mobile golems resembled the Rabbi, the Stone Golem itself is a portrait of that noble Visigoth /amir/, Radonic.

The silt hides colour, of course, makes everything a uniform brown-green in the million-candlepower lights. The stonework itself I think is granite, or red sandstone. I cannot tell you the quality of the workmanship. What seems to have corroded are the metal joints of the arms, wrists, and hands.

Below, it is part of a dais. As far as I can tell, the torso joins seamlessly to a surface of marble or sandstone. Pressured jets of water might clear some of the silt, to see if there are markings on the dais, but Isobel and the team are frantically taking film footage of this, they won't touch it until everything has been recorded, recorded beyond a shadow of a doubt, beyond all necessity for proof, no proof needed, because it is, it IS, the Stone Golem, Ash's MACHINA REI MILITARIS.

And I'll tell you something, Anna. Even Isobel isn't trying to come up with a method by which somebody can fake THIS.

What I need to know—what I can't know, because it has been non-functional and lost under the sea for five hundred years—is, is this the MACHINA REI MILITARIS that 'Fraxinus' says it is? Is it a temple statue, a religious icon—it can't be anything else, can it, Anna? Anything else is because I haven't slept for I can't remember how long, and I haven't eaten, and I'm light-headed but I can't stop thinking it: IS it a mechanical chess-player? IS it a war-machine?

Oh, suppose it was something more. Suppose it WAS the voice that spoke to her?

Two-thirds of a mile down, in the deep trench that an earth-quake might have left, in the cold and the dark, five hundred years under the sea that has seen enough wars since then—fighting ships, aircraft, mines; I can't help wondering, would the MACHINA REI MILI-

TARIS cope with combined-ops warfare, if Ash were alive what would it tell her now, if it HAD a voice?

Isobel needs this computer now. Anna, please, you said to me once, if the golem are true, what else is? This is. The ruins of Visigoth Carthage: an archaeological site on the bed of the sea. _There_are_no_50_billion_dollar_frauds,_ and that is what this would have to be.

Anna, this supports everything that's in the 'Fraxinus' manuscript!

But how could the carbon-dating on the messenger-golem be wrong? Tell me what to think, I'm so exhausted I don't know.

--Pierce

Message: #143 (Pierce Ratcliff)
Subject: Ash
Date: 03/12/00 at 11.53 p.m.
From: Longman@

format address deleted
other details encrypted and non-recoverably deleted

Pierce--

Jesus Christ!

I won't breathe a word, I promise. Not until the expedition's ready. Oh, Pierce, this is SO BIG! I'm so sorry I doubted you!

Pierce, you have _got_ to send me the next part you have of /Fraxinus/ that's translated. Send me the text. If _two_ of us are looking at it, there's more chance we might pick up clues, things you need to tell Dr Napier-Grant about. I won't even keep it in the office, I'll take it home with me—I'll keep it in my briefcase all the time, it won't get more than arm's-length away from me!

And you _have_ to finish the translation!!

Love,
Anna

Message: #237 (Anna Longman)
Subject: Ash/Carthage
Date: 04/12/00 at 01.36 a.m.
From: Ngrant@

format address deleted
other details encrypted
by non-discoverable personal
key

Anna--

I know. I know! Now we need 'Fraxinus' more than ever! But there are nonetheless _problems_ in the later part of 'Fraxinus' that we cannot afford to be blind to!

I had always planned to send you an explanatory note with the penultimate part of 'Fraxinus', 'Knight of the Wasteland'. Even without the problems of golem, C14 dating, and inauthentic manuscripts, 'Fraxinus me fecit' still ends on a cliff-hanger in November 1476: it doesn't tell us what happened *afterwards*!

I have skipped over the final pages of the 'Angelotti' ms. Ash's ships sail from the North African coast on or around 12 September 1476. I omit a short passage which deals with the expedition's return to mainland Europe. (I would like to include this in the final text of the book. The details of daily life on board a Venetian galley are fascinating!) Their retreat to Marseilles occupies around three weeks. I calculate that the ships left Carthage on the night of the 10th September 1476, and—with storms, and bad navigation, and a stop at Malta to take on food and put off the sick who would otherwise have died—the voyage took until 30 September. The ships then landed (during the moon's last quarter) at Marseilles.

It seems, from the 'Angelotti' manuscript, to have taken between three and four days for the company to have regrouped, acquired mules and supplies, and set out for the north. Antonio Angelotti devotes a large part of his text to regretting his lost cannon, which he describes in great technical detail. He spends rather less time—a bare two lines—on the direction in which the exiled Earl of Oxford decided to take ship again and to sail away with his own men.

It is at this point that the 'Angelotti' ms. cuts off (a few final pages are missing from the 'Missaglia' treatise). 'Fraxinus me fecit' adds only a few bald sentences: that the country was, by this time, in a state of emergency, with famine, cold, and hysteria emptying the towns and devastating the countryside.

Evidently, from the little we can glean from Angelotti, the company disembarked at Marseilles, in conditions that we would now think of as resembling a nuclear winter. With Ash leading them, they proceeded on a forced march up the valley of the Rhone River, from Marseilles north to Avignon, and further north towards Lyons. It says something for Ash as a commander that she could have groups of armed men travel several hundred miles under very loose control, during unprecedentedly terrible weather conditions—a force with less effective leadership would surely have been far more likely to hole up in a local hamlet or village outside Marseilles, and hope to wait out the 'sunless' winter.

Given their lack of horses, and the fact that a starving peasantry had eaten the countryside bare of crops and draught animals, stealing river ships was probably their easiest option. Moreover, in a countryside that is pitch-dark twenty-four hours a day, without reliable maps or guides, following the Rhone valley at least ensured that the company would not get hopelessly lost. A fragmentary reference indicates that they gave up river-travel itself just south of Lyons when the Rhone froze over completely, and marched towards the Burgundian border, following the Saône north from Lyons.

It is not recorded that any of the French ducs reacted to this incursion on their territory. They may have had too much to cope with themselves, with famine, insurrection, and war likely. More probably, in the winter and night conditions, they simply didn't notice.

Given the logistics of getting two hundred and fifty men across Europe in darkness, together with all the baggage they could carry on their backs, and the number of starving survivors who began to attach themselves to the company (either to give sexual favours for food, or to attempt to rob them)—given the sheer work involved in keeping her men on the road, keeping them fed, keeping them from mutiny or plain desertion, it is perhaps not surprising that 'Fraxinus' details almost no interaction on a personal level between Ash and anyone else in the company until the hiatus immediately following their arrival outside Dijon.

We do know, from the beginning of the 'Fraxinus' manuscript, that the company gained a position very close to Dijon itself without being seen by Visigoth scouts. The company moved along the cultivated edges of the true wildwood—the virgin forested areas that still, at this point, covered a great deal of Europe. Travel would be slow, especially if weapons and baggage were to be transported, but it would be sure. It would be almost the only certain way of reaching Dijon without being wiped out by a detachment of one of the Visigoth armies.

'Fraxinus' states that the journey occupied almost seven weeks (the period from 4th October to 14 November). By 14 November 1476, then, Ash and between two and three hundred of her armed men, with mules and baggage train, but without horses or guns, are five miles west of Dijon, just south-west of the main road to Auxonne.

Anna, I *did* think the 'Fraxinus' manuscript was either written or dictated by Ash herself; I was certain it was a reliable primary source. Now—with Carthage 1000 metres below me!—I'm even MORE certain!

BUT—there was always going to be *a* problem. You see, I had always hoped that the discovery of the 'Fraxinus' document would allow me my niche in academic history as the person who solved the 'missing summer' problem. Although, in fact, given the problem with dates—some of Ash's exploits fit far better into what we know of the events of 1475; others can only have taken place in 1476; and the texts treat them all as one continuous series of events—it may be a 'missing year and a half' problem!

Records appear to document Ash fighting against Charles the Bold's forces in June 1475/6. She is unaccounted for over what appears to be the summer of 1476; turns up again in winter; and dies fighting at Nancy (5 January 1476/7). There are some missing weeks between the end of 'Fraxinus' (mid-November 1476), and the point where conventional history picks Ash up again. (Some mysteries must be left for other scholars, after all!) 'Fraxinus' breaks off abruptly, evidently incomplete.

If 'Fraxinus' does not mesh seamlessly with recorded history, that is not a problem.

The *problem* is, that in the autumn of 1476, Charles the Bold is involved in his campaign against Lorraine, besieging Nancy on 22 October. He stays at that siege all through November and December; and dies there in January, fighting against Duke René's reinforcements (an army of Lorrainers and volunteer Swiss).

I had initially expected this latter part of 'Fraxinus' to indicate that Ash returns to a Europe in which the Visigoth raid has failed and is in retreat.

It does not. 'Fraxinus' has the Visigoths _still_ *present* in Europe in force as late as the November of 1476.

It has France and the Duchy of Savoy at peace, by treaty, with the Carthaginian Empire; it has the ex-Emperor Frederick III of the Holy Roman Empire—now controlled from Carthage—making inroads into ruling the Swiss Cantons as a Visigoth satrap, hand in hand with Daniel de Quesada. It has, in fact, everything you would expect to see if the Visigoth invasion had _succeeded_.

If this is 1476, where is Charles's war against Lorraine? Conversely, if this is 1475, then my theory that the incursion of the Visigoths was forgotten in the collapse of Burgundy falls apart, since that won't occur for another twelve months!

I can only assume that something in the dates within this text is deeply misleading, and that I have not yet understood it completely.

Whatever we have not yet understood, I do understand this much: 'Fraxinus' has given us Carthage. Isobel says being able to identify a site this early is amazing!

I will send you my final version of the last section as soon as I can—but how can I stay away from the ROV cameras!!!

I am looking at *Carthage.*

I keep thinking about FRAXINUS's 'wild machines'.

–Pierce

PART ONE

14 November AD 1476–15 November AD 1476

KNIGHT OF THE WASTELAND

I

RAIN STREAMED OFF the raised visor of her helmet, streamed off the sodden demi-gown and brigandine that she wore, and soaked her hose inside her high boots. Ash could feel it, but not see it—the sound of falling water and the unobstructed blisteringly cold air told her she must be close to the tree line, but she could see nothing in the pitch-darkness of the forest.

Someone—Rickard?—blundered into her shoulder, throwing her forward into the slick, hard bark of a tree trunk. It grazed her mittened hand. An unseen spray of soaked autumn leaves slapped her across the face, dashing cold water into her eyes and mouth.

"Shit!"

"Sorry, boss."

Ash waved the boy Rickard to silence, realized he couldn't see her, and groped until she caught his sodden wool shoulder, and pulled his ear down level with her mouth:

"There are umpteen thousand Visigoths out there: would you mind keeping *quiet*!"

Cold rain soaked through her belted demi-gown, and through the velvet-and-steel plates of the brigandine, making the arming doublet against her warm flesh uncomfortably cold and damp. The constant rattle of rain in the darkness, and the whispering creak of trees swaying in the night wind, prevented her hearing anything more than a few paces away. She took another cautious step, arms outstretched, and simultaneously hooked her scabbard into a low-hanging branch, and skidded her heel into a mud rut six inches deep.

"Shit on a fucking *stick*! Where's John Price? Where are the fucking scouts!"

She heard something suspiciously like a chuckle, under the noise of the falling rain. Rickard's shoulder, against hers, juddered.

"Madonna," a quiet voice said, to her left and below her, "light the lamp. There's a great deal of forest between here and Dijon; how much of it would you like us to cover?"

"Ah, shit—okay. Rickard . . ."

Several minutes passed. Occasionally the boy's arm or elbow jogged her, as he wrestled with a pierced iron lantern, a candle, and presumably the lit slow match he had brought with him. Ash smelled smoldering powder. The velvet blackness pressed against her face. Cold drops of rain spattered her head as she turned her face up, letting her night vision attempt to distinguish between the crowns of trees and the invisible sky.

Nothing.

She flinched, repeatedly, as rain struck her on the cheeks and eyes and mouth. Sheltering her face with one soaked sheepskin mitten, she thought she distinguished a faint alteration of darkness and blackness.

"Angelotti? You think this rain's stopping?"

"No!"

Rickard's dark lantern finally glimmered, a weak yellow light in the surrounding pitch-darkness. Ash caught a glimpse of another figure shrouded in heavy woollen hood and cloak, seemingly kneeling at her side—a sucking sound made her startle. The kneeling figure stood up.

"Fucking *mud*," Master Gunner Angelotti said.

The light from the lantern failed, serving only to illuminate the silver streaks of falling water droplets. Before that, Ash had one glimpse of Angelotti, his cloak torn and his boots clotted with mud to his upper thighs. She grinned briefly to herself.

"Look on the bright side," she said. "This is a whole lot better than the conditions we've just come through to get here—it's *warmer*! And, any raghead patrols are going to stay really close to home in this murk."

"But we won't see anything!" Rickard's face above the lantern, in his hood, was a chiaroscuro demon-mask. "Boss, maybe we should go back to the camp."

"John Price said he saw broken cloud. I'm betting the rain's going to ease up before long. Green Christ! Does anybody know where we *are*?"

"In a dark wood," her Italian master gunner said, with sardonic satisfaction. "Madonna, the guide from Price's lance is lost, I think."

"Don't go yelling for him . . ."

Ash faced away from the lantern's tiny glow. She let the dark into her eyes again, gazing blindly into blackness and rain. The sleeting drops found the gap between sleeve and mitten at her wrist; eased cold rivulets of water down between sallet-tail and gown collar. The cold water made her hot flesh shudder and begin to chill.

"This way," she decided.

Reaching out a hand, she grasped Rickard's arm and Angelotti's gloved hand. Stumbling and lurching through the mud and thick leaf mold underfoot, she banged against branches, shook down water from trees, unwilling to take her eyes from the faintest of silhouettes in front of her—the waving twigs of hornbeam trees against the open night sky beyond the wood.

"Maybe around—*whuff*!" Her numbed, cold hand slid off Rickard's arm. Angelotti's strong fingers gripped, tightly; she slid down onto one knee and hung from his grasp, momentarily unable to get her feet under her. Boot soles skidded in the mud. Her leg went out from under her, and she sat down heavily and unguardedly in a mass of wet leaves, sharp twigs, and cold mud.

"Son of a *bitch*!" She hauled her twisted sword belt back round, feeling sightlessly down the hilt to the scabbard—trapped under her leg—for breaks in the thin wood. "*Shit*!"

"Keep that fucking noise down!" A voice whispered. "Put that fucking lantern out! Do you want an entire fucking Visigoth legion up here? The old battle-ax will have your fucking arse!"

Ash, in English, said, "Too damn right she will, Master Price."

"Boss?"

"Yeah." She grinned, invisible in the black night. Grabbing for arms and hands at random, she found herself pulled back onto her feet. The cold was bitter enough to make her body shake, and she beat her hands against her arms—seeing neither, in the darkness. A flurry of rain made her duck her head, then turn her wet face in the direction of the unobstructed wind.

"We're on the wood's edge?" she said. "Lucky you found us, Sergeant."

Price muttered something in a northern dialect, in which "making enough noise for six pair of yoked oxen" was the only phrase Ash clearly overheard.

"We're farther along here, on top of the bluff," the man added. "Rain's been easing this last hour. Reckon you'll get sight of the city from here, soon, boss."

"Where's the ragheads now?"

A movement in the black night, which might have been a waving arm. "Down there, someplace."

Green Christ! If I could just ask the machina rei militaris:

Dijon, southern border of the Duchy of Burgundy: strength and disposition of siege camp. Ask the Stone Golem: *name of battle commander, tactical plans for the next week—*

A shudder went through her skin that was nothing to do with the bone-chilling rain. For a moment, the darkness was not the mulch-odored, bitter-cold, open night blackness of a Frankish forest, but the shit-smelling, stomach-turning darkness under the Citadel of Carthage, kneeling with a dead man's body in the sewers, and hearing voices louder than God blast through her head, in that solitude where she is used to hearing only the *machina rei militaris*.

And for a heart-stopping moment she whipped her head around, glaring into the darkness, afraid of seeing the same celestial light that had burned in the desert outside Carthage, seven weeks before. The aurora that glimmers above the red silt-brick pyramids . . .

Nothing but wet night.

Don't be stupid, girl. The Wild Machines want you dead—but they can't know where you are.

Not unless I tell the Stone Golem.

If I can live nine weeks without asking tactical advice, Ash thought grimly—*if I could manage the road from Marseilles to Lyon,* Christus Viridianus!, *without advice—I don't need to ask now.* I don't need to.

Faint rustles in the undergrowth made her suppose Price's men and their lost guide had come up to join them. Other than the lighter darkness in front of her, and the solid darkness behind, there was no way to distinguish anything in the blackness in which they stood. The infinite, invisible, random dropping of water on her was a continuous soaking presence.

"The moon will have risen by now, madonna," Angelotti's soft voice said, beside her. "A first quarter, by my calculations. *If* we see it."

"I trust your celestial mechanics," Ash murmured, groping blindly with a cold-numbed hand to check her sword hilt and scabbard again. "Got any predictions about this fucking rain?"

"If it has rained for eighteen days solid, madonna, why should it stop now!"

"Ah, well done, Angeli. I only keep you on the company books for your morale value, you know."

One of Price's men rumbled a chuckle. By common consent, they moved back into the underbrush, squatting down in any scrap of cover: she heard their movement without seeing them. Ash, hand up to keep invisible briars out of her eyes, rested a knee in the sodden, puddled grass. After a while, she felt the heat of her flesh warm it; and then, the cold begin to suck the heat from her body. The pattering of the rain on the leafless trees faded into the background.

Filthy weather, enemy pickets: this could be any campaign I've been on these last ten years. Treat it that way. *Forget anything else.*

"There." She reached out blindly, at last; eyes on the sky, and touched a shoulder. "A star."

"Cloud's breaking up," Price's voice said.

His shoulder had been visible, Ash realized, as she lowered her head, a darker silhouette against the sky. She quickly glanced backward and forward, seeing the black swaying branches of trees, and two or three other silhouettes distinguishably human: nothing else in nature is head-and-shoulder-shaped.

"We all secure here?"

"We're on the bluff above the Suzon River, west of the Auxonne road." Price grunted. "Not skylined. Wood's behind us; no one could see us up here without they were on top of us."

"Okay: make sure all helmets are covered by hoods. If we do get any moonlight, I don't want us flashing away like heliographs."

John Price turned away to mutter orders. Ash realized she was seeing his breath, white in the cold air. She stripped off her wet sheepskin mittens and, with numb fingers, unbuckled her sallet. Rickard received it, concealing it under a fold of his sodden cloak. Clean, bitter-cold air bit at her ears, cheeks, and chin.

The rain ceased, suddenly, within the space of a minute. A constant dripping came from the trees around her, but the wind dropped. With that came a new, intense cold; and she glanced up to see the trailing ragged end of a black cloud against a gray sky, the cloud bank running high and fast into the east.

What's it like here, now?

Cold biting to the bone, she finds her flesh remembering Dijon of the golden strip-fields and heavy vines; Dijon with blue sky and blazing sun seen over its white walls and blue-tiled roofs; the company's camp in Dijon's meadows smelling of sweat and horse dung and the thick sweetness of cow parsley.

Stout-walled Dijon: richest capital of southern Burgundy, stiff with merchants wealthy enough to show off and keep architects, masons, painters, and embroiderers in business; Dijon thronging with the household and army and ordnance of Charles, Great Duke of the West . . . A white jewel in a rich countryside.

Before we rode out to Auxonne, and got our asses kicked.

Her own breath smoked white before her face. The night became full of the noise of dripping water, gaunt bark shedding still-clinging rain. She realized that the shapes of trees were becoming more apparent. Grass and dead bracken had a visible verge, two yards in front of her.

Beyond that was a drop.

Far out across the open air in front of her, a gray pearl of cloud parted in the east and became a shatteringly bright silver semicircle.

"That river's up," she murmured, her night vision dazzled by the moon, edging forward on all fours, the cold puddles seeping through her hose.

Eyes adjusting to the half-moon's light, she could see the slope of a bluff dropping down in front of her, too steep to be climbed easily. A hundred paces below, scrub and bushes were an impenetrable darkness. Beyond them, she would not have known where to look for the road to Auxonne, but she saw it glimmering: one long sheet of puddles and water-filled ruts reflecting the moon. A black silhouette of limestone wooded hills, to the south. *And we marched down that road with the Burgundian army how long ago—three months? De Vere said they were holding out, but that was nine or ten weeks ago . . .*

Roberto, are you down there?

Further east, by a half mile or more, the silver light shone back from swelling waters that lapped up close to the road—the Suzon River, flooding. Squint as she might in the moonlight, Ash could not make out anything beyond it, no black obstruction that might be Dijon's city walls. Glimmers of light might be the other river, the Ouche; or the slates on roofs. A glance at the stars told her it was not long past Lauds.[1]

"Sergeant Price? What do the scouts report?" Ash said, switching without thought into the military-camp version of English that she knew.

The first-quarter moon made white chalk of the man's face beside her. John Price, made a Sergeant of Bill in Car-

[1] 3 a.m.

racci's place, after Carthage—momentarily she saw, not Price's moon-whitened features, but Carracci's face: skin blackened by fire, eyelids crisped away . . . She put the thought from her.

"The ragheads are down there like you thought, boss."[2] Price squatted, pointing, bulky in mail shirt and huke. The war-hat buckled over his coif was far too rusty to catch the moon's light and betray their position. Dirty ringlets snaked out from under his coif.

Ash followed his direction. In the mile or more of dark land between her and the town, she began to make out intermittent dots of fire. Campfires, being relit after the rain. Regularly spaced. Two or three hundred, by guess; and there would be more, not visible from her position.

"Patrols come out every hour," Price added briefly. "Got it covered, but we shouldn't stay here long."

"Right. So, we have enemy encampments on the land between the road and the river—what's down there?"

Price rubbed at a runny nose with fingers that were ingrained with dirt, his thick nails cracked and bitten, then shoved his hands back into sheepskin mittens.

"Okay, boss. In front of us now, we've got the main north–south road. From here, Dijon's on the far side of the road and the river—we're looking at the western wall, but you can't see it. There's water meadows along the river, the other side of the road—that's where they've got their main artillery. There's reports of some infantry up the road to the north, just up at the crossroads." Price shrugged, a move-

[2] There is no mention in conventional histories of a siege of Dijon in the autumn of 1476. Since the 'Fraxinus' document depicts it, one must assume that it is an exaggeration, by Ash or by Visigoth chroniclers, of a minor military incident that history has ignored. Fraxinus's narrative breaks off in November 1476: there is then a gap between the end of the 'Fraxinus' text and Ash's presence in the Nancy campaign.

ment entirely visible in the white light. "Could be. I know for sure there's infantry blocking the road south to Auxonne; I went down that way myself. They've got raghead boats chained together across the river, so no one's going to get downriver from Dijon."

"Just siege machinery down there?" Squinting, Ash could make out nothing more than Visigoth campfires between herself and the invisible city walls. "What about golems?"

John Price grunted. "My lads did good enough to get in close and tell it was an engineers' camp. You want to know what the ragheads had for supper as well?"

Ash gave him a look that the bright moonlight did nothing to hide. "I'd be surprised if your lot couldn't tell me!"

Price unexpectedly grinned. "You won't get any chivalric nonsense out of billmen. We're better at sneaking around than those damn knights in their tin cans. You know knights, boss—'death before dismount'!"

"Oh, quite," Ash said dryly. "That'll be why de Vere took you lot to Carthage, and left the heavy armoured guys behind here . . ."

"Sure, boss. Half *my* lads are poachers."

"And the other half thieves," she observed, with rather more accuracy than tact. "Okay, what about north of Dijon? And what about on the east side, over the Ouche?"

"We've scouted all round. Dijon's just north of where the two rivers join." Price's fingers sketched a shield-shape in the moonlit air. "The city takes up all the ground in between, right down to the junction. Over this side, the Suzon comes right up close to the walls—acts as a moat. Over the east side, there's broken ground between the city walls and the river Ouche, and broken ground on the far bank, too. Scrub, cliffs, swampy ground. *Bad* ground.

Some of my lads ran into raghead patrols there, earlier tonight."

"And?"

"And they'll be missed." Price's teeth showed bright. "God rot us, boss, we had little enough choice in the matter."

"So assume that, by now, the Visigoths know there are enemy forces around. Bit of luck, they'll think we're some gang of peasants, or burghers from a burned town; they must be getting a lot of that." Ash squinted. "Okay, there's a road comes in from the east, to Dijon's northeast gate, I remember that . . ."

"They've got men and guns sitting on the hills above the eastern bridge. Looks like there's been artillery used from inside the town. That area's churned up pretty bad." John Price wiped his nose and blew into his sheepskin mittens for warmth. "Twenty culverins and serpentines and a bombard[3] up on the hill, we think. You won't get in from the east."

Antonio Angelotti's voice startled Ash, coming from her shoulder, where he had crawled up to peer out from the top of the bluff. "Give me twenty guns, and I could keep that eastern gate of Dijon impassable. I looked round, when we were here before."

"So they got artillery over there, and here?"

"Moats work two ways, madonna. If the Visigoth *amirs* cannot order an infantry attack over the Suzon at Dijon's west wall, then neither can the defenders sally out and attack the siege engines. The *amirs* can bombard Dijon with impunity from here."

---

[3] Bombard: the great siege gun, often not firing more than one or two of their 550 lb. shot per day. The smaller cannon—culverins, serpentines, and others—kept up a more rapid fire.

And they will have done. How close is this city to falling?

Shit, we've taken too long to get here!

Ash grunted. "What about the country to the north? What have they got up there?"

John Price answered, "Better part of a legion and a half. 'S true, boss. Saw the XIV Utica and the VI Leptis Parva."[4]

There was a second's silence.

Absently, whimsically, Ash murmured, "So much for Plan B . . ."

Been bad enough on the road here, avoiding their forces, skirmishing if we had to—shit, I was hoping we wouldn't find anything like this concentration of forces here! But it was an even chance we were going to . . .

"Where, exactly?" Ash asked.

"See the crossroads, where the road comes in from the west?"

Trying to see a mile and more in moonlight, Ash could glimpse nothing more than an obstruction to the glint of the river, which might be a bridge across it, and which might argue a road coming in. "Can't see it, but I remember it; goes out toward the French border. And?"

"They got guns covering the northwest gate of the city,

---

[4] Presumably Visigoth legions named for the areas from which troops were initially raised. Judging by the text, these 'legions' resemble the Classical pattern in their strength (within the 3,000–6,000 men of the Roman legion at various periods), and conceivably their infantry/cavalry/auxiliary structure, if one supposes the place of the auxiliaries to have been taken by Visigoth slaves. There is, however, no mention of them dividing their legions into cohorts or centuries. I suspect the Visigoth fighting force otherwise resembles the Western European mediaeval model, but with some additions—religious terms, and some ranks—in keeping with their concept of themselves as the successors of the Roman Empire.

same as they got guns covering the northeast gate." Price shrugged. The movement released a musty, damp smell from his clothing. "They've got a *lot* of people up beyond there, boss. All their main battles are camped up from the water meadows, where we were in the summer. They've got troops dug in all across the open ground in front of the woods, right over to the east river."

Ash, trying to squint in the silver darkness, had a brief memory of the Lion standard hanging listless in the heated air, by the Suzon River, and the chapel and the nunnery nestled under the eaves of the wildwood, a little to the north.

"What's Dijon's northern defense?"

"Speaking from memory, madonna, a moat dug between the Suzon and the Ouche, and stout city walls. Otherwise, the land north of the city is flat meadowland, until the forest. Do I remember well, Sergeant?"

Price nodded.

"That's the weakest spot, then. That's why the ragheads have got their main force there." *More* than six thousand men. Maybe seven. *Christus Viridianus!* "Hang on, what about the south gate?"

"Someone's thrown that bridge down. No one's getting in or out of Dijon's south gate."

"That was probably the idea . . ." Ash tapped her fingers together, then laid them cold against her lips. "Okay, that's a *lot* of troops. Not just your ordinary siege. Something *is* going on here . . ."

Antonio Angelotti touched her shoulder. "You could ask your voice, madonna."

"And hear *what*?"

It has been weeks, but the overwhelming fear of the *Ferae Natura Machinae*, the Wild Machines, is still with her. Squat stone pyramids in the desert south of Carthage, sullenly bright under the Eternal Twilight; their nature hidden for so many aeons . . .

She kept her voice low with an effort.

"If I *did* ask the *machina rei militaris* questions, the ragheads could just ask it what I'd wanted to know. Then they'd work out where the company is—right here on their doorstep, just handy for their six thousand troops!" She drew a breath. "I'm willing to bet Lord-*Amir* Leofric asks it daily—'is the bastard Ash alive, does she speak to you? If she has asked questions, what do they tell us about where she is, the strength of her force, her intentions?' . . . Assuming *Leofric's* still alive. He may be dead. But *I can't ask!*"

"Unless they have heard the Wild Machines, madonna, some *amir* will be using the *machina*, even if Lord-*Amir* Leofric is dead. We know it was not destroyed." Momentarily, there was a ragged note in Angelotti's whisper. "*If* you were to ask the *machina rei militaris* what orders are being passed between Carthage and the Faris-General, you could tell us how this war goes. I see that you can't ask. But you could . . . listen?"

A shudder that was not the bitter cold of the night, not the cold of the rain-soaked underbrush, went through her body.

"I *listened*, in Carthage. An earthquake flattened the city. I can't listen to the Stone Golem without the Wild Machines knowing, Angeli. And we've left them behind in North Africa, they don't know where we are, and I'm *fucked* if I'll ever have anything to do with that again! The Wild Machines want Burgundy? That isn't my problem!"

Except that I've made it my problem, by coming back here.

John Price, rumbling his deep voice on the other side of her, said, "Didn't like the look of them pyramids, in

Carthage. Didn't like the look of the ragheads, neither. Bunch of fucking nutters. Better they don't find out where we are. Don't you go telling 'em, boss."

If anything could have warmed the stone coldness inside her, it would have been the Englishman's stolid humor. She remained numb at a level deeper than camaraderie could reach.

Ash forced herself to smile at the straggle-haired bill-man, knowing her expression to be visible in the moonlight. "What, you think they won't be pleased to see us? I guess not. After the state we left Carthage in, I don't think we'll be winning any popularity contests with the King-Caliph. . . . That's if his mighty highness King-Caliph Gelimer is still with us, of course."

Rickard unexpectedly said, "Would the *amirs* still have a crusade in Christendom if Gelimer were dead?"

"Of course they will. The *machina rei militaris* will be telling whoever's King-Caliph to push the campaign for all he's worth. Because that's what the Wild Machines are saying, through it. Rickard, that's nothing to do with the Company of the Lion." Ash saw moonlit disbelief on his face. She shrugged and turned back to the Sergeant of Bill. John Price looked at her, as if for orders; she saw fear and trust in his expression.

"This gives us an answer. I'll bet on it." Ash reached down and rubbed her booted thighs, easing her cold and sodden legs back into life. "Numbers like this. . . . First, even if he *was* wounded at Auxonne, Duke Charles is still alive. Second: he hasn't escaped into northern Burgundy. The Visigoths wouldn't have this much force sitting outside one town in the south if Charles *Temaraire*[5] was dead or in Flanders. They'd be up there trying to finish this."

---

[5] 'The Bold,' or 'the Rash,' according to taste.

"You think he's in Dijon, boss?"

"I think so. Can't see any other reason for all this." Ash put her hand on Price's mailed shoulder. "But let's get to the important bit. Have the scouts seen Lion liveries on the city walls?"

"Yes!"

Evident, from his expression, what crucial hope rides on this.

"It's our lot in there! We saw the Lion Passant Guardant okay, boss! Burren's lads saw a standard before it got dark. I'd trust his boys to know the Blue Lion, boss."

Rickard, as abrupt as young men are, demanded, "Can we attack the Visigoths? Raise the siege and get Master Anselm out?"

If Robert's there, and alive . . . Ash snorted under her breath. "Optimist! Do it on your own, Rickard, will you?"

"We're a legion. We're soldiers. We can do it."

"I must stop getting you to read me Vegetius . . ."

There was a chuckle from the men around her at that.

Ash paused momentarily. A new cold dread sat in her stomach, and gnawed at her: *I'm going to make a decision based on this information, and it won't be one hundred percent right—it never is.*

She spoke. "Okay, guys—now we're committed. I'm betting that the rest of the company *didn't* break out, go to France or Flanders; they're still in there, with Duke Charles as their employer. So, if the other half of the Lion Azure is sitting inside that siege, we don't give a fuck about weird shit in Carthage, or *anything* else, we sort out our lads first."

"Yes," Angelotti agreed.

"On our own, boss—well, we ain't going to get no backup. It's all bandit country and Visigoths we've come through," John Price said disgustedly. "Burgundy's the only place that's still fighting."

"They should have attacked the Turk," Angelotti said quietly. "We know now, madonna, why the Lord-*amirs* chose to attack Christendom and leave the Empire of Mehmet whole on their flank."

"The Stone Golem gave them that strategy."

Abrupt in her memory, she hears the voices that spoke through the *machina rei militaris* in Carthage: 'BURGUNDY *MUST* FALL—WE MUST MAKE BURGUNDY AS THOUGH IT HAD NEVER BEEN—'

And her own voice, speaking to the Wild Machines: *Why does Burgundy* matter*?*

The cold mud slid away under her heels as she stood up, chill in the wet moonlit night.

I still don't know why.

I don't want to know!

The tension between what she felt, and what she could say in front of these men, momentarily silenced her. Quietness and cold made her shudder. Dripping trees sprayed her with water, as the wind blew up briefly before dropping; the stillness of predawn not many hours off.

She looked around at their white faces in the moonlight. "Remember who's in there. The other side of the guns and siege engines and six thousand Carthaginians. Just remember."

Antonio Angelotti got to his feet, mud-soaked. "The city's held out nearly three months, madonna. Things will not be good in there."

The same thought in both their minds: a memory of empty French villages, frozen under the eternally black sky where day never dawns. Half-timbered houses burned and abandoned; charred wood covered with snow. Sties empty; paddocks scraped down to flint and clay. A child's ragged linen shirt left frozen in the muddy ice, with preserved boot marks treading it down. Houses, farms, all empty; their reeves leading the people away; lords and their bailiffs gone beforehand; towns left with empty, devastated streets, not the neigh of a horse, nor the stink of a gutter remaining. And those who could not flee dead of starvation, and stacked like icy kindling wood; not all the bodies untouched.

In a siege, there is nowhere to flee to.

Angelotti added, "We should get Roberto and the men out."

Ash turned back to Price. "There's the three main gates into the city. . . . Any sally ports?"

Price nodded. "Yeah, my lads were looking at 'em when we were here in the summer. There's about half a dozen postern gates, mostly over the east side. There's two water gates down this side, where they diverted the river through the town to the mills. You want us to sneak Master Anselm and the company out down a millrace, boss?"

"That's right, Sergeant." Deadpan, Ash looked at him. "One at a time. It should take, oh, about three days, provided we do it in the dark, and nobody notices!"

John Price gave a short, choked laugh. He wiped his nose on the back of his sodden mitten. "Fair enough."

She thought, *I want to despise him for responding to so blatant a manipulation.* A wry smile moved her mouth. *But all I wish is that someone would do the same for* my *morale. We are committed, that's for sure.*

Ash turned until she could see Angelotti's dirty angelic features, as well as Price. Rickard hovered behind her, with Price's men.

"Send the scouts out again." Her voice dropped chill into the bitter air, warm breath turning to white mist as she spoke. "I need to know if the overall commander of the Visigoth forces is here, too. I need to know if the Faris is here at Dijon."

"She will be," Angelotti muttered. "If the Duke is."

"I need to be sure!"

"Got you, boss," Price said.

Ash squinted in the white light: a calculating look at the distant fires in the western camp of the Visigoth army. "Angeli, can you get one of your people up through the engineers' camp to the walls without being noticed?"

"Not difficult, madonna. One gunner looks very like another, without livery."

"Not a gunner. Find me a crossbowman. I want to send a message in over the walls. Tied to a crossbow bolt is as good a way as any. . . ."

"Geraint will object, madonna? To my telling his missile troops what to do?"

"Find me a man or woman that you trust." Ash turned away from the valley. The ground squelched under her boots as she staggered back toward the cover of the waist-high soaking bracken and the wet trees.

In memory—not in, never in, the silent recesses of her soul, now—in memory she hears the Wild Machines say 'BURGUNDY *MUST* FALL!' And a sardonic, quite different part of herself asks *How long do you plan to ignore this?*

"Find me Geraint, and Father Faversham," she ordered Rickard; waiting at the edge of the black depths of the wood. "Euen Huw, Thomas Rochester, Ludmilla Rostovnaya, Pieter Tyrrell. And Henri Brant, and Wat Rodway. Officer meeting, soon as we're back at HQ. Okay, let's *go*!"

Avoiding sodden branches and keeping a footing on the rough ground and undergrowth took all her attention, and she gladly surrendered herself to that necessity. Ten or so armed men lumbered up out of the bracken and briar, cursing at the wet darkness under the trees, and took up their places around Ash as she went. She heard them muttering about the fucking *size* of the fucking raghead army, God love us; and the lack of game in the woods, not even a God-rotted squirrel.

The true wildwood, even in winter, would have been impassable; progress measured in yards, not leagues, per day. Here on the cultivated edges, where charcoal burners and swineherds lived, it was possible to move fairly quickly—or would have been, by daylight.

The sun! Ash thought; one hand on the shoulder of the man in front, one arm cocked up to shield her face, able to see nothing but blackness. *Dear God, two months traveling in pitch-darkness, twenty-four hours a day: I hate the night, now!*

A league or so away, they paused to light lanterns and went on more easily. Ash swatted a wet, leafless hornbeam branch out of her face, following the back of the man in front, a crossbowman, sergeant of Mowlett's lance. His mud-drenched cloak swung in her vision, held down by the leather straps of belt, bag, and bolt-case. A twisted rag had been tied around his war-hat, above the brim; it might once have been yellow.

"John Burren." She grinned, pushing her way through wet briar to walk beside him. "Well, what's *your* men's guess—how many ragheads down there?"

He rasped, "A legion plus artillery. And a devil."

That raised her brows. " 'Devil'?"

"She hears devil-machines, don't she? Those damned things in the desert, like you showed us? That makes her a devil. Fucking bitch," he added, without emphasis.

Ash staggered sideways in time to avoid a tree, looming black in the faint lamplight. Confronted by his broad back, she said wryly and on impulse, "I heard them too, John Burren."

He looked over his shoulder, his expression in the darkness uncomfortable. "Yeah, but you're the boss, boss. As for her . . . We all got bad blood in families." He skidded, avoiding underbrush; regained his balance, and stifled the noise of a phlegmy sniff in his cupped hand. "And anyway, you didn't need no voices at *all* to get us out of that ambush outside Genoa. So you don't need 'em now, Lion *or* Wild Machine, do you, boss?"

Ash thumped him on the back. She found a smile creasing her mouth. *Well, hey, how about that? I said I wanted someone to improve my morale . . .*

Green Christ, I wish I thought he was right! I do need to ask the machina rei militaris. *And I can't. I mustn't.*

An hour traveling in the dark with lanterns brought them to the pickets and the muzzled, silenced dogs. They passed over the dug-trench-and-brushwood walls into the camp: two hundred men and their followers encamped under mature beech forest.

Most of the beech trees were already de-barked to above the height of a man's reach, feeding the meager fires that gave the only light now. The borders of a streamlet were trodden down into a wet, black slick. On the far side, Wat Rodway's baggage-train helpers clustered around iron cook pots on tripods. Ash, muddy and wet to the thigh, made first for the banked fires and accepted a bowl of pottage from one of the servers. She stood talking with the women there for a few minutes, laughing, as if nothing in the world could be a worry to her, before handing back a bowl scraped dry.

Angelotti, bright-eyed, huddled his cloak even more tightly around his lean shoulders and pushed in beside her again, close to the flames. His face bore the mark of weeks on basic rations, but it did not seem to have depressed his spirits; if anything, there was an odd, reckless gaiety about him.

"Another one of Mowlett's men has come back here before us, madonna. You could have spared yourself sending those other scouts—he has the answer to your question. Her livery's been seen, and her person. The Faris is here."

The blast of heat from a windblown flame of the campfire does not make her flinch: she is momentarily lost in memory of a woman who is nameless, whose name is her rank;[6] whose face is the face that Ash sees in her mirror, but flawless, unscarred. Who is the overall military commander of perhaps thirty thousand Visigoth troops in Christendom. And who is more than that, although she may not know it.

"I'd have bet money on it. It's where the Stone Golem will have told her to be." Ash corrected herself: "Where the Wild Machines will have said, through the *machina rei militaris*, that they want her."

"Madonna—"

"Ash!" Another figure shoved in beside Ash, through the press of people. Patches of firelight picked the woman out, the brown and green of her male dress: hose and cloak nearly invisible against mud, bare trees, stacked kindling wood, and wet crumpled briar.

"I want a word with you," Floria del Guiz demanded.

---

[6] 'Faris': cavalryman; knight.

ii

"YEAH, SOON AS I'm done here—" Ash wiped her mouth with her sleeve, chewing the crust of dark bread that Rickard shoved into her hand, sipping springwater from a cup he thrust at her, eating on the move, as ever. She nodded abstractly to Florian, noting also, now, Rickard, Henri Brant, and two of the armourers, all waiting to speak to her; and turned back to Angelotti.

"No," Florian interrupted the group. "A word with you *now*. In my tent. Surgeon's orders!"

"Y'okay . . ." The chill springwater made Ash's teeth ache. She swallowed down the bread, told Henri Brant and the other men briefly, "Clear it all with Angeli and Geraint Morgan!", and nodded Rickard toward the warmth of the fires. She turned to speak to Floria del Guiz, to find the woman already striding away through the slopping leaf mulch and mud and darkness.

"Flaming hell, woman! I've got stuff to set up before morning!"

The tall, skinny figure halted, looking over her shoulder. Night hid most of her. Firelight made an orange straggle of her hair, still no longer than a man's, that curled at the level of her chin. She had obviously raked it back with muddy fingers at some point: brown streaks clotted the blond hairs, and her freckled cheekbones were smeared dark.

"Okay, I know you don't bother me for no reason. What is it *this* time? More on the sick list?" Moving too fast, Ash skidded, and put her boot down in a pothole hidden in shadow. Her hose were wet enough that she scarcely felt the cold through the soaked leather.

"No. I told you: I want a word."

Florian held up the flap of the surgeon's tent, where it had with difficulty been pitched among the shallow roots of the beech trees. Canvas yawed and sagged alarmingly, shadow and reflected firelight shifting with the movement. Ash ducked, entering the dim, musty-smelling interior, and let her eyes adjust to the light of one of the last candles, set aside for the dispensary. The pallets on the earthen floor appeared empty.

"I'm out of Saint John's-Wort and witch hazel," Florian said briskly, "and damn near out of gut for surgery. I'm not looking forward to tomorrow. I shan't need you, deacon."

She continued to hold the tent flap up. One of her lay priests abandoned his mortar and pestle and nodded to her as he scrambled out of the tent into the darkness. Nothing in his demeanor suggested he was in any way uncomfortable this close to a woman dressed as a man.

"There you are, Florian. Told you so." Ash seated herself at one of the benches, leaning her elbows on the herb-preparation table. She looked up at the female surgeon in the half-light. "You sewed them up after Carthage—you went to Carthage *with* them, under fire. You've stuck with us all the way back. Far as the company's concerned, it's, 'We don't care if she's a dyke, she's *our* dyke.' "

The woman slung her lean, long-legged body down on a wooden folding chair. Her expression was not clear in the candlelight. Her voice stung with bitterness. "Oh, no *shit*? Am I supposed to be pleased? How magnanimous of them!"

"Florian—"

"Maybe I should start saying the same about them—'so, they're a bunch of muggers and rapists, but hey, they're *my*—' Hell! I'm not a . . . not a . . . company *mascot*!" Her hand hit the table, flat, making a loud crack in the cold tent. The yellow flame shifted with the movement of the air.

"Not quite fair," Ash said mildly.

Florian's clear green eyes reflected the light. Her voice calmed. "I must be catching your mood. What I meant to say was, if I took a woman into my tent, then we'd find out how much I'm 'theirs.' "

"*My* mood?"

"We're going to be fighting today or tomorrow." Florian did not inflect it as a question. "This isn't the right time to say this, but then, there may not be a right time later. We might both be dead. I've watched you, all the way here. You don't talk, Ash. You haven't talked since we left Carthage."

"When was there time?" Ash realized she still held the wooden cup in her numb, cold fingers. There was no water left in it. "There any wine tucked away in here?"

"No. If there was, I'd be keeping it for the sick."

Pupils dilating with night vision, Ash could make out Floria's expression. Her bony, intelligent face had lines from bad diet and hard marching, but none of the marks of a surfeit of wine or beer. *I haven't seen her drunk in weeks*, Ash thought.

"You haven't been talking," the other woman said deliberately, "since those things in the desert scared the living shit out of you."

Cold tension knotted in her gut, released a pulse of fear that left her dizzy.

Florian added, "You were all right at the time. I watched you. Shock set in afterward, when we were crossing the Med. And you're *still* avoiding thinking about it now!"

"I hate defeats. We came so near to taking out the Stone Golem. All we've done is make sure they know they need to protect it." Ash watched her own knuckles squeezing the wooden cup, trying to stop it rattling against the planks of the table. "I keep thinking that I should have done more. I *could* have."

"Can't keep refighting old battles."

Ash shrugged. "I know there was a breach into House Leofric somewhere below ground level—I'd seen his damn white rats escaped into the sewers! If I could have found the breach, maybe we could have got down to the sixth floor, maybe we could have taken out the Stone Golem, maybe now there'd be no way the Wild Machines could ever say anything to anyone again!"

"*White* rats? You didn't tell me about this." Florian leaned across the table. The candlelight threw her features into sharp relief: her expression intense, as if she pried into chinks in masonry. "Leofric—the lord who owns you? And owns the Faris, one supposes. The one whose house we were trying to knock down? *Rats?*"

Ash put her other hand around the cup, looking down into the shadow inside it. It felt marginally warmer in the tent than in the forest, but she yearned for the scorching heat back at the bonfire.

"Lord-*Amir* Leofric doesn't just breed slaves like me. He breeds rats. They're not natural rat-color. Those ones I saw had to mean the earthquake cracked House Leofric open underground. But, it might not have been the same quadrant of the House that has the Stone Golem in, it *might* not have been a wide enough breach to get men through . . ." She left it unfinished.

" 'Coulda, woulda, shoulda.' " Floria's expression altered. "You told me about Godfrey in the middle of that firefight. Just, 'He's dead.' I haven't had any more out of you since."

Ash saw the darkness in the empty cup blur. It was quite

genuinely several seconds before she realized tears were in her eyes.

"Godfrey died when the Citadel palace came down, in the earthquake." Her voice gravel, sardonic, she added, "A rock fell on him. Even a priest's luck has to run out, I suppose. Florian, we're a mercenary company, people *die*."

"I knew Godfrey for five years," the woman mused. Ash heard her voice out of the candlelit darkness of the predawn, did not look up to see her face.

"He changed, when he knew I was no man." Florian coughed. "I wish he hadn't; I could remember him with more charity now. But I only knew him a few years, Ash. You knew him for a decade, he was all the family you'll ever have."

Ash leaned back on her bench and met the woman's gaze. "*Okay*. The private word you wanted to have with me is: you don't think I've grieved for Godfrey. Fine. I'll do it when I have *time*."

"You had *time* to go out with the scouts, instead of letting them report in like normal! That's make-work, Ash!"

Anger, or perhaps fear of the immediate future, kicked in Ash's belly, and came out as spite. "If you want to do something useful, grieve for your useless shit of a brother, instead—because no one else is going to!"

Florian's mouth unexpectedly quirked. "Fernando may not be dead. You may not be a widow. You may still have a husband. With all his faults."

There was no discernible pain in Floria's expression. *I can't read her*, Ash thought. *There's, what, five, ten years between us? It could be fifty!*

Ash got her feet under her, pushing herself up from the table. The earth was slick under the soles of her boots. The tent smelled of mold and rot.

"Fernando did try to stand up for me in front of the

King-Caliph. . . . For all the good it did him. I didn't see him after the roof fell in. Sorry, Florian. I thought this was something serious. I *haven't* got time for this."

She moved toward the tent flap. Night air billowed the mildew-crusted canvas walls, shifted the light from the candle. Florian's hand came up and gripped her sleeve.

Ash looked at the long, muddy fingers knotting into the velvet of her demi-gown.

"I've watched you narrow down your vision." Florian didn't relax her grip on the cloth. "Yes, being that focused has got us across Christendom to here. *It won't keep you alive now*. I've known you for five years, and I've watched how you look at *everything* before a fight. You're . . ."

Florian's fingers loosened, and she looked up, features in shadow, hair brilliant in the candle-shine, searching for words.

"For two months, you've been . . . closed in on yourself. Carthage scared you. The Wild Machines have scared you into not thinking! You have to start again. You're going to miss things; opportunities, mistakes. You're going to get people killed! You're going to get *yourself* killed."

After a second, Ash closed her hand over Florian's, squeezing the chill fingers briefly. She sat down on the bench beside the surgeon, facing her. Momentarily, she dug at her brows with her fingers, grinding the flesh as if to release pressure.

"Yeah . . ." Some emotion crystallized, pushing to the forefront of her mind. "Yeah. This is like Auxonne, the night before the battle. Knowing you can't avoid decisions anymore. I need to get my shit together." A memory tugged at her. "I was in this tent, then, too, wasn't I? Talking to you. I . . . always meant to apologize, and thank you for coming back to the company."

She looked up to see Florian watching her with a closed,

pale face. She explained, "It was the shock of finding I was pregnant. I misinterpreted what you said."

Florian's thick, gold brows dipped. "You ought to let me examine you."

Ash spoke concisely. "It's been a couple of months since I miscarried; everything's back as it should be. You can ask the washerwomen about the clouts."[7]

"But—"

Ash interrupted. "But now I've mentioned it—I should apologize for what I said then. I *don't* think you were being jealous that I could have a baby. And . . . well, I know now that you weren't—well—making a pass at me. Sorry for thinking that you would."

"But I would," Floria said.

Relief at finally having made her apology overwhelmed her, so that she almost missed Florian's reply. She stopped, still beside her in the half dark, on the cold wooden bench, and stared at the other woman.

"Oh, I would," Florian repeated, "but what's the use? You don't watch women. You never look at women. I've seen you, Ash—you've got *hot* women in this company, and *you don't ever look at them.* The most you'll do is put your arm around them when you're showing them a sword cut—and it means nothing, does it?"

Ash's chest hurt; Floria's vehemence left her breathless.

Floria said, "Say what you like about being 'one of the boys'—I watch you flirt with half the male commanders you've got here. You can call it *charisma* if you like. Maybe none of you realize what it is. But you *respond* to guys. Especially to my slut of a brother! And *not* to women. Now what would be the use of me making a pass at you?"

---

[7] 'Clouts'—cloths; in this case presumably menstrual.

Ash stared, her mouth slightly open, no words coming into her mind. The chill of the night made her eyes and her nose run; she absently wiped a sopping velvet sleeve across her face, still with her gaze fixed on the older woman. She strained for words, finding only a complete absence of anything to say.

"Don't worry." A brittle note entered Florian's voice. "I wasn't then, and I won't now. Not because I don't want you. Because it's not in you to want me."

The harshness of her tone increased. Caught between revulsion and an overwhelming desire to console the woman—*Florian, this is Florian; Jesu, she's one of the few people I call friend*—Ash began to reach out a hand, and then let it drop.

"Why say this now?"

"We may both be killed before the end of tomorrow."

Ash's silver brows came down. "That's been true before. Often."

"Maybe I just wanted to wake you up." The fair-haired woman leaned back on the bench, as if it were a movement of relaxation, and only coincidentally one that moved her farther away from Ash. She might have been thoughtful, might have been smiling slightly, or frowning; the dim light made it impossible to know.

"Have I upset you?" Florian asked, after a moment's utter quiet.

"I . . . don't think so. I knew that you and Margaret Schmidt—but it never occurred to me that you'd look at *me* like that—I'm . . . flattered, I guess."

A splutter of edged laughter came from farther down the bench. "Better than I'd hoped for. At least you're not treating it as a management problem!"

That was so much Florian—knowing perfectly well what Ash's first reaction would be—that Ash had to smile.

"Well . . . Okay, I'm flattered it turns out I'm a woman you could fancy! Same as with a man, I guess. I deal with this from time to time in the company. I tell them, they'll find a good woman—it just isn't me."

In a deliberately casual tone, Floria del Guiz said, "I can handle that."

"Well, okay." An unaccustomed feeling that she should do something, or say something more, made Ash stand up quickly, her footing uncertain on the wet, earthen floor. She looked at the seated woman. "What am I . . . supposed to do with this?"

"Nothing." A wry smile touched Florian's features, and faded. "Do what you like with it. Ash, wake up! This isn't just getting half the company out of a siege. We're back in the Duchy; you spent one night on the beach outside Carthage telling us that these"—her voice hesitated—"these *ferae machinae*[8] have spent two hundred years tricking House Leofric into breeding a slave for them to conquer Burgundy with—and you've said nothing since. Now you're here, Ash. This is Burgundy. This isn't a war that people had anything to do with. Are you going to carry on acting like it's just another campaign? Like you and your—sister—are just war-leaders?"

Ash was unaware that her face had a peculiarly unfocused expression, as if she were still listening to the echoes of machine-voices in her head. She snapped her gaze to the woman's face, suddenly. "No, you're right, Florian. No, I'm not."

"Then what?"

"This isn't 'just another campaign.' But—don't take this wrong—Burgundy isn't my business. *Or* yours."

"But Carthage is."

---

[8] 'Wild machines.'

Ash turned her head away from the woman's uncompromising expression, hearing the familiar voices of her lance leaders outside the tent. "Time for the officer meeting. I want to hear what state we're in. You come with me. If there aren't any wounded you should be looking after?"

"We lost the last of the *non*walking wounded just north of Lyons." There was a rasp in the woman's tone.

Ash turned toward the tent doorway, the candle casting her shadow dark in front of her, and she groped blindly for the flap and pushed it open. Stiff, cold canvas scraped her bare fingers. She tugged her sodden, frozen mittens on. Aware of Florian at her shoulder, she stepped out into the firelit darkness.

"I haven't *completely* lost it," Ash added. "I have spent some of the time we took getting here working out what the fuck we could do if we ever *got* here. . . ."

She heard Florian's familiar cynical snort. Ash halted, staring off through the darkness. In one place, among branch-shelters, the distinctive smoke of burning green wood went up. "Put that fucking fire out!"

Geraint ab Morgan, walking up with most of his belongings hanging off his belt and a greatsword resting over his shoulder, turned to shout at a provost-sergeant, who set off at the trot. "Yes, boss. Hey, boss, council of war's set up. The rest of 'em are in your pavilion."

There were only two tents put up on the difficult open ground within the edge of the wood: the surgeon's infirmary tent and the commander's pavilion. Most shelters were ripped-down branches, or muddy canvas tied between trees. Ash fell in beside Morgan in the firelit darkness, walking in the wake of her other lance leaders heading toward her tent—a drooping structure pegged between the roots of beeches, partly tied to branches, lurching as the wet night loosened the guy ropes.

"How many men do we have now, Geraint?"

The big man scratched under his coif at his russet-colored, short-cropped hair. "Down to one hundred and ninety-three men, aren't we? Men who can fight. The baggage train is up to three or four hundred, but we're getting civilians tagging on."

"Sort that out." Ash met Geraint ab Morgan's gaze mildly. "Do it before we eat breakfast."

"Some of the men here have taken women from the road. If we drive the women off, they'll starve. The lads won't like that, boss."

"Shit!" Ash hit one fist into her mittened palm. "Leave it, then. More trouble than it's worth, to get rid of them."

Floria del Guiz, stumbling across the broken ground with them, a wry smile only just visible in the fire's light, murmured, "Pragmatist . . ."

A night's camp had left autumn undergrowth trodden into the mud or ripped up for bedding. No goats or chickens ran underfoot. Something like five hundred people and their pack beasts, crowded into the oblong camp erected in the strip of land along the edge of the wildwood. Archers and lightly armored men-at-arms crouched around fires, in the wet, eating the sparse rations.

A bray came from the pack mules tied to trees farther down the length of the camp; and Ash breathed into her mail-covered mittens as she walked, letting her breath warm her frozen face, watching by the fires' shifting illumination—squires and pages talking as they cared for the pack mules, billmen and hackbutters chivvied into clearing up by sergeants and corporals; and the women and children who roamed everywhere, the newcomers underfoot, pinched of face, with the look of deep shock in their eyes. Judging morale.

"We lost another two men-at-arms, then?"

"Last night, before we made camp. That's fewer than in the south."

We didn't get here a minute too soon.

Geraint frowned. "Boss, I've been reorganizing some of the understrength lances into provost units, and this lot are far more scared of me now than they are of deserting. But I wish you'd let me leave missile-troop duty to Angelotti; we got all the damn company archers with us; it's taking up too much of my time."

Ash nodded thoughtfully. "You're a damn sight better provost than you ever were Sergeant of Archers! Okay, I guess you'd better keep it up, then."

She made for the commander's tent, Morgan and the surgeon with her. Geraint ab Morgan shoved his way past Floria del Guiz to enter, halted with comical suddenness, and jumped back to let her pass.

"God's *blood*! You can't show me your pubic lice and then expect me to want to be treated like a lady," Floria rasped, striding past him into the pitch-dark tent.

Ash caught sight of his expression, and, for all her own bitter confusion, almost burst into laughter.

"Quiet down," she said, smiling, walking into the canvas-darkened, already occupied interior. "Rickard, open the flap; let's have some firelight in here."

"I could light lamps, boss."

"Not unless Father Faversham here helps you with a miracle. We're out of lamp oil. Aren't we, Henri?"

"Yes, boss. That and a lot of other things. We can't keep going forever on what we scavenge from abandoned towns."

"*If* they were abandoned before you 'scavenged' . . ." Floria, feeling her way, sat herself down on one of Ash's back-stools, with a caustic glance at Thomas Rochester, and at Euen Huw, as the Welsh lance leader scuttled in, late.

"Most of them were. Mostly." Euen Huw's dirty, rough features assumed an injured expression. "Who can tell in the Dark? Spoils of war, isn't it, boss?"

Ash ignored the banter. She glanced around in the dim light. The Rus woman Rostovnaya came in on Euen's heels. Geraint ab Morgan muttered to Pieter Tyrrell, Tyrrell listening to the Welshman and massaging the leather glove sewn over the remaining finger and thumb of his half hand. Wat Rodway leaned up against the center pole and sharpened his cook's knife on a whetstone, Henri Brant now talking to him in an urgent undertone.

"Henri," she said, "what's the state of play with the food?"

The broad-faced man turned around. "You've run it too fine, boss. Half rations for the last week, and I've had armed guards on the pack mules. There's no more hot food after today; we're down to dark bread; maybe two days' worth. Then nothing."

"That's definite?"

"You've given me five hundred people to feed; yes, I'm definite, it can't be done! I have nothing left to bake!"

Ash held up one hand, calming his red-faced anxiety, keeping her own stomach-churning apprehension off her face. "It's not a problem, Henri. Don't worry about it. Geraint, what is it?"

Geraint ab Morgan's deep voice filled the musty air, in the flickering gold light. "We don't think it's a good idea to attack the city."

The unexpected challenge jolted her. "Who's 'we'?"

"Fuck this, boss." Ludmilla Rostovnaya didn't answer directly. "Go on, tell us all about getting the rest of the company out of Dijon, 'n' on the road to England. What we gonna do, boss, *spit* at the fucking ragheads?"

"Yeah, spit 'n' the walls fall down," Geraint growled.

Ash, catching the eye of Thomas Rochester, shook her head fractionally.

"You know what?" she said, conversationally, "I don't give a fuck what you think isn't a good idea, Geraint. I expect my officers to keep themselves informed of what's going on."

"Demons." The big russet-haired man stared at her through the gloom. "The King-Caliph's got *demons* telling him what to do!"

"Demons, Wild Machines, call them what you like. Right now, those legions of Visigoths outside Dijon are a bigger problem!"

Geraint scratched in his cod, still gaping at Ash, and then shot a glance at Ludmilla Rostovnaya.

"Your arm okay?" Ash asked the Rus woman, and at her hesitant nod, said, "Right. Report to Angelotti. He's got a job for you, and your crossbow snipers. I'm going to write a dozen messages for the company inside Dijon, and I want them shot over the walls—and I want you to wait then for a message back from Captain Anselm. You got that?"

Given something to do, the crossbowwoman looked reassured. "Now, boss?"

"Angelotti's with the hackbutters. Get going."

In the shuffling rearrangement of bodies as the woman left the pavilion, Geraint ab Morgan said, "I don't agree with what you're doing! It's madness, an assault on Dijon. The men won't follow you."

At that rasping complaint, the pavilion became silent. Ash nodded once to herself. She glanced around in the dimness at the lance leaders, steward, and surgeon.

"You're going to have to trust me," she said, her eyes finally meeting Geraint's pale blue, bloodshot gaze. "I know we're hungry, we're exhausted, but we're *here*. Now you either trust me to take it from here, or you don't. Which is it, Geraint?"

The big Welshman glanced to one side, as if seeking Euen Huw's support. The wiry, dirty lance leader shook his head, lips pursed together. Thomas Rochester rumbled something under his breath. The only other sound came from Wat Rodway stropping his knife on the whetstone.

"Well?" Ash gazed around in the flickering shadows at the pavilion full of men, their breaths smoking in the freezing air; big bodies slung about with belts, daggers, swords, arrow-bags. In that company of soldiers, she noted that Floria got up and went to stand with the steward and cook.

"I'm with you," Floria said, as she walked past Ash. Henri Brant nodded; Wat Rodway glanced up with piggish eyes and inclined his head, sharply, once.

"Master Morgan?"

"Don't like it," Geraint ab Morgan said suddenly. He did not drop his gaze. "Bad enough the enemy's being led by a demon, isn't it? Now we are, too."

" 'We'?" Ash queried gently.

"Saw it at the galleys. You were going to go into the desert. Find them old pyramids, maybe. Maybe listen to their orders. What are we doing here, boss? Why are we here?"

"Because the rest of the company is—inside Dijon." Ash moved to one side, by feel; seating herself on the edge of the trestle table, covered in maps, on which she had earlier been attempting to work out their route of march.

She gazed around at her officers sitting on back-stools, at Floria lounging beside Wat Rodway at the tent pole, and Brant shifting from foot to foot on the bracken-strewn earth. Richard Faversham hulked at the back. The light from the open tent flap illuminated profiles, only.

She nodded to Rickard, gesturing him to pull the canvas back wider, and heard him exchange some comment with the guards outside.

"Okay," Ash said. "Here's how it is. First I'm going to talk to you; then I'm going to talk to all the lance leaders, and then to the lads. First I'm going to tell you what we're doing here. Then I'm going to tell you what we're going to do next. Is everybody clear on that?"

Nods.

"We all know," she said, her words quiet in the silence, and her gaze mostly on Geraint ab Morgan, "that there's an enemy behind the enemy. Christendom's been fighting Visigoths, Burgundy's been fighting Visigoths—but that isn't all there is to it, is there?"

It was a rhetorical question: she was momentarily off-balance when Geraint muttered, "That's what I said, isn't it? Led by a demon. She *is*. Their Faris, their general."

"Yes. She is." Ash rested both hands beside her, on the table. "She hears a demon. And so do I."

The Welsh archer winced at that; but Euen Huw and Thomas Rochester shrugged.

"More than one bloody demon," Rochester said, his voice elaborately casual. "Bloody desert down there's full of them, ain't it, boss?"

"It's okay, Tom. It scares me shitless, too."

Momentarily, they are silent; their minds full of the southern lights, of the dark desert illuminated by silver, scarlet, ice blue. Seeing again the lined ranks of pyramids, stark against the silver fire.

"I used to think I was hearing the Lion—but it was their Stone Golem," Ash said. "And you all know that I heard the Wild Machines at Carthage. The voices *behind* the Stone Golem. I don't know if the Faris even knows they're there, Geraint. I don't know if anyone—House Leofric, or the

Caliph, or the Faris—knows a damn thing about the voices of the Wild Machines." She held Geraint's gaze in the dim light. "But we know. We know Leofric was a puppet, and the Wild Machines bred his slave-daughter. We know this isn't normal war. It hasn't been, not from day one."

Geraint said, "I don't like it, boss."

She noted the slump of his shoulders, his second glance around for support, and gave him a smile of great friendliness. She shifted herself off the table and moved to stand in front of him.

"Hell, I don't like it either! But I won't go to the Wild Machines. I haven't felt the pull of them since we sailed from North Africa. Trust me." She gripped his forearms.

Standing there, in the red and golden filtered light, she is a strong, filthy, mud-stained woman, white scars on her face and hands, flesh dimpled with old wounds; wearing orange-rusted mail mittens and a sword as if it were a matter of course. And grinning at him with apparent utter confidence.

Geraint straightened his shoulders. "Don't like it, boss," he repeated. He looked down at her hands. "Nor do the lads. We don't know what this war's for, anymore."

Floria, her face in shadow, said vitriolically: "Loot, pay, rapine, drunkenness, and fornication, Master Morgan?"

"We're still out here to beat any other company in the field," Euen Huw said as if it were self-evident.

"Master Anselm and the others!" Rickard croaked.

An edge of tension informed all their voices. Ash let go of Geraint Morgan's arms, giving him a friendly slap. She looked around at the others, unconsciously bracing herself before she spoke again.

"No. He's right. Geraint's right. We *don't* know what this war is for." She paused for a moment. "And the *Visigoths* don't know what this war's for. That's the key. They think it's a crusade against Christendom. But it's far more than that."

Slowly, she stripped off her armored sheepskin mittens, rubbing her frozen fingers together.

"I know the Wild Machines have fed ideas to Leofric, and through him to the King-Caliph. They speak through the Stone Golem. The Visigoth armies are here because the Wild Machines sent them here. Not to Constantinople, or anywhere in the east—*here*, so they could get Burgundy overrun and destroyed."

From the back of the tent, Richard Faversham said in English, "Why Burgundy?"

"Yeah: why Burgundy?" Ash repeated in camp patois. "I don't know, Richard. In fact, I don't know why they've brought an army here at all."

Geraint ab Morgan spluttered an amazed laugh. Unselfconsciously falling back into his rank, he blurted, "Boss, you're mad! How else would they fight Duke Charles?"

Ash looked past him. "Richard, we need more light in this tent."

The apparent non sequitur silenced them all. She had a moment to watch as the English priest lumbered up off his stool and knelt, Thomas Rochester shifting out of the way, Floria turning to look at Ash in amazement, Wat Rodway stuffing his whetstone back in his purse, and his skinning knife into its sheath.

"In nomine Christi Viridiani . . ."[9]

Richard Faversham's surprising high tenor silenced them.

". . . *Christi Luciferi,*[10] *Iesu Christi Viridiani . . .*"

The prayer went on; their voices joined in. Ash

[9] 'In the name of the Green Christ.'

[10] 'Christ the Light-bringer.'

watched them, with their lowered heads and clasped hands, even Rickard at the tent flap turning and kneeling in the cold mud.

"God will grant this, to you," Faversham announced, "in your need."

A low, yellow light, like the light of a candle, shone from the air.

A shiver went up from her belly. Ash shut her eyes, involuntarily. A faint warmth touched her scarred cheeks. She opened her eyes again, seeing their faces clearly now in the calm light: Euen Huw, Thomas Rochester, Wat Rodway, Henri Brant, Floria del Guiz—and, slipping in, Antonio Angelotti, his wet, mud-draggled hair and face taking on a smirched, unearthly beauty.

"Blessed be." The gunner touched his doublet, above his heart. "What is here?"

"Light in darkness. God forgive me," Ash said, resting her hand on Richard Faversham's shoulder. She raised her head, gazing around now at parchment-colored canvas, at swords and a few last herbs hanging from the roof-wheel. Shadows leaped; shrank. "I had no need of it, except to show it could be done. Richard, I'm sorry for using you."

The honey light clung about her. Sparkles of white light flickered at the edges of her vision. Richard Faversham kissed the Briar Cross he held and stood up, heavily, his hose black with leaf mold.

He murmured, "Man calls on God eternally, Captain Ash, and for greater than this; yet all seems, to Him, as small as a candle flame. And in any case, small miracles are what I'm with the company for."

Ash knelt, briefly. "Bless me."

"*Ego te absolvo*," the priest recited.

Ash got to her feet.

"Geraint, you asked me a question. You said, how else

would the Visigoths fight Duke Charles? This is how."

The provost-captain shook his cropped head. "Don't get it, boss."

The luminous air shifted, granular.

"With miracles," Ash said, gazing around. "Not like this one. Not from God. With evil; with devil's miracles. I know this from the Wild Machines—they bred the Faris from Gundobad's line. They bred her from the Wonder-Worker's blood, to be another saint, another Prophet, another Gundobad. But not for Christ. They've bred her so she can be *their* power on earth and to perform *their* miracles. On their compulsion—and they can compel."

In the miraculous light, Richard Faversham licked his dry lips. "God wouldn't permit it."

"God may not have. But we don't know that." Ash paused. "What we do know is, the Faris isn't the King-Caliph's design, nor *Amir* Leofric's. The Faris belongs to the Wild Machines. They bred her to make a devil's miracle and wipe Burgundy off the face of the earth. So—why has she come with an army?"

There was a momentary silence.

Richard Faversham suggested, "Her power for miracles may be small, everyday. No more than a priest or deacon. If that is so, then of course she must bring an army."

Floria frowned at the priest. "Or . . . not come into her power yet?"

"Or their breeding may have failed." Antonio Angelotti stood, not looking at Ash, smiling gently in the luminous air. "Perhaps God is good, and she can do no evil miracles? *You* can't."

Ash looked ruefully back at the English priest. "No. I can't even do tiny miracles. Richard will tell you how many nights on this trek I've spent praying with him! I'll never make a priest. All I can do is hear the Stone Golem.

And the Wild Machines. She could be more than I am. And yet, here she is, *fighting* her way in. . . ."

Antonio Angelotti shook his head. "If I hadn't known you so long, madonna, and if I hadn't seen what we saw in the desert, I'd think you were crazy or drunk or possessed!" His bright eyes flicked up to meet her gaze. "As it is, I must believe you. Clearly, you heard them. But if the Faris knows nothing of their existence, and if the Wild Machines only speak to her in the disguise of the Stone Golem's voice, she may not know yet what we know."

Richard Faversham demanded, "And when she does know, will she make a desolation here for them?"

Angelotti shrugged. "The Visigoth armies have already made a desolation. Nothing stands where Milano stood, not a wall, not a roof. Venice is burnt. A generation of young men are dead in the Swiss Cantons . . . Madonna, I trust you, but tell us this at least—why Burgundy?"

There were murmurs of agreement; faces turned toward her.

"Oh, I'd tell you—if I knew. I asked the Wild Machines questions, and got my soul nearly blasted out of my body. I don't know, and I can't think why." Ash wiped her nose on her sleeve again, conscious of the stink of mildew in this pavilion, too. "Florian, you're Burgundian-born. Why these lands? Why not France, or the Germanies? Why this Duke, and why Burgundy?"

The woman surgeon shook her head. "We've been on the road well over two months. Every night I've thought about it. I don't know. I don't know why these 'Wild Machines' care about anything human, never mind the Burgundians." Sardonic, Florian added, "Don't try asking them! Not now."

"No," Ash said, something naked about her expression. The miraculous light dimmed a little, the air turning thin and dark again. Ash glanced at Richard Faversham. An expression of pain, or the concentration of prayer, passed across his face.

Even our miracles are becoming weaker.

She turned her gaze back to Geraint, Euen, Thomas Rochester, Angelotti. The tent was full of the smell of sodden wool and male sweat.

"All we know for sure," she said, "is that there's a war behind the war. If I've got you guys involved because of what I am, then that's regrettable—but remember that we would have been in this war anyway. It's what we do." She hesitated. "And if their Faris hasn't done a devil's miracle yet, we can hope that she won't do any in the future. Then it's down to steel and guns. And *that's* what we do."

Reservations were plain on their faces, but no more so than during any campaign. Not even Geraint Morgan, she noted.

"Boss?" the provost-captain asked diffidently, as her gaze fell on him.

"What is it, Geraint?"

"If she does conquer Burgundy, if she does kill their old Duke for them, whether it's by a war or a miracle—what happens then, boss?"

Ash suddenly laughed. "You know—your guess is as good as mine!"

"What do you care, Morgan?" Euen Huw demanded, roughly good-humored. "By the time that happens you'll be back in Bristol, with all the money you can spend, and clap enough to keep the doctors rich for years!"

Wat Rodway, who had said nothing yet, regarded the fading miraculous light in the tent with jaundiced reverence. "Boss, can I go back and fix food to break our fast? Look—either she can bring some demonic retribution down on us, or she can't. Either way, I'm about to cook the last pottage we're going to see before we attack Dijon. You want it or don't you?"

" 'You want it or don't you, *boss*'," Ash said.

"Oh, I'm not bothered with this. I'm off. Meal in an hour. Tell the lads." Rodway strode out of the tent, with a word to the guards in the same abrupt and entirely offensive tone.

Ash shook her head. "You know, if that man couldn't cook, I'd stick him in the pillory."

"He can't cook," Floria snapped.

"No, that's right. Hmm." Ash, with a smile still stretching her cheeks, felt a cold wind blow through the open tent flap, bringing the smell of unwashed men, excrement, wet trees, woodsmoke and mule dung.

Nearly Prime, and the air has started to move—

"Angelotti, Thomas, Euen, Geraint, the rest of you, come outside." She stepped forward, grabbing for the tent flap. "Florian—"

Geraint ab Morgan leaned over, blocking her way.

"The men won't like it," he repeated, stubbornly. "They don't want to attack the town."

"Come outside," Ash repeated, cheerfully and with an edge of authority. "I'm going to show you another reason why we're here."

Loud squawks and croaks from ravens echoed across the clearing as she stepped outside, past Geraint. She saw the black birds dropping down to the middens by the cook-wagons, strutting unfed, complaining raucously—and realized that she could see them clearly between the spaced beeches, twenty yards away.

Ash turned her face up to the sky.

The air moved across her skin.

"Look!" She pointed.

Deep in the trees, the first half hour of it must have

passed without notice. Now—men and women getting up off their knees in the mud, where they had been hearing Digorie Paston's service of Prime—now all the leafless twigs and bare branches on the eastern horizon of the clearing stood out clearly against the sky.

Ash barely looked at the moon, bone white and sinking to the west. She felt a tightness in her chest, became aware that she was holding her breath, heard a muttering from the people thronging out into the empty space between the camp's perimeter ditches.

The eastern sky turned slowly, slowly from gray to white to the palest eggshell blue.

The minutes passing could have been no time, or all time; Ash felt that she simultaneously endured an eternity, waiting, and at the same time, that it happened all in an instant—that one minute the clearing in the wood was dark, and the next, a line of bright yellow light lay across the trunks of the western trees, and a sliver of imperishable gold rose up over the eastern mist.

"Oh, Jesu!" Euen Huw plonked down on his knees in the mud.

"God be thanked!" Richard Faversham's deep voice shouted out.

Ash, for once not hearing the shouts, or seeing people running—Geraint ab Morgan and Thomas Rochester grabbing each other in wild hugs, tears streaming down their cheeks at this continuing miracle—Ash stood watching as, for only the fourth morning since the twenty-first day of August, she saw the sun rise in the eastern sky.

The end of three months of darkness.

A shoulder brushed hers. Dazed, she looked to see Floria beside her.

"You're still not thinking this is our business," Florian said quietly. "Just something for us to avoid."

Ash almost reached out and thumped the woman's shoulder, as she would have done an hour ago. She stopped herself from making physical contact.

" 'Our business'?" She stared around her at the men, kneeling. "I'll tell you what 'our business' is, right now! We can't stay camped here—I give it twenty-four hours maximum before we've got Visigoth scouts up our ass. We can't *eat* here—and they got supply lines bringing in all the food they want. We're outnumbered, what, thirty to one?"

She found herself grinning at Florian, but there was more blind exhilaration than humor in it.

"And then there's this. It's still happening! Light!"

"They won't retreat now," the surgeon said. "You realize that?"

Ash's fist clenched. "You're right. I won't be able to lead them back under the Penitence. I know that. We can't go back. And we can't stay here. We *have* to move forward."

Floria del Guiz, for the first time since Ash had known her, and quite unconsciously, reached up with dirty fingers and crossed herself. "You told me on the beach. The 'Penitence' is nothing to do with the Visigoths. You told me the Wild Machines put out the sun over Christendom this summer. That they've made two hundred years of the Eternal Twilight, over Carthage, by drawing down the sun."

Cold air moved against Ash's face. A sudden cold tear ran down her scarred cheek at the brightness.

"Burgundy, again," Florian said. "In the summer the Wild Machines made a darkness that stretches across Italy, the Cantons, the Germanies, now France . . . and when we cross the border, here, we're out of it. Out of the Eternal Twilight, again. Into this."

Ash looked down. The line of sunlight bisected her body, illuminated the dirt-ingrained skin of her hands, bringing out every whorl in her fingertips. Wet velvet sleeves began to steam under the infinitesimal warmth.

Florian's voice said, "Before this year, the Twilight was only over Carthage. It spread. But not here. Have you thought? Maybe *that's* why the Faris is here with an army. We may be beyond where the Wild Machines can reach."

"Even if we are, that might not last."

Ash looked up at the sky. Automatically, still, this being Florian, she added aloud what was in her mind:

"Remember 'Burgundy must be destroyed'? This is their main target area. Florian, I had no choice about bringing us back here—but now we're standing right on ground zero."

iii

LOWERING HER FACE from the faint but perceptible warmth of the risen sun, Ash wiped her muddy palm across her scarred cheeks.

Beside her, the woman took her gaze from the eastern sky and shivered in the cold morning.

"Girl, I wouldn't want your job right now!" Florian briskly blew on her bare fingers, looking around at the camp. "We can't go back. *Can* we go forward? What are you going to tell them?"

"That?" Ash, for the first time in weeks, gave a genuinely relaxed smile. "Oh, *that's* not the difficult part. Okay: here we go . . ."

Ash walked on, out into the middle of the clearing, clapping her hands.

Five hundred people stopped talking fast enough, gathering around once they saw it was her: men in mail, and rusted plate, or padded jacks, standing, or squatting on the mud where it was too filthy to sit down. Some few diced in the wet. Rather more were drinking small ale. She gazed around her, at their faces that kept turning away in wonder to the sky.

"Well," Ash said. "Will you look at *your* sorry asses!"

"We can take it, boss!" one of the Tydder brothers yelled: Simon or Thomas, Ash was momentarily unsure which. He ducked a shower of punches, mudballs, and insults.

"Creep!" Ash remarked. Laughter started, unstrained, going round the crowd.

Well, well. Geraint was wrong. And I was right.

She rubbed her hands together and grinned broadly back at the laughter on drawn faces. "Okay, lads. We're broke again. Not for the first time—won't be the last. It means a day or two more on bread rations, but hey, we're rough, we're tough, we can hack it."

The other one of the Tydder brothers whimpered in a shrill falsetto. "Mummy!"

Ash took the laughter that followed as an opportunity to look at them closely. The Tydders and a lot of the younger men-at-arms were elbowing each other in the ribs, laughing, one with his lancemate's head wrestled under his arm. Two hundred fighting men with faded liveries and ragged hose, bundled up in every garment they owned; mud-stained, fingers white with chilblains, noses dripping clear liquid. She took the feel of them, electric in the air, read from their faces that they seemed tighter, more exultant, high on being rough, ragged, tough, and soldiers in a world of refugees.

It's because there's sun. We've come across the border. For the first time in weeks, there's the sun. . . .

And they've got out of Carthage in one piece and force-marched the better part of a hundred leagues in moonlight and darkness: right now, they think they're shit-hot.

And they are.

Please God it's not all for nothing.

As the laughter died down, Ash lifted her head and looked around at the muddy encampment, and the mud-stained men in front of her.

"We're the Lion company. Never forget it. We're *fucking amazing*. We've come across a hundred leagues of this, through night and bitter cold; it's taken us weeks, but we're still here, we're still together, we're still a company. That's because we're disciplined, and we're the best. There isn't any argument about it. Whatever happens from now on in, we're the best, and you know it."

There was a ragged, good-natured cheer: if only because they knew the amount of truth in what she said. Some men were nodding, others gazed at her in silence. She watched faces, alert for fright, for arrogance, for the imperceptible loosening of bonds between men.

Ash pointed over her shoulder, in the general direction of the river valley and Dijon. She showed teeth in a fierce smile. "You're expecting me to tell you how we're going to batter those walls down and rescue Anselm and the lads. Well, guys, I've been up ahead to look. And I've got news for you. Those walls aren't going down, they're fucking solid."

One of Carracci's billmen put his hand up.

"Felipe?"

"Then how the fuck are we going to get the rest of the Lions out, boss?"

"We're not." She repeated it, more loudly: "*We're not.*"

A noise of confusion.

"That's a siege going on up there," Ash said, pitching her voice to carry. "Now most people are trying to break *out* of a siege."

"With the exception of the enemy," Thomas Rochester put in helpfully, behind her.

Antonio Angelotti snickered. A number of the men took it up, appreciative of the backchat.

Ash, who knew very well why—in the midst of Visigoths, twenty-four-hour-a-day darkness, and speaking stone pyramids—both her officers were doing this, contented herself with a glare.

"All right," she said, breath smoking on the icy air. "*Apart* from the enemy. Pair of bloody smart-asses."

"That's why you pay us, madonna . . ."

"He gets *paid*?" Euen Huw complained, in broad Welsh.

Ash held up her hands. "Shut up and listen, you dozy shower of shit!"

A voice from the back of the ranks murmured whimsically, " 'We're the best' . . ."

The outburst of laughter made even Ash grin. She stood, nodding and waiting, until quiet returned, then wiped her red, runny nose with her sleeve, put her hands on her hips, and projected her voice out to them:

"Here's the situation. We're in the middle of hostile countryside. There's two Carthaginian legions just down the road in front of us—the Legio XIV Utica and some of the Legio VI Leptis Parva: six or seven thousand men between them."

Murmurs. She went on:

"The rest of their forces are behind us in French territory, and up north in Flanders. Okay, it isn't winter here yet, like it is under the Dark—but there's corn rotted in the fields and grapes rotted on the vine. There's no game, because they've hunted it all. There's nowhere left to loot, because every town and village for miles around has been stripped. This land is *bare*." She stopped, waiting, looking around; hard, dirty faces scowled back at her.

"No need to look at me like that," Ash added, "since you looted your share on the way up here. . . ."

An archer's voice: "Fuckin' right."

"You bastards carried away everything that wasn't tied down. Well, I got news for you. It's gone. I've talked to Steward Brant, and it's—all—gone."

Ash gave that a slow emphasis, saw it sink in. A billman crouched down a few feet away looked at the hunk of dark bread in his hand, and thoughtfully tucked it away in his purse.

"What we gonna do, boss?" a crossbowwoman called.

"We've done one hell of a forced march," Ash said, "and we're not finished yet. We're in the middle of a war here. We're about to run out of rations. Now, most people are trying to break *out* of a siege . . ."

She flirted a quick glance at Angelotti, gave Florian a grin, and turned her attention back to the men yowling questions:

"Most people. Not us. We're going to break *in*."

Those in the front row bawled their amazement.

"Okay, I'll tell you again." Ash paused, for emphasis. "We're not going to break Robert Anselm and the lads *out* of Dijon. *We're* going to break *in*."

Simon (or Thomas) Tydder blurted out, "Boss, you're mad!" and blushed bright red. He stared down at his boots.

She let the buzz die down. "Anyone else got anything to say?"

"Dijon's under *siege*!" Thomas Morgan, Euen Huw's second-in-command, protested. "They got the whole bloody Visigoth army in front of their gates!"

"And they have had—*for three months*. Without taking the city! So what better place to be than safe inside Dijon?

If they find us out here," Ash said, looking around at faces again, "we're catsmeat. We're in the open. Most of our heavy armor's in Dijon. And we're outnumbered thirty to one. We can't face a Visigoth legion in the field—not even you guys can do that. Now we *are* here, there isn't any option. We need walls between us and the Visigoth army, or that's the end of the Lion Azure, right now."

She had the experience to wait then, while a hubbub of talk rose up—to wait with her arms folded, weight back on one hip, her bare cropped silver hair exposed to the wintry light under the trees—a woman no longer beautiful, but in mail coat and sword, and with her pages, squire, and officers ranked behind her.

One of the billmen stood up. "We'd be safe in Dijon!"

"Yeah, till the Goths batter the gate down!" a man-at-arms in Flemish livery remarked.

Until we find out what the Wild Machines have bred the Faris for.

Ash stepped forward and held her arms up.

"Okay!" She let their noise die down. "I'm getting in contact with our people inside Dijon. I'm arranging for a gate to be opened tonight. De Vere picked you guys to move fast, for the raid on Carthage, so moving fast is what we're going to do! We won't have to fight our way in—but I'll want volunteers for a diversionary attack."

The Englishman John Price nodded and stood up, his mates with him. "We'll do it, boss."

Ash spoke quickly, not letting any more questions be asked.

"You, Master Price, and thirty men. You'll attack tonight, two hours after moonrise. Angelotti, give them whatever slow match and powder we've got left. You guys: wear your shirts over your armor: kill anything that doesn't show up white."

"That won't work, boss," Price's lancemate objected. "All them fuckers wear white robes!"

"Shit." Ash let them see her look amused. "Y'know—you're right. Sort out your own recognition signal, then. I want you down at the west bank of the Suzon, setting fire to their siege engines—that'll bring the whole army awake, siege machines are expensive! When you've done it, fall back into the forest. We'll pick you up in a boat tomorrow evening and bring you in through one of the water gates."

Ash turned to her officers.

"That'll give the rest of us time enough to move. Okay, we've got ten hours before dark. We're leaving any carts: I want everything in the baggage train either on someone's back or slung out. I want the mules blindfolded." She gauged spirit, looking around at all the faces she could see in the November morning. "Your lance leaders will tell you where you are in line of march—and when we go in tonight, we go in with weapons muffled, and wearing dark clothes over armor. And we don't hang about! They won't know we're here until we're in."

There was still some murmuring. She made a point of making eye contact with the dissenters, gazing around at white, pinched faces, cheeks flushed with small beer and bravado.

"Remember this." She looked around at their faces. "That's your mates up ahead in Dijon. We're the Lion—and we don't leave our own. We may be broke, it may be winter, we may need a siege-proof roof over our heads right now, but don't forget this—with the whole company together, we can kick *any* damn Visigoth's ass from here to breakfast! Okay. We go in, we assess the situation, and when we move on out later on, we move out with all the armor and guns we had to leave here—and we move as a full-strength company. You got that?"

Mutters.

"I *said*, you got that?"

The familiar bullying tone cheered them, enabled a complicit cheer:

"YES, BOSS!"

"Dismiss."

In the resulting ordered chaos of men running, shelters being demolished, and weapons being packed up, she found herself standing beside Floria again.

A sudden awkwardness made her avoid the woman's eye. If Florian, too, was uncomfortable, she showed no sign of it.

But she will be.

"Don't—" Ash coughed, getting rid of some congestion in her throat. "Don't do a Godfrey on me, Florian. Don't *you* vanish off out of the company."

She surprised a sudden unmonitored expression on Florian's face, a raw anguish, gone before she could be sure it was anything more than a cynical, brilliant grin.

"No danger of that." Florian folded her arms across her body. "So . . . You've solved the immediate military problem. If it works. We get into Dijon. What then?"

"Then we're part of the siege."

"For how long? Do you think Dijon will hold out? Against *those* numbers?"

Ash looked levelly at the Burgundian woman. *There will be unease,* she thought. *Not enough to matter—and not for long. Because it* is *still Florian.*

"I'll tell you what I *think*," Ash said, with a release of breath and tension, in sudden honesty. "*I* think I made a shit-lousy mistake in coming here—but once we landed at Marseilles, once we were committed, there hasn't been a damn thing I can do about it."

Floria blinked. "Good God, woman. You've been keeping this lot on the road by sheer willpower. And you think we're *wrong* to be here?"

"Like I said on the beach at Carthage—I think we should have sailed for England then." Ash shivered in the morning cold. "Or for Constantinople, even, with John de Vere, and taken service with the Turk. Got as far away from the Wild Machines as possible, and left the Faris to whatever shit there's going to be in Burgundy."

"Oh, bollocks!" Floria put her fists on her hips. "*You*? Leave Robert Anselm and the rest of the company here? Don't make me laugh! We were always coming back here, whatever happened at Carthage."

"Maybe. The *smart* thing to do would be to cut our losses and start again with the men I've got here. Except that people don't sign up with commanders who dump their people."

Some internal honesty prompted, unexpectedly: *But she's right, we were always coming back here.*

She squinted into the morning wind, her eyes tearing, thinking, *Weather's bad even for November, and that's a weak sun. And it's been so cold, south of here, for so long now. There won't have been a harvest.*

"Too late now," she said, hearing herself sound almost philosophical. She smiled at Florian. "Now we *are* here—there isn't anywhere else to go, except behind the nearest walls! Better dead tomorrow than dead today, right? So you can pick between Dijon falling sometime soon, and the legions up ahead finding us tomorrow. . . ."

She felt an immense release, as if from a weight, or an unrelenting grip. Fear flooded through her, but she recognized it and rode it, let herself become fully aware, again, that it is not merely the usual business of war that concerns her.

Floria snorted, shaking her head. "I'll get my deacons

praying. Fix where we'll be in line of march. Where will you be, on this moonlight flit? In front, as usual?"

"I won't be with the company. I'll join you in the city, before dawn."

"You'll *what?*"

Ash beat her cold hands together. Warming circulation pricked at the impacts. Cool, damp air touched her face.

Her gaze met Florian's: whimsical, bright, utterly determined.

"While the company's making an entry into Dijon tonight, I'm going to get some answers. I'm going to go down to the Visigoth camp and talk to the Faris."

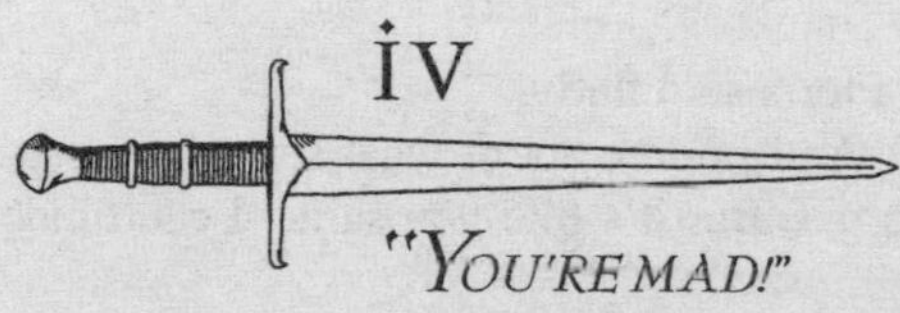

IV

"YOU'RE MAD!"

In the wet, muddy daylight, Ash suddenly grinned to herself. *I can still talk to Florian. At least I still have that.*

"No. I'm not mad. Yes: we had a defeat at Carthage. Yes: I needed to *think*. Yes: I am going to do something." Half-teasing, she added, "Once my banner goes up in Dijon, the Faris will know I'm alive anyway."

"So don't raise it!" Exasperated, unguarded, Floria waved her hands in the air. "Come off it, Ash. Forget chivalry. Keep your banner rolled up. Sneak out when we *do* leave Dijon! But don't tell me you're going out there to try and *talk* to her!"

"I could tell you a lot of good reasons why I should

talk to a Visigoth army commander." Ash wiped her muddy hands together, took her sheepskin mittens from her belt, and put them on: still damp and uncomfortable. "We're mercenaries. I'm expected to do this. I've got to look for the best deal. She might just give us a *condotta*."

Florian looked appalled. "I know you're joking. After Basle? After *Carthage*? The minute you show your face, they'll ship you back across the Med! They'll string you up for the raid! And then Leofric will poke around in what's left!"

Ash stretched her arms, feeling the ache in her muscles from the night's exertions, watching the camp beginning to pack up. "I'd take any help I can get, including Visigoth, if it means getting the company out of here before whatever the Wild Machines have planned for Burgundy starts happening."

"You're nuts," Floria said flatly.

"No. I'm not. And I agree about what sort of a reception I'm likely to get. But it's like you said—I can't hide from this forever."

Florian's dirty face scowled.

"This is the craziest thing I've ever heard you say. You can't put yourself in that much danger!"

"Even if we get into Dijon okay, we're only hiding. Temporarily." Ash paused. "Florian—she's the only other person on God's earth who hears the Stone Golem."

In the silence, Ash turned back to find Florian looking at her.

"So?"

"So I need to know . . . if she hears the Wild Machines, too." Ash held up her hands. "Or if it's just in my head. I need to know, Florian. You all saw the Tombs of the Caliphs.

You all believe me. But she's the only other person on God's earth who *knows*. Who will have heard what I heard!"

"And if she didn't?"

Ash shrugged.

After a pause, the surgeon asked, "And . . . if she did?"

Ash shrugged again.

"You think she knows something about this that you don't?"

"She's the real one. I'm just the mistake. Who knows what's different about her?" Ash heard bitterness in her own voice. She cocked a silver brow at the woman surgeon and deliberately grinned. "And she's the only one who can tell me I'm not nuts."

Shrugging sardonically, Florian muttered, "You've been nuts for years!"

There was nothing unfamiliar in the woman's affection. Or unfamiliar about her complicit, unverbalized consent. Ash found herself smiling at the dirty, tall woman. "You're a doctor, you'd know!"

A sharp *thock*! made Ash turn her head: she caught sight of Rickard and his slingshot—and tree bark scarred down to raw, white wood thirty yards away, from his practice shot.

"If you show yourself," Florian said, "the Faris won't be the only one who'll find out where you are. Carthage; the King-Caliph; the *Ferae Natura Machinae*."

"Yes," Ash said. "I know. But I have to do it. It's like Roberto always says—I could be wrong. What use am I, if I'm not sane?"

At dusk of that day—it came early, from a frozen sky empty of clouds, under which her officers complained lengthily after the announcement of her decision—Ash gave penultimate orders.

"A first-quarter moon rises about Compline.[11] We move then, after mass. If there's messages from Anselm, send them to me. Call me if it clouds over. Otherwise—I'm getting a couple of hours' sleep first!"

A last tallow candle, unearthed from the bottom of a pack, stank and flickered in the command tent as she entered. Rickard stood up, a book in his hands.

"You want me to read to you, boss?"

She has two books remaining, they live in Rickard's pack: Vegetius and Christine de Pisan.[12] Ash walked to the box bed and flopped down on the cold palliasse and goatskins.

"Yeah. Read me de Pisan on sieges."

The black-haired young man muttered under his breath, reading the chapter headings to himself, holding the book up close to the taper. His breath whitened the air. He wore all his clothes: two shirts, two pairs of hose, a pourpoint, a doublet, and a ragged cloak belted over the top of them. His nose showed red under the rim of his hood.

Ash rolled over onto her back on her pallet. Damp chill drafts crept in, no matter how tightly the tent flap was laced down. "At least we didn't have to eat the mules yet. . . ."

"Boss, you want me to read?"

"Yeah, read, read." Before he could open his mouth, Ash added, "We've got a moon just past first quarter; that's going to give us some light, but it's rough country out here."

---

[11] 9 p.m.

[12] Daughter of an astrologer-physician, herself widowed with three small children, Christine de Pisan earned her living as a professional writer. She produced, among her many other works, *The Book of Feats of Arms and of Chivalry* (begun AD 1409), a revision of Vegetius, and a practical manual of warfare much used in the field by the great captains of her era. This is most probably the book of hers to which 'Fraxinus' is referring here.

"*Boss* . . ."

"No, sorry: read."

A minute later she spoke again, a bare few sentences into his reading, and she could not have said what he had read to her about. "Have any messages come out of Dijon yet?"

"Don't know, boss. No. Someone would've come and said."

She stared at the pavilion wheel spokes. The cold burned her toes, through her boots and footed hose. She rolled over onto her side, curling up. "You'll have to arm me in two hours. What have they been saying about Dijon?"

Rickard's eyes sparkled. "It's great! Pieter Tyrrell's lance are blacking their faces. They're betting they can get into the city before the Italian gunners, because they'll be dragging Mistress Gunner's—"

Ash coughed.

"—Master Angelotti's swivel-guns!"[13]

She rumbled a laugh under her breath.

"Some of them don't like it," Rickard added. "Master Geraint was complaining, over at the mule lines. Are you going to get rid of him like you got rid of Master van Mander?"

Preparations for the battle of Auxonne, when the sun was still in Leo: it seems a lifetime ago. She barely remembers the Flemish knight's florid face.

Ash curled herself tighter against the cold. Her breath left dampness on the wool of her hood, by her mouth. "No. Joscelyn van Mander came in this season, with a hundred and thirty men; he never made himself part of the company; it made sense to bounce him back out again." She sought the boy's face in the dim light, seeing his flaring

[13] Two-man-portable weapon; between the size of a hackbut and a small cannon.

brows, his unpremeditated scowl. "Most of the disaffected men around Geraint have been with me for two or three years now. I'll try to give them something of what they want."

"They don't want to be stuck in a town with a bloody big army on the outside!"

The guy ropes creaked. The tent wall flapped.

"I'll find a compromise for Geraint and his sympathizers."

"Why don't you just order them?" Rickard demanded.

She felt her lips move in a wry smile. "Because they may say 'no'! There isn't much difference between five hundred soldiers, and five hundred refugee peasants. You've never seen a company stop being a company. You don't want to. I'll find some way of satisfying their gripes—but we're still going to Dijon." She grinned at him. "Okay; read."

The young man held the book up to the taper.

"It isn't that bad a tactical situation," she added, a moment later. "Dijon's a big city, must have ten thousand people in it, even without what's left of Charles's army; the Faris can't have her people cover every yard of the walls. She'll be covering roads, gates. If the sergeants can get us moving and keep us moving, we'll get inside, maybe without fighting at all."

Rickard rested his finger on one illuminated page and closed the cover of the book. The tallow candle gave hardly enough light to show his expression.

He said suddenly, "I don't want to be Anselm's squire. I want to be your squire. I've been your page. Make me your squire!"

" 'Captain Anselm,' " Ash corrected automatically. She reached over her shoulder, hauling goatskins and sheepskins over her fully dressed body.

"If I don't get to be your squire, they'll say it's because

I'm not good enough. I've been your page again since Bertrand ran off. Since we found you in Carthage! I fought at the field at Auxonne!"

On that outraged protest, his voice slid up the scale to squeak, and down to croak. Ash flinched with embarrassment. She snuggled the sides of her hood back, ears bitten with cold, so that she could hear him more clearly. He rose and banged about in the dark tent for some minutes, in silence.

"You're good enough," Ash said.

"You're not going to do it!" He sounded suspiciously close to tears.

Ash's voice, when it came, was tired. "You didn't fight Auxonne. You've *seen* what it's like in the line, Rickard, you just don't *know* what it's like."

The edges of swords and axes slice the air, in her mind:

"It's a storm of razors."

"I'm going to fight. I'll go to Captain Anselm."

Ash heard no pique in his tone, only a sullen, excited determination. She shifted herself up on her elbow to look at Rickard.

"He'll take you," she said. "I'll tell you why. Out of every hundred men we get, ten or fifteen will know what to do in the field when the shit hits the fan, without being told, either by instinct or training. Seventy men or so will fight once someone else trains them, and then tells them how and where. And another ten or fifteen will run around like headless chickens no matter *what* you train into 'em or tell 'em."

In the line of battle, she has grabbed men by their liveries and thrown them bodily back into the fight.

"I've watched you train," she finished. "You're a natural swordsman, and you're one of the ten or fifteen any commander picks out and goes, 'you're my sub-commander.' I want you alive the next two years, Rickard, so I can give you a lance to command when the time comes. Try not to get killed before that."

"Boss!"

The warmth from the furs hit some level that allowed her body to stop shivering. A wave of tiredness rose up, drowning her; she barely had time to register Rickard's pleased, inarticulate, aggressive surprise; then sleep took her down like a fall from a horse, no impact, only oblivion.

She was aware that she rolled on the pallet, under the blankets.

Something gave, under her body.

She heard a hollow crack, a noise like a man putting his foot through a waxed leather bottle. Close to her. She stirred, heard guards and dogs beyond the canvas walls, shifted one arm sideways, and felt some obstruction give under her ribs.

The solidness cracked, broke with a wet noise.

Ash slapped her hand across the pallet, down by her side. Something slick and solid impaled itself on her thumb. She felt the nail resisted by obstruction, then whatever it was split, squelchy as a ripe plum. Her hand became suddenly slimy and wet.

She smelled a familiar odor: a sweet richness, mixed with the excremental stink of battle, thought *blood* and opened her eyes.

A baby lay half-under her body. She had rolled over and crushed it. Its tight swaddling-bands were sopping with something dark, seeping down from the head. Its fuzz-haired scalp ran red. White bone glinted, the child's skull fractured from ear to ear, the back of it crushed where she had rolled over. Her hand rested over its face, her thumb deep in a ruined eye socket.

The other eye blinked at her. So light a brown as to be amber, gold.

A baby, no more than a few weeks old.

"*Rickard*!"

The scream left her mouth before she knew she had given voice. Dizzy, blackness seething in front of her eyes, she dug her heels into the bedding and pushed herself bodily back, off the pallet, onto the mud, away.

Boots sucked out of mud, outside the tent flap; the tent laces gave way to a dagger slash.

A dark figure ducked into the tent, and Ash saw that his hair was golden, although it was Rickard.

"You killed our baby," he said.

"It isn't mine." Ash tried to reach out and pull the sleeping furs over the bundled body, but she didn't have the strength to drag them to her. The baby's skin was fine, soft; the tent smelled like a hard-fought field. "Fernando! I didn't kill it! It isn't mine!"

The boy turned and left the tent. In another man's voice, he said, "You were careless. Only a moment, and you could have saved it."

"They *beat* me—"

Ash reached out, but the cold dead skin of the child felt hot under her fingers, as if her fingers burned. She scrabbled back across the floor of the pavilion, and abruptly sprang up and ran out of the door.

White snow shone under a blue sky.

No night sky. Noon: and a bright sun.

There were no tents.

Ash walked into an empty wood. The snow sucked at her bare feet, pulling her down. She kept slipping, landing heavily, struggling to her feet. Snow plastered every twig, every leafless winter bud, every crooked branch. She floundered, wet, bitten with the chill, her hands red and blue in the freezing whiteness.

She heard grunting.

She stopped moving. Carefully, she turned her head.

A line of wild boar rooted through the snow. Their hard snouts plowed up the whiteness, leaving troughs of black leaf mold exposed. They softly grunted. Ash saw their teeth. No tusks. Sows. Razorback sows, moving between the trees, in the bright sunshine. Their winter coats were thick and white, they smelled of pig dung, and their long lashes shaded their limpid eyes against the light.

A dozen or more striped boarlets ran between their mothers' legs.

"They're too young!" Ash cried, crawling on hands and knees through the snow. "You shouldn't have littered them yet. It's too early. Winter's here; they'll die; you had them at the wrong time! Take them back."

Snow fell from branches onto snow on briars, white hoops against the trunks of trees. The boars moved slowly, methodically, ignoring Ash. She sat back in the snow, on her knees. The stripy little ones, about the size of a fresh-baked loaf, trotted past her with their stringy tails whipping against the snow, their chisel-hooves kicking up whiteness.

"They'll die! They'll *die*!"

A red-breasted bird flew down, landing beside the biggest sow's forefoot. She nosed toward the robin momentarily. Her head swung back to root under the snow. The robin's beak dipped for worms.

The boarlets strayed farther from the herd, into the white forest.

"They'll die!" Ash felt her throat tighten. She began to sob, wretchedly, felt the muscles of her throat moving, felt her eyes dry and without tears, felt the hard stuffed canvas of the palliasse under her back.

The tallow candle had burned down to a stump.

Rickard made a huddled lump, sleeping across the door.

"They'll die," Ash whispered, looking for orange-and-brown-striped flanks, for trotting hooves, and for brown eyes shaded by delicate long, long lashes. She smelled the air for blood, or dung.

"I didn't kill it!"

I miscarried. I was beaten, and I miscarried.

Her eyes remained dry. If there was weeping, she could not do it. Aches and cold and bodily discomfort reasserted themselves.

A voice said, *—Making friends with the shy, fierce, wild boar.*

Ash relaxed back against the skins and furs. "Shit. God sent me a nightmare, Godfrey. My hands . . ."

She strained to see them, in the dimmest light. She could not see if her fingers were stained with anything. She lifted them cautiously to her nostrils: sniffed.

"Why does He want me to see dead babies?"

—I don't know, child. You're presumptuous, perhaps, to think He troubles Himself to trouble your sleep.

"You sound troubled." Ash frowned. She stared around, in the all-but-dark; could not see the priest.

—I am troubled.

"Godfrey?"

—I am dead, child.

"Are you dead, Godfrey?"

—The boars are a dream, child. I am dead.

"Then why are you talking to me?"

In the part of her that listens, the part of her soul that she is used to sharing with a voice, she feels something: a kind of warmth. Amusement, perhaps. And then, again, the voice:

—I thought that, since I could call boars, I could call you. When I was a boy, in the forest, using nothing but stillness, I made friends with those of God's creatures whose tusks could rip my belly in a moment. You are one of God's creatures with tusks, child. It took me so long to get you to trust in me.

"And then you went and died on me. Are you in the Communion of Saints, Godfrey?"

—I was not worthy. I am tormented by great Devils! Purgatory, perhaps, this is. Where I am now.

"Close to God, then. Ask God, for me, why do the Wild Machines want Burgundy wiped out?"

A chill pain sliced through her mind. At the same moment, Rickard said sleepily from the door, "Who are you talking to, boss?"

He reached up from where he lay, in his blanket roll, and pulled the tent flap open. Moonlight slanted into the command tent. It shone on his face, his white breath, on Ash's clean hands, on her furs, clothes, sword, pallet.

"I—"

No transition. No transition from dream to waking. Ash sat up, suddenly, none of the languor of sleep in her muscles. Her head was clear. *I have been awake for more than a few minutes*, she realized, and peered around: the tent remained dirty, familiar, corporeal. Rickard stared expectantly at her.

I have been awake.

"Oh *shit*." Ash bent over, gagging. Memories momentarily overwhelmed her. The single moment of vision, Godfrey's body flopping back, the smashed and missing top of his skull, this stays with her, details imprinted on her inner eye. "*Christus!*"

Dimly, she was aware that Rickard put his head out of the tent and called to someone, that he left, that someone else came in, bustling—Ash could not have said how much time had passed—and then she lifted her head and found herself staring at Floria.

"Godfrey," Ash said. "I heard his voice. I heard Godfrey. I *spoke* to him."

Silver and black in the moonlight, there are people moving outside the tent.

Floria's voice said, "If he's still alive, perhaps you dreamed of him where he is—"

"He's dead." Tears welled up in Ash's eyes. She let them fall, in the dark interior of the tent. "Christ, Florian, he had the top of his head smashed *off*. If you think I would have left him if he wasn't dead—!"

The long, slender fingers of the surgeon came out of the darkness, turning her face to the light. She felt no awkwardness, no fear of the woman's touch. Floria crouched in front of her, sniffed at her mouth—for wine, Ash realized—touched her cool forehead; finally sat back, and shook her head.

"Why should he haunt your sleep?"

"I wasn't asleep."

She made to get up, to call Rickard to arm her, since it was plain that moonrise was well advanced, silver light streaming down between trees. Without warning, a sharp pain stabbed through her nose, eyes, and throat. She choked. Her mouth distorted; tears ran out of her eyes. She dragged in a breath, sobbed tightly.

"Shit. He's dead. I let them kill him."

"He died in the earthquake in Carthage," Floria snapped.

"He was there because of me, he was doing what I told him to do."

"Yeah, and so have half a hundred soldiers been, when you got them killed in some battle." The woman's voice changed. "Baby, no. You didn't kill him."

"I heard him—"

"How?"

" 'How'?" Ash's wet eyes burned. The question stopped the sobs in her throat.

"When *you* say you hear voices," Floria observed, sardonic in the cold moonlight, "then I want to know what you mean."

Ash stared at her for a long moment.

"Rickard," she said abruptly, and stood up so quick that she left the surgeon kneeling at her feet. "Find my arming doublet; let's get moving. *Now*."

"Ash," Floria began.

"Later." She put her hands on Floria's shoulders as the woman stood up. "You're right, but later. When we're in Dijon."

"If you risk trying to get to the Faris, you might not *get* into Dijon!" More quietly, under the noise of Rickard rummaging in the baggage, Floria added, "Not a dream. A voice."

"*After* a dream. It was very like him." Ash was surprised at how much her composure returned, with the words. She reached out, and after a second's hesitation, Floria took her hands.

"In Dijon," Ash promised. "I'll be there. I'll come back."

Rickard blurted, from the dark corner of the pavilion, "Ash always comes back. That's what they've been saying since Carthage. That you'll always come back to the company. You will come back, boss?"

"Though all the army of the Visigoths lie between," Ash said lightly, mock-grandly, and was rewarded by a grin as the boy armed her: brigandine, sallet, and sword. She shrugged her cloak back over everything, stepping outside with Rickard and Floria, to be immediately overwhelmed in a moonlit wood by men with questions, sergeants coming for orders, and messengers shoving through the crowd.

She took a roll of paper from Ludmilla Rostovnaya, bending her head to listen while Rickard read it out to her under a horn lantern; nodded decisively, and gave a string of orders.

"I take it we're expected?" Floria del Guiz said, in a momentary break.

Without even time to realize her own searing relief, Ash confirmed: "Robert's still alive and giving orders, if that's what you mean. There'll be a gate open. Now all we have to do is get there. . . ." Ash spoke absently, peering through the crowds in the semidarkness. "Thomas Rochester!"

She strode forward, picking up Angelotti on the way, pulling the two men into a huddle with her, in the freezing moonlit muddy woodland.

"I've told the lance leaders and sergeants to come to you," she said, without preamble. "Angelotti, I want you with the guns and all the missile troops. Just get them inside the walls. Henri Brant and Blanche and Baldina will handle the train. Thomas, I want you leading the foot troops."

His dark, unshaven face showed sudden confusion. "Aren't you leading the foot, boss? Won't you be back before we leave?"

"I'll be back before you're inside Dijon. You'll have Euen Huw and Pieter Tyrrell as your officers. Geraint will keep any stragglers under control—won't you?" she added, as the big Welshman plodded up to them through the mud.

She studied his unreadable features, thought for the hundredth time, *Perhaps nothing* does *go on behind that face*, and watched him draw himself up, a large, dirty man in mail, cloak, and archer's sallet.

"You know I don't agree with this, boss."

"I know, Master Geraint. You can disagree all you like, once we're in Dijon." She let her expression soften. "We can debate what we do as a company, after that. What you're doing now is going into the city. Right?"

Tension left his stance. "Right. And you'll be with the enemy commander, boss? Okay."

A glance from Angelotti's calm, Byzantine features made her feel more disquiet than Geraint ab Morgan's blunt acceptance.

"With the Faris," Ash confirmed. And then: "I'm the one who can walk into the Visigoth camp and no one will say a thing."

She reached up and touched her cheek, fingers taking scars entirely for granted.

"It's still her face. She's still my twin."

[Original e-mail documents found inserted, folded, in British Library copy of 3rd Edition, Ash: The Lost History of Burgundy, (2001) — possibly in chronological order of editing original typescript?]

Message: #147 (Pierce Ratcliff/misc.)
Subject: Ash/Carthage
Date: 04/12/00 at 09.57 a.m.
From: Longman@

format address deleted
other details encrypted and non-recoverably deleted

Pierce–

I want to know what's going on! Are you still on the ship? What else have you found???

Are you sure—no, of course you're sure. _Visigoth_ Carthage!!! No wonder the existing site on land didn't match the description in 'Fraxinus'!

I don't expect you to answer lots of questions right now, but I've got to have _some_ information if I'm going to stop the book/documentary project being suspended.

Just ask Dr Isobel: _when_ can I pass on the news about her discovery to my managing director?

Oh my _God_, what a book we're going to have.

Oh, yes—is this the last of the 'Fraxinus' manuscript? Or is there one more section to come? Do hurry up and finish the translation! I swear I won't let it out of my hands!

–Anna

Message: #150 (Pierce Ratcliff/misc.)
Subject: Ash/Carthage
Date: 04/12/00 at 04.40 p.m.
From: Longman@

format address deleted
other details encrypted
and non-recoverably deleted

Pierce--

I'm stalling people.

Please get Dr Isobel to mail me. Just a sentence. Just 'we've found something amazing that verifies Dr Ratcliff's book'. Just something I can show Jon Stanley!

I may be out for a few hours tomorrow, as Nadia phoned me, but I'll take the satellite notebook-PC and check regularly.

We're probably okay till the end of the week, since I successfully managed to fudge everybody today—but if I go in Friday morning and find the plug's been pulled, I'm going to need convincing evidence that I can _show_ them.

It's been nearly a whole day, I WANT TO KNOW MORE ABOUT WHAT YOU'VE FOUND ON THE SEABED. PLEASE!!!

Love,

Message: #256 (Anna Longman/misc.)
Subject: Carthage
Date: 04/12/00 at 05.03 p.m.
From: Ngrant@

format address deleted
other details encrypted by non-discoverable personal key

Ms Longman,
>>Just ask Dr Isobel: _when_ can I pass on the news about her
>>discovery to my managing director?

If _absolutely necessary_ to the survival of Dr Ratcliff's book, you may disclose his 3/12/00 mailing to your managing director. This is on condition that it goes no further, until I am ready to put out a press release.

You may tell him that I endorse every word Dr Ratcliff has written. We have Visigoth Carthage.

I. Napier-Grant

PART TWO

15 November AD 1476

SIEGE PERILOUS[14]

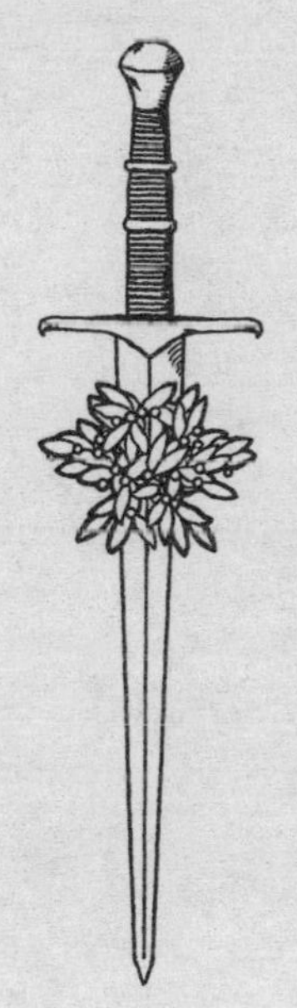

[14] Final part of the document 'Fraxinus me fecit,' presumed written c.1480(?).

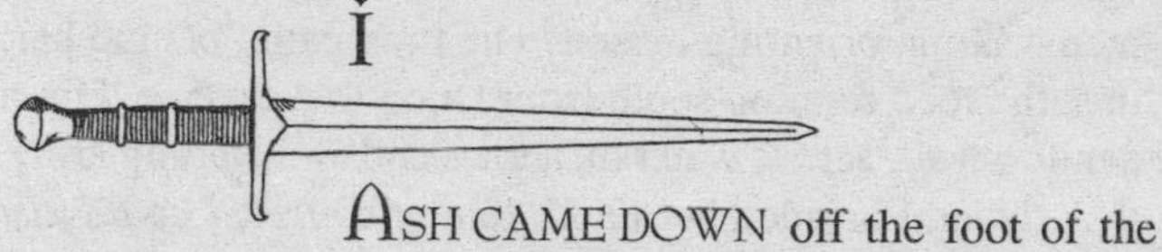

I

ASH CAME DOWN off the foot of the bluff in a clatter of clods of earth, into the exposing light of the moon.

Her eyes adjusted from night vision in the forest. The cold moon, clear of clouds, shone down on the road where she crouched.

Shit! I'm surrounded by bodies!

A clear sky brought lower temperatures: frost glittering on the mud; cat-ice forming a skin on puddles, water-filled holes, and expanses of quagmire. Around her, crammed together in the slopping impassable mud ruts, horse-drawn carts and people—horses with bony, arched spines, heads hanging down in sleep or exhaustion. And men, men and women bundled up on the ground, filthy, careless of the mud that froze around and on them as they slept, or sprawled dead in the night.

Ash froze, squatting down in the bitter cold, listening for shouts.

Nothing.

She rubbed the wind's cold tears from her eyes, thought: *No; it only* looks *like a field of battle—but there's no dead bodies piled up man high, no scavengers looting, no crows and rats, no drying blood; it doesn't* smell *like a skirmish, an ambush, a massacre.*

These men are sleeping, not dead.

Refugees.

Sleeping, exhausted, wherever they were when darkness fell tonight.

She remained perfectly still, alert for any movement of men waking, orienting herself. The Lion camp behind her; this, the road running south from Dijon to Auxonne. Dijon a mile ahead, across water meadows and an invading army.

A thought invaded her mind. *But, of course, I could just keep going. Stay clear of Dijon. Keep going: leave Floria and the Faris, the company and the Wild Machines, behind me: leave everything, because it's all different now; I only ever wanted to be a soldier—*

That ended on the beach at Carthage. That ended when something made *me start walking toward the pyramids, toward the Wild Machines.*

South of her, she heard the distant bugling of a wolf's call. Another; two more; then, silence.

Still want to run?

She felt her mouth move, wryly.

I am *a soldier. I have a couple of hundred living, breathing reasons behind me for why I need answers* right now.

Of course, I could fuck off and leave Tom Rochester in charge. Go someplace else. Sign on as a grunt. Stop trying to hold all this together—

A twist of unease in her bowels made her aware of the extent of her fear. Greater than she expected.

Is that because going to the Visigoths now is lunatic? It is *lunatic. Some damn guard can hack me down without a question asked. The Faris can have me executed. Or on a ship back to Carthage—what's left of it. I think, after Basle, I know her—but do I? It's stupidly dangerous!*

And that's before *I get my questions answered.*

Lose the armor, lose the sword, Ash thought. *Lie down to sleep beside one of these women, get up in the morning, and carry on walking. I'd keep my face hidden, but no one's going to recognize me; not among this lot.*

There must be hundreds of thousands of refugees in this war. I'd just be one more. Even if they manipulated the Faris's army, the Wild Machines wouldn't find me. I could get out of Burgundy. I could stay hidden for months. For years.

Yeah: lose the armor, lose the sword; get raped and murdered because I still own a pair of boots.

No one stirred out of their exhaustion.

She got carefully to her feet. The demi-gown buckled over her brigandine and the cloak over all, kept her armor from being obvious. She kept one hand on the scabbard of her sword. Under the hood, and helmet, her face felt naked. The cold wind whipped her hair against her scarred cheeks, hair too short now to get in her eyes.

I'd stay alive, she thought. *At least until I starved.*

The taste of urine settled into her mouth. The road stank of piss and excrement. She stepped across deep cart ruts, moving quietly on the sodden earth between groups of slumped bodies: men and women so exhausted that they had collapsed where they stood, waiting for tomorrow's dawn.

It was a minute before she realized that she was seeing children everywhere, almost every family with swaddled babies or small brats. Someone far off coughed; a young baby cried. Ash blinked, in the night chill.

At that age, I was one of a slave's litter in Carthage. Waiting for the knife.

Moving through the mud with the quietness of an animal—and there were no dogs here, few horses; only people on foot, with what they could carry on their backs—she placed her boots with care, avoiding potholes, and crossed the track. She had an impulse to leave her cloak spread over one child, but her automatic stealthy movement carried her past before she could give way to it.

The Faris and me, we have more in common with each other than we do with these people.

Her breath smoked on the chill, moonlit air. Without hesitation, she turned north, trudging toward the crossroads and bridge north of the town.

I'm not going to run. Not with Robert and the rest in Dijon. The company knows it, and I know it: that's why we've never had a choice about coming here.

Damn the Earl of Oxford, damn John de Vere; why didn't he bring all *my men to Carthage—! I could be half the world away!*

Done, now.

I'd still be hearing a dead man's voice—

Godfrey—ah, Jesu! I miss Godfrey!

Bad enough to remember him so clearly I think I hear him?

She plodded on, through frozen scrubland, across ground it would have taken her minutes to cross in daylight. She spared a glance for the moon, saw that something under an hour had passed, and with that came over a rise and in sight of the bridge and the great north part of the siege camp.

"Son of a *bitch* . . ."

Seeing it from the bluff with John Price, she had only seen west of the river: tents spread out across three or four miles of what had been vine-covered hills and cornfields and water meadows. Across the bridge, north of the town, there was nothing *but* tents, hundreds of them, white in the moon; and farther over, dark structures might have been field-forts, thrown up as winter quarters. And more great siege machinery: trebuchets, and the square silhouettes of hide-covered towers.

No golems visible.

The bridge was dark, only a campfire here and there on the perimeter this side, and the intermittent movement of guards around them. The remains of old crucifixions hung from trees: mute reminder of what happens to refugees. She began to catch snatches of voices, across the cold air: Carthaginian Latin.

I've got an hour before John Price does his stuff. I hope. Don't get it wrong, rosbif . . .

It is easy, in the night, the confusion, the lack of timing and command and control, for everything to go to hell in very short order. She knows this, wonders for a moment if she should go back, and on that doubt straightens her shoulders and walks forward, down the muddy slope, onto the road that leads to the bridge and the perimeter of the Visigoth camp.

"Halt!"

"Okay, okay," Ash called, good-humoredly, "I'm halting." She held her gauntlets out from her side, open palms clearly displayed.

"We ain't got no fucking food!" a despairing voice bawled in French. "Now bugger off!"

Another, deeper male voice said in Carthaginian, "Put a bolt over their heads, *nazir*, they'll run."

"Oh, *what*?" Ash snuffled a laugh. Excitement fizzed in her blood. She found herself grinning so broadly that her mouth hurt, and the night cold stung her teeth. "Green Christ up a fucking Tree! *Alderic*? *'Arif* Alderic?"

There was a brief moment of complete silence, in which she had time to think *No, of course you were mistaken, girl, don't be such a bloody idiot*; and then, from one of the dark figures at the wagon gate, the same male voice said, "*Jund*?[15] Is that you, *jund* Ash?"

"Hell's great gaping gates! I don't believe it!"

"Step forward and be recognized!"

Ash wiped the moisture off her upper lip with the cold

---

[15] 'Jund': a mercenary.

sleeve of her demi-gown and tucked her arm back under her cloak. She stepped forward, stumbling on muddy ground, night vision gone with having looked into their fire, and came down onto the trodden mud around the wicker gate, between wagons that blocked the bridge.

Half a dozen men with spears came forward, a bearded, helmeted officer at their head.

"Ash!"

"Alderic!" She reached out, at the same moment that he did; they gripped arms and stood grinning at each other for a stunned second. "Keeping an eye on your perimeter guards, huh?"

"You know how it is." The big Carthaginian chuckled, letting go of her, running his hand over his braided beard.

"So—who'd you upset, to get posted back up here?"

That jolted him, she saw it; made him focus himself again as a soldier, and an enemy. His shadowed face became severe. "Many died in your attack on House Leofric."

"Many of my men, too."

A thoughtful nod. The *'arif* snapped his fingers, muttered something to a guard, and the man set off at a run back into the camp. Ash saw him slow, once away from the guiding firelight at the gate.

"I suppose I should consider you my prisoner," Alderic said, stolidly. He moved, and the firelight shone onto his face. Ash saw, along with the amazement that he was concealing, a brief spurt of amusement. "God in His mercy damn you. I did not believe a woman could do what you did. Where is the English *jund*, the white mullet livery? Is he with you here? Who is with you?"

"No one's with me."

Her mouth dried as she spoke. She thought, *Damn, it had to be him, he knows me, he'll turn the camp guards out, John Price will have his work cut out for him down at the siege engines.*

Well, he's a hard bastard, he can take it.

"What you see is what you get," Ash remarked, keeping her gauntleted hands in plain view. "Yes, I am bearing a sword; I'd like to keep it."

The *'arif* Alderic shook his head. He gave a deep bellowing laugh. With a good- natured cheerfulness, beckoning his men forward, he said, "I wouldn't trust you with a blunt spoon, *jund*, never mind with a sword."

Ash shrugged. "Okay. If I were you, though, I'd ask the Faris first."

Alderic himself put back her cloak, while two of the guards held her arms, and began unbuckling her sword belt. His fingers were quick, even in the chill. Straightening up, her scabbarded blade in his hands, he said, "Don't try to convince me the General knows you're here."

"No. Of course not. You'd better tell her." Ash met his gaze. "You'd better tell her Ash is here to negotiate with her. Sorry I didn't bring my white flag."

She could see in a second that the cheek of it appealed to him. The *'arif* turned, gave orders to the gate-guards, and the men either side of Ash pushed her forward, not particularly roughly, into the camp. The river rustled below, as they crossed the bridge, walking out into muddy lanes between tents, that showed clear in the white moonlight.

The sheer reality of her presence, here, now, among armed men who will have absolutely no hesitation in killing her—that reality makes her eyes open wide to the freezing night wind, as if to imprint the moonlit silhouettes of hundreds of frost-rimed pavilions; her ears take in the noise their feet make, crunching through the mud. It nonetheless seems unreal. *I should be with my company: this is crazy!*

Ash, walking in the *'arif*'s wake, heard a hound bark once, a pale, lean-bodied shadow in the night, nosing at rubbish abandoned outside one of the big barrack-tents—almost no small tents, she noted; the Visigoths like to keep their men in bigger units—and an owl flicked like the white shadow of death over her head, brought her heart into her mouth with the memory of hunting, in Carthage's darkness, among the pyramids.

They skidded, walking up and down slopes, walking for half a mile or more, still within the camp, hardly closer to the north wall of Dijon. Moonlight glinted from something—the artillery-battered tiles on Dijon's turreted roofs.

Somewhere a sally gate is being opened. Please God.

"Seven men of my forty died when you attacked the House," Alderic said, dropping back to walk beside her. He still gazed ahead, profile stark in silver light. "*Nazir* Theudibert. Troopers Gaina, Barbas, Gaiseric . . ."

Ash let a little of the bleakness she felt into her voice. "Those are men I would have killed personally."

Looking at his bearded face, she thought him entirely aware—as a good commander should be—of the beating that had lost her her child, who had done it, their names.

"You are too seasoned a campaigner to let it become personal. Besides, *jund*, you did not die in our Citadel when it fell. God spares you for something: other children, perhaps."

At that, she stared up at the big Carthaginian.

He knows I lost a child: not that I can't have another. He knows I got out of Carthage: he doesn't know about the Wild Machines. He's assuming I'm here for another contract. A condotta.

If he knows anything, it's barrack stories that I'm another Faris, I hear the Stone Golem.

If they'd had reason to stop using the machina rei militaris—*and he's House Leofric; he'd know!—he'd be* afraid *of me.*

As if to confirm her thoughts, the *'arif* Alderic continued calmly: "If I were you, *jund*, I would not risk myself within reach of the *Amir* Leofric's family again. But our General is a fighting woman, she may well have a better use for you with us, here."

She registered that *Leofric's family* rather than plain *Leofric*.

"The old man's dead, huh?" she said bluntly.

In the sharp contrast of moonlight and shadow, she could see Alderic raise his eyebrows. When he spoke, it was still in the tone of one professional colleague to another:

"Sick, I thank you, *jund*; but recovering well. What else might we expect, now that God blesses us so clearly?"

"He *does*?"

A flicker of amusement. "You could not know, in Dijon. God touches His earth, at Carthage, with the light of His blessing; and any man may see His cold fire burning over the Tombs of the King-Caliphs. A seer told me it presages a speedy end to our crusade here."

She blinked, thought, *He assumes I've made my way* out of Dijon? and then, *Cold fire over the tombs—*

Over the pyramids.

The aurora of the Wild Machines.

"And you think it's a sign of God's *favor*?" she blurted.

"How else? You yourself, *jund*, were there when the earth shook the Citadel and the palace fell. And, all in one moment, the first Fire of the Blessing was seen, and King-Caliph Gelimer was spared from death in the earthquake."

"But—!"

There was no time to formulate questions: they were arriving on the heels of the *'arif*'s messenger; the man still shouting at the guards on what Ash saw, by the livery, was the Faris's quarters. No tent there: raw timber had been knocked together into a long, low, turf-roofed building, surrounded by braziers and troops and slaves waking from their sleep.

About to persist, she shut up when a white-clad figure opened the arched doorway and stepped out.

The automatic attention of the men would have told her it was the Faris, if nothing else; but the moon on the river fall of silver-blond hair, falling down about her shoulders to her thighs, was unmistakable. Ash, watching and not yet seen, had a second to think *I used to look exactly like that,* before she strode forward, long-legged and gawky, arms wrapped in her cloak, and said in a cheerful voice, "This is a parley. You want to talk to me."

With absolutely no hesitation, the Visigoth woman said, "Yes. I do. *'Arif*, bring her inside."

The Faris turned and walked back through the doorway. Her white garment was a heavy robe of marten fur and silk, swathing her body. Unarmed, bareheaded, barely awake, she seemed still in complete possession of herself. Ash stumbled on the wooden steps, her feet numbed by the cold.

Two golem stood, one either side of the door, oil lamps held in their stone hands.

They might have been merely statues of men: one in white marble, the other in carved red sandstone. An artificer's hand had certainly shaped the muscled arms, the long limbs and sculpted torso, given form to the aquiline features. Then the bright polished bronze of shoulder and elbow joints flashed in the light, as the marble golem raised its lamp higher. Ash heard the infinitesimal sound of greased metal sliding on metal. The red golem mirrored the movement, the vast weight of its stone body shifting.

"Follow!"

At the Faris's word the two golems fell in behind her, their stone tread making the wooden floor creak. A flickering light danced on the tapestried walls.

Ash stared at the back of the golems. *I was so damn close. So damn close to the Stone Golem itself, the* machina rei militaris . . .

She called ahead, "You want to speak to me privately, Faris."

"Yes. I do." The Visigoth General walked without hesitation into an arch hung with silk curtains, and hands pulled the material back for her to pass. Ash, as she followed, glanced to one side and saw fair-haired slaves in woollen tunics, House slaves, sent up from the African coast, even one or two men she knew by sight from House Leofric. But not—a swift searching glance—the man Leovigild, or the child Violante.

Leovigild, who tried to talk to me in my cell; Violante, who brought me blankets.

Of course they might be dead.

"Isn't it nice when you get important enough that people don't kill you out of hand?" Ash said sardonically, walking into the low, lanternlit chamber and throwing herself down onto a stool in front of the nearest brazier. She didn't look at Alderic or the Faris for a moment, putting back her hood, stripping off gauntlets and sallet, and stretching her hands out to the heat. When she did, it was with a look of complete confidence. "Not won Dijon, yet, then?"

It was the *'arif* who rumbled, "Not yet."

She had one dizzy moment, literally light-headed, looking at the *'arif* commander Alderic and seeing how he watched herself and the Faris. *Identical sisters. One, you've followed around Iberia, and trusted your life to in combat. And the other—you cut the throat of, when she was fourteen weeks old.*

Ash's hand moved. She put it down again, not wanting to reach up to the unseen scar on her neck. She settled for grinning at Alderic and watching him wince at her scarred face. There was still sympathy in his expression, but not to excess. Professional, military . . . evidently he felt his semiresponsibility discharged with his own confession to her in Carthage.

"Dijon is not yet won by assault." The Faris wrapped her arms around her body, lifting her robe as she turned. The light on her perfect face showed her tired, but not drawn, campaigning hard, but not starving.

"Assaults don't end sieges. Hunger, disease, and treachery end sieges." Ash lifted a brow, at Alderic. "I want to talk to your boss, *'arif*."

The Faris said something quietly to him. Alderic nodded. As the big man left, the Faris signaled to the slaves, and remained standing while food and drink was brought in by men wiping suddenly broken sleep out of their faces.

The long chamber contained trestle tables, chests, a box bed; all of it European and probably looted. Among these Frankish items, the war gear of the Visigoth General, and the red clay and white marble of the golems, seemed jarring.

"Why interrupt my sleep?" the Visigoth woman said, suddenly quizzical. "You could have waited until morning to be a traitor?"

Both of them? Ash thought, nothing registering on her face. *Without my saying anything—they're both assuming I've been in Dijon all this time?*

Of course*—because the Faris will have seen men in my livery on the walls! And since I haven't talked to the* machina rei militaris, *it can't have told her where I've really been.*

She thinks I'm here to give her the city.

Let *her think that. I've got about thirty minutes. I only have to keep them guessing for that long. Stay alive for that long.*

And meantime do what I came for.

The Faris stared for a moment. She walked back to the chamber door, past her mail hauberk hanging on a body form, and gave quiet orders to the slaves. The men left the room. Turning, she said, "The golem will tear you apart if you attack me. I need no guards."

"I'm not here to kill you."

"I will doubt that, for my own survival." The Visigoth woman walked closer, seating herself in a carved chair farther off from the brazier. It was as she sat, her body dropping limply down onto the silken cushions, that Ash realized how weary she was. Long silver lashes drooped over her eyes for a moment.

Still with her eyes closed, and as if completing long thoughts, the Faris said, "But you wouldn't be here, after I've taken the city, would you? You're too afraid of being taken to Carthage again. You haunt me," the woman added unexpectedly.

"Dijon," Ash said neutrally.

"You will have your price for opening a gate." The Faris put her hands in her lap. The fur gown slid back, exposing her leg to the charcoal brazier's heat. Red light gleamed on her fine, pale skin. A self-possessed woman, little different from the woman Ash had seen at Basle.

Looking at the Faris's hands in her lap, Ash saw that the flesh at the sides of her perfect nails was ripped, bitten; fragments of skin stripped out and the meat showing red beneath.

"The safety of my company is paramount," Ash said. As if it were a normal negotiation—and *might* it be?—she added, "We march out with full honors of war. All our kit. Give an undertaking not to contract to the Empire's enemies in Christendom."

As if she did not want to look, but could not stop herself, the Faris met Ash's gaze. With a quiet fretfulness, she said, "Our lord Gelimer presses me hard. Messengers, pigeons, as well as the *machina rei militaris*. 'Press the siege, press hard'—but other commanders could hold the siege, my place is with my field armies! Give me the city, and I am in a mood to make it worth your while."

So Gelimer did *make it out of the palace alive. Damn. That's one rumor down.*

Ash briefly considered asking, *Is my husband Fernando alive?* and dismissed both the thought and the odd stab of grief that came with it.

And are they still fighting up in Flanders?

"My money was on Gelimer thinking the campaign's going to have to stop for the winter, the crusade's succeeded so far, it can all wait till spring. Meanwhile Gelimer makes himself a *secure* elected monarch." Ash rubbed her cold hands together. "If the real action's in Flanders, Gelimer won't send you orders. You're Leofric's toy; Gelimer doesn't want him looking good at the moment."

She spared a glance to see how the Faris was taking her familiarity with Carthaginian politics.

"You're wrong. Nothing matters to our King-Caliph but the death of the Duke and the fall of Burgundy." As if they were sisters, the Visigoth woman said, "Father is ill; he took injuries in the earth tremor. Cousin Sisnandus commands the House. I speak with Sisnandus, through the Stone Golem—he assures me Father will be well, soon."

At the mention of the *machina rei militaris*, Ash felt the

nape of her neck turn cold. "You can still speak to it? To the Stone Golem?"

The Faris's gaze slid away. "Why should I not?"

Something in her tone made Ash freeze, hardly breathing, trying to pick up every nuance.

"I tell the Stone Golem what the tactical situation is, and Sisnandus and the King tell me to continue here. I would sooner hear it from Father . . ." She sighed, rubbing at her eyes. "He must recover, soon. It takes two weeks, a month, to go back in person: I cannot leave here."

Her eyes opened: her dark gaze met Ash's. Ash thought, *There is something different about you*, but could not work out what it might be.

"You've heard the other voices," Ash said. Not knowing, until she heard herself say it, that it must be true. "You've heard the Wild Machines!"

"Nonsense!"

The Faris looked for a moment as if she might jump to her feet. Her robe fell back farther, disclosing that the woman was wearing her shift, with a belt and dagger fastened over it any-old-how, the signs of a sudden waking alarm. Her hand moved down to caress the curved knife's hilt.

The Faris glanced over toward the nearest golem. Lamplight shone on its red stone limbs, its eyeless face. " 'Wild Machines' . . . ?"

"They told me Friar Bacon called them that."

"They *told* you . . ." The woman stumbled over her words. Her voice strengthened. "I—yes—I heard what the *machina rei militaris* reported, on the night of your attack on Carthage. The tremor disturbed it, obviously: it told me nothing but some myth or legend that someone once read into it. Garbled nonsense!"

Ash felt the palms of her hands become cold, wet, with sweat. "You heard it. You heard them!"

"I heard the Stone Golem!"

"You heard something speaking *through* the Stone Golem," Ash said, leaning forward intensely. "I made them tell me—they weren't expecting it—I can't do it again. But you heard them say what they were: *Ferae Natura Machinae*. And you heard them say what they want—"

"Fiction! Nothing but fiction!" The Faris shifted around in the chair, so that she no longer looked at Ash. "Sisnandus assures me it is a made-up story some slave must have read into the Stone Golem at some point—probably some slave with a grudge. He has executed many slaves in retribution. A temporary glitch, nothing more."

Oh Lord. Ash stared down at the Carthaginian woman. *And I thought* I *was avoiding thinking about this. . . .*

"You can't believe that," she said gently. "Faris. Where there was one voice, I heard many. You heard them, too. Didn't you?"

"I didn't listen. They told me nothing! I won't hear."

"Faris—"

"There *are* no other machines!"

"There's more than the voice of the Stone Golem—"

"I will not listen!"

"What have you asked them?"

"Nothing."

To an outsider—and Ash suddenly conceives of that hypothetical outsider, perhaps because she wonders if slaves or guards are listening at doors—this would seem uncanny: two women with the same face, talking to each other with the same voice. She has to touch her scars to reassure herself, seek out the fading tan that masks the Visigoth woman's eyes, to know that they are not the same person, that she is not in the same place as the dead baby and the boar wood.

"I don't believe you haven't spoken to them," Ash said flatly. "What, not even to find out what they are?"

The woman's cheeks flushed slightly.

"There is no *them*. What do you want with me, *jund*?"

Ash leaned forward to the brazier. "I'm your bastard sister."

"And that means?"

"I don't know what it means." Ash smiled, quickly and ruefully. "On the most pragmatic level, it means I hear what you hear. I've heard the Wild Machines telling me what they are. And I've heard them say why they've manipulated House Leofric for the past two hundred years, trying to breed you—"

"No!"

"Oh yes." Ash's smile glinted. "You're Gundobad's child."

"I have heard none of this!"

"Your—our father, Leofric; he's been used. Is *being* used." Ash stood up. She gave a sudden, wary glance at the golems. They remained still. "Faris, in the name of Christ! You're the one, you've been hearing the Stone Golem since you were born, you've got to tell me what you've been hearing from the Wild Machines!"

"*Nothing*." The woman also rose. She stood barefoot on the furs thrown down on the rough-hewn oak boards, her eyes on a level with Ash's. Her head tilted a little to one side, studying. "This is some fantasy of a discontented slave. How can it be anything else?"

"This isn't your war. It isn't Leofric's war. It isn't even the fucking *King-Caliph's* war." Ash turned her back, stalking up and down the chamber, in and out of lamplight and brazier light. "It's the Wild Machines' war. Why? Why, Faris? Why?"

"I don't know!"

"Then bloody ask!" Ash roared. "*You* might get an answer!"

The nearest golem shifted on its stone feet. Ash froze, waiting until it returned to complete immobility, as she might have done for a large, fierce, not very intelligent dog.

The woman said, "I . . . heard voices. Once! And—It is some error. Leofric will correct it, as soon as he is well!"

"You know what they are—I bet you've even seen them, in the desert—Alderic called it 'God's blessing'—"

"Be quiet." The Visigoth General spoke with a sudden, immense authority. A little helplessly, Ash stopped pacing. She felt herself to be in the presence of a woman who had fought a dozen Iberian campaigns before she ever set foot in Christendom. Unarmored, without weapons, the woman was nonetheless a warrior. The only crack in her composure came with her shifting, inadequate gaze.

"Look at it from my point of view, *jund*," the Faris said quietly. Her voice shook. "I have three armies in the field. That's my priority. That gives me enough work, twenty-four hours of the day. I do not need to bother with some *rumor*. Where would these other *machinae* be? How would we not know of them, and the *amirs* who must have built them?"

"But you know it's no rumor: you *heard*—" Ash broke off.

She isn't listening to me. She knows what she heard. But she won't admit it—even to herself.

Do I tell her what I *know?*

A gleam in the corner of the chamber resolved itself into another body form, covered by a white harness. Seeking a diversion of the Faris's attention, Ash moved closer to it. She reached up and touched the breastplate, slid her fingers down over the fauld to the left lower lame, and the newly riveted strap on the tasset of the completely familiar Milanese armor.

"Bloody *hell.* Been carting this around with you, then? All the way from Basle? But then, I suppose it fits *you*, too!"

Ash ran her fingers back up her own armor, where it hung on the body form, giving the strap that buckled plackart to breastplate a solid tug. "Buckles could do with a polish. All these bloody slaves, you'd think you could manage that."

"Sit down, mercenary."

With that reminder of enmity, Ash remembered the matter of time, saw no clock in the chamber, could see no moon through the tapestried doorway. *I won't know,* she realized. *When all hell breaks loose, I won't know whether it's John Price putting his attack in, or the rest of the company being caught on their way in through the sally port.*

"You know this isn't about armies," Ash said, turning to face the Visigoth woman. "If it was, you'd be fighting the Turk, not Burgundy. Whatever they are, whatever they want, these Wild Machines: they're getting stronger. You must know that *they* make the darkness, not some damn Rabbi's curse. And now it's spreading—"

The Faris shook her head, loose hair shimmering. "I don't *listen*!"

"Do they call you 'Gundobad's child'?"

Dark eyes, under silver brows, watched her with a flat lack of affect. The Faris said mechanically, "Nothing speaks to me except the tactical machine. Anything else is history, legends that someone once read into the golem. Nothing else speaks to me."

She isn't seeing me, Ash thought. *She isn't even talking to me.*

Is this what she said to *Leofric*? The day that it happened?

The realization was sudden, but absolute; Ash imagined

both the woman's first tentative questions to her adoptive father and the lord-*amir*'s instant, panicky replies. And now her denial.

But how long has Leofric been ill? Ever since the 'quake, two months ago? Christus! *Was* he injured in the earth tremor, or is it something else—?

And who's this cousin Sisnandus? How much does he know? About the Wild Machines, about any of this. . . . How ill *is* Leofric?

"So what's 'Father' said to all this?" Ash demanded, sardonically.

The woman looked up. "I shall hardly bother him with such nonsense, until he recovers his full health."

Aware of being on dangerous ground, Ash only watched the woman, saying nothing.

Have the Wild Machines already spoken through the machina *and made House Leofric set a guard on it? Can I ask her that?*

No. I'm not getting through to this woman. Whatever I'd ask her—she doesn't want to know. She's shut down for the duration.

And I don't know what she'll repeat through the Stone Golem.

The Faris leaned back in her chair. The orange light from the oil lamps limned her brow, cheek, chin, shoulder. She passed a hand over her face. Some of the weariness went, and with it, strangely, some of her authority. She looked up at Ash, her expression acutely indecisive.

"Is your confessor with you?" the Faris said, suddenly, into the silence.

Ash gave a startled laugh. "My *confessor*? You're going to have me executed? Isn't that a bit extreme?"

"Your priest, the man Gottfried, Geoffroi—"

"Godfrey?" Stunned, Ash said, "Godfrey Maximillian's dead. He died trying to get out of Carthage."

The Faris put her arms on the back of her chair, resting her weight on it. Ash watched her look up at the plank-and-earthen roof, as if the answers were somewhere in the dirt, and look down again, meeting Ash's gaze.

"I . . . have questions I would have asked a Frankish priest."

"You'll have to try someone else. They don't come much deader than Godfrey when I saw him last," Ash said coarsely.

"You're certain?"

A chill that was nothing to do with winter twisted in her gut. "What's one priest, to you? When did Godfrey Maximillian ever meet you?"

The Faris looked away. "We never met. I had heard his name at Basle, as a priest of your company."

Spurred, impulsive, Ash blurted, "Would you know his voice?"

The color of the woman's face altered, subtly; she looked now as if she were unwell.

"You are the only other one," the Faris said suddenly. "*You* hear. You and I, both. How else am I to know I am not sunstruck-crazy?"

". . . Because we hear the same thing?" Ash said.

It was no more than a whisper: "Yes."

Armor, golems, the Visigoth camp outside: all forgotten. Nothing else exists but the realization: *She isn't talking about the Wild Machines now*.

Cold sweat slicked Ash's palms. Dry-mouthed, she asked, "What *do* you hear, Faris?"

"I hear a heretic priest, persuading me that I should betray my religion and my King-Caliph. I hear a heretic priest telling me that my *machina rei militaris* is not to be *trusted*—"

On the last word, risen an octave, she cut herself off.

Almost in a whisper, the Faris finished: "I hear great voices, tormenting a heretic's soul."

Ash, holding her breath, released air slowly and silently through her nostrils. The golems' perfumed lamps made the atmosphere heavy, both cold and stifling. Aware that one wrong word or gesture could lose it, she said quietly, "A 'heretic priest' . . . yes, it is; it must be. Godfrey Maximillian. I . . . heard him too."

With that, the realization hit home. She momentarily forgot where she stood; was back in the command tent, her dream of boars and snow fading, hearing a voice—

It really is *him. Godfrey, dead Godfrey; if she hears him, too, it* has *to be!*

She pushed the heel of her hand into her eye sockets, one after the other, smearing away water. Rapidly, remembering the woman in front of her, she said, "And the 'great voices' you hear are the Wild Machines."

"A dead heretic, and ancient machine-minds?" The Faris's perfect face moved in an expression of sardonic humor, fear, forgiveness: all in a second. "And you'll tell me, too, that I can't trust the Stone Golem to win my battles for me, now. Ash—what else *would* you say to me? You're fighting with the Burgundians."

"And if you pay me to fight on the same side as your men," Ash said steadily, "I'll tell you exactly the same thing."

"I will not trust an enemy!"

"But you'll trust the Stone Golem, after *this*?"

"Be quiet!"

The flickering light of oil lamps gleamed on armor, on mail, on the red stone limbs of the golem.

Godfrey, Ash thought, dazed. *But how?*

"I could hire your men," the Faris said absently, "but not to fight under your command: I would need you elsewhere. Father wants you," she added. "He told me so, before he grew ill. Sisnandus tells me he still orders your presence."

Oh shit, I bet he does!

"Your 'father' Leofric wants to dissect me, to know how *you* work." Ash lifted her eyes to discover an expression of bewilderment on the woman's face. "Didn't you know that? Probably he'd want it even more badly, now! If you and I can hear a *dead* man—"

A voice outside bellowed, "To arms!"

Oh, Christus, not now! What a time to be interrupted!

A fist hammered at the outer door of the command building. Ash heard shouting, did not shift her gaze from the Visigoth woman's face.

"Maybe," Ash said, "it isn't just Leofric and this Sisnandus who want me in Carthage. Do you *know* who's giving you orders, Faris?"

"*To arms!*" a male voice bawled again, outside the chamber door.

The Faris swung around, breaking eye contact with Ash, marched to the door, and flung the curtains aside, just before a slave male could do it.

"Give me a proper report, *'arif*," she snapped.

The man-at-arms, with the *'arif*'s rank on his livery, gasped, "They're attacking the camp—!"

"Which perimeter?"

"Southwest. I think, *al-sayyid*."[16]

"Ah. That will be a diversion. Get me the *qa'id* for the engineers' camp, but first, send a message to alert the *qa'id*

---

[16] 'Boss.'

of the east camp. Get me *'arif* Alderic and his troop, here, now. Slaves! Clothe me!"

She flung back into the room, brushing past Ash, who had to take a step back to keep her balance. Jolted, Ash had time to think *Is that what* I *look like when I get in gear?*

"I'm not sending you to Carthage, yet. Father will have to wait. I need the city. I'm sending you back to Dijon, *jund*." The Faris looked up from the clothing on her bed, with a brief, surprising smile. "With an escort. Just in case you get ambushed on the way."

Back to Dijon. *Into* Dijon!

A handful of slaves pushed past Ash, two or three of them showing stark surprise and recognition at seeing her. They began to strip robe and shift from the Visigoth General, and dress her from the skin out.

"You're giving me an *escort*?"

"Dijon is where you are crucial to me, now. I need the city! We will talk again. About these . . . Wild Machines. And your dead priest. Later."

Ash shook her head, spluttering between frustration and anger. "No. *Now*, Faris. You know what war is! Don't leave something because you think you can do it tomorrow."

The other *'arif* rushed back in. "Now they are attacking the eastern perimeter, *al-sayyid*!"

Ash opened her mouth, all but said, aloud and incredulously, *Two* attacks? She shut her mouth again.

"And that will be the true attack. Get your men to arms! You were a distraction, to allow these sallies out of the city? Well, you may still have your price!" Not waiting for a confirmation, and still with a wicked smile covering her immense weariness, the Visigoth woman put her arms up as her slaves lowered her mail hauberk over her head, wriggling arms and body and neck until the mail snugged down over her body.

I need another hour with her! Ash thought, frustrated. *She* wants *to talk, I can* feel *it—*

As a child tied the waist of the hauberk to her belt with aiglettes, the Faris continued:

"Alderic will take you to the gates, once we have contained these attacks. We *will* talk again—sister."

Stunned at the swiftness of it, Ash found herself stumbling out, down steps into the moonlit camp, into a flurry of lanterns, men running with spears and recurved bows, *nazirs* bawling hoarse orders; all the ordered confusion one might wish to see in a camp surprised by a night attack. By the time she got her helmet on and her night vision back, she was being hurried along between two of *'arif* Alderic's men, boots ringing on the frosted earth, toward the great dark bulk of the city walls of Dijon.

She can't just send me off like this! Not without answers—!

Torches moved outside the impromptu holding area. Her feet grew numb in her boots.

From somewhere to the east she heard steel blades slamming together.

Two *attacks? One will be mine. I wonder if Robert's sent a force out of the sally gate himself? It'd be like him. Twice the confusion.*

" 'Hurry up and wait,' " she remarked, to Alderic's *nazir*, a small spare man in well-worn mail. He said nothing, but he gave a brief smile. *No different in* this *man's army.*

After an interminable wait, the sounds of combat moved off. Nothing then, but torches moving in the Visigoth camp, legionaries on fire watch shouting in frustration, warhorses neighing from their lines. She considered asking if the cooks been woken up too, decided against it, and found herself almost falling asleep on her feet, the length of the wait blurring in her mind.

"*Nazir*!" The *'arif* Alderic strode back into the circle of torchlight, nodded abruptly at his men, and they all moved off, Ash in the middle of the eight, the cold forcing her half-sleeping mind back to alertness.

She stumbled down trenches, behind palisades, the smell of earth and powder thick in her nostrils, then out into the open, beyond the last of the defensive barriers. Ahead, across a wide expanse of blasted, raw earth, torches already began to flare—up on the hoardings hanging out from the battlements, above the northwest gate.

"Best of luck," the *'arif* said brusquely. Glimpsing Alderic's face, she saw the last of his guilt-induced kindness.

He and his men vanished back into the trenches, the darkness, the flames.

"God *damn* it!" Ash remarked into the cold air.

She let me go. Yeah. Because she can. She's sending me into a siege. Because she wants me to betray Dijon. She doesn't think I'm going any*where.*

And she thinks she can get me for Leofric anytime . . .

"Cow!"

Ash stopped dead, on the battered, rutted, rough ground, up to her ankles in mud. Cold wind made her eyes leak tears down her numb, scarred cheeks. Through the helmet's padding, she could hear the river running somewhere off on her right-hand side, water not yet frozen over. Closer, dancing in her vision, she saw sheer towering walls and lights in front of her, over the northwest gate of Dijon.

"Oh, the cow. She's *already* got my armor. Now she's kept my bloody *sword*, too!"

A nervous voice came from the parapet above the

portcullis and gates. "Sarge, there's someone out there *laughing*."

Ash wiped her eyes. *Goddammit, they should have had word about me—fine time to go down to friendly fire!*

"Some crazy rag'ead tart," a second, invisible male voice commented. "You going to go down there and give 'er one?"

"Yo, the wall!" She walked forward, at an easy pace, into the circle of light now spread by the lanterns, keeping an eye on the combat-ready and twitchy men lining the parapet of the gate above her. She squinted. In the poor light, their livery was unclear.

"Whose men?" she sang out.

"De la Marche!" a beer-roughened voice bawled, arrogantly.

"Who the fuck are *you*?" another, anonymous, voice demanded.

Ash looked up at bows, bills, one man in armor with a poleax.

"Don't for the Green Christ's sake shoot me now," she said unsteadily. "Not after what I've just been through! Go tell your boss he wants to see me."

There was a silence of sheer, dumbstruck amazement.

"You *what*?"

"I said, go tell your boss de la Marche he wants to see me. He does. So open the gate!"

One of the Burgundian men-at-arms snorted. "Cheeky *bitch*!"

"Who is that?"

"Can't see, sir. Not in the cloak. It's a woman, sir."

Still grinning, Ash put her cloak back over her shoulders.

Over her brigandine, dirty yellow but perfectly distinct, the livery of the Lion Azure shone in the light of their torches.

A clutch of Burgundian men-at-arms, swords drawn, hustled her through the man-high door cut into Dijon's great gates, hustled her into darkness, and echoes off masonry, and the smell of sweat and shit and pitch torches burned down to the socket.

I'm in! I'm inside the walls*!*

The relief of such safety deafened her, for a second, to the voices of men and officers.

"She could be a spy!" an overexcited billman shouted.

"A woman dressed as a man? *Whore!*"

A lance leader stuttered, "No, last August I s-saw her in the English Earl's affinity—"

She blinked, eyes gradually adjusting to the torchlight in the long tunnel of the gates, and the faint glimmer of light—dawn? torches?—at the arched exit.

And I'm sane. Or—a smile hidden by helmet and hood—*as sane as the Faris, anyway, which may not be saying much.*

Her smile faded.

And it *is* Godfrey . . . dear God: *how*?

Ash returned her attention: raised her voice. "I have to find my men—!"

I'm in. Are they*? Fuck!*

And—if we are—now, how the hell do I get us out again?

ii

GROWING FIRST LIGHT showed her devastation—a shattered no-man's-land stretching two hundred yards from the northwest gate back into the city, and as far to either side as she could see. Dawn picked out man-high heaps of rubble, the broken beams of bombard-wrecked houses and shops; scarred cobbles, burned thatch; one teetering, remaining wall.

Ash stumbled, between the Burgundian soldiers, the cold wind numbing her scarred cheeks. She spared a glance for heraldry and faces: definitely Olivier de la Marche's troops. And therefore Charles of Burgundy's loyal men.

We were with them at Auxonne, they'll be assuming we're still hired on with them—

But we might just be a damn sight better off selling Dijon to the Visigoths and heading east to the Sultan and his armies. Mercenaries are always welcome.

If we're not all dead out there.

Noise shocked the air.

Above Ash's head, in the chill prelight before dawn, the bells of Dijon suddenly began to peal out. Church after church, St. Philibert and Notre Dame, noise running back from the street where she stood; abbey and monastery, within the city walls; all their great bells pealing out high and low, shrill and clear, shaking the birds up from the roofs and the citizens awake in their houses: the bells of Dijon clamoring out into the morning, cascading with joy.

"What the fuck—?" Ash yelled.

The Burgundian officers fell back. She glimpsed Thomas Rochester shoving his way through the pack—Christus, *the first familiar face in hours*!—battered, not badly injured; safe in the city; an escort of company men-at-arms with him under the tattered Lion standard. Seeing her, he signaled, and one of the men-at-arms unrolled and raised her personal banner beside it.

"Where the fuck have *you* been?" Ash bellowed.

The dark Englishman shouted something, inaudible in the Dijon street for the noise. Pushing in close, shoulder to shoulder, he lowered his mouth close to her ear, and she thumbed up one side of her sallet to hear him shouting:

"... got in! They swam rope-bridges across at the south gate! Where the bridge has been mined?"

The scent of summer dust is suddenly heavy in her memory: she recalls riding into Dijon by that bridge, at the side of John de Vere, Earl of Oxford. Into a white, fair city.

Floria del Guiz appeared from behind Rochester, yelling, so that Ash read her lips rather than heard her above the bells and the shouting: "News has got out! I thought we'd never find you!"

"Where's Robert? *What* news?"

The woman grinned: might have said, "Sometimes you're *slow*!"

Voices shrieked at windows above Ash's head. She glanced up, listening—the earth still darker than the lightening sky—and a body cannoned into her and Thomas Rochester together. She caught her balance, shoving back at a burly man tumbling out of his scarred wooden front door, a fat woman fumbling at his shoulder and tying his points; two small children howling underfoot.

"Jesu *wept*!"

Amazed, Ash signaled to the banner, attempting to back off across the trebuchet-battered cobbled streets. Among the familiar military silhouettes in the crowd—pinch-waisted doublets, hose, bill-points, and sallets—there were civilian men bundling themselves into their gowns, cramming on their tall felt hats: neighbor shrieking to neighbors, all questions, all demands.

"Find me Roberto!" Ash directed Thomas Rochester, at battlefield pitch. The Englishman nodded, and signaled to the men-at-arms.

Now bodies pressed up against Ash from all sides. Their breaths whitened the air; the smell of old sweat and dirt filled her nostrils. She shoved. *Hopeless!* she thought. There was no way to move without using force. Rochester looked back at her and raised his shoulders, in the press of bodies. She shook her head at him, ruefully, almost relaxing into the chaos, still dazzled by the implicit safety of the city's towering walls.

The press of bodies swayed against her, the narrow street spilling people out into the no-man's-land of demolished streets and burned-out houses. Not all civilians, Ash noted; Burgundian-liveried men in mail and plate, or in archer's jacks, were also running out across the bombarded ground, toward the northwest gate and walls of the city. The pressure of the crowd began to push her inexorably in that direction.

"Okay, guys! Listen up! Better find out what the fuss is . . ."

The aches of the night's exertions and the lack of sleep blurred her mind. It was a minute before she realized she and her escort were stomping up stone steps—up to the walls, in the wake of armed men; deafened still by the bells.

Is this . . . ?

She automatically glanced back down the flight of stone steps, looking for a house with a bush hanging from it, to signify an inn. *Is this where Godfrey came to me, on the walls of Dijon, and told me he wanted me?*

There were no undamaged buildings below: everything at the foot of the wall was a mess of beams, broken plaster, scrambled roof tiles, and abandoned furniture; and masonry scorched black.

No: we must have been farther down the west wall, I remember looking down at the southern bridge. . . .

Wry humor made her smile; there was nothing other than cynicism and adrenaline to keep her going now:

. . . The same day I saw Fernando in the Duke's palace, was it? Or the day we beat up Florian's aunt? Christus!

She crowded between a priest and a tanner and a nun, pushing her way toward the crenellations, where the soldiers were leaning out under the wooden brattices[17] and shouting down off the city's north wall.

At her elbow, a monk in green robes bellowed, "It's a miracle! We have prayed, and it has been granted to us! *Deo gratias!*"

To Rochester and Floria del Guiz, impartially, Ash bawled, "What the fuck *is* this?"

Prime,[18] on the morning of the fifteenth of November, 1476: Ash tastes the chill of winter in her mouth, on the wind that blows from the northeast. She has time to notice the streaming lines of people running up to the walls—used to estimating numbers on the field, she thought: *the better part of two thousand men, women, and children.* Leaning into an embrasure, she touched her hand to the walls above Dijon's northwest gate, feeling their protection.

She cupped her gauntlet, shielding her eyes from the sun that rose on her right hand, listening for what was being so rhythmically shouted. The sight in front of her put it clear out of her mind.

A greater "town" surrounds the walls of Dijon—the town that is the Visigoth siege camp. Clear in the daylight, it has its own streets and muster grounds, its own turf-roofed barracks and Arian chapels and army markets. Two months is long enough to make them seem frighteningly established and permanent. Rank upon rank of weather-worn, bleached tents stretch out, too, into the white-misted

---

[17] Hoardings.

[18] 6 a.m.

distance. They cover all the acres between Dijon and the forests to the north.

Cold air making her eyes water, Ash let her gaze travel across the sweep of the Visigoth camp: pavises, shelters; fenced siege-engine parks; saps and trenches snaking toward the walls of the town . . . and thousands upon thousands of armed men.

Jesu! Now we're in *here—what have I done?*

Leaning out, looking west, she picked out the burned ruins of great wooden pavises that had sheltered at least four massive bombards. The cannon seemed apparently untouched—their distant crews beginning to crawl out of their bashas and poke campfires into more life.

Frost limned every blade of grass. Amid the dozens of intact mangonels, ballistas, trebuchets, and cannon, she saw a few blackened areas of grass and collapsed canvas. White-haired slaves desultorily cleared up the mess, cold-fingered and slow; she heard *nazirs* bellowing at them. Their voices came clear across the cold air.

Glancing east, she saw no sign whatsoever of any attack there, not even burned canvas.

Two attacks didn't even dent them.

She leaned forward, feeling her men crowding in beside her, moving her gaze to the north.

Men are small, three or four hundred yards away, beyond the trenches and outside bowshot and arquebus range; but livery is still visible. She could not make out the Faris's Brazen Head livery on any of them. Wind-tears blurred the edges of pavilions and the colors of pennants. She lifted her head, looking farther out from the walls.

"Jesus fucking Christ, there's thousands of them!"

Down on the Visigoth horse-lines, men fetching feed stopped, listening to the sudden noise from Dijon. The low morning sun shone on Carthaginian spearpoints, and men's helmets, on the camp perimeter. The sound of barked orders came clear across the open air. Down toward the western bridge, half-hidden by pavises, men sprinted to serve guns—a puff of white smoke came from the muzzle of one mortar, and perceptible seconds later, the *thump!* of its firing.

Fat crows flew up from camp middens.

"And a good morning to you ragheads, too!" Rochester growled, beside her, in profile against the yellow eastern sky.

Ash squinted, head whipping round, not able to see where the mortar shot hit—lobbed somewhere inside the burned streets of Dijon, back of her.

Another flat *thwack!* brought her head back around. Ten yards down the parapet, the crowd of men folded in on itself: a swirl of figures in belted gowns and chaperon hats; one voice raised in high, shocked agony. The constant shout of the crowd lining the walls drowned him out.

Shit. There is *a whole legion out there. Oh,* shit. . . .

No wonder the Faris thinks that all a "betrayal" would save her is time.

A man-at-arms in Lion livery leaned precariously out from under the hoardings, yelling down at the frost-glittering tents of the Visigoths, four hundred yards out from the walls, spit spraying out from his mouth:

"*Your city's fucked! Your Caliph's dead! How about that, motherfuckers!*"

A great cheer went up along the walls of Dijon. With Rochester and the banner at her shoulder, Ash pushed in close. The man-at-arms, a redhead she remembered as one of Ned Mowlett's men, all but lost his grip on the brattice strut he held. A mate hauled him back.

"Pearson!" Ash thumped him on armored shoulders, hauling him around to look at the first one of the men who had stayed in Dijon—filthy with mud, straggle-haired, and with a healing scar across one eyebrow.

"*Boss*!" Pearson bellowed: sweating, surprised, happy, transcendent. "Those fuckers are *done* for, aren't they, boss?"

His gold-and-blue livery was unaltered, her own device of the azure Lion Passant Guardant,[19] nothing added or subtracted by Robert Anselm. She contented herself with another slap on his shoulder.

A second priest called, "*Deo gratias,* the Visigoths and their stone demons are thrown down!"

Two yards away, a Burgundian man-at-arms yelled down, "We didn't even have to *be* there! You're outside of our city, and our walls stand! We didn't even have to *go* to Carthage and it's fucking *flattened*!"

Someone farther down the north city wall blew a herald's horn, wildly. More men-at-arms entered the crowd, unshaven men in Lion livery pushing through the press toward the frost-stiff blue and gold of the Lion Affronté on her personal banner. Behind them, men in rich gowns with their faces full of sleep—sergeants with staffs, constables, burghers—made vain attempts to clear the parapet. The deep, flat crack of mortar fire sounded again: two shots, five, and then a slow, erratic succession of explosions.

The soldiers, starting with the Lion Company men clustered around her, leaned out off the brattices, and started to chant:

"Carthage fell *down*! Carthage fell *down*! Carthage fell *down*!"

---

[19] More properly referred to as a 'lioncel,' or 'leopard'; 'Fraxinus,' however, prefers the more unorthodox usage. Presumably this reflects Ash's religious devotion to the 'Heraldic Beast' of her childhood: the mythical 'Lion born of a Virgin.'

"But it—" *wasn't quite like that!* Ash mentally protested.

A company archer, one of Euen Huw's men, shouted, "Yer Caliph's *dead* and yer city fell *down*!"

"But it was a quake—"

Floria del Guiz' voice, at her ear, bellowed, "They know that!"

Despite the precariousness of being an exposed target, Ash could only grin helplessly as the sound grew, a chant that was deep, male voices bellowing, loud enough to reach the enemy lines and then some; and she put her face up to the dawn breeze, grinning out at more Visigoth men who began to collect along the front line, muttering and gathering in groups.

" 'Ware trebuchets!" Thomas Rochester touched her arm and pointed west across the Suzon River to the big counterweight siege weapons, their crews visible now, tiny figures staring at the city walls. Eighty or ninety percent of the engines undamaged, she thought.

"Jesu, this lot aren't bright! You couldn't shift 'em with bombards!" Ash shrieked back. "Let 'em have their shout, Tom, then start moving them back down off the walls! I want us across the broken ground and *out* of here!"

"THE CALIPH IS *DEAD*! CARTHAGE FELL *DOWN*!"

The wind shifted, coming from the east as the sun rose up. She focused into the distance—up on the northern slopes, above the water meadows, an empty shell stood: nothing now but fire-blackened stone. *I wonder what happened to Soeur Simeon and the nuns?*

Ash's throat tightened. She wiped at her watering eyes.

Half the population of Dijon up on the defenses now: despite the rapid tremble of the stone parapet underfoot, where mangonel boulders struck home against the outside wall.

"They're getting the range!" she yelled to Floria, her mouth at the woman's ear to be heard over bells, men shouting, women shouting, children shrieking.

"THE CALIPH IS *DEAD*! CARTHAGE FELL *DOWN*!"

"But Caliph Theodoric died before the earthquake!" Floria yelled back, her mouth now to Ash's ear, warm damp breath feathering her skin. "And they elected another one!"

"And Gelimer's still with us. These people don't care about *that*. Oh, the hell with it! The Caliph is dead!" Ash raised her voice: "Carthage fell *down*!"

Several men in armor and Burgundian livery jackets came pushing through the crowd toward her banner. Ash let herself down off the masonry. She inclined her head, bowing a speechless greeting.

Behind the men, squads of foot soldiers began clearing the walls, heaving people back from the brattices. She blinked, hearing the faintest diminution in the sound volume. Two of the men she recognized from the summer: an elderly chamberlain-counselor of the Duke's court, and a nobleman she knew to be one of Olivier de la Marche's aides.

"It's her!" the chamberlain-counselor exclaimed.

"Messire—" Ash managed to remember his name: "—Ternant. What can I do for you? Tom, *get these bloody idiots down from here!* Green Christ on a crutch, I didn't get them back here to have them shot off the walls! Sorry, messire Ternant, what is it?"

"We expected Captain Anselm!" de la Marche's aide bellowed, his face a picture of sheer incredulity.

"Well, you've got Captain Ash!" She shifted as the first

of her men filed back off the brattices, boots booming on the hollow wooden floors.

"In that case—it is your presence that the siege council requests, Captain!" Ternant bawled, his voice cracking with age and effort.

" 'Siege council'—? Never mind!" Ash nodded emphatically. "I'll come! I'm settling my men here in their quarters first! When? What time?"

"The hour before Terce.[20] Demoiselle, we are hearing such rumors—"

She waved him to silence, in the face of the wall of sound. "Later! I'll be there, messire!"

"CARTHAGE FELL *DOWN*! CARTHAGE FELL *DOWN*!"

"I give up." Floria stood up on her toes, grabbing at Thomas Rochester's mail-shirted shoulder for support. She bellowed toward the open air, "Down with the Caliph! Carthage fell down!"

Thomas Rochester gave a snort. Abruptly, the dark Englishman caught Ash's eye and pointed. At the standards set up at different points in the enemy camp, she realized. Standing aside to let the last of her men past, she looked out from the walls at the tents Rochester indicated.

Frankish pavilions, not Visigoth barracks.

"What? *Oh*. Uh-huh . . . oh, *right* . . ."

Five hundred yards away, men were gathering in a businesslike way under a great white standard, bearing a lamb surrounded by rays of gold. It flapped in the frosty air on the eastern side of the camp.

Under the sound of bells, impacting rocks, and the chant that had got up a rhythm now—the men and women of

---

[20] i.e., 8 a.m.

Dijon struggling not to be herded off the walls—Thomas Rochester yelled, "We can kick *his* ass, boss!"

Besides Agnus Dei's standard, in what was obviously the mercenaries' part of the Visigoth camp, Ash picked out the banner of Jacobo Rossano—*wondered who was paying him after Emperor Frederick!*—and half a dozen other small mercenary companies. One standard, a naked sword, teased her memory. She blinked, the air up on this wall, a hundred and fifty feet above the ground, cold enough to make her eyes run.

"Shit, that's Onorata Rodiani."

"What?" Floria screamed.

"I *said*, that's *Onorata*—" Ash broke off. The rising wind unwrapped the standard next to Rodiani's. It was the ripped, scarred and triumphant banner carried onto a hundred fields by Cola de Monforte and his sons.

The surgeon's voice, at her ear, breathed, "The bastards! Those are *Burgundian* mercenaries!"

"Not anymore! He must have gone over, after Auxonne! That's a lot of men out there. Cola doesn't have a company. He has a small army." Ash narrowed her eyes against the slanting brilliance from the east. "Looks like nobody gives a shit for this city's chances—"

Floria's hand tightened on her arm. Ash glanced where the surgeon stared, into the now-sunlit Visigoth camp. When she saw it, she did not know how she had missed it before. In the Frankish tents back of Monforte's pavilions, a silver-and-blue banner: the Ship and Crescent Moon.

"Joscelyn van Mander," she said bleakly.

Thomas Rochester swore. "Fucking Flemish cocksucker! What's he doing out there!"

"Ah, shit, Tom! He's a mercenary!"

A stench of woodsmoke filled the air. She winced, as the

paving stones under foot juddered, and glanced toward the northwest gate. The nearest brattice was on fire.

"Fucking incendiaries now!"

The rhythm of sound broke: men and women only too eager, finally, to struggle down the steps and off the walls. Distantly, the creaking of siege weapons being wound up for a shot came to her. In the Visigoth artillery park, the red-sandstone arms of a golem glinted, raising the great trebuchet counterweight at four times the speed of a human crew.

A succession of badly aimed, jagged missiles slammed into the wall above the gate; a merlon flew apart in stone fragments, and the press of bodies lurched, cannoning into each other, screams audible above the noise.

And just in case the Visigoths also *have a gunner who can show you the brick in the castle wall that he's about to hit—*

"Time to go," Ash murmured, turning, as Rochester raised the banner.

"No: look!" Floria took another step forward, until she stood pressed against the hide-covered wooden frame of the brattice. Ash heard the surgeon's harsh intake of breath. "Sweet Green Christ . . ."

Far over, under the pale sun, the distances of the river valley were plainly visible now. On the far side of the Suzon and its bridge, people on foot plodded to the south. Too far to see who they were—peasants and craftsmen, goodwives and maids, a few deserting men-at-arms, maybe; maybe even a priest. Indistinguishable figures wrapped in cloaks and blankets, plodding, head down in the biting wind; small figures—children or old men—huddled by the side of the road, some still crying out to those that had left them.

Hungry, frozen, exhausted, the column of walking

refugees snaked on down the track, no end of them in sight.

"They're *still* coming," Floria breathed, almost inaudible over the roaring mob hanging off the walls.

Rather less interested than her surgeon, Ash grabbed Florian's arm, pulling her back from the wall. "Let's go!"

"Ash, those aren't soldiers, those are *people*!"

"Well, don't sweat it; the ragheads are leaving them alone. We appear to still have some of the rules of war operating . . ." The press of bodies on the parapet lessened. Ash tugged the surgeon toward the steps, in the wake of her men, Rochester and the banner at her shoulder.

Shrill, Floria yelled, "I expect they come down and rape and rob a few, when it gets boring in camp—don't you think, girl?"

"Depends how good her discipline is. I'd want them concentrating on getting inside these walls, if it was my troops." Ash looked back over her shoulder at the distant road and the thick clogging masses of people.

"You know what it is?" Floria said suddenly. "They're heading *south*. To the border at Auxonne. Look at them, they'd rather go under the Sunless Sky than stay here!"

Too far, up there on the walls, to hear human voices; only the shriek of ungreased axles came up through the still air, and the scream of a driven packhorse. A dot—a person—lurched and fell down, got up on his or her feet, fell again, got up, and trudged on.

Floria said, "Darkness or sun, they don't care where they're going. They just want to get away from here. These are Duchy people, townsmen, farmers, villagers, craftsmen; they're just *going*, Ash. They don't care what's in front of them."

"I'll *tell* you what's in front of them—starvation!"

The *crack*! of a small-caliber cannon: a ball thwacked

off the eastern gate tower. A huge roar of contempt and adrenaline went up from the remaining people crowding the walls:

"THE CALIPH IS *DEAD*! CARTHAGE FELL *DOWN*!"

In a moment of stillness, Ash looked out from the walls at the refugees. Despite what Florian said, she could see people trudging north, too, farther into Burgundian territory, into sunlit cold and famine.

That could be us. I can't feed my people, not out there, there's no land to live off. The war chest won't buy anything if there's nothing for money to buy. There was no harvest: we're due a famine. And out there it's dark, and cold. *We'd fall apart as a company inside three days.*

Let's hope it's better in here.

For however long this lasts.

Because the only way out of here is treachery.

Ash clapped her hand on Rochester's shoulder. "Okay, if the civilians want to get themselves killed, fine—we're leaving! *Lions, to the banner*!"

There was a pleasing amount of legionary discipline in the way that men wearing Lion livery detached themselves from the crowds to follow her banner, tugging in the wind above their heads. They scrambled across the devastation, into city streets again—away from the chanting crowd that now sank to its knees in prayer, still deafened by celebratory bells.

"Company billet's this way, boss!" Rochester pointed southeast into winding streets.

"Let's go!"

Green Christ, this place has been battered about!

They shouldered their way down narrow cobbled streets, under heavily timbered overhanging buildings. Glass and tiles covered the cobbles, clattering underfoot, slippery in the frost. Coming out into the open again—crossing a bridge into a square, beside the walls of silent mills—she recognized it. In the summer, a dozen Burgundian noblemen had reined in their horses there, to let a duck and her chicks waddle past to the water.

The memory took all her attention for a second; not until Rochester called the men to a halt did she rouse from her reverie, focus eyes gritty with lack of sleep, and realize she was at the company billet.

The shadow of a square, squat tower blocked out what November sun there was. Over its surrounding wall, she saw it was old, brutal in its construction, with featureless sides and narrow arrow-slit windows. Four, maybe five stories high.

She opened her mouth to speak. A gust of wind down the cramped street snatched the breath out of her mouth. She swallowed, eyes running in the sudden, bitter blast.

One of the men-at-arms swore and stepped back as a roof tile fell, hit, and sprayed fragments across the dung-covered cobbles. "*Jesu*! Fuckin' *storms* coming again!"

Ash recognized him as another of the men who had stayed behind in Dijon; one of di Conti's Savoyards, remaining after his captain quit. She looked up, beyond the tower's flat roof, at a sky that was rapidly losing morning clarity, turning gray and cold. "Storms?"

"Since August, boss," Thomas Rochester said, at her elbow. "I've got reports. They've been having foul weather here. Rain, wind, snow, sleet; and storms every two or three days. *Bad* storms."

"That's . . . I should have thought of that. Shit."

A darkness freezing Christendom beyond the Burgundian border—the border that is barely forty miles away.

The body of air around her shifted. Even down between those buildings, it tugged hard at the silk of her rectangular banner, the material cracking loudly in the wind. A scurry of white dust—almost too powdery to be snow—blew into her face. Under velvet and steel, her warm flesh shivered at the sudden chill.

"Son of a bitch. Welcome to Dijon . . ."

It got a laugh, as she knew it would. Only Florian's face remained serious. Despite reddening cheeks and nose, the tall woman spoke with gravitas:

"It's been dark over Christendom for five months. We can be sure of one thing while we're here. This weather isn't going to get any better."

The effect of her words was immediately visible on the faces of the men around her. Ash contemplated some jovial or profane remark, caught sight of Thomas Rochester's superstitious scowl, and changed her mind.

"You keep one thing in mind," she said, loudly enough to be heard over the gusting wind. "That's one fuck of a big army out there. Soldiers, engines, guns, you name it. But we've still got one thing they haven't."

Evidently regretting her unguarded remark, Florian provided the required question. "*What* have we got that they haven't?"

"A commander who isn't cracking up." Ash cast another glance up at the heavy bellies of the clouds, aware of the men-at-arms listening. "I saw her last night, Florian. Trust me. The woman's going completely bug-fuck."

iii

THE BANNER AND escort moved forward, under the arch of the tower's guard-wall.

"Sorry," Floria del Guiz murmured. "That was stupid of me."

Ash kept her tone equally low. "Let's deal with current problems. We're in here now. Now we worry about what happens next! You're Burgundian—what's this 'siege council' likely to be?"

The woman frowned. "I don't know. He didn't mention the Duke?"

"No. But no one except Duke Charles will be giving orders for the defense." Ash huddled her cloak around her as they strode toward the tower entrance. "Unless he's *not* here. Maybe I'm wrong. Maybe he did die at Auxonne, and they're keeping it quiet. *Shit* . . . Florian, go talk to the physicians."

The tall woman nodded, said breathlessly: "If they'll let me."

"You try it while I go to this 'council.' We haven't got much time. C'mon."

Over the arched main gate of the tower, a painted heraldry plaque bore the arms of an obscure Burgundian noble—*obscure enough not to be here*, Ash thought. *Or maybe his household is up north, besieged in Ghent or Bruges?*

This situation is looking stickier by the minute.

Loping from the courtyard up the steps to the first floor,

she met Angelotti, Geraint ab Morgan, and Euen Huw at the keep door.

"We got everybody?" she questioned sharply. "Everybody inside, last night?"

"Yes, boss," Geraint nodded breathlessly.

"Baggage train as well?"

"All of them."

"Casualties? John Price's lot?"

Antonio Angelotti said, "We're picking Price up tonight, after sunset. We have no one lost that we know of."

"Fucking hell, I don't believe it!" Ash looked to Euen Huw. "Robert's lot put in an attack, too, didn't they? They all get back?"

"Been checking 'em on the roll, boss, haven't I? The attack force is here."

"And Anselm?"

"He was leading it." Euen's unshaven face creased in a grin. "He's upstairs, boss."

"Okay, let's go. I've got to be at this damn 'siege council' in half an hour."

The inside of the keep was darker than the morning outside, but less chill. She nodded a brief greeting to the startled guards, loping with her officers up the steps as her sight adjusted to the lanterns. Rough gray masonry and brick lined the stairwell, bleakly strong. Walls fifteen or twenty feet thick, she gauged. Old, solid, undecorated, unsubtle.

Behind her, she heard bill-shafts thumped against the flagstones, someone bawling "Ash!" as loudly as they called it on a field of battle.

Guards pulled leather hangings back at the second-floor entrance. She had one moment to take it all in: nothing but one hall, wooden-floored, as wide as the keep itself, stinking of humanity. Men and women crowded it, wall to wall.

She rapidly identified faces—troops she had brought from Carthage—and saw no immediately apparent absences. There are men missing—casualties of Auxonne, but Rochester has warned her about them; and inevitably there will be some from the attrition of the siege.

Nine dead at Carthage, a score of deserters on the way here; with what we've got in Dijon, are we four hundred, four-fifty strong? I'll call a muster.

"*Ash*!" Baggage-train officers not seen for months—bowyer, tailor, falconer, Master of Horse—jumped to their feet.

Washerwomen hugged each other, talking; children scrambled about; two or three couples were industriously having sex. The floor was hidden under their new heaps of baggage rolls, wicker baskets, mail shirts in rusted heaps, bills propped up against the stark walls. Wet clothes hung from makeshift lines, steaming dry after immersion in the Suzon River. A fire smoked in the hearth. As, one by one, lance by lance, they saw the banner at the doorway, saw *her*, men and women scrambled to their feet, the sound of a ragged cheer battering back off the stone walls:

"Ash! *Ash*! ASH!"

"Okay, *pack it in*!"

A brace of mastiffs ran across the hall, splaying plates, cups, and costrels aside in their enthusiasm.

"Bonniau! Brifault! Down!" Ash neatly grabbed their studded collars, forcing the mastiffs down. They wriggled at her feet, growling happily, smelling of dog.

Despite the lanterns, and the light from the arrow-slit windows, it was a second before she saw Robert Anselm stomping across the cluttered floor toward her. She was at the center of a crowd in seconds: Anselm shouldered through them without effort.

"Green fucking Christ up a Tree!" he snarled.

Ash snapped her fingers, quieting the mastiffs.

Three months—or hunger—had put lines in his face. Other than that, he was no different. His hose were torn at the knee, and his demi-gown had half its lead buttons ripped off; there was the glint of a mail standard at his throat. Stubble blackened his cheeks. His shaven head shone with sweat, despite the chill morning. She met his dark gaze.

If he's going to challenge my authority, now's the time. It's been his company for three months; I've been dead.

"Fucking hell, woman!"

At his tone, at his expression, she couldn't help but laugh.

"You wouldn't like to try that again, would you, Roberto?"

Euen Huw had his hand over his mouth; some of the others were openly grinning.

"Fucking hell, *Captain Ash*." Robert Anselm shook his head, bearlike, and for a second she did not know whether he was about to yell at her, attempt to hit her, or laugh. He reached out. His strong hands gripped her shoulders painfully hard. "Christ, girl, you took your time! Just like a bloody woman. Always late!"

"Too right!" Ash, when the gale of laughter died down, added, "Sorry, I dragged it out as long as I could—I hoped the war'd be over before we got back here!"

"Damn right!" one of the archers yelled.

"We've been waiting three months." The big man looked down at her with a familiar, amazed amusement. Robert Anselm, battered and broad-shouldered; the familiar rasp of his *rosbif* accent unbelievably welcome. "You're getting a reputation. 'Ash always comes back.' "

"I like it. Let's try and keep it that way," Ash said sardonically. She looked at him, at the men around him, was aware of no friction yet between those who had gone to Carthage and those who had stayed in Dijon. "Find me one of the clerks. I need to write some retrospective commissions of array—Euen Huw and Thomas Rochester to be made sub-captains; Angelotti in overall charge of all missile troops as well as guns, Rostovnaya and Katherine as his subordinates to take over the crossbows and longbows."

There was a murmur of pleasure and approval. She kept her face bland when Geraint ab Morgan looked at her.

"Geraint, I want you to take over as head of the provosts. I need a man I can trust to keep discipline in the camp."

Morgan's face flushed with pride. "I'll do that, boss, don't you worry!"

I won't worry—not with you out of the combat line. Let's keep you and your doubts where they can't do any damage—and see if you can learn something about discipline while you're enforcing it. . . .

"Robert, you'll have your own recommendations for promotions with the guys here." She added, "Consider them okayed. Now we get our asses in gear, the city council want to talk to me, and I want an officer meeting before we go, Robert, what's that?"

She finished, breathless, staring at a horse.

Snickers sounded from the men-at-arms; she could feel them grinning without looking at them. The ones that grinned were mainly the troops who had stayed in Dijon.

"It's a horse," Robert Anselm said unnecessarily.

"I can *see* it's a fucking—" Ash took a quick glance under the beast, where it stood by one wall, head contentedly down in a feed bag. "—a mare. What's it doing *here*?"

Robert Anselm lifted bland brows. A couple of the resident lance leaders chuckled.

Ash picked her way between people's kit, across the dormitory floor, to the straw-strewn area liberally dotted with horse dung that housed the large chestnut mare. The beast flickered a dark eye at her. "I'm not even going to ask how you persuaded it up the stairs . . ."

"Blindfolded," Anselm answered, striding up beside her. "We picked her up in the early hours of this morning."

"Robert—where from?"

"The Visigoth horse-lines." The big man kept a straight face. "No one wanted her at the time. Even with this."

At his signal, a billman and a groom unfolded between them a filthy length of cloth. Horse caparisons, she saw. With the Brazen Head livery still visible through the filth.

"Great Boar! That's the Faris's horse!"

"Is it? Well, well. Who'd have guessed?" Anselm smiled down at her. "Welcome home."

Their pleasure was noisy, and extensive; and she gave way to it wholeheartedly. She slapped Robert Anselm on the arm. "Everything they ever said about mercenaries is true! We're nothing but a bunch of horse thieves!"

"Takes talent to be a good horse thief," Euen Huw remarked professionally, and flushed. "Not that I'd know, see."

"Perish the thought. . . ." Ash did not approach the mare too closely, reading *warhorse* in her conformation. "Where's Digorie Paston?"

"Here, ma'am."

As the clerk pushed his way to the front of the men, she said, "Digorie, write me a message. To the Faris. Have a herald take it down to the Visigoth camp. 'Chestnut mare, thirteen hands, Barb blood, livery supplied—will exchange for one harness, Milanese plate, complete; and my bloody best sword!' "

A roar.

"I'll take it!" Rickard emerged from the press of men, flushed.

"Yeah, okay, you and Digorie; but I'll need you for the council. Take a parley flag. Don't be cheeky, and wear a clean livery. She'll be expecting a message from me—" Ash stopped, grinned cynically, and added: "—just not the one you're taking her. Meanwhile . . ."

She lifted her head, looking at her company.

"Food," she announced, pointedly.

Within a few minutes, sitting on someone's wicker rucksack, she was tearing dark bread apart with her teeth, greeting men and women not seen for nearly twelve weeks, alert to any signs that they might now be two different companies. They sat or knelt around her, on the floor, the hall full to the point that the window embrasures were crowded with sitting men, swapping stories at full volume.

"Is the Earl still out there?" Robert Anselm asked, squatting beside her.

He smelled of woodsmoke condensed in confined quarters, eye-wateringly strong. Ash grinned at him through a mouthful of bread. "Oxford's not in Burgundy as far as I know."

Anselm's jerk of the head took in all the company occupying the hall. "If it wasn't for him, we wouldn't be here. He made it a retreat, not a rout. Four days back from Auxonne, all the Burgundian leaders dead or wounded, Oxford holding everybody together, step by step by step."

"With the ragheads snapping at your ass all the way?"

"Yeah. If we hadn't held together as fighting units, they'd have wiped out the rest of the Burgundian army right there." Anselm rubbed his hands together, and reached out for some of the bread. Through it, thickly, he added, "If not for de Vere, there wouldn't be a siege going on here. All of south Burgundy would be overrun."

"The man's a soldier." Ash, aware that they were being listened to, said carefully, "As far as I know, and if he's been lucky, my lord of Oxford is currently in the court of the Sultan at Constantinople."

Anselm sprayed wet crumbs. "He's *what*?"

Over a general murmur, Ash said, "Don't bust your points. If Burgundy is weakening, now's a good time for the Turks to hit the Visigoths. Before they get too strong. Make the ragheads fight a war on two fronts."

"Make them the jam in the shit sandwich."

"Robert Anselm, you have a real way with words. . . ."

His brow furrowed. "How much chance of my lord Oxford getting Turkish help?"

"God in His mercy knows, Robert. I don't." Ash made a rapid change of subject, jerking her thumb at the nearest window and the graying sky. She said briskly, "I see there's a tiltyard down the end there. Some of the lads could do to get up to speed on weapons practice. After that hike, I'd like to give them a day or two training before we put them into the field."

Robert Anselm shook his head. "Boss, you didn't see Auxonne."

"Not the end of it, no," Ash remarked dryly. "What's your point, Captain?"

"As far as casualties are concerned, Auxonne was Agincourt and the Burgundians went down like the French."[21]

Blankly amazed, Ash said, "Fuck me."

"*I'd* be out with the Goths," Anselm said grimly, "if I didn't know what treatment the Lion Azure can expect. We got about a tenth left of the Duke's army—between two

---

[21] At the Battle of Agincourt (1421) an English force of perhaps 6,000 men (five-sixths of whom were archers) defeated upwards of 25,000 French cavalry and foot, wiping out the heart of the French nobility for a generation. Henry V's English army is reported as suffering 'a few hundred' casualties; the French had 6,000 dead and many more captured for ransom.

and a half, three thousand men. And the city militia, for what they're worth—I give 'em this; on their home ground, they're determined. And we got an entire city wall to defend."

Ash looked at him in silence.

"You brought back two hundred fighting men," Robert Anselm said. "Girl, you don't know how much of a difference two hundred men can make right now."

Ash raised silver brows. "Man, I *thought* I was popular! So that's why this 'siege council' wants to talk to me."

"That and the fact that 'Carthage fell down,' " Anselm completed her thought.

Ash nodded, consideringly, and looked at the men around her.

"Robert, I don't know how much Angelotti and Geraint have told you—"

"These new demon-machines in the south?"

Warmed by his quickness, and by the lack of any alteration in the way he spoke to her, Ash nodded and moved closer to the hearth. There was a scurry of men-at-arms moving their kit out of the way; the escort sitting down on the floorboards a yard or two off, giving at least an illusion of privacy. Ash sat down on a joint stool, resting her elbows on her knees and letting her cloak fall open to the fire's warmth.

"Sit down, Robert. There are things you need to hear from me."

He squatted beside her. "Are we staying?"

It was blunt.

"You came back for us," Anselm elaborated. "What's the options now, girl? Do we stick with this siege? Or try to negotiate a way out past the Visigoth lines?"

"You saw what food we brought in, Robert. Fuck-all. It took a *lot* longer getting here than I'd bargained for. . . .

We'd have to negotiate with the Visigoths themselves for supplies, for a forced march. I know the Faris is anxious for a quick end to the siege. As for leaving here . . ." Ash turned her gaze away from the burning wood's scarlet buttresses, on the hearth. She looked at Robert Anselm's sweating face.

"Robert, there's stuff you need to know. About the 'demon-machines,' yes, and the Stone Golem. About my sister, the Faris—and why she's so damn determined to keep this crusade here in Burgundy."

Distant in her memory, her own voice asking a question comes to her: *why Burgundy?*

She reached out; touched Robert Anselm's dirty sleeve. "And about Godfrey Maximillian."

Anselm rubbed both bare hands back over his scalp; she heard stubble rasp.

"Florian told me. He's dead."

Aware suddenly of the three-month hiatus between them—aware that she may not know, yet, how Robert Anselm has changed, three months in command of his own men—Ash nodded, slowly.

I could wait. Leave it; tell him later.

We're either one company, or we're not. I either trust him, or I don't. I have to risk it.

"Godfrey's dead," she said, "but I've heard his voice, Roberto. Exactly the way I've always heard the Lion—the *machina rei militaris*. And—so has the Faris."

Some fifteen minutes later, Ash rejoined her men.

To Baldina, Henri Brant, and a woman called Hildegarde, a sutler who appeared to have stepped into Wat Rodway's place in his absence from Dijon, she said, "How are we off for supplies, here?"

"I've shown Henri the cellars, boss." Hildegarde's red face creased. "Town supplies aren't good."

"They're not? I thought they'd have a year's supplies put by—they've had sieges here before."

Henri Brant said sardonically, "They had all of the Duke's standing army billeted here for weeks before Auxonne. I've been checking—it's bloodmonth, and they've had fuck-all to slaughter![22] They ate the place all but bare, boss."

Hildegarde put in, "But we won't need to worry, will we? Not now the Goths are beaten."

"Beaten?" Ash exclaimed.

The woman shrugged, a movement which strained the laces of her bodice. "Only a matter of time, my dear, isn't it? With their demon-city fallen in bits about their ears. What's their army to do? They'll lift the siege before solstice."

By the nods of agreement around her, Hildegarde was not the only one of that opinion. Ash caught Floria's eye, where the surgeon sat with her long legs sprawled out on the floor—and a rapidly emptying wine bottle beside her.

"There's still a government in Carthage," Floria pointed out. "That army out there hasn't surrendered!"

"Never argue with morale," Ash murmured. "No—never argue with *high* morale."

"Why am I surrounded by idiots?" Florian remarked, rhetorically.

"*Dottore*, you should consider that thought very carefully." Angelotti chuckled, where he sat between Geraint and Euen Huw. "As the *rosbifs* have it, 'like calls to like'!"

---

[22] During November—Anglo-Saxon 'bloodmonath'—it was the usual practice to slaughter all animals except the breeding stock for meat, to enable communities to survive through the winter.

The heat of the hall began at last to penetrate. Ash put her hands up and slid her hood back, stripped her gauntlets and helmet off, and looked up to find Robert Anselm and a whole lot of the garrison troops staring at her, suddenly silent.

She becomes aware again of her roughly cropped short hair. Aware that the river fall of shining glory is gone, that she is only a leggy, dirty, strong woman with her hair cropped as close as a slave's, shorter than most of the men's. That the one in armor and glory, now, is the Faris.

"At least now you can tell me and the Visigoth bitch apart," she remarked dryly, into the silence.

Robert Anselm said, "We always could. You're the ugly one."

There was a split second of belly-chilling silence, in which the men around her worked out firstly that only Anselm could have said it, and secondly that his brutal grin was being answered by one of Ash's own.

"Hey," she said. "I had to get scars before *I* could frighten children."

Anselm's grin widened. "Some of us do it with natural talent."

"Yeah." She threw a gauntlet at him; he snagged it out of the air. "Robert, I don't know if you frighten the enemy, but you scare the shit out of me. . . ."

There was a glow in the room, nothing material, that came from the garrison's appreciation of the banter, came with their realization that Anselm would not challenge her for the company, came with her arrival beyond hope out of the unknown sunless south. Ash basked in it, for a moment. She took a look around, at the lances eating together, deep in exchange of stories, catching up on old quarrels and gossip.

Okay, she thought. *No time like the present.*

"You guys better listen up." She raised her voice, addressing the room generally. "Because I'm going to tell you why you'll be better off without me."

It got their attention, as she thought it might. Talk died down. Men and women looked at their lancemates, and moved closer, to be able to hear. A baggage-cart child said something that made her friend giggle. Ash let the hall become silent.

"Your lance leaders and officers will bring you up to speed on this," she said. "You guys hold a company meeting, while I'm at this siege council. The main thing you need to know is, I saw the Faris last night—"

"And got out again?" one of Mowlett's archers surprised himself into saying out loud. Ash grinned at the man.

"And got out again. Hell, she even gave me an escort, so I wouldn't get lost on the way. . . ."

"What does she want?" Geraint ab Morgan demanded, drowned out by other questions.

"What do you mean, better off without you?" Robert Anselm demanded bluntly over the hubbub. "The company needs you in command!"

There was a murmur, expressions of agreement on most of the faces she could see; and that startled her, slightly. *They've done without me for three months. I know damn well some of them will be thinking exactly that, right now. Won't they?*

"Okay." Ash moved forward, to be seen by them all. "Do we stay in Dijon, do we look for a contract in Burgundy? If not, if there are any supplies left here, we *might* manage a forced march east."

But not if the Burgundians know we're going to ransack the place and go . . . and they must at least be thinking that's a possibility.

"We *might* negotiate a way out past the ragheads. We

might give them the city." A quick, weighing glance: *have any of them developed a loyalty for what they've been defending*? "Okay. Over the next few hours, I want you guys thinking about this. There's a chance the Visigoths might let you guys march out anyway; it would weaken the defense here. But this is what you should bear in mind—as far as the Faris and House Leofric are concerned, they want *me*. Me, personally. Not you guys, not the Lion. Me."

Euen Huw said something in Thomas Rochester's ear that she did not catch. The two Tydder boys, at the back, seemed to be explaining something in confused excitement to garrison lancemates. Blanche and Baldina, mother and daughter faces all but identical now under dyed yellow hair, looked identically bemused.

"Why'd they want you?" Baldina shouted.

"Okay, we'll take it from the top." Ash brushed crumbs off the front of her demi-gown. "If it's been long enough since you came through the sally port for rumors to get out among the citizens, then it's more than long enough for rumors to get round the company, I know that!"

She raised her voice, over the noise: "These are facts. The old King-Caliph Theodoric died. They've got a new one—he's crap, but they've got one. That's King-Caliph Gelimer. The city of Carthage was flattened by an earthquake. But, sadly, as far as I can tell from the Faris's camp, Gelimer survived, and there's still a functioning government."

Euen Huw, in deep Welsh gloom, remarked, "Oh *shit*," and then narrowed his black eyes in surprise as half the company burst out laughing.

One of the younger garrison crossbowmen thumped his fist on the floor. "Get us a contract with the attackers, boss! That's safer. Fight *with* the Visigoths."

A woman beside him, in archer's gear, muttered in English: "I heard rumors they'd pay us twice as much as they're paying Cola de Monforte if we go over. One of van Mander's lads got word back to me last week."

Before Ash could comment, one of the sergeants leaned over the woman's shoulder: a hatchet-faced Italian, Giovanni Petro.

"Sure they might sign us up for twice the money," he rasped, "and who do you think would get to walk up and mine the walls? Or bring a siege tower up to the gate? Or go through the first breach? There's a lot of shit jobs in a siege, and we'd get them all. We'd never live to collect."

Pieter Tyrrell said flatly, "I don't want a contract, after Basle. Not after they broke the *condotta*."

There were many heads nodding in agreement. A babble of suggestions, contradictions, and complaints broke out. Ash let it go on for a minute or so, then raised her hands for quiet.

"Whether you could sign up with them and survive it or not—and you're tough motherfuckers, I still think it's your best chance—the Visigoths want *me*," she repeated. "That's why they sent a snatch squad in at Auxonne. That's why the scientist-magus Leofric tried to take me apart in Carthage. And I do mean 'take me apart'—maybe he's been learning from our surgeon!"

She took the opportunity of the unsubtle joke to check on Floria. The woman raised her wine jug, acknowledging the subdued rumble. Ash saw no hint in her expression of any loyalty to the country of her birth. *Fuck knows it was hard enough for her last time we were here—but she can't start drinking again because of that.*

"Why don't they want you alive, boss?" Jean Bertran, one of the armorers, yelled from the back. She lifted a hand, acknowledging him, soot-blackened, unchanged in her absence. He shouted across, "Two's better than one, right? And you hear their old machine, too!"

Another man-at-arms who had stayed with the garrison stood, hauling up his drooping hose. "Yeah, boss, if you're another Faris, and you hear the Stone Golem, too, why won't she employ us? Fuck, the ragheads would flatten everybody, then!"

Ash, head tilted slightly sideways, eyed the footman. "You know, next time I'm going to have feudal levies, not bloody mercenaries, then I can just tell them what to do without all these fucking questions. Listen up, dickheads! I'll say it again. House Leofric and the King-Caliph don't give a fart in a thunderstorm about the Company of the Lion. If you guys decide to get out of here—maybe go look for the Turk, maybe go north—then you'll get no more trouble than you ever do. If I'm with you, we're the prize target. *Without me, you can leave Dijon.*"

"We can take 'em! Fuck the ragheads!" Simon Tydder yelled, to general approval.

"How about a bit less morale and a bit more intelligence?" Ash's hands dropped to her side. "Now fucking listen. This isn't war. No—shut up! Right. This isn't human war."

The hall hushed.

"There are other powers in the world besides men. God gives his miracles to those who believe in Him. And the devil gives power to his own."

Into an almost total silence, Ash went on:

"Those of you who were with me at Carthage saw it. The Visigoths won't admit it, but their empire is founded on demons. We've seen them. Stone demons, stone engines, wild machines in the desert. *They* put the sun out, not the *amirs*."

Now the silence became total. The better part of three hundred men and women of the baggage train; forty lances of fighting men who will pass this word on to those of the Lion Azure out on guard duty or elsewhere; the children and the mastiffs—all still, and watching her face.

"*They're* spreading this darkness. Not the Visigoths—it's the Wild Machines who tell the King-Caliph and his Faris what to do. They speak to her through the Stone Golem. I hear them. *She* hears them. *She* knows the Stone Golem's possessed by demons. And she's scared!"

Richard Faversham got to his feet. "These Wild Machines killed Father Maximillian!"

"No, that was an earthquake," Floria called out.

"Doctor; priest!"

A sudden, private shudder threatens to demolish this public argument: *Godfrey*! she thinks; aware of sweat cold now against her skin.

"*Later*. Now listen up! I know you guys don't give a shit about demons. You'd scare the ass off demons, anyway!"

A cheer.

"But the demons—" Ash put her fists on her hips. "—the demons are only after *me*. Maybe the demons want another Faris. But if they do—" A shrug. "It isn't to lead their army! As far as they're concerned, I'm a loose cannon. I'm a Faris they don't control. So House Leofric wants me dead, the King-Caliph wants me dead, the demon Wild Machines want me dead." Her mouth moved into a grin, lopsided with private emotion. "I don't kill so easy. You know that."

"Fucking right, boss!"

"But they won't sign a *condotta* with *me*. I'm giving you guys—advice, let's say. Take Robert Anselm as your commander. Sell Dijon to the Goths. Break out and head for Dalmatia. Take Visigoth money, rob this city of supplies if you have to, and head for the Turks."

It is cold advice, standing there in this beleaguered city that has held out for three long, bitter months. Advice that the *machina rei militaris* might have given her, if she could have asked it.

"The Sultan isn't going to see the Visigoth Empire take over Christendom without doing something about it. You could get a *condotta* with him—"

Over the great confusion of noise, shouting, men springing to their feet, sergeants trying to restore order, Robert Anselm got to his feet.

"I won't take the command! You're our commander!"

"Never mind the fucking heroics!" Ash shouted, roughly. "Never mind the fucking company flag and loyalty. *Think about this*. Do you really want a captain who the Visigoths and their demons are determined to kill? Because if you do, we're stuck in here!"

"Screw the fucking ragheads!" Euen Huw, also on his feet, punched the air with his fist.

Ludmilla Rostovnaya yelled, "Nah, we want to fight with you, boss!"

A wall of sound hit Ash: it was a second before she realized it was agreement.

"Ash wins battles!" Pieter Tyrrell shouted.

"Ash gets us *out* of the shit!" bellowed Geraint ab Morgan. "Got us back from fucking Carthage, didn't you, boss?"

"*This isn't your fight!*" She paced, nearing the window embrasure. The weak sunlight of a clouded day touched her, showing clearly a woman in stained and muddy brigandine and hose, a dagger at her belt, her face white with exhaustion. Nothing about her that is fire except her eyes.

Trying to guess at the mood of the meeting, the necessity of reducing four or five hundred interior lives, complicated souls, to names on a muster roll and a gestalt mood:

this bewilders her, sometimes. She stared around at faces. Those she would have automatically picked out before to be troublemakers and authority-grabbers—Geraint Morgan, Wat Rodway—did not avoid her eye. Both men, and others like them, watched her with a raw loyalty that frightened her.

Part of it's that no one wants to be boss right now, and have to take these decisions. They're afraid they might lose if I'm not in charge—and that's not reason: war doesn't depend much on rational thought.

But that's still only part of it.

"For Christ's sake," Ash said, voice rough. "You don't know what you're getting into."

"A *fortunate* commander is worth much," Antonio Angelotti remarked, as if it were a proverb.

Ludmilla Rostovnaya stood up, facing Ash.

"Look, boss," the raw-featured Rus woman said reasonably, "we don't give a fuck whose fight it is. I never fought for any lord or country. I keep my eye on my lancemates' backs, and they watch mine. You're a fucking awkward boss sometimes, but you get us through. You got us out of Basle. And Carthage. You'll get us out of here. So we'll stick with you." A dazzling, gap-toothed smile toward the shaven-headed soldier beside Ash: "No offense, Captain Anselm!"

"None taken," Anselm rumbled, confidently amused.

Jolted, Ash demanded, "What do you mean, 'awkward'?"

"You spend half your time playing up to the local nobs." Ludmilla shrugged. "Like with German Emperor Frederick? All this social-climbing shit? I was *embarrassed*, boss. But we kicked ass at Neuss anyway."

Thomas Rochester unexpectedly said, "And I've covered more miles as your escort than I ever did in the entire Yorkist war! Can't you ever stay in one place on the fucking battlefield, boss?"

"Yeah, then the runners would know where to find you!" a sergeant of archers called.

"*Excuse* me." Ash began a protest.

"And you don't get drunk half often enough!" Wat Rodway called. Baldina from the wagons added, "Not with us, anyway!"

Ash, trying to press home the seriousness of it, began to laugh. "Are you *quite* finished!"

"Not yet, madonna, there's plenty more. The gunners haven't even started."

"Thank you, Master Angelotti!"

The hall filled with a buzz of friendly, foul-mouthed harassment. Ash put her fingers through her cropped hair, at a loss. Opening her mouth, and not sure what she was going to say as she did, she was interrupted.

"Boss . . ."

A raw voice. She turned around, trying to locate the man who had spoken; found Floria del Guiz on her feet, grabbing at the arm of a man on crutches.

Black bandages looped his face, covering the cauterized sockets of his eyes. Above them, white scars gave way to wisps of white hair. He snarled something at the surgeon, hitching his crutches under his armpits, tilting his head up, listening, sightlessly staring off into a corner of the roof.

"Carracci," Ash began.

"Let me speak," the ex–Sergeant of Bill cut in, his head turning approximately to face her.

Ash nodded; then realized. She said aloud, "What is it, Carracci?"

"Just this." His blind head weaved a little, as if he were trying to face all of the company there, or as if he wanted to be clearly seen by them. "You didn't have to bring me back from Carthage. I'll never be any use again. I'm not the only one you brought back, boss. That's all."

A different quality of silence fell. Ash reached out, gently closing her hand over his forearm, where corded overdeveloped muscles trembled with the tension of balancing upright. There were people nodding all through the hall, a few men shifting uncomfortably or going back to their rations, but most murmuring quiet agreement. A voice said, "Right on, Carracci."

"We don't leave our own," Robert Anselm said. "Works both ways. No more shit, girl."

She turned her head sharply to one side, momentarily not in control of her expression.

There is no way to escape this: not if you are asking men to pick up swords and axes and walk out into wet fields, and end up facedown in the mud; no way *not* to create that fierce mixture of fear and affection that—she admits to herself—will lead them to this refusal, nine times out of ten.

Could've been the tenth time, she thought, somewhere between black humor and appalled resignation. *I'd better be able to handle this now I've got it.*

A clatter of feet and weapons at the stair broke the silence. Still holding Carracci's arm, Ash yelled across, "What is it?"

A harassed company guard entered the hall, behind him a dozen or so men in armor and Burgundian liveries. She saw in an automatic glance that their swords were in their sheaths, that the leader carried a white baton.

"Captain Ash," their leader called across the hall. "My lord Olivier de la Marche has sent us. He wishes you to be suitably escorted to the Viscount-Mayor's siege council. It is my honor to ask, will you come with us now?"

"You go," Ash said instantly to Robert Anselm. "Assuming I'm right, and he's here, I've got more important things to do—if you're all set on staying here, I need to talk to the Duke."

"To Charles?" Anselm lowered his voice. "They won't let you in, girl."

"Why not?"

"You don't know yet? Fuck. I should have told you." Anselm hitched up the belt that held his purse and ballock dagger, settling it under his beer belly. His gaze on the Burgundian men, he said, "You know Duke Charles was wounded at Auxonne? Yeah? That was three months ago. They tell us he still hasn't recovered enough to leave his bed."

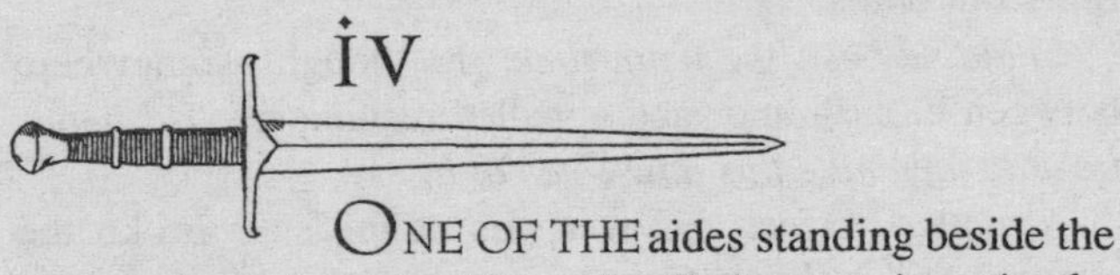

IV

ONE OF THE aides standing beside the Burgundian with the white rod called across impatiently, "Are you *deaf*, woman? The council's *waiting*!"

Jolted, she turned her head: found herself among men-at-arms swearing, straightening their shoulders, beginning to move. She made the abrupt mental gear change necessary to realize that violence is about to happen—especially now; especially after Carracci—and nodded at Geraint, watching as he and his provosts brought the lances to order.

"Son of a bitch!" Robert Anselm muttered, from his tone, as disoriented as she was.

The leader of the Burgundian officers—Joussey? Jonvelle?—said something sharply condemnatory in French to his companion. He shrugged a very informal half apology toward Ash. His expression, as far as Ash could decipher it in the dim, high-roofed hall, was embarrassed. His gaze went up and down her, head to foot.

"He's got a point," Ash said grimly.

The night-before-last's sodden rain still blackened her brigandine's blue velvet and buff straps. She glanced down at the high boots pointed to her doublet skirts, and the mud drying black and crusted on them. One moment of feeling naked without cuisses and greaves—without armor—then she realized, too, that the brass-headed studs on her brigandine were dull, and her sallet (where Rickard, blushing, picked it up) was glazed orange and brown with rust.

"Get me a sword," Ash said abruptly.

"*And* the rest . . ." Robert Anselm gave her one assessing glance, already signaling to one of his squires. The boy came back across the hall with his hands full of straps, scabbard, and sword.

"Arm me." Anselm, stripping off his demi-gown, stood with his arms outstretched, while his pages pointed and strapped leg armor and cuirass to his arming doublet. As if they weren't there, he stared around at the men-at-arms, and finally fixed on the master gunner. He showed his teeth. "*Tony!*"

Angelotti, kneeling by a bucket, lifted his head and threw a quantity of wet gold hair back, spraying his own squires with dirty water. His face was a little cleaner, still showing traces of having come in through mud, rain, and freezing slush. He looked first at Anselm, then at the Burgundians, scowled, and muttered something mellifluous and filthy.

"Yeah, yeah. I *know* you. You got clean stuff in your pack, wrapped up dry. Right?" Robert Anselm kicked at the Italian gunner's kit with his sabatons, as his pages laced his arm defenses onto his obviously newly repaired arming doublet. "You're about her size. That demi-gown. The one you always wear when you're on the pull . . . You manage to bring that all the way back from North Africa?"

Ash covered her mouth with her hand, feeling a sudden grin under her palm. Angelotti knelt, unwrapped a pack of leather and waxed pelts, and stood up and turned, a garment across his arms.

A white silk damask demi-gown. Spotless. Furred at the high collar, skirts, and slit sleeves with the soft, multiple grays of wolf fur.

"Can't 'ave boss going out there looking shite," Anselm said, giving the Burgundians a brawl-starting grin. "Now can we, Tony? Get the Lion a bad name."

Long minutes, while the Burgundian officers waited meekly: two pages brushing her boots, Rickard pointing and buttoning the spotless demi-gown on over her filthy brigandine and calling to a mate of his for the loan of a polished archer's sallet. He deftly twisted blue-and-yellow silk ribbon around the open-face helmet, and skewered a white plume into the holder.

The soft wolf fur lining Angelotti's collar stroked her scarred cheek.

"Sword!" Anselm beckoned his squire forward. Ash automatically raised her arms for the squire to kneel at her side.

Anselm reached across and took the weapon from the boy, with a deliberate, expansive physicality that always brought him far more clearly into her mind than anything else.

He stepped forward and knelt on the flagstones in front of her, an armored man now but for his helmet and gauntlets. He began to buckle the sword belt and weapon on around her waist, over the shining demi-gown.

She dropped her hand down, encountering a hand-and-a-half grip: blue velvet bound with gold wire. She touched the flutes of a writhen brass pommel and cross, the metal polished to a deep, glimmering brightness.

"This is your best sword, Robert."

"I'll wear my other one." He snicked a buckle home, expertly threaded the tail of the belt through itself in a knot, and let the blue leather strap, studded with brass mullets, hang down over the pleated white damask skirts of her demi-gown. "You ain't at Neuss now, girl."

The memory of kneeling before the Holy Roman Emperor is sharp in her mind's eye. Silver hair rippling to her knees; young, scarred, beautiful; a woman in full Milanese plate shining so brilliantly in the sun that it hurts the eye, leaves dazzles on the vision—and says, as clearly as a shout: *This is what I earned as a mercenary captain, I'm* good.

They're going to look at me now and think: she can't even afford plate armor. Well, shit, I'm down to a helmet and gauntlets: that's it. *Everything else—spare leg harness, borrowed cuirass—is lost, damaged beyond repair, or out there with the fucking Faris. . . .*

Is this going to be enough?

Ash reached out and took the borrowed sallet, prodding the padding for a better fit. She lifted her chin as Rickard tied the fastenings of a clean, dry livery jacket, and buckled the sallet's strap.

"Looks like I'm going to the council. Angelotti, Anselm; with me. Geraint, I want a complete muster roll of the whole company before I get back. Okay, let's move it!"

A cluster of men sorted themselves out into a remarkably clean, if now unspectacularly dressed, Angelotti; a Thomas Rochester, equally rapidly cleaned up and wearing other people's kit; and his lance of twelve as escort with Ash's banner. Ash strode at their head, out of the shadow of the doorway, into the open air. The courtyard scurried with pigs and a few remaining hens, chased by screaming children, clanged with the noise of the armory sheds that lined the inside of the tower's perimeter wall.

A *crack!* made her whole body startle—the invisible impact of a rock, not far off. Animals and children simultaneously froze for a second. Pale sun struck her face: her chest suddenly constricted, her breath coming shallow.

"Hitting up at the northwest gate again," Anselm rumbled, glancing automatically and uselessly at the sky and reaching up to buckle on his sallet.

Beside him, Rickard flinched. Ash reached out to shake his shoulder companionably. Unexpectedly, she felt sweat cutting runnels in the dirt on her face. *What's wrong with me now? This is just the usual shit for a siege.* She made herself start to walk down the stone steps, toward the men and horses in the courtyard.

There was a brief moment of the confusion that she has been used to for over a decade, armored men mounting into the saddles of warhorses: trained, restless stallions. As the Burgundians mounted up, Rickard led forward a mouse-colored dun stallion with black points and tail visible under the caparisons.

"Borrow Orgueil,"[23] Anselm said. "I don't suppose you picked up any remounts on the way back from Carthage."

The dun's shining black eyes looked into Ash's face,

---

[23] 'Pride.' There is a certain knowing defiance about this name, pride being in the mediaeval mind a great sin—and one that goes before a fall.

dark nostrils flaring. Anselm's rough, sardonic tone demanded humor, or at least comradeship.

"Boss?"

"What?"

"Wrong time of the month for a stallion? We can find you a gelding."

"No. 'S okay, Roberto. . . ."

Momentarily—reaching up to put a firm hand against the beast's soft muzzle; feel warm horse-breath on her bare, cold skin—she is stopped dead: incapacitated with loss.

Six months ago, she owned destrier, palfrey, and riding horse. All gone. Iron gray Godluc, wide-chested, bossy, and protective. Lady's flaxen chestnut sweetness and greed. The Sod's dirty water gray coloring and foul temperament. For one second her heart hurts, thinking of the golden foal that Lady might have had, and The Sod's viciousness (nipping at her leg when least expected, nuzzling at her chest equally unexpectedly), all lost in the rout from Basle. And Godluc—*I swear*, she thought, eyes stinging, mouth twisting with black humour; *I swear he thought of me as a horse; some misbehaving mare*!—skewered and dead at Auxonne.

Easier to grieve for horses than men? she wonders, remembering the dead buried on rocky, inhospitable Malta.

"We'll get you another warhorse," Anselm said, appearing at a loss when she did not speak. "Shouldn't have to lay out more than a couple of pounds. There's been enough dead knights won't need 'em anymore."

"Jeez, Roberto, you're an ever-present trouble in time of help. . . ."

The Englishman snorted. She cast an eye around at the armored knights on their warhorses, the bright richness of rounded steel plate. Her own blue-and-gold liveries on the mounted archers shone out brilliant in the gray morning; men with open-faced steel helmets and mailed sleeves mounting up—she guessed—on some of the riding horses the garrison still maintained. Jutting bow-staves and her striped banner-pole pierced the air. A careful eye could have picked out rusted cuisses and poleyns, and boot leather blackened and cracked by wet and cold.

". . . Let's go."

They rode in the wake of the Burgundian officers, out into a crowded street where cold air moved against her face. Her escort formed up around her. Dust blew, filling the air; and old ashes skirled across the cobbles, spooking two of the geldings. Groups of people standing talking on the corner moved back out of the way of the armed men. She laid the rein over to avoid a man hauling a handcart of rubble away from a collapsed shop. In the space of a hundred yards, she picked half a dozen constables out of the crowds.

Another heavy *crack!* and boom of something landing and exploding into fragments echoed through the morning air over Dijon. Orgueil fluffed a plume of breath into the chill air, and she felt him shift discontentedly under her. Another succession of sharp impacts sounded, to the north. The Burgundians rode on, with an unconsciously hunched posture—men used to shrinking, however pointlessly, away from what the sky might deliver to them.

"Shit, that's close!"

"Couple of streets. Sometimes they play silly buggers like this all day." Robert Anselm shrugged. "Limestone. Reckon they're quarrying rocks all the way down the Auxonne road by now. It's just harassment." Riding up to her side, he jerked his thumb at a church farther on down the street. Ash saw it was a blackened shell. "When they're *serious*, they use Greek Fire."

"Shit."

"Too fucking right!"

"I've been up on the walls. They must have upwards of three hundred petriers[24] out there," Angelotti called, his voice thinning. Careful on the flagstones, he brought his brown gelding over closer on her other side. "Perhaps twenty-five trebuchets that I can see, madonna. They shelter their mangonels and ballistae with hides; difficult to count them. Perhaps another hundred engines—but truly bad weather will make at least their catapults unusable. But . . . they have golem."

Wryly, Ash said, "I thought they might."

Angelotti said, "But do we fight here, madonna?"

Our options are narrowing all the time—

The Burgundian officers, picking up the pace, struck off diagonally down a narrower street, riding from the cover of one house to the next. Here there were fewer broken roofs and burned-out houses. Under the iron hooves of the horses, rubble strewing the cobbles made footing uncertain.

Deliberately not answering his question, Ash asked, "If you were their *magister ingeniator*,[25] Angeli, what would you be doing right now?"

"I would look to undermine the north wall, or break one of those two gates." The Italian's oval-lidded eyes narrowed, looking past her to study Anselm's reaction. "To weaken morale first, I would have had men up on the bluff, to draw me a map of what could be seen in the city; then I would concentrate my barrage on public targets. Markets, where people congregate. Churches. Guild halls. The ducal palace."

---

[24] Small siege engines: stone-throwers that operate by winching a wooden beam down and using the tension as a spring to propel rocks.

[25] 'Master Engineer': specifically, here, a military siege engineer.

"Got it in one!" Anselm snorted.

The churning in her stomach, and the tightness in her chest, both increased. A man desperately nailing boards across his remaining windows paused as she passed, pulling off his hat, then ducked into his doorway as another spray of rocks cracked and whined across the rooftops.

"Ah, *fuck* it!" Ash exclaimed. "Now I remember how much I *hate* bloody siege engines. I like something I can get within ax-reach of!"

"No shit? I'll tell Raimon the Carpenter that." Robert Anselm: sardonic. At her inquiring look, he added, "Had to make someone Enguynnur,[26] with Tony here buggered off to Africa and likely dead."

Doubled-up commands aren't going to make anyone's life easy. . . .

"*Christus Viridianus!*" Ash shook her head. "So much for 'safe inside Dijon.' We're sitting smack in the gold![27] Okay, brief me, before we get to this damn council—what's been happening, Roberto?"

"Okay. Debrief." Robert Anselm wiped his hand across his nose. There was a slight awkwardness about the movement that she guessed meant a wound taken during a Visigoth assault; knew he would not mention it himself.

"They bottled us up here after Auxonne. We could see the sky on fire, every night—burning towns, off in the boonies. First off they set up their engines and guns, gave us a major artillery barrage. Those big trebuchets? They had 'em lobbing dead bodies in, dead horses, our own casualties from Auxonne. That was when they set up the

---

[26] The 'Fraxinus' text uses this indiscriminately with both 'enginur' and 'enguigniur'; all mean 'engineer,' in the sense of 'combat engineer.'

[27] Presumably a reference to the gold ring at the centre of targets used for archery.

flamethrowers opposite the three gates, 'bout fifteen to a gate, covering the walls and river. We blew up the south bridge; they started mining in from the north."

"Didn't miss a trick." She blinked at the backs of the men and horses she followed, as they rode into a larger public square, where a slide of bricks blocked half the road. *I wish I couldn't picture everything he says.*

What's wrong with me? This stuff never bothers me!

"Oh, they done their best to fuck us, all right," Anselm said grimly. "Been bombarding us from the end of August, soon as they found they couldn't take the city straight off. They couldn't get no bombards and siege engines over on the east of the Ouche River, ground's too broken, so they stuck their artillery north and west of the city. Plowed up as much of the place as we thought was in their range."

He looked down, bringing his mount around a crater that gouged the flagstones. As they passed it, Ash saw that the sandstone walls of a church were pocked with holes.

"This lot started shifting their people down into the southeast quarter of the city," he added. "For safety. Well, about the beginning of October, the Goths let loose with everything they had—on the southeast quarter. Stone shot. Greek Fire. Fucking golem war machines—'*course* they were in range. They just wanted to give the civilians a chance to pack up tight in one area. . . . The Burgundians lost a lot of troops, too. Since then, it's been 'guess the target area, and where in the city do you want to sleep tonight?' "

'The company's tower looks sound."

"They've put the fighting men in places that'll stand bombardment." He looked across at her. "Then the human-wave assaults started on the walls. That's been hot. The ragheads are losing men—and they don't *need* to. They've got two or three *fucking* big saps under way. Going for the northwest gate. Where you come in? Up there. You get down in the foundations of the gate tower, and you can fucking *hear* them coming. They don't need to keep piling up the wall at us!"

"How long has this place got?"

Confronted with a direct question, Robert Anselm didn't answer. He looked at her with a slow smile. "By God, girl, you look different, but you don't sound it. Carthage 'asn't changed you that much."

" 'Course not. Long way to go to get a haircut, that's all."

They exchanged glances.

Strong winds snapped the Lion Affronté over her head. The group of men riding around her speeded their pace a little, unconsciously. She didn't counter it.

"How often *do* the Goths try and come over the walls?"

"Well, they ain't relying on hunger and disease to break this city. It's been fucking hot up at the northwest gate," Anselm admitted. He lifted a hand, scarred as a smith's or farmer's hands, to signal the banner-bearer to slow to a less panicky pace. "You spoke to their boss. The ragheads want Dijon. Never mind Antwerp, Bruges, Ghent. I reckon they must want the Duke—if he don't die of his wounds, first. That means assaults. It's been every few days. Some nights. Fucking *stupid* siege tactics."

"Yeah. It is. But, looking out there, they must outnumber the Burgundians four or five to one. . . ."

Searing cold air cut her face. Overhead, ragged clouds ran south on a high wind. A white facade—a Guild hall?—was visible now, over the heads of the Burgundian escort. She didn't recognize the area from the summer. The group of riders straggled to a halt. Looking ahead, Ash saw the leader of the Burgundians in fluent discussion with some civilian at the foot of the Guild hall steps.

"Strong roof over our heads would be nice," she murmured, quietening Orgueil. "'Till some bugger drops a ton of rock on it, I suppose. . . ."

The banner-bearer murmured, "Looks like we're moving, boss."

What had delayed them had evidently been some debate about ceremony: as they dismounted and entered the Viscount-Mayor's hall, a herald's clarion rang out under its painted, vaulted roof.

The nobles, merchants, and Mayor of Dijon looked up from seats at a long, beech-wood table. The tapestried chamber filled with their voices. A flock of armed men and civilians sat, or stood. A few, Ash judged by the hennin headdresses lost in the crowd, must be female, merchant's wives, traders on their own accounts, minor nobility. She took note of the liveries on the armed men with them. Not all Burgundian households.

"Frenchmen? Germans?" she murmured.

"Noble refugees," Anselm said, with a wealth of cynicism.

"Who want to carry the war on against the Visigoths?"

"So they say."

In full armor, with Chamberlain-Counselor Ternant beside him, Olivier de la Marche stood up from the chair of state. He looked, Ash thought, tired and dirty and not at all like the man who had commanded the Duke of Burgundy's army at Auxonne. She frowned.

"As the deputy of the Duke," Olivier de la Marche said without preamble, "I welcome the hero of Carthage into our company. Demoiselle-Captain Ash, we bid you and your men welcome. Welcome!"

De la Marche bowed, formally, to her.

"The—" Ash kept her face expressionless with an effort.

Hero of Carthage! She returned the bow; awkward; as ever, not knowing whether a curtsy would have been better. "Thank you, my lord."

Seats toward the head of the table were rapidly vacated. She sat down, muttering under her breath to her officers, "'Hero' of Carthage? 'Hero'!"

Robert Anselm's grim face looked twenty years younger as he snuffled back a laugh. "Don't ask *me*. God only knows what rumors have been being spread here!"

"Inaccurate ones, madonna!" Angelotti said softly.

Ash finally grinned. "So. A hero, by accident. Well—that makes up for the dozens of utterly splendid things I've done that nobody ever noticed!" She sobered. "Trouble with being a hero is, people expect things of you. I don't think I do 'hero,' guys."

Anselm punched her shoulder, briefly and very fast. "Girl, I don't think you have a choice!"

Thomas Rochester and the escort took up places behind them. Ash looked around, grateful for Angelotti's evidently blisteringly expensive demi-gown, seeing every reaction from contempt to awe on the faces down the table. She beamed, broadly, at the man across the table, with the Viscount-Mayor of Dijon's chain resting on his rich robes, a man bundled up in furs and velvets, who was glowering covertly at "the hero of Carthage."

"Yes, madonna," Angelotti said, before she could speak, "that is the man who would allow no merchant to give us credit, when we first arrived here from Basle and you were sick. The Viscount-Mayor, Richard Follo."

"Called us 'scruffy mercenaries,' didn't he?" Ash beamed. "Which I doubt he repeated to John de Vere! Well, that's Rota Fortuna[28] for you."

---

[28] 'The Wheel of Fortune.'

Ash looked around at the assembly of Burgundians and the foreign nobles present, those who had precedence sitting at the long table, those who had not crowding the room to the walls behind them. An air of aggressive desperation, familiar to her from other sieges, hung about them. What friction there might be between lords, burghers, the Viscount-Mayor, and the people of Dijon itself, she decided she would not concern herself with at the moment.

"We bid you welcome," de la Marche concluded, seating himself.

She caught his eye, thought *Let's throw the cat in the fire, then!* and spoke. "My lord, it's taken me and my men the better part of two months to get here from Carthage. My intelligence isn't current or good. I need to know, on behalf of my company—how strong is this city, and how much Burgundian territory is still holding out against the Visigoths?"

"Our lands?" De la Marche rumbled. "The Duchy, Franche-Comté, the north; Lorraine is not certain—"

A thin-faced noble hammered his hand on the table, turning to Olivier de la Marche. "You *see*! Our Duke should consider. I have lands in Charolais. Where is his loyalty to our king? If you would only seek King Louis's protection—"

"—or call on the feudal ties he has with the Empire—"

Ash barely realized the second voice was speaking in German when the two Burgundian knights, almost in unison, finished: "And sign a peace with the King-Caliph!"

Anselm muttered, "Shit, why not? Everywhere else in Christendom has!"

The hundred or so men and women in the hall began to shout, in at least four different languages.

"*Silence!*"

De la Marche's full-throated shout—*you could hear that over cannon*! Ash reflected—banged off the roof beams and brought a shuffling quiet to the council hall.

"Jesus, what a dog-fight!" Ash muttered. She realized she had been heard, and felt her face heat. Fear—of the army outside, of a twin, of all the incestuous south, of all the lack of answers there or here—made her bad-tempered. She shrugged at de la Marche. "I'll be frank. I wondered what Cola de Monforte and his boys were doing out there with the Visigoths. I'm starting to see why. Burgundy's coming apart at the seams, isn't it?"

Unexpectedly, the chamberlain-counselor who sat beside de la Marche, Philippe Ternant, chuckled. "No, Demoiselle-Captain, no more than usual! These are family quarrels. They grow heated when our father the Duke is out of the room."

Ash, seeing Ternant's watery blue eyes and age-spotted hands, weighed up his probable experience of Burgundian politics. She said politely, "As you say, messire," and flicked a glance at Robert Anselm. *I need to take decisions! I thought—if we got here—at least we'd have a breathing-space—*

"What is Burgundy?" de la Marche demanded, his weather-beaten face turning toward Ash. "Demoiselle-Captain, what are we? Here in the south, we're two Burgundies: both the Duchy and the County. Then the conquered province, Lorraine. All the northern lands: Hainault, Holland, Flanders . . . [29] What our Duke does not owe as a French fief to King Louis, he owes as an Imperial

[29] At this time, at the height of its power, Burgundy consisted of the Duchy of Burgundy, the County of Burgundy (Franche-Comté), Flanders, Artois, Rethel, Nevers, Brabant, Limbourg, Hainault, Holland, Zeeland, Luxembourg, Guelders, and—briefly, in 1475—the duchy of Lorraine.

fief to the Emperor Frederick! Demoiselle, we speak French in the two Burgundies, Dutch and Flemish in Flanders, and Imperial German in Luxembourg! Only one thing holds us together—one man—Duke Charles. Without it, we would collapse again into a hundred quarreling properties of other kingdoms."[30]

Philippe Ternant looked amused. "My lord, much as I bow to your military prowess, let me say that a single chancellor, chancery, and system of tax binds us equally—"

"And that would last *how* long, without Duke Charles?" Olivier de la Marche's hand came down flat on the wooden table, with a bang that startled all of the crowded room. "The Duke unifies us!"

A flicker of green cloth: Ash caught sight of an abbot, his face hidden from her in the crush of bodies farther down the Guild hall.

"We are the ancient German people of Burgundia," the abbot said, still invisible; "and we have been the Kingdom of Arles, when Christendom was divided into Neustria and Austrasia. We are older than the Valois Dukes."

His deep voice reminded her briefly of Godfrey Maximillian: she was unaware of the sharp crease that appeared in the flesh between her eyebrows.

"Names do not matter, my lord de la Marche. Here in the forests of the south, there in the cities of the north, we are one people. From Holland to Lake Geneva, *we are one.* Our lord the Duke is the embodiment of that, as his father was before him; but Burgundy will outlast Charles of Valois. Of that I am certain."

---

[30] This is, broadly speaking, what happened when Charles the Bold died in 1477, having failed to sire a male heir, or arrange the marriage of his only daughter and heir, Mary. Had Charles lived, his ambition to be a European monarch might well have succeeded.

Into the hush, Ash found herself saying thoughtfully, "Not if someone doesn't do something about the Visigoth army out there!"

Faces turned toward her, white discs in the sunlight that now streamed in through the ancient stone windows.

"The Duke unites us." The Viscount-Mayor, Follo, spoke up. "And therefore, since he is here—the north will come south and rescue us."

It will? Restraining a sudden, blind hope, Ash turned toward de la Marche. "What's the news from the north?"

"The last message spoke of fighting around Bruges; but that news was a month old when it arrived. The armies of the lady Margaret may have won a victory by now."

"Will they come? Just for one town under siege?"

"Dijon is not merely 'one town under siege,' " the chamberlain-counselor Philippe Ternant said, looking at Ash. "You stand in the heart of Burgundy, here; in the Duchy itself."

"My Duke," Olivier de la Marche said, "wrote, three years ago, that God has instituted and ordained princes to rule principalities and lordships so that the regions, provinces, and peoples are joined together and organized in union, concord, and loyal discipline.[31] Since the Duke is here—they will come."

About to ask *What strength are the forces in the north?*, Ash found herself interrupted.

Olivier de la Marche, briskly now, said, "Demoiselle-Captain, you and your men have more recently seen what lies beyond these walls."

"In Carthage?"

De la Marche's weather-beaten face twisted, as if with some pain. "In what you have seen south of Burgundy first,

[31] Charles the Bold, ordinance of Thionville, 1473.

demoiselle. We know little of the lands outside our borders, these past two months. Except that there are refugees every day on the roads outside the city."

"Yes, messire." Ash got to her feet again, and realized that was out of pure habit, to let them see that she was a woman wearing a sword, even if it was without armor and thus not a customary thing to do.[32] *I'm not used to being a hero of anywhere. . . .*

"We came in through the French King's territories, under the darkness," she began. "They say there that the dark extends north to the Loire—at least, they were saying that two or three weeks ago. We didn't see any fighting—" She grinned, toothily. "Not against the *Visigoths*, anyway. So I suppose the peace treaty is holding."

"Motherfuckers!" de la Marche spat, explosively. Some of the merchant princes looked startled at his language, but not, Ash thought, as if they disagreed with the sentiment. There was a rumble from the few refugee French knights present.

Ash shrugged. "That's the Universal Spider[33] for you."

"God rot him," de la Marche observed, in his battle-loud voice. Merchants and noblemen who would have winced at the champion's loudness in peace now looked, Ash thought, as if the big Burgundian were their last hope.

"God rot him, *and* German Frederick!"[34] de la Marche finished.

She has a brief memory of some of these noble German

---

[32] The practice of wearing a sword over 'civilian' clothing does not, in Western Europe, really begin until the 16th century. In 1476, a sword is normally only worn with armour or other war-gear. (The wearing of a knife, however, would be universal.)

[33] Louis XI of France.

[34] The Holy Roman Emperor, Frederick III.

and French refugees when they stood in the cathedral at Cologne, at her marriage to Fernando del Guiz: all of them in bright liveries, then, and with well-fed faces. Not now.

"Messire—"

Getting a second wind, de la Marche thumped the long table. "Why should their lands be spared, treacherous sons of bitches? Just because the groveling little shits signed 'treaties' with these Visigoth bastards!"

"Not all of us are traitors!" A knight in Gothic armor sprang to his feet, crashing his plate gauntlet down on the table. "And at least *we* do not wish to continue to cringe behind these walls, Duke's man!"

De la Marche ignored him. "What else, Demoiselle-Captain?"

"Their lands aren't being 'spared' much of anything. Whoever wins this war—there's going to be major famine." Ash looked around the table, at jowled faces somewhat bitten by short rations.

What had been prosperous townships, on the rivers of southern Burgundy, what had been rich abbeys, all of these are in her memory, under weak autumn sunlight. Burned-out, deserted.

"I don't know what stores are like here in Dijon. There's nothing going to come in to you, even if the Visigoth army didn't have this place sewn up tight. I've seen so many deserted farms and villages on the way north that I can't count them, messires. There aren't any people left. Cold's ruined the harvest. The fields are rotten. There are no cattle or swine left: they've been eaten. On the march, we saw babies left out, exposed. There isn't a surviving township between Dijon and the sea."

"This isn't war, this is obscenity!" one of the merchants snarled.

"It's bad war," Ash corrected him. "You don't wipe out

what makes a land productive if you're trying to conquer it. There's nothing left for the winner. My lord, I'd guess your refugees out there are turning for Savoy, or southern France, or even the Cantons. But it's no better there—and they'll be under the Darkness. There's still sun over south Burgundy. But outside, it's already winter. Has been since Auxonne, as far as I can see. And it's staying that way."

"Winter like in the Rus lands."

Ash turned her head, recognizing Ludmilla Rostovnaya's voice from where the crossbowwoman stood with Thomas Rochester. She signaled her to continue.

Ludmilla Rostovnaya's red hose and russet doublet were thick with candle grease, under her cloak. She shifted from foot to foot, conscious of eyes on her, and spoke more to Ash than to the assembled nobles.

"Far north, the winter comes with ice," she said. "Great sheets of it, eight months of the year. There are men in my village who can remember Czar Peter's port[35] freezing one June, ships cracking like eggs. *That's* winter. That's what it's like at Marseilles, when we landed."

A priest at the far end of the table, between two Burgundian knights, spoke up. "You see, my lord de la Marche? This is what I have said. In France and the Germanies, Italy and eastern Iberia, they no longer see the sun—and yet he has not entirely forsaken us, here. Some of his heat must touch our earth, still. We are not yet Under the Penance."

Ash opened her mouth to say *Penance be damned, it's the Wild Machines!*, and shut it again. She looked to her officers. Robert Anselm, lips pushed together, shook his head.

---

[35] Some textual corruption here? If St Petersburg/Leningrad is intended, conceivably an addition by a later hand—Peter the Great did not found the city until 1703.

Antonio Angelotti first glanced at her for permission, then spoke aloud. "Messires, I am a master gunner. I've fought in the lands under the penitence, with Lord-*Amir* Childeric. There was *warmth* there, then. As of a warm night. Not enough for seed, but still, not winter."

Ash nodded thanks to the crossbowwoman and the gunner.

"Angelotti's right. I'll tell you what I saw, not two months ago, my lords—*it isn't warm in Carthage anymore*. There's ice on the desert. Snow. And it was still getting colder when I left."

"Is it a greater Penance?" The priest—another abbot, by his pectoral Briar Cross—leaned forward. "Are they the more damned, now that they take their guidance from demons? Will this greater punishment spread with their conquests?"

De la Marche met Ash's gaze, his eyes shrewd. "The last news I have is that impenetrable darkness covers France as far north as Tours and Orléans, now; covers half the Black Forest; stretches as far east as Vienna, and Cyprus. Only our middle lands, as far as Flanders, still witness the sun."[36]

Aw, *shit*! "Burgundy is the only land—?"

"I know nothing of the lands of the Turk. But as for what I do know—yes, Demoiselle-Captain. Daily, the dark spreads north. The sun is seen over Burgundy alone, now." Olivier de la Marche grunted. "As well as what you see fleeing away, we have hordes of refugees traveling *into* our lands, Demoiselle-Captain. Because of the sun."

---

[36] It is interesting to plot these and the other geographical points mentioned on a map of Europe and the Mediterranean. In fact, they form more than half of an ellipse, with the northeastern coast of Tunisia as its hypothetical centre.

"We cannot feed them!" the Viscount-Mayor protested, stung, as if this were part of a long debate.

"Use them!" the German knight who had spoken before snarled. "War will cease over winter. We might win free of this poxy town, as soon as spring comes, and fight a decisive battle. Take them in as levies and train them! We have the Duke's army, we have the hero of Carthage here, Demoiselle Ash; in God's name let us *fight*!"

Ash winced, imperceptibly, both at the mention of her name and at Robert Anselm's snort. She waited for the Duke's deputy to build on it, propose some heroic and doubtless foolhardy exploit for the hero of Carthage to perform to help raise the siege.

We ain't going to fight a hopeless *war. There ain't enough money to pay us for that.*

What are *we going to do?*

Olivier de la Marche, as if the German knight had not spoken, demanded abruptly, "Demoiselle-Captain Ash, will the Visigoth army stay in the field now? How much of Carthage is destroyed?"

The white masonry of the ogee windows glittered, sun flickering between clouds. Frost starred the stone. A scent of something burning drifted in on the chill air, over and above the great fire that the servants kept burning in the hearth. Ash tasted coldness on her lips.

"Nothing like as much as rumor says, my lord. An earthquake threw down the Citadel. I believe the new King-Caliph, Gelimer, to be alive." She repeated, for emphasis: "My lord, it's snowing on the coast of Africa—and they didn't expect it any more than we did. The *amirs* I met are shit-scared. They started this war on the word of their King-Caliph, and now the countries they've conquered are under Darkness, and back home in Carthage they're freezing their asses off. They know Iberia's the grain basket of

Carthage—and they know that, if the sun doesn't come back, they won't have a harvest next year. *We* won't have a harvest. The longer this goes on—the worse things will be in six months' time."

Near a hundred faces stare back at her, civilians and soldiers, some of the nobles' escorts probably, inevitably, in the pay of men outside the walls of Dijon.

"Anything else," she said flatly, "isn't for open council; it's for your Duke."

At her dismissal, a hubbub of noise filled the room, particularly from the foreign knights and nobles. Olivier de la Marche spoke over it effortlessly:

"This cold, does it come from the demons your men speak of? These 'Wild Machines'?"

Exchanging glances with Robert Anselm, Ash thought, *Damn. My lads have got big mouths. I bet there's half a hundred garbled stories going the rounds.*

"I'm trying to stop rumor. The rest's for your Duke," she repeated doggedly. *I'm not going to be palmed off with underlings!*

De la Marche looked bluntly unwilling to let it go at that. Tension painfully tightened her shoulders. Ash rubbed at the muscles of her neck, under the back of the demi-gown's collar. It did not ease the ache. Regarding their white faces, all turned to her in the morning light, she felt a pulse of fear in her bowels. Memory chills her: voices that say '*WE HAVE DRAWN DOWN THE SUN*.'

"Fucking mercenary *whore*!" someone shouted, in German.

There was no hearing anything for the next few minutes, the council and the foreign knights raising their voices in ferocious, excited discussion and argument. Ash put her hands on the table and leaned her weight on them, momentarily. Anselm put his elbow on the back of her chair, leaning behind her to talk to Angelotti.

I should sit down, she thought, *let them get on with it. This lot is hopeless!*

"My lord de la Marche." She waited until the Duke's deputy turned his attention to her again.

"Demoiselle-Captain?"

"*I* have a question, my lord."

If I hadn't, I might not have bothered with this damn stupid council!

She took a breath. "If I were the King-Caliph, I wouldn't have started a crusade here without taking out the Turks first. And if I *had* done it, I'd be looking to make peace about now—the Visigoths have got most of Christendom to hold down. But the Goths aren't stopping. You say they're fighting in Ghent and Bruges in the north, they're trashing Lorraine. They're here at Dijon. My lord, you tell me—what's so important? *Why Burgundy?*"

A woman's voice spoke before the Duke's deputy could, and spoke in the tone of one citing a proverb: "Upon Burgundy's health depends the health of the world."

"What?"

The voice tugged at Ash's memory.

She leaned farther forward across the table, and found herself looking into the pinched white face of Jeanne Châlon.

She was, for once, glad Floria del Guiz was not present.

Abruptly, she flinched from the memory of August in Dijon, and the death that had followed the disclosure of Floria del Guiz as a woman. *But* why*? There have been deaths since that one. The man I killed might well have died in battle by now.*

"Mademoiselle." Ash stared at the surgeon's aunt. "With

respect—I don't want superstitious twaddle: I want an answer!"

The Burgundian woman's eyes widened, her face full of shock. She stumbled back from the table, pushing her way through the confused crowd and the servants, and fled.

"You always have that effect on people?" Anselm rumbled.

"I think she just remembered, we've met." An ironic smile twisted Ash's lips, fading quickly. " 'Upon Burgundy's health—' "

A knight in French livery completed: " '—depends the health of the world.' It is an old proverb, and a meretricious one; nothing more than self-justification by the Valois Dukes."

Ash glanced around. No Burgundian appeared willing to speak.

The French knight added, "Demoiselle-Captain, let us have no more nonsense of demons. We do not doubt the Visigoth army has many engines and devices. We have only to look out from the walls here to see that! I do not doubt, they have more engines in their cities in the south, perhaps greater ones than they have here. You say you have seen them. Yes. But what of this? We must fight the Visigoth crusade *here*!"

A buzz of approval sounded around the chamber. Ash noted it came mainly from the foreign knights. The Burgundians—de la Marche in particular—merely looked grim.

"We know better," Antonio Angelotti murmured under his breath.

Ash waved him to silence.

"Suppose, messire—?" Ash waited until the French knight responded:

"Armand de Lannoy."

"—Suppose, messire de Lannoy, that the Visigoths are not fighting this war with their engines. Suppose it is the 'engines' which fight, using the Visigoths."

Armand de Lannoy slammed his palms flat on the table. "This is nonsense, and an ugly girl's nonsense at that!"

The breath went out of her. Ash sat down, amid a babble of French and German.

Shit, she thought bleakly. *Had to happen. I don't have how I look to count on anymore. To use. Shit*. Shit.

Beside her, there was a low, unconscious, ratcheting growl from Robert Anselm, almost entirely identical to the sound that the mastiffs Brifault or Bonniau might make.

She grabbed his arm. "Let—it—go."

Olivier de la Marche's voice rose, a bellow that ripped the air in the hall apart, brought adrenaline into Ash's body even if it were not directed at her. He and the French knight, de Lannoy, both stood and shouted into each other's faces across the table.

Ash winced. "This is worse than Frederick's court! Christ. Burgundy was better than this, the first time we came."

"The place wasn't full of factious refugees, madonna," Angelotti put in, "and the Duke, besides, was ruling then."

"I've sent Florian to talk to the doctors. See what state he's really in." Aware of some disturbance among Thomas Rochester and her escort, behind her, Ash turned her head. The men-at-arms parted, letting through the elderly Burgundian chamberlain-counselor.

"Messire . . ." Ash got hastily to her feet.

Philippe Ternant regarded her for a moment. He put his hand on the shoulder of a boy beside him, a page in puffed-sleeve white doublet, gold aiglettes pointing doublet to hose.

"You are summoned. Jean, here, will guide you," he said quietly. "Demoiselle- Captain, I am ordered to bring you to attend on the Duke."

V

"DUKE CHARLES?" ASH said, startled. "I thought he was sick."

"He is. You will be allowed in for a short time. It would weary the noble Duke to see many people; therefore, you must bring no crowd. Perhaps one man-at-arms, if you will have a bodyguard with you." Ternant's lined mouth smiled. "As I know, to my cost, here, a knight must have his entourage, be it never so small."

Ash, catching the chamberlain-counselor's eyes on de Lannoy and his single archer escort, nodded companionably. "Quite. Robert, Angeli; take over for me here. Thomas Rochester, you come with me." She signaled to the page, before her officers could do more than nod obedience. "Lead on."

At last!

Following the boy Jean, her hand automatically went to her scabbard, steadying Anselm's sword. Any likelihood of assassination would be small; nonetheless she kept a keen eye out as they crossed the streets to the palace—flinching at the noise of bombardment, over toward the west side of the city—and entered, and traversed white-walled passages cut deep into stone; climbing stairs where stained-glass windows spilled pale light on the floor. She noticed fewer Burgundian men-at-arms in the palace than when she had first visited it, in the summer.

"Maybe he's dead, boss," Thomas Rochester suddenly ventured.

"What, the Duke?"

"No, the asshole—your husband."

Just as Rochester said it, she recognized the vaulted chamber they were passing through. Banners still hung from the walls, although the muted light made less of the stained glass's reflections on the flagstones.

The qa'id *Sancho Lebrija is doubtless with the crusade, Agnes Dei's banner is outside these walls, but Fernando? God and the Green Christ know where Fernando is now—or if he's even alive.*

This is where she last touched him—her warm fingers entwined with his. Where she struck him. In Carthage, later, he was as weak, as much of a pawn as he was here. Until the last moments before the earth tremor—*But he could afford to speak up for me: no one was going to* care *about a disgraced, turncoat German knight!*

"I choose to assume I'm a widow," she said grimly, and followed the page Jean and the chamberlain-counselor Philippe Ternant as they began to climb the stairs of a tower.

The chamberlain-counselor passed them through great numbers of Burgundian guardsmen, into a high-vaulted chamber packed with any number of people: squires; pages; men-at-arms; rich nobles in gowns and chaperon hats; women in nun's headdresses; an austringer with his hawk; a bitch and a litter of pups in the straw by the great hearth.

"It is the Duke's sickroom," Philippe Ternant said to

Ash, as he went on into the mass of people. "Wait here: he will call on your attendance when he desires it."

Thomas Rochester said, low-voiced, for her ear, "Don't reckon that 'siege council' is much more than a sop to keep the civilians quiet, boss."

"You think the real power's here?" Ash glanced around the crowded ducal chamber. "Possible."

There were enough men in full armor present, wearing liveries, for her to identify the notable military nobles of Burgundy—all who had survived Auxonne, presumably—and all of the major mercenary commanders with the exception of Cola de Monforte and his two sons.

"Monforte's leaving could have been political, not strictly military," she murmured.

The dark Englishman's brow creased under his visor; and then his face cleared. "Beginning to think we'd had it, boss, listening to that council. But if the captains are still here—"

"Then they might still stand a chance of kicking ass." Ash completed the English knight's train of thought. "Thomas, I know you'll stick close to my back here."

"Yes, boss." Thomas Rochester sounded cheerful at her confidence in him.

"Not that I expect to get nailed in the middle of the Duke's sickroom. . . ." Ash stepped back automatically as a Soeur-Viridianus came past with a basin. Bandages with old blood and filth filled the copper pan.

"If it isn't my patient!" the big woman exclaimed.

The green robes and tight wimple of a soeur still made Ash's hackles rise. At the gruff greeting, she found herself startled into looking up into the broad white face of the Soeur Maîtresse of the convent of *filles de pénitence*—up, and farther up than Ash had realized while being nursed; the woman was tall as well as solidly big.

"Soeur Simeon!" Ash sketched a genuflection scarcely

worth the term, but with a brilliant smile that more than made up for that. "I saw they trashed the convent—glad you made it into the city."

"How is your head?"

Moderately impressed at the woman's memory, Ash made a bow of rather more respect. "I'll live, Soeur. No thanks to the Visigoths, who tried to undo your good works. But I'll live."

"I am glad to hear it." The Soeur Maîtresse spoke without change of tone to someone beyond Ash: "More linen, and another priest: *be quick.*"

Another nun dipped a curtsy. "Yes, Soeur Maîtresse!"

Ash, trying to see the little nun's face, was startled when Simeon said thoughtfully, "I shall wish to visit your quarters, Captain. I am missing one of my girls this morning. Your—surgeon, 'Florian'—may, I feel, be able to help me."

Little Margaret Schmidt, Ash thought. *I'd put money on it. Goddammit.*

"How long has your soeur been missing, Maîtresse?"

"Since last night."

That's my Florian . . .

Her private smile faded. She was conscious of an uneasy relief. *After what she said to me—it's safer if she's with someone else.*

"I'll make inquiries." Ash met Thomas Rochester's blue eyes briefly. "We're contract soldiers, Soeur. If your soeur's signed up with the baggage train . . . well. There's an end of it. We look after our own."

She watched the English knight more than the Soeur Maîtresse, looking for the slightest flinch. If the idea of keeping the surgeon's woman lover away from a nunnery was disturbing Thomas Rochester, he didn't show it.

But if he knew Margaret Schmidt isn't the only woman here that Florian's attracted to?

"I'll see you later," Simeon cried, her tone too determined for Ash to make out whether that was threat or grim promise, before the big woman strode out through the crowd that parted in front of her.

"Can't we sign up that one, boss?" Thomas Rochester said whimsically. "Better have her than some bimbo the surgeon fancies! Stick the Soeur Maîtresse in the line-fight beside me—and I'll hide right behind her! Scare the shit out of the ragheads, she would."

The page, Jean, appearing at her elbow, hauled off his hat and gabbled, "The Duke summons you!"

Ash followed the boy through the crush, overhearing the many guildsmen and merchants present discussing civilian matters, keeping only enough attention on them to estimate morale. A large number of confident men in armor came past her from the far end of the chamber, their aides carrying maps; Ash moved through them and found herself confronting the Duke of Burgundy.

The walls were pale stone, saint's icons set into niches with candles burning before them; and a great tester bed occupied this whole end of the chamber, between two windows blocked with clear leaded glass.

The Duke was not in the great bed.

He lay, on his left side, on a truckle bed no more splendid than any she had seen in the field, apart from some carvings of saints on the wooden box frame. Braziers surrounded the bed. Two priests stood back as Ash, the page, and her bodyguard approached; and Duke Charles waved them aside decisively.

"We will speak privately," he ordered. "Captain Ash, it is good to see you returned at last from Carthage."

"Yeah, I think so, too, Your Grace. I've been up and down Christendom like a dog at a fair."

No smile touched his face. She had forgotten he was not

to be moved by a sense of humor, or by charm. Since it had been a reflex remark, made entirely to hide her shock at seeing him, she did not waste time regretting it, only stood silent and tried not to let her thoughts appear on her face.

Bolsters kept the Duke propped up on his left side on the hard bed. Books and papers surrounded him, and a clerk knelt by his side, hastily returning what Ash saw to be maps of the city defenses to order. A rich blue velvet gown covered Charles of Burgundy and the bed together; under it she could see that he was wearing a fine linen shirt.

His black hair stuck, sweat-tangled, to his skull. This end of the ducal chamber stank of the sickroom. As he looked up to meet her gaze, Ash took in his sallow skin and prominent feverish eyes, the ridges of cheekbones that stood up now in his face, his cheeks sunken in. His left hand, closing around the cross hanging from his neck, was frighteningly thin.

She thought, quite coldly, *Burgundy's fucked.*

As if he were not in pain—but by the sweat that continually rolled down his face, he must be—Duke Charles ordered, "Master priests, you may leave me; you also, Soeur. Guard, clear this end of the chamber."

The page Jean moved back with the rest. Ash glanced uncertainly toward Thomas Rochester. She noted that the Duke's bodyguard, a big man with archer's shoulders and a padded jack, did not move away from his station behind the Duke.

"Send your man away, Captain," Charles said.

Ash's question must have been apparent on her face. The Duke spared a brief glance for the archer, towering over him.

"I believe you to be honorable," he said, "but, were a man to come before me with a stiletto up his sleeve, and if there were no other way to stop him, Paul here would put himself between me and such a weapon, and take the blow into his own body. I cannot honorably send aside a man prepared to do this."

"Thomas, stand back."

Ash stood, waiting.

"We have much to say to each other. First, go to that window," the Duke said, indicating one of the chamber's two glassed windows, "and tell me what you see."

Ash crossed the two yards' space in a stride or so. The tiny, thick panes of glass distorted the view below, but she made out that she was looking south, under a low gray sky, clouds racing on a rough wind that rattled the window in its frame. And that she was high enough that she must be, now, standing in the Tour Philippe le Bon, the palace's notorious lookout post.

Doesn't look any fucking better from up here . . . !

Wind yanked at the withy barriers surrounding rows of catapults. Squinting, she could make out men crowding around the jutting beams of trebuchets, long lines passing rocks up to the slings, and loaded oxen dragging carts full of quarried stone through the flooded Auxonne road.

"I can see as far as the joining of the Ouche and Suzon Rivers, beyond the walls," she said, loudly enough for the sick man to hear her, "and the enemy siege-machine camp in the west. River's up: there's even less of a chance to assault across it at those engines."

"What can you see of their strength?"

She automatically put her hand up to shield her eyes, as if the rattling wind were not outside the glass. The sun—somewhere around the fourth hour of the morning[37]—was a barely visible gray light, low in the southern sky.

"Unusual lot of cannon, for Visigoths, Your Grace. Sak-

---

[37] c. 10 a.m.

ers, serpentines, bombards, and fowlers. I heard mortars when we were coming in. Maybe they're concentrating all their powder weapons with these legions? Above three hundred engines: arbalests, mangonels, trebuchets—shit."

A great tower began to roll forward as she watched, toward the bastion where the southernmost bridge over the river had been thrown down. A fragment of escaping sunlight glanced back from its red sides.

A tower shaped like a dragon, bottle-mouthed—she glimpsed the muzzle of a saker projecting from between the teeth—but with no soaked hides coating it to protect it against fire arrows.

A wheeled tower made of stone, twenty-five feet high.

"*Christus Imperator . . .*"

No slaves pushed the tower forward to the river's edge.

Instead, it rolled forward of itself, upon brass-bound stone wheels twice the height of a man, which settled deep into the mud. As it came closer, she could just see a Visigoth gun crew inside the tower's carved head, furiously sponging and loading their cannon.

The window glass distorted a commotion on the city walls. Feeling cut off, Ash watched men running, crossbows being winched, spanned; steel bolts shot into the chill wind, all in silence, up here in the Duke's tower. A bang and crack from a Visigoth saker came muffled to her, and the whine of plaster fragments spraying from the bastion wall.

Arbalest and crossbow crews crowded the city's battlements. Anxiety sharpened her eyesight. *Any Lion liveries? No!*

A thick bolt-storm rattled against the sides of the stone dragon-tower, sending its gun crew scuttling deeper inside for shelter.

Stomach churning, she watched. The tower lurched. One

wheel bit deeper into the mud, sinking to the axle. A throng of Carthaginian slaves, herded out of the legion camp with whips, began casting fence posts and planks down under the great stone wheel for traction; falling man by man under a constant arrow fire from the city walls. As Ash watched, they ran away from the siege tower, leaving it and its crew desolate.

Evidently the Faris believes in keeping up the pressure.

"If I had to find a word for . . . for golem-*towers*," Ash said, still staring, her tone somewhere between awe and black humor, "I think my voice would call them 'self-propelled artillery' . . ."

The Duke of Burgundy's voice came from behind her. "They are stone and river silt, as the walking golem are. Fire will crack their stone. Arquebus bullets will not. Cannon have cracked their bodies. The Faris has ten towers, we have immobilized three. Go to the north window, Captain Ash."

This time, knowing what to look for, it was easier for Ash to rub moisture from the glass and lead and pick out details of the northern part of the encircling forces. There, she saw the great camp between the two rivers laid out—the moats in front of Dijon's north wall half-full of bundles of faggots, dead horses rotting in the no-man's-land of open ground.

It took her a while to pick it out from the tents, pavises, barricades, and men queuing outside the cook tents. A blink of brightness from the southern sun caught her eye, gleaming from a brass-and-marble engine longer than three wagons.

"They've got a ram. . . ."

A marble pillar as thick around as a horse's body hung sheathed in brass, suspended between posts, on a great stone-wheeled carriage. Men could not have swung the weight of that ram, or have wheeled the body of it up to the gates, but if the wheels would turn of themselves, the great metal-sheathed point slam into the timbers and portcullis of Dijon's north gate . . .

"If it hits too hard, it'll disintegrate." Ash turned back to face the Duke. "That's why they use their ordinary golems for messengers, not combat, Your Grace. Bolts or bullets will chip them away. That ram, if it hits too hard, will crack its own clay and marble. Then it'll just be a lump of rock, for all the *amirs* can do."

As she walked back to stand in front of the Duke's austere bed, he said authoritatively, "You have not seen the most dangerous of their engines—nor will you. They have golem-diggers, tunneling saps toward the walls of Dijon."

"Yeah, Your Grace, my captain Anselm's told me about those."

"My *magistri ingeniatores* have been kept employed in countermining them. But they need neither sleep nor rest, these engines of the scientist-magi, they dig twenty-four hours a day."

Ash said nothing to that, but could not entirely hide her expression.

"Dijon will stand."

She couldn't keep the sudden scepticism off her face. She waited for his anger. He said nothing. A sudden spurt of fear moved her to snap, "I didn't bring these men halfway across hell just to get them killed on your walls!"

He did not appear offended. "How interesting. That is not what I expect to hear from a mercenary commander. I would expect, as I heard from Cola de Monforte on his leaving, to hear you say that war is good, good for business, and however many men are killed, twice as many will flock to take their place in a successful company. You speak like a feudal lord, as if there were mutual loyalties involved."

Caught wrong-footed, Ash reached for words and failed to find anything to say. At last, she managed, "I expect to see my men killed. That's business. I don't expect to *waste* an asset, Your Grace."

She kept her eyes stubbornly on his face, refusing to identify, even for the briefest moment, a nagging dread.

"How are your men made up?" the Duke demanded. "Of what lands?"

Ash folded her hands in front of her to stop the sudden tremble in her fingers. She ran through the muster in her mind: the comforting neutrality of names written on paper, read to her. "For the most part, English, Welsh, German, and Italian, Your Grace. A few French, a couple of Swiss gun crews; the rest who-knows-what."

She did not say *why*? but it was plain in her expression.

"You had some of my Flemings?"

"I split the company, before Auxonne. Those Flemings are out there with the Faris, Your Grace. Orders," she said, "will only take you so far. Van Mander was a liability. I want my men fighting because they want to, not because they have to."

"So do I," the Duke said emphatically.

Feeling verbally trapped, Ash spelled out the necessary conclusion. "Here in Dijon, you mean."

Charles's face tightened. He gave no other sign of pain. Momentarily, he looked around for a page to wipe the sweat from his face; they having been sent away, he wiped his sleeve across his mouth, and raised his dark eyes to look at her with determined authority.

"I show you the worst, first. The enemy. Now. Your men will be one in five, or one in six, of my total forces here." A sharp jerk of the head, toward his captains farther down the chamber. "It is my intent to bring you into my counsel, Captain, since you form a sizable part of the defenses. If I will not always take your advice, I will listen to it nonetheless."

That's the respect he'd show a male captain.

She said soberly, and completely neutrally, "Yes, Your Grace."

"But in that event you will say that you and your men are, nonetheless, fighting only because you must. Because you must fight to eat."

Oh, you're good. Ash met his keen, black gaze. He was not very many years older than her, a decade, perhaps.[38] Lines cut down the skin at the sides of his mouth, put there both by authority and, more recently, she guessed, by pain.

"Your Grace, I'm a mercenary. If I think my men should leave, we will. This isn't our fight."

Charles said, "Therefore, I intend to offer you a contract."

"Can't take it." She shook her head, her answer immediate.

"Why not?"

Ash spared a glance for the big archer behind the Duke, wondered momentarily how close mouthed the man might be, and then mentally shrugged. *The rumor mill will have had everything around the city before Sext,*[39] *no matter what I say.*

"For one thing—I signed my name on a contract with the Earl of Oxford," Ash said measuredly. "He's employing me right now. If I knew for certain where he was, Your Grace, I'd feel obliged either to get his orders, or to take the company and leave to rejoin him. As it happens, I have no idea where he is, or even whether he's alive—from Carthage to the Bosphorus is a damn long way, right now,

---

[38] In fact, Charles of Burgundy had been born, in Dijon, in AD 1432.

[39] The canonical sixth hour of the day: noon.

through war and freezing winter, and who knows what mood the Sultan's in? I guess that my lord of Oxford may have a better idea where *I* am. He may get word to me here. He may not."

None of what she said appeared to come to the Duke as a surprise. *At least his intelligence is reasonable.*

"I wondered what you would finally say to me when I asked for your commitment."

So did I.

She became aware that her heartbeat increased.

"I kept you from Visigoth hands, Captain, last summer." Charles leaned forward in the bed, as if his back pained him. "You feel no obligation to me?"

"Personally, perhaps." Saying that, unsure, she decided to let it stand. "This is business. What happened in Basle to the contrary, I don't break contracts, Your Grace. John de Vere is my employer."

"He may be lost. Imprisoned. Or dead these many weeks. Sit." The Duke pointed.

A three-legged stool stood not far from the ducal bed. Ash sat, carefully, balancing her weight in the brigandine, wishing she could turn around and see people's expressions. It is not everybody who is invited to sit in the presence.

"Yes, Your Grace?"

"You doubt my competence as a leader, now," Charles said.

It was a forthright statement, with no uncertainty about the uncomfortable fact, given with a kind of confidence nonetheless. Ash, startled, could think of nothing to say that would not get her into trouble. *It's true. I do.*

"You're wounded, Your Grace," she said at last.

"Wounded, but not dead. I still command my officers and captains. I will continue to do so. If I fall, de la

Marche, or my wife, who commands in the north, are both perfectly capable of withstanding the invading army and relieving the siege here."

Ash let no doubt show in her voice. "Yes, Your Grace."

"I want you to fight for me," Charles said. "Not because towns and cities have been destroyed, and out there on the horizon the dark is closing in on us, and you have nowhere else to go. I want you to fight for me because you trust me to lead you, and win."

He continued to hold her gaze, where she sat. His voice became quieter.

"When I first ordered you into my presence, this summer past, you were concerned that your own men might not follow you, you having been wounded at Basle. I think that you wondered, later, if they would have rescued you at Auxonne—if that wound, and their doubt of you, had not held them back. Then, when your men came to Carthage, it was not for you, but for the Stone Golem. You are still partly troubled over their loyalty, even if you do not express your concern." Charles gave a small smile. "Or do I read you wrong, Captain Ash?"

"Shit." Ash stared blankly at him.

"I've been in the field since I was a boy. I read men." The Duke's smile faded. "And women, too. War makes nothing of that distinction."

How the fuck *do you know what I've been thinking?*

Ash shook her head, unaware that she did so—not so much a negative as a rejection of the thoughts in herself.

"You're right, Your Grace. I thought exactly that. Up to today. Now . . . I've just had a demonstration of—loyalty, I guess. That's even harder to cope with."

The Duke surveyed her for a long moment.

"You may sign a contract with me that leaves de Vere

your master," he said, abruptly. "If orders come from him, or if you hear of his whereabouts, you and your men are free to go. Until then, remain here, fight for me. When you agree, I will have you fed along with my men, which is worth more than coin in this city now; and you and your officers will have a say in the defense of the city. As for the rest—"

Charles broke off again. This time it was clearly pain. One of the green-robed soeurs edged closer, glaring at Ash in unmistakable anger. Ash got to her feet, the previous night's exertions aching in her muscles.

"Your Grace, I'll retire until you're well."

"You will retire when you are given leave."

"Yes, *sir*," Ash said under her breath.

Her gaze weighed him, as she stood before him, a woman in man's demi-gown and hose, her own bodyguard holding her sword belt and weapons six paces away.

Whatever wound he had taken at Auxonne, it still pained him. She looked away from his sallow face, caught by his gesture as he waved the nun away. His right hand was blotched, at the first knuckle of the middle finger, with black oak-gall ink.

He's still up to writing orders and ordinances, however sick he is.

That's a good sign.

He'll probably stand by his word, too, if the past's anything to go by.

That's a better one.

He's no John de Vere. On the other hand, he's certainly no Frederick of Hapsburg.

She remained silent, weighing him on the one hand with the English soldier-Earl, on the other with the political acumen of the Holy Roman Emperor, realizing without much surprise that—even with his little humor and less social grace—what she felt comfortable with was the soldier in him, rather than the Duke.

There are six thousand men and three hundred engines out there, minimum. Against some vague hope of a relieving force from Flanders. And the minute this guy keels over—the city goes.

And he has more than men for enemies.

"Follow me, and trust me," Charles said. He spoke with a brisk, awkward confidence, but nonetheless a confidence that was total. Looking at this man, even on his sickbed, Ash found she could not imagine him in defeat.

Dead, yes, but not defeated. That's good. If they're that confident, we might settle this before his death's an issue.

"You believe you're going to win, Your Grace."

"I conquered Paris, and Lorraine." He spoke without boasting. "My army here, though much reduced, is better equipped, and made up of better men than the Visigoths. There is another army of mine in the north, under Margaret's command, in Bruges. She will come south soon. Yes, Captain, we shall win."

Whether you will, or whether you won't—right now, I can't feed my men without you.

She met his dark gaze. "Upon condition, I can sign a *condotta* that's limited to what you've just said, Your Grace." And then, an irrepressible grin breaking out, born of relief at having taken any decision, no matter how temporary: "I guess we're with you for the moment!"

"I welcome that much trust. I shall ask you questions that you will not answer unless you trust me, Captain."

He gestured. She sat down again. He shifted on the hard bed, a grimace of pain twisting his features. One of the priests moved forward. Charles of Burgundy waved him back.

"Dijon is in danger because its Duke is here," he added

reflectively. "This Goth crusade is determined to conquer Burgundy, and they know they cannot do it except by my death. Therefore, the storm falls on the place I am."

"Fire magnet," Ash said absently. At his questioning look, she said, "As a lodestone draws iron, Your Grace. The war follows you, wherever you are."

"Yes. A useful term. 'Fire magnet.' "

"I learned it from my voice."

She rested her forearms on her thighs, supporting herself on the stool, and gave him a look that said *pick the bones out of that!* as clearly as if she had voiced it. Let's see *how* good your intelligence is.

He made as if to lay his shoulders back into the bolster and stopped. No pain showed on his face, but visible droplets of sweat ran down his sallow, shaven cheeks; drenched the chopped-straight black hair that lay across his forehead. With illness and with the Valois features, nose and lip, he made a singularly ugly young man in some respects, Ash reflected.

As if it cost him nothing, the Duke shifted himself up into a sitting position.

"Your men are concerned that you will no longer consult with the *machina rei militaris*," he said. "It is said—"

"My men? Since when do you know about my men?"

He frowned at her bald interruption.

"If you would be treated with respect, behave as a commander does. Reports are made to me of rumors, tavern talk. You are far too well known for them not to speculate about you, Captain Ash."

A little shaken, Ash said, "Sorry, Your Grace."

He inclined his head slightly. "Their concerns are mine, to a degree, Captain. It seems to me that, even if this *machina rei militaris* is a tool of the Visigoths, there is nothing to stop you consulting it, perhaps learning of their tactics and plans, also. Knowledge would make our numbers seem greater. We would know where and when to strike."

His black stare challenged her.

Ash put her palms flat on her thighs, staring down at her gauntlets.

"You see darkness when you look at the horizon, Your Grace. Do you want to know what I see?" She raised her head. "I see pyramids, Your Grace. Across the Middle Sea, I see the desert, and the light, and the Wild Machines. They're what I'd hear, if I spoke to the Stone Golem. And they'd hear me. And then I'd be dead." Irrespective of his sense of humor, Ash added, "You're not the only fire magnet in Dijon, Your Grace."

He ignored her pleasantry. "These Wild Machines are not merely more Visigoth engines? Think. You could be mistaken."

"No. They're nothing made by any lord-*amir*."

"Might they have been destroyed, in the earthquake that destroyed Carthage?"

"No. They're still there. The ragheads think they're a sign!" Ash, bleak, saw that her hands had made fists, without her intention. She unclenched her fingers. "Lord Duke, put yourself in my position. I hear a Visigoth tactics machine. By accident. And what I hear is itself a puppet. It isn't the King-Caliph who wanted war with Burgundy, Your Grace. It isn't Lord-*Amir* Leofric who wanted to breed the Faris to talk to the Stone Golem. This is the Wild Machines' war."

Charles nodded absently. "Yet, now your sister knows you are here, she will communicate that fact to the *machina rei militaris*. So these greater machines will—overhear—that you are in Dijon. May already have heard."

A hot wire of fear twisted in her guts at the thought. "I know that, my lord."

Charles of Burgundy said firmly, "You are mine, for now, commander. Speak to your voice. Let us learn what we can, while we can. The Visigoths may find some way to stop you from hearing the *machina rei militaris*, and then we have lost an advantage."

"*If* she's still using it . . . This isn't my business! My business is to command my men in the field!"

"Not your business, perhaps, but your responsibility." The Duke leaned forward, black eyes feverish. Very deliberately, he said, "You visited your sister, under parley, to speak of this. She will look for answers, as you do. And she may move freely to seek them."

He held her gaze.

"You say this is the Wild Machines' war. *You* are all I have that will aid me in finding out what these machines are, and why I am at war."

Charles's body shifted, on the hard bed; and he took more of his weight on his right arm, not leaning back at all.

He said, "We have no Faris, but we have you. And no great time to waste. I will not let Burgundy fall because of one woman's fear."

Ash looked from side to side. The white stone walls of the palace reflected back the day's gray light. The chamber seemed suddenly constricting. *Dijon is a trap in more than one way.*

Pages busily took wine around among the men behind her, near the hearth-fire. She heard the high-pitched yelp of one of the pups, seeking its bitch, and an urgent buzz of talk.

"Let me tell you something, Your Grace." The urge to lie, to conceal, to prevaricate, all but overwhelmed her. "You made the worst mistake of your life before Auxonne."

An expression of affront crossed his face, gone almost

before she could register it. Charles of Burgundy said, "You are blunt. Give me your reason for saying this."

"Two mistakes." Ash ticked them off on her gauntleted fingers: "First, you didn't finance my company to go south with Oxford, before Auxonne. If you'd supported the raid on Carthage, we might have taken out the Stone Golem months ago. Second, when you did let the Earl raid Carthage, you kept half my company back here. If we'd had more men, we might have broken House Leofric—high casualties, but we might just have done it. And we'd have broken the Stone Golem into rubble."

"When my lord of Oxford traveled to Africa, I spared him all the fighting men I could. The rest I needed to man the walls of Dijon. I grant you, a raid in force, beforehand, might have been better. In retrospect, I misjudged it."

Son of a bitch, Ash thought, looking at the man in the sickbed with a new respect.

Charles of Burgundy's voice went on steadily: "Denying the use of the *machina rei militaris* to their Faris would both weaken her, since I believe she relies upon it, and by morale, weaken her men. I cannot see, however, that failing to bring that about is the worst mistake of my life. Who knows but that may be yet to come?"

She met his fever-bright eyes, detecting a slight—a very slight—glint of humor. Behind her, she heard movement. The Duke of Burgundy signaled past her, to pages, who shepherded back the armed nobles anxious to speak with him.

"I've had the Wild Machines in my head," she said, watching him steadily. "You haven't. They're louder than God, Your Grace. I've had them turn me around and walk me toward them—"

He interrupted: "Possession by demons? I have seen you brave in the field, but, yes, any man would fear that."

Since he seemed entirely oblivious of that *any man*, Ash let it go. She leaned forward, speaking with intensity:

"They're machines, stones that live; the ancient peoples made them first, I think, and then they grew of themselves." She held the Duke's gaze. "I do know, Your Grace. I listened to them. I—think I *made* them tell me, all in a second. Maybe because they weren't expecting it, weren't expecting me. After that, I ran; I ran from Carthage, and the desert, and I kept on running. And I wish that was *all*—"

She reached for her sword's pommel; remembered it to be in Rochester's hands, farther down the chamber; and clasped her fingers together again to stop them shaking. She could, for a moment, only try to quiet her rapid, shallow breathing.

"If it wasn't for my company, I wouldn't be in Dijon, I'd still be running!"

Confident, he reached to clasp her hands in his. "You are here, and will fight in whatever way you can. Even if it means talking to the *machina rei militaris* for me."

She took her hands away, bleak. "When I said that not destroying it was the worst mistake of your life, I meant it. The Wild Machines could speak to Gundobad because he was a Wonder-Worker, a miraculous prophet. And then—Your Grace, *then they spent centuries in silence until Friar Roger Bacon built a Brazen Head in Carthage, and House Leofric built the Stone Golem.*"

The Duke stared. Back down the chamber, a hooded hawk cried: brief, high, pained. As if it jolted him, he said, "They speak through the *machina rei militaris*."

"*Only* through it."

"You are certain of this?"

"It's their knowledge, not mine." Ash wiped a hand over her face, hot with sweat, but did not shift her stool away from the charcoal brazier. "I think they need a channel of some kind to speak to us, Your Grace. Those like the Green Christ or the Prophet Gundobad aren't born more than once or twice in a thousand years. The Wild Machines need Bacon's devices, or Leofric's; otherwise, they're dumb. They've been secretly manipulating the Stone Golem ever since it was made. If they could have manipulated the Visigoth Empire any other way, by now they would have!"

Looking at him, she surprised a look of pain on the Duke's face that had nothing to do with any wound.

"What would they have had now," she said bitterly, "if I could have destroyed the Stone Golem last summer? Nothing! They're *stone*. They can't move or speak. They might compel the earth to shake, but only in Carthage."

Memories of falling masonry invade her mind: she pushes them away.

"If I'd managed to take it out, we'd have been safe! There'd be peace by now. The Visigoth Empire's overextended, they need to consolidate what they've taken. It's only because the damn Stone Golem keeps telling them to take Burgundy that they're keeping on with this campaign! And the Stone Golem's only relaying the words of the Wild Machines."

"Then we must see if we cannot mount another raid," Charles of Burgundy said, "more successfully."

In the overheated ducal chamber, seated by a wounded man, Ash found herself suddenly and unwillingly invaded by hope.

"No shit? They're probably manipulating to get a hell of a guard on House Leofric now. . . ."

"It might be done." Charles frowned, ignoring her coarseness, calculating. "I cannot weaken the defense here. If orders could be got north, to Flanders, and my wife's army, she might send a major force out by the Narrow Sea, and south down the coast of Iberia. You will talk to my captains. Perhaps now, when the Goths are overextended, and before Carthage has recovered its defenses. . . ."

Something unexpected moved her. She recognized it as the perception of possibility. *Could we do it? Go back to Carthage, trash the place? If we could—oh, if we could! Damn, I knew there had to be* some *reason the Burgundians followed this man!*

Taking instant decisions, as battles have taught her to, Ash said, "Count me in."

"Good. All the more important, now, that you speak with the *machina rei militaris*, Captain Ash. And, when you hear these 'Wild Machines,' that you tell me what they are planning."

All her hope vanished in a rush of fear.

Can't get away from it; can't not *tell him—*

I can try not to.

"Your Grace, what happens when *they* hear *me*? I could be controlled—" She caught his expression. "You said yourself, anyone would be afraid! You pray, Your Grace, but you wouldn't want the voice of God in your head, I promise you."

"These 'Wild Machines' are not God." His voice was gentle. "God permits them to exist, for a time. We must deal with them as we can. With courage."

By the way he looked at her, she thought Charles of Burgundy might have his own doubts about her piety.

"I *know* what they're planning!" she protested. "Trust me, there isn't any need to ask twice! All I heard from them in Carthage was *Burgundy must be destroyed*!"

" '*Burgundia delenda est*' . . ."

"Yes. *Why*?" She sounded loud, brash, brutal. "Why, Your Grace? Burgundy's rich—or it was—and powerful, but that isn't it. France and the Germanies were allowed surrender. What's so important about Burgundy that they want it razed to the ground, and then they want to piss on the ashes?"

The Duke drew himself together, having considerable presence despite his sickbed. He looked at her keenly.

"I may give you no reason why they should wish Burgundy destroyed."

His ambiguity was plain.

Not sure if it were trust or resignation that she felt, Ash merely looked at him.

"Destroy this link," Charles said, "and we have only the Visigoth Empire to meet in the field. That, I believe we can do. We have taken harder blows than this and come back with victory. So you must listen for me, Master Captain, if we are to attempt Africa again. Call your voices to you."

Carried on his words, she came to herself with a shock as cold as springwater. She sat back on the stool

"Your Grace, I don't think I'll be much good to you."

Ash looked away from his face. She said steadily:

"The last time I—listened to where my voice is, I heard the voice of my priest, Father Maximillian. That was yesterday. Godfrey Maximillian died, in Carthage, two months ago."

Charles watched her, neither judgment nor condemnation in his face.

She protested, "If you think I'm hearing illusions, Your Grace, you won't think that *any* voice I hear can be trusted!"

" 'Illusions.' " Charles, Duke of Burgundy, reached out among the papers that surrounded him, uncovering one with an effort. As he read, he said, "You *would* call it that, Captain Ash. You say nothing of demons, or of temptation by the devil. Or even that this Father Maximillian may be with the saints, and this the answer to your sorrow at losing him."

"If it *is* Godfrey—" Ash clenched her fist. "It is Godfrey. The Faris hears him, too. A 'heretic priest,' she said. If *both* of us . . . I think when he died, there, as they shook the earth, his soul went into the machine—he's trapped, his soul is trapped in the *machina rei militaris*. And whatever's left of him—not a whole man—is there for the Wild Machines to pick apart. . . ."

He reached out to grip her arm.

"You do not grieve easily, or well."

Ash pressed her lips together. "You've lost men under your leadership, so you know how it is, Your Grace. You carry on with the ones you've got."

"War has made you hard, not strong."

His tone was not condemnatory, but kind. His grip on her arm did not feel like that of a sick man. She flinched. Charles released her.

"Captain Ash, I have noted down on this paper, here, that I spoke to your Father Maximillian, some days before the field of Auxonne. He came to me for a letter of passage across these lands, and for a letter requesting the Abbot of Marseilles to find him a place on a ship to the south."

"To *you*?"

"I gave him his letters. It was clear to me he is—was—no traitor, but a devout man seeking to help a friend, in charity and love. If anything of his soul does remain, fear for it, but do not fear it."

Ash blinked rapidly. One hot drop of water broke from her eye before she blinked it clear, coursing down her cheek. She scrubbed her wrist across her face.

"Grief is part of the honor of a soldier," Charles said, awkwardly, as if the tears of a woman moved him more than the tears of a man might have.

"Grief is a fucking pain in the ass," Ash said, on a shaky,

indrawn breath; and then with the brilliant smile that was all hers, she said, "Sorry, Your Grace."

"Ask for what help you need," the Duke said.

"Your Grace?"

The young black-haired man in the embroidered gown finally smiled at her. There was nothing of malice in it, only plain kindness, and a weary joy, as if he were making things very clear, as if she might not otherwise hear his meaning.

"I will not use force." His eyes shut, for a split second, and then he was looking at her again. "Nor shall I in any way compel you to speak to the *machina rei militaris*. I *ask* you to do it."

"Shit," Ash said miserably.

"I ask you to answer the question of why you hear a dead man's voice. I ask you to discover what these machines beyond the *machina rei militaris* will do now. I want," Charles said, looking at her keenly, "to know why you have been saying that the Visigoth Faris has been bred to work a great and evil miracle against Burgundy. And whether it is true that she has the power to do this."

Ash looked at him dumbly. *Nothing wrong with his intelligence at all.*

"I offer any help you may need. Priests, doctors, armorers, astrologers: whosoever of my people can help you, you shall have them. Name help, and you shall have it."

Ash opened her mouth to answer him, and had no answer to make.

Charles of Burgundy said, "Nor will I use underhand methods. If you and your men desire it, I will welcome you as one of my captains, whether you do this or not. You are a field commander I would wish to have serve me."

Dumb, she could only stare at him. *He means this. I wish I thought he didn't. He means what he says.*

"Do it," he said, holding her gaze, completely confident, all his awkwardness for once gone. "For yourself, for your men, for Dijon, for Burgundy. For me."

Ash said flatly, "I've been forced back here, I'm sitting smack in the center of a target, and *I don't know why it's a target.* Your Grace, I'm going to need to know that. If not now, then very soon."

She studied his sallow face, and the hollow gaps between socket and eye, where the flesh of his eyelids had sunk in. No weakness showed in his expression.

"I offered whatever help you need. Speak with your dead priest." He watched her with authority and determination. "If it proves needful—come back to me. You shall know whatever I can tell you."

At last, painfully, she said, "Give me time."

"Yes. Since you need it, you shall have that, too."

Ash, sweat running down her body under her armor, light-headed with fear, stood and looked down at the Duke of Burgundy.

"Not time to decide," she said. "This was always going to happen, here or anywhere else. I've decided. Give me time to do it."

[Original e-mail documents found inserted, folded, in British Library copy of 3rd edition, Ash: The Lost History of Burgundy, (2001) — possibly in chronological order of editing original typescript?]

Message: #258 (Anna Longman)
Subject: Carthage
Date: 04/12/00 at 05.19 p.m.
From: Ngrant@

format address deleted
other details encrypted by non-discoverable personal key

Anna--

Is Isobel's mail what you needed? Let me know later today. We're so busy here, you wouldn't believe it! Or perhaps you would!

Everybody is being very nice to me, and not pointing out that I have no particular authorisation to be here except for 'Fraxinus', and that I'm continually underfoot. I think we're all too excited to care. A genuine, untouched, DOCUMENTED seabed site—even Isobel can't bring herself to call it anything other than Carthage!

Anna, *that* is the final part of 'Fraxinus me fecit'. My last piece of translation. The manuscript breaks off there, plainly incomplete.

I cannot answer any of the questions it raises!

Other historical documentation picks Ash up again, but only in the initial part of January 1476/77. We may never know why the 'siege of Dijon' section gives such an unconventional rendering of European history, and of Charles the Bold's character—in some ways, it is much closer to a portrait of his father, Duke Philip the Good—but *he* died in 1467! We may never know what happened to Ash in the winter before her death at the battle of Nancy, or why this text places Charles in Dijon!

In the light of current events, does it *matter*?

I don't believe, now, that I'm worried about what results the metallurgy team will come up with when they re-test the 'messenger golem'.

Suppose carbon-dating *does* put it in this half of the 20th century? It is not *completely* impossible that someone else saw the 'Fraxinus' document before I did. Nor is it *completely* impossible that a fake 'golem' might be made—Isobel tells me there is a substantial market in archaeological fakes to the more gullible private collectors.

Carthage is not a fake. Carthage is a fact.

Of course, archaeologically speaking, there is the question of what, as a fact, this implies. Has this inundated site any connection with the Liby-Phoenicians who settled the original 'Carthage' in 814 BC—did they perhaps land here, and only later move to the land site that has been excavated outside Tunis? It seems unlikely: this is not the Carthage that the Romans sacked. But it is Visigothic Carthage.

You see, Anna, I have been positing a settlement made in the AD 1400s—and from the ROV images, this site already seems much older than that! Perhaps this is Vandal Carthage? Or perhaps this is a much *older* Visigothic site? After all, if a storm had not sunk their fleet in AD 416, the Spanish Visigoths would have taken over Roman Carthage thirteen years before the Vandals did just that!

So much—so _much_ to be discovered now.

My initial theory posited a late-mediaeval, short-lived settlement. Any continuously-occupied site, from AD 416, gives us much *more* of a problem—I can believe that 'my' Visigoth settlement on the North African coast, lasting perhaps 70–80 years in total, could go unnoticed, or at least have such evidence as survives 'swept under the carpet' for any number of reasons. However, nine and a half centuries of continuous occupation would show up in Arabic chronicles, even if the 'Franks' managed to ignore it!! I grant you there are tens of thousands of surviving mediaeval Islamic manuscripts, and many libraries throughout North Africa and the Middle East that have yet to be fully catalogued—but, no mention of 1060 years of Carthage?! *Anywhere?*

I do need to talk to Isobel about this.

I've said that we are all in a state of exaltation—that's true, but, I would expect Isobel to be more joyful. She seems concerned.

I suppose that, if I were responsible for confidentiality on the site of the biggest archaeological discovery this century, *I* might look a little frazzled and haggard, too!

There are new images coming through from the ROVs every few minutes—will contact you again when I can—isn't this *wonderful*?

--Pierce

Message: #158 (Pierce Ratcliff/misc.)
Subject: Ash, manuscript
Date: 05/12/00 at 07.19 p.m.
From: Longman@

format address deleted

other details encrypted and non-recoverably deleted

Pierce--

There is a manuscript.

I wanted you to know that first. I've been to Sible Hedingham, I've spoken to Professor Davies' brother, who's been remarkably candid with me, but first—THERE IS A MANUSCRIPT.

It isn't an unpublished work by Vaughan Davies.

It's original.

Pierce, I've no idea if this is important or not. I don't even know if it's from the right era. Or if it's a fake.

The brother, William Davies, says Vaughan referred to it as a 'hunting treatise.' The cover bound onto it does have a woodcut of a deer being chased through the woods by riders. I hope you are not going to be disappointed. My (small) Latin's Classical, not mediaeval, so I can't pick out anything much except a few references to 'Burgundia'. For all I know, the rest of it could be about hound breeding! I hope it isn't; I really hope it isn't, Pierce. I'm going to feel I've let you down if it is.

William has let me scan it. Given the condition the paper is in, I'm not sure I should have allowed him to—but I had to. He's contacting Sotheby's and Christie's. I have talked him out of contacting the British Library at the moment. It won't be long before he insists.

If this is genuine—important—even useful, I can use this discovery to support the combined book-and-documentary project, without having to involve what you and Dr Isobel are doing at the sea site yet. I do realise she needs total security at the moment.

I'll start sending some scanned text after this. I know what sort of chaos there'll be where you are—you're still on the ship, right?—but how soon can you translate these first pages?!

Here's its provenance—

I went up to East Anglia with Nadia, on the pretence that she might want to buy some of the remaining bric-a-brac. (Not a pretence, as it turned out: she did negotiate for some pieces.) William Davies turned out to be a nice old man, a retired surgeon and an ex–Spitfire pilot; so I came clean and told him I was your publisher, you were in Africa, but you were doing a re-edition of his brother's work on ASH. (Thought this was most tactful.)

As far as I could find out by talking to him, William Davies never had much to do with his brother before Vaughan came to Sible Hedingham. They were brought up in an upper middle class family somewhere in Wiltshire. Vaughan went to Oxford and stayed there, William went to London, studied medicine, married, and came into the Sible Hedingham property on his wife's early death. (She was only 21.) After that, he only saw Vaughan while on leave from the RAF, and they didn't talk much.

What relevant family history I've picked up from him is as follows: Vaughan Davies moved from Oxford to Sible Hedingham in the late 1930s. William remembers it as 1937 or 1938. William owned the house, but was in the process of joining the RAF, and was prepared to let it to Vaughan. I get the feeling they wouldn't have moved in together—listening between the lines, Vaughan sounds bloody impossible to live with. Vaughan was on a sabbatical from Oxford, finishing the 'Ash' manuscript for publication.

According to William, Vaughan then lived the life of a hermit; but no one in the village much minded. I think he must have been very abrasive. In any case, as a newcomer, he wasn't made welcome. He 'bothered' (William's word) the family who owns Hedingham Castle for access to it, and made himself a real pain; so much so that they told him to go away.

I think William thinks this manuscript comes from Hedingham Castle.

I think he thinks Vaughan stole it.

He didn't see Vaughan Davies after the war because Vaughan vanished in 1940.

I'm not kidding, Pierce. He vanished. William was shot down over the Channel that summer, and spent considerable time in hospital. He still has burn-scars, you can see them. By the time he was invalided out, the house at Sible Hedingham was deserted. There were the usual rumours for the time of Vaughan having been a German spy, but all William could find out was that his brother had left for London.

Being war-time, the police investigations were a bit scanty. Now it's sixty years later, the trail's cold.

William says he always assumed his brother was caught in the Blitz, killed in the bombing, his body blown up or burned so as to be facially unidentifiable. He had no hesitation in saying this to me in just those words. Gruesome. Maybe it's being a surgeon.

William Davies is selling the Sible Hedingham house because he's going into sheltered accommodation. He must be in his eighties, now. He's very sharp. When he says there's no mystery over his brother's death, I want to believe him.

No—what I _want_ is to go back to the office and pretend that none of this is happening. I've always loved academic publishing, but what I want now is for there to be more distance between me and history. All this is uncomfortably close, somehow.

What you're finding on the Mediterranean seabed—Pierce if this manuscript _is_ something we need, I don't know what I'll do. Take my annual holiday, fly to the Florida Keys, and pretend that none of it is happening! It's too much.

No.

As your editor—as a friend—I'll be here. I know you can't do the translation instantly, I know you're busy examining the new site, but can you at least give me some idea of whether this is a valuable document or not, before the end of the day?

--Anna

Message: #270 (Anna Longman/misc.)
Subject: Ash/Visigoths
Date: 05/12/00 at 10.59 p.m.
From: Ngrant@

format address deleted
other details encrypted
by non-discoverable
personal key

Anna--

Good God, even as separate files, they're taking *forever* to download! I'm using Isobel's other notebook while they're coming in; and I'm looking at the first page at this moment—

One thing I can tell you immediately. If these images have scanned in correctly, this document is by the same hand that wrote 'Fraxinus'.

Anna, I KNOW this handwriting—I can read it as fast as I can read my own! I know all the tricks of phraseology and contractions and spelling. I should do, I've been studying and translating this hand for the last eight years!

And if that's the case—

This *has* to be a continuation of 'Fraxinus'.

'Fraxinus me fecit' is quite definitely Ash's autobiography. Either written or (more likely, given her illiteracy) dictated by her.

If Vaughan Davies had access to *this* document, why doesn't he mention it in his Second Edition of the 'Ash' chronicles?! All right, he didn't have 'Fraxinus', but even this—the little I've read so far—it's plainly and evidently Ash; why didn't he *publish*!

Encrypt the rest and send it; I don't care _how_ long it takes to scan or download!

--Pierce

Message: #277 (Anna Longman/misc.)
Subject: Sible Hedingham ms.
Date: 10/12/00 at 11:20 p.m.
From: Ngrant@

format address deleted
other details encrypted by non-discoverable personal key

Anna--

It *carries on* from 'Fraxinus'—is a missing part of the document—a *continuation*—covers autumn of 1476!!! But I don't know how MUCH it covers!!!

Evidently one or more pages are missing at the start—perhaps torn away over the intervening five hundred years—BUT, I don't think we're missing more than a few hours of 15/11/1476!!

From the internal textual evidence, these events MUST belong in the same 24-hour period as Ash's first entry into Dijon! Or at least no later than the following day. Given the correspondence between details of dress and weather in the 'Fraxinus' ms., this HAS to be a bare few hours after Ash's interview with Charles of Burgundy, and is therefore 15 November 1476.

I don't think there can be anything missing except some initial call to arms!

Was there anything written on the binding (if any) and could that be scanned?

Later:

Here is 1st part, quick & dirty, tidy up later. Been at this for five days straight. Can't *believe* what we have here!

--Pierce

PART THREE

15 November AD 1476–16 November AD 1476

UNDER THE PENITENCE[40]

[40] Sible Hedingham mss., part 1. (PR)

[. . .] COMMAND GROUP ON Dijon's walls.[41]

"What the fuck is she *doing*?" Robert Anselm shrieked above the noise. "I thought you said she was waiting for us to sell her a gate!"

"Maybe she's trying to concentrate our minds!"

Ash is conscious, in the back of her thoughts, of the heavy protection of steel on head and hands; of the thin layers of mail and wool and linen that are all that cover her limbs. The desire for Milanese harness is strong enough for her to taste.

"Fucking hell! All that talk, and we can lose this city *right now*—"

She forced herself to stand upright on the parapet and stare out between the merlons[42] at the empty ground– covered suddenly, now, in running figures.

A horde of men running forward toward Dijon's north-west walls, planting screens, kneeling to shoot—Carthaginian archers, behind mantlets,[43] with wicked

[41] The first part of this sentence has been lost with the missing page(s) of the Sible Hedingham mss.

[42] The solid parts of battlements, as opposed to the 'crenels' or gaps between them.

[43] *Mantlet*: a protective screen which can be moved to enable archers and gunners to advance closer to besieged walls.

black recurve bows. The *thwick*! of arrowheads against stone tightened her belly. A crackle of arquebus fire sounded all along the parapet, Angelotti's and Ludmilla's voices raised in shrill orders, and the rapid, repetitive thrum of longbows went up into the air: sweating archers bellowing foul-mouthed congratulations at each other.

A black wave of men rose up from the earthworks in front of the Visigoth camp. At the same second, a whistling shrillness sounded. Ash glanced to her left: could not see past the tower to the northwest gate—but a sound of impacts and screaming rose over the clamor. She looked back—only a split second—and the ground below was covered with running men holding siege ladders and shields above their heads, some already falling under the steady fire from the battlements.

"Auxiliaries!" Robert Anselm bellowed in her ear. She heard him through the helmet's muffling lining.

"What about *them*?" She leaned into the gap in the stonework, staring out and down. Along with the black tunic-wearing men with spears and hatchets, forty or fifty Europeans were running.

"Prisoners!" Anselm bellowed.

A glance told her he was right—captured townsfolk, Dijonnais taken sometime this autumn and pressed into service, due now to die either on the walls or by the hand of the Visigoth *nazirs* behind them. Abruptly she broke off from hearing messengers and giving orders, tapped Anselm's breastplate, and pointed.

Anselm shoved his visor up, squinting, then bellowed a coarse laugh. "Tough fucking shit, Jos!"

In the wake of the auxiliary troops and condemned prisoners, men in blue livery with the Ship and Crescent Moon on it jogged forward, soaked hides over their shoulders, carrying ladders of their own. Ash found herself squinting, trying to see if she could see Joscelyn van Mander's personal banner, but in the confusion of flying rock splinters, dirt, arquebus smoke, and distance, she couldn't make it out.

"Here they come," Ash began, steadily, trying to stop her voice shaking.

As the first of the men hit the edge of the moat below, throwing down more wood faggots on the piles that almost filled it, she turned back to the parapet.

"Anselm! Get the billmen up on the walls, *now*! Ludmilla: move the archers back to give 'em room! Angelotti—"

Over the noise of men in mail and plate jogging up the steps to the parapet, and the archers determined to get off every last shaft, a great *crack!* and *boom!* sounded to her left. *Main gate*, she realized. *Shit!*

She turned away to look for Angelotti, failed to see him, and took a step toward the nearest mangonel. Two of the winch crew squatted down behind the arrow-studded wooden screens, and, as Ash looked, Dickon Stour gave the wooden frame a solid whack with a hammer, straightened up, stepped back, and slapped the cup-shaft with an expression of satisfaction. "Okay? Try it now?"

"Where's Captain Angelotti gone?" Ash bawled.

The lanky armorer, straw-colored hair jutting out under the rim of his war-hat, shouted over his shoulder at her. "Down by—"

A stupendous explosion deafened her.

The parapet jumped under her feet: the air filled with screaming fragments of rock. Two merlons gaped, whitely; half the masonry to each side blown away, a crater gaping in the surface of the battlements.

Something vast glanced past her and on into the town below. Body shivering with shock, she first realized *I'm not hurt!* and then *Direct hit on the mangonel!*

The wooden protective screens hung in flinders. A shattered tangle of wood and rope looked nothing like the frame and cup. One man rolled, screeching. In among the white splinters of wood in front of Ash, ragged joints of meat leaked wetly; and a leg hung, still inside a perfectly whole boot. Another man lay dead on the parapet. There was no sign of Dickon Stour. Only a red-splashed, jagged scar, dug six inches deep in the cracked flagstones.

Ash put her hand up and wiped hair out of her mouth. It was not her hair. She spat at the taste, ridding her mouth of a fragment of bone.

Within a fractured moment, a second trebuchet missile hit, farther down the wall: a lump of limestone half the size of a cart. She saw a mess of ropes and wood and men on their knees, on their backs, blown halfway down the steps. A boulder shattered into fragments, hurtling down into the no-man's-land behind the walls.

The shrill whistling of clay pots trailing flames sounded overhead.

Ash winced, ducking. Clay vessels hit, one after another, all down the length of the walls from her, spraying Greek Fire bright into the hoardings and lines of men. The *whoof*! of igniting flame made her shudder.

"ANSELM—!"

A shoulder barged her to one side. Overhead, her banner dipped, fell to a diagonal, and slowly moved away from her in the press of a crowd of men—archers and billmen all shoving past her, back away from the walls, pressing toward the steps.

"*HOLD!*" she bellowed, lung-crackingly loud.

A gaggle of Rochester's billmen shove her hard up between themselves and one damaged merlon: she has a momentary glimpse of yards of empty air, and men and ladders beneath. The nearness of the fall jolts her stomach.

Off toward the gate, she hears hook-guns firing, and

their fortified ballistae shooting hard and fast, but the Carthaginians are in under their minimum range now—

"Fucking *stand*!" she screamed, and grabbed one man's shoulder, another by the belt. Both pulled free. Over the helmets of the routing men, she saw her banner gradually come back upright, and toward her—and then fall.

Without hesitation, Ash ducked into the melee of running men, scooped up the pole, and raised the banner over her head. Awkward and unwieldy, it wavered. She heard Anselm's voice, louder, at the steps, grabbing the bearer of the Lion standard and bellowing: "—*right* where you fucking are!" She saw his arm and sword blade go up.

"ON ME!" she yelled. Rickard's face appeared in front of her, in the press of people. She shoved the Lion Affronté into his hands, grabbing at the short ax he carried for her. Shouldering her way against the crowd, shouting into men's faces, she sensed the slowest possible hesitation.

"*Follow* me!"

Farther down toward the White Tower, the brattice[44] was alight, and the stone surface of the parapet alive with unquenchable flames of spilled Greek Fire. The nearest brattice was untouched. Faintly above the shrieking and yelling, she heard noise from below; she switched to a two-handed grip on the ax, and put all her weight into shoving two archers and a gunner's mate back out of her way.

"Bring that fucking flag!" she snarled at Rickard, not stopping to see what the white-faced boy did, slammed her gauntlet into the back of one man's helmet, and cleared herself a way up into the embrasure.

"*On me, you fucking sons of bitches!*"

She felt her own voice come out muffled, the sound

[44] Wooden structure built out from the walls to allow missiles, etc., to be dropped through holes in the floor.

reflected back by the wood and hide roof of the brattice; had a second to think Jesu Christus! *I wish I could have worn a bevor,*[45] *or even a sallet with a visor!*, and flipped the shaft of the poleax over in her hand. It slapped home into the linen palms of her gauntlets.

A face appeared up through the hole in the wooden hoarding in front of her.

In a conscious irony entirely separate from the combat awareness of her mind, she thought, *What I'd give to be able to talk to the* machina rei militaris *right now.*

The wooden shaft of the ax fitted smoothly and familiarly into her grip: left hand forward, right hand in support. She let the ax head go back, then thrust forward with the shaft, and slammed the butt-spike into the Visigoth auxiliary's face.

The point skidded off his helmet's nasal-bar.

The man's bearded mouth opened: shock or anger. He roared. He thrust himself up on the top of a scaling ladder, invisible beneath the planks of the brattice, hauling his sword through the gap.

She let the weapon's momentum carry her body forward a step. Breath coming hard in her throat, whole body tensed in anticipation of his blow, she mentally screamed at herself *I'm not moving fast enough!* and let the ax swing round and back and over her head, sliding her right hand down to the bottom of the ax shaft to join her left, accelerating the cutting edge of the weapon over and down. Four pounds of metal, but moving in a tight four-foot arc. She slammed the blade into his face as he looked up.

A spray of wet speckled her arms. She felt the edge bite: couldn't hear his screaming for the shouts behind her, the clash of edged steel, the cracks of arquebuses, and the

---

[45] A bevor is a plate lower-face defence, covering the mouth.

sound of other men shrieking. Not a mortal wound, not enough to put a man down—

A spear-point jabbed up between her feet. It caught in the roughly sawn planks: jammed.

She leaped back. One of her heels caught on the edge of the embrasure behind her. The poleax flew up in her grasp, ripped the soaked hides that roofed the brattice as she fell backward, and sat down hard in one of the crenellations. The impact jolted her whole spine.

Quietly, without fuss, and from a sitting position, she lifted up the ax and slammed the butt-spike forward again, punching a hole just below the brow of the steel helmet of the first man.

His eyes stayed open, fixed on the planks, as he fell forward, half-in, half-out of the gap. Thick, dark red blood and brain matter came out with the spike as she twisted it free.

No footsteps behind her, no banner, no shout from Rickard. A shrieking, bellowing clamor from below—

For all I know, I'm alone up here now—

"*On me, for fuck's sake!*"

The spearpoint levered itself out of the planking from below. The dead body jerked, the Visigoth soldier being pulled down by others on the ladder beneath; she heard them shrieking orders, swearing. Unaware that she was very grimly smiling, she got back up onto her feet.

"Boss!" Euen Huw leaped over the battlements and slammed into her side. He staggered. Blood soaked his hose from thigh to knee.

"Oh, thank fuck! Where's Rickard? Where's my banner! Ludmilla, get your archers up here! It's a fucking bird shoot!" Ash slapped the shoulders of Huw's infantry and Rostovnaya's archers, ten or fifteen men piling onto the brattice now, feeding them on past her. She swung herself over the dead man by gripping a beam above her, and ran down to the next gap. Her boots echoed on the planking.

As she lopes, feet shifting sideways, she keeps her back to the safety of the wall, head switching rapidly from side to side, trying to watch for an attack from any quarter. The tingling vulnerability of exposed unarmored thighs, shins, forearms, elbows, all of this fires her to extreme perceptiveness, extreme efficiency.

"*Here!* Get the ones below, on the ladder!"

An archer, whose greasy ringlets and unshaven face shone with sweat, loped up and ducked his head down through the gap in front of her. Within seconds, he bawled at his pavise mate for more shafts, stood astride the gap, drawing his bow with difficulty in the confined space, shot down at the foot of the siege ladder, fifty feet below.

Two crossbowmen rapidly elbowed him out of the way: more room for their weapons in the gap.

Ash bent her head for a quick squint out through an archery port in the planks. *If they can storm—If they come over the wall, it's all irrelevant: voices, everything!*

A constant *thunk!* of bolts and shafts echoed along the brattice now, points hitting wood and stone. Her body tensed against the searing rush of Greek Fire. *No, not while their own men are scaling the walls—*

The hook of a scaling ladder thumped into another brattice, farther along the wall; she had a bare second to see that the men with swords and axes beginning to swarm up it were not Visigoth auxiliary troops but men with Crescent Moons on blue livery jackets.

She's seen my banner on this section of the wall—this is deliberate—sending men we've fought beside—a psychological attack: getting Frankish mercenaries to kill each other—

"Look who it ain't!" Euen Huw bellowed, slamming his

wiry body between the wall and her. Over his shoulder as he ran on, he bawled, "Been 'aving it easy, 'aven't they? See about that!"

A glance back along the hoarding showed her Angelotti's brilliant curls under the edge of a sallet, his heavy-bladed falchion rising and falling in an appalling close-combat press of bodies jammed together. His left arm hung, bleeding, buckler gone somewhere. His men crowded that side: warding him.

Christ, half the Visigoth army's on its way!

"Boss!" Robert Anselm, Rickard, and the banner appeared at the embrasure behind her, the older man limping, his face twisted in a bellowed warning.

Ash swung around, saw in a second that the dead auxiliary's body was dislodged now, two soldiers wearing the Crescent Moon scrambling up scaling ladders and through the openings in the plank floor.

Euen Huw parried the first man's sword down with his own in a shower of sparks and kicked the man's leg under the edge of his mail hauberk. Two or three pounds' pressure will pop a kneecap. The man—no time to guess at the face; if this is someone known, or someone Joscelyn van Mander has picked up in the months since he left the Lion Azure—the man fell forward deadweight, like a sack of grain.

The roof and beams cramped her. Ash stuck the shaft of her poleax forward past Euen as he recovered his balance. She hooked the curved back edge of the blade behind the second man's knee. Bracing both feet, she yanked.

The razor edge of the ax hooked the man's knee forward, his mouth opening in a scream as the cut hamstrung him. He went over, onto his back, crumpling against the front wall of the brattice. Euen Huw stabbed with his sword, up between the legs, under his hauberk, into his groin.

The first man struggled upright, onto one knee, his other leg jutting at a twisted angle. Too close. Ash dropped the ax, grabbed her dagger out of its scabbard with her right hand, and threw herself down onto his back, where he was struggling upright up from being on his hands and knee.

She wrapped her forearm around his helmet, twisted his head around, and slammed the blade down into his eye socket, straight into the brain.

Despite helmet, despite blood and the scream and the disfigurement of his face, she had a moment to recognize the man. *Bartolemey St. John—Joscelyn's second—I know him!*

Knew him.

Only a second or so had elapsed. Anselm bellowed something. Two or three dozen men in Lion livery piled over the battlements into the brattice, iron cook pots maneuvered gingerly between them on bill-shafts. The first two tipped their cauldrons, and a white mist of steam hissed up: boiling water spilling through the gaps and planks alike. More men: Henri Brant and Wat Rodway heaving a cauldron between them, *laughing* under the clamor, tipping hot sand down through the nearest opening—

A yard under Ash's feet, men screamed, shrieked; there was the recognizable crack of a siege ladder shattering under panicking men's weights. Screams diminishing, bodies falling into the bright air.

"Shit, boss, that was close!" Euen bellowed, mouth at her ear, one hand reached out absently to pull her to her feet.

Ash grabbed the ax with her free hand, hauling it out from under Bartolomey St. John's dead body. Her hands were, she realized, shaking; with the same uncontrollable tremor that one has when badly injured. *But nothing's touched me: the blood isn't mine!*

She lifted her head, couldn't see Anselm, could hear him

and her sergeants yelling orders back on the battlements—*he's done it, we're holding!*

"Euen, send a runner! The Byward Tower, *now*. What the fuck are the Burgundians doing up there? We need covering fire! They've got no business letting these guys get anywhere near the foot of this wall!"

One of Euen's squires pelted off down the brattice, regained the battlements, and vanished in the direction of the nearest tower. *Can we cover it still, from the Byward Tower to the White Tower?*

Ash ducked back and stepped off the hoardings onto the walls. Only the backs of men visible, now; a hundred or so here: blue-and-yellow Lion livery for the most part; a couple of Burgundian red X's. Farther along, where the brattices had been on fire, and chopped away because of that, she saw swords, axes, men hooking bills over the tops of ladders—no time for anything subtle: slam them into position along the battlements and tip down everything available onto the scaling ladders below.

Robert Anselm jogged up in a clatter of armor and hard breathing. "I've sent my lance to the tower to kick some sense into the Burgundian missile troops!"

"Good! We got 'em turned round here, Roberto!"

Something bright and burning dropped out of the sky, with the whistle of flames fanned by the wind.

The stench of it warned her.

"*Greek Fire!*"

Oh, sweet Jesu, they will *fire on their own men if it means getting us too, they just don't care!*

She threw herself back across the battlements to the inside of the wall, hauling Anselm with her, yelling orders: "Back! Off the walls! *Away from the walls!*"

Fire hit and splashed.

Inside a second, the nearer brattices burst into flame.

She saw the flaming greasy liquid splash and spread. One high voice shrieked. No use to call for water—

"Cut the hoardings free!" she ordered, swinging her ax up and over, chopping down at the supporting beams. Inside a couple of seconds she stood back as the men of three more lances took over.

The shrieking figure rolled on the stone battlements, Greek Fire clinging, a stench of burning coming from blackened skin. Ash recognized red hose and brown padded jack, and the frizzled hair under the melting steel of her sallet: Ludmilla Rostovnaya, half her torso and one arm coated in gelatinous, burning fire.

Anselm yelled, "Thomas Tydder!"

The boy and the rest of his fire detail rushed up along the wall, doused leather buckets of sand over the screaming woman, scraping the stuff away. Ash glimpsed their hands going red in the process.

"Stand aside!" Floria del Guiz sprinted past her with a stretcher team.

The brattice creaked, tilted, gave way with a rush. Flaming wood tipped out into the empty air.

Ash moved forward to the wall. Below, she saw siege ladders falling back, screaming men falling from them. Bodies in twenties and thirties plummeted to the broken ground at the foot of the city wall. Visigoth slaves—without armor, without weapons—ran about on the escarpment, darting forward, lifting and carrying men with broken limbs.

As she watched, one pale-haired slave fell with a bolt in him. A few yards away, a soldier wearing the Crescent Moon knelt beside another trooper who writhed with a broken back, gave him the *coup de grâce* with his dagger, and ran on, leaving the slave jerking and twitching and alive.

Ash looked up to the Byward Tower. Archers and crossbow troops surged past to the shuttered embrasures and arrow loops, some of the Welsh longbowmen recklessly shooting over the merlons.

Another bolt of Greek Fire impacted, farther down the wall.

Under her breath, Ash muttered, "Come *on*. Take that machine *out!*"

She grabbed the edges of the battlements, staring out from the walls. Under the pale sun, four carved limbs of turning stone flashed white in the November day. Four carved marble cups, on stone beams, like the cups of a mangonel, revolved around a stone spindle. There wasn't a soldier or a slave within yards of it to wind it. Ash watched it moving, golemlike, of itself.

Stone chips exploded off it, under a hail of crossbow bolts.

A shrill voice from the Byward Tower yelled, "*Gotcha!*"

As Ash watched, the brass-bound wheels of its carriage began to turn, and it swiveled away from the walls and back toward the Visigoth camp to reload. Blue flickers of fire still burned in the cups at the end of each of its four arms.

"We're holding!" Ash yelled at Anselm.

"Only just!" Ordering the sergeants back to the wall, Robert Anselm broke off to add: "They got the ram going against the main gate! *This* is just a diversion!"

"Yeah, I could've guessed that!" Ash wiped her mouth, took her hand away bloody. "Are they holding the gate?"

"Up till now!"

Breathless, Ash could only nod.

"Motherfuckers!" Robert Anselm narrowed his eyes against the light. " 'Ere they come again. Auxiliaries and mercenaries again. Wait till they fucking *mean* it."

Aware now that her chest was heaving to gain air, Ash

snatched a second to look out at the distant enemy camp. Three or four hundred men, massing in preparation for the assault's success. "No eagles!"

Robert Anselm tilted his sallet down, against the sun that showed the dirt and stubble on his face. "Not yet!"

Another stone machine edged forward out of the makeshift vast city that is the Visigoth camp. Ash watched. The cups were loaded: fragile clay pots with fuses already lit, shimmering with heat.

"Look at that! They're not supporting that engine. Robert, send to de la Marche, tell him to sally out and take out those bloody engines! Tell him if he won't, we'll be happy to!"

As Anselm signaled a runner, Ash narrowed her eyes in the sunlight. Below, the ground before the walls was strewn with the dead, already, in what must be the first fifteen minutes of fighting. The moat was full of bodies, moving feebly, or still and broken, bleeding onto the faggots and mud and shattered rock.

Two or three riderless horses wandered aimlessly. Carts with pavises mounted on them, slave-hauled, began to recover enemy wounded.

And this wasn't even an attack. A feint. Just so they can get the ram or the saps up to the northwest gate.

It isn't what we can see. It's what we can't see.

With that thought, and almost as she thought it, a great section of the city wall five hundred yards to her right, past the White Tower to the east, first rose up slightly—mortar puffing out between the masonry—and then slumped by ten or eleven inches.

A hot wind blasted her: a thunderous muffled roar shook the paving stones under her feet.

"Fucking saps!" Thomas Rochester thrust through the

command group, joining her. His scream was almost hysterical. "They had *another* fucking sap!"

The high-pitched painful ringing in her ears began to deaden a little.

Euen Huw yelled, "I thought we were supposed to be countermining!"

Now a vast number of men came running forward from the Visigoth lines, obviously at this signal, dozens of scaling ladders carried aloft over their heads. Ash heard Ludmilla Rostovnaya's lancemate, Katherine Hammel, yell a shrill "Nock! Loose!" and hundreds of shafts whirred blackly into the middle air from the Lion archers, twelve per minute; vanishing into the mass of men, impossible to see any single strike.

"They've fucked it!" Ash slapped her palm down hard on Rochester's shoulder, grinned at Euen Huw. "They didn't bring the fucking wall *down*. You must be right about the countermine!

She stared at the point where the wall now dipped, and the unsafe battlements along it. Hoardings smoldered. Burgundian men with red St. Andrew's crosses on their padded jacks were moving slowly out of the wreckage, a few men being carried.

They may not have brought the wall down. But that's going to be a hell of a weak spot from now on.

"We'll have to hold the wall for them while they sort it! Every second man! Robert, Euen, Rochester: on me!"

Reckless of the likelihood of collapsing masonry, she ran lightly down onto the broken section of wall, the company swarming through the White Tower after her. Rapidly hammering out orders, Ash saw the tops of scaling ladders appear; and hand-to-hand fighting start all along the wall. Four hundred men, a line three and four deep in places;

war-hats bright in the light, the spiked blades of bills throwing up a fine red mist into the light. Behind, on the parapet, the Burgundian troops regrouped.

"They blew it!" Ash yelled to Robert Anselm, over the shrieks, the harsh bellowing of "A Lion! A Lion!", and the bang of swivel guns brought down from the far end of the wall. She saw men-at-arms, sunlight glinting off their war-hats, passing up hooked poles, shoving scaling ladders off the walls; and more than one lance was picking up the shattered fragments of trebuchet and mangonel missiles and dropping chunks of masonry back down off the battlements.

Onto the men below.

"The wall didn't come down in front of 'em!" Robert Anselm bellowed. "They ain't got *nowhere* to go!"

Antonio Angelotti, arriving with more swivel guns, showed eyes that were the only white thing in his black face. He yelled to her, "We *must* have countermined some of their mines! Else this whole section would be down!"

"At least we're doing something right—let's hope de la Marche can hold the fucking *gate*!"

It seemed long—was probably not, probably only another fifteen minutes—before the only things visible on the walls were the backs of her own men, ignoring any wounds, still high on adrenaline, leaning over the battlements and shouting their raw, violent, contempt down at the dying men below. One billman stood up on top of the battlement, his cod-flap unlaced, urinating off the wall. Two of his mates grabbed dead stripped Visigoths by wrists and ankles, and slung them out through the embrasures.

She did not draw breath again until the Burgundian combat engineers had shored up the fallen section of wall with forty-foot planks as thick as a man's arm, supported by wooden buttresses; and the attack on the northwest gate had petered out into a rout, under missile fire, men running back behind the wooden palisades of the Visigoth camp, the golem-ram abandoned sunk over the axles in mud.

"*Shit . . .*"

Standing with her command group, she made an assessment of the sagging wall in front of her, almost without thinking of it. Merlons broken, like jagged teeth. Men-at-arms moving back from the walls as the sergeants stood them down, leaving anything else to the missile troops.

When they come again, this is where they'll come.

"Can we stand them *all* down?" Angelotti demanded. He appeared oblivious to the blood dripping onto the stone from the fingers of his left hand. "My boys, too?"

"Yeah. Pointless wasting ammunition."

Her gaze went up and down the parapet. One crossbowman had his foot planted firmly in the stirrup of his crossbow, winding the winch, but with little urgency now. A handgunner in breastplate and war-hat was kneeling, leaning over, hook-gun braced against the edge of the crenellation. As Ash watched, her lancemate touched a slow match to the touchhole; then stuck it back in a sand barrel, unconcerned by the noise of the shot.

The gunner, as she bent her head to reload and her face became visible, was Margaret Schmidt.

"Stop wasting your fucking ammunition!" Angelotti's sergeant, Giovanni Petro, bawled, as Ash opened her mouth to give the order. "Don't shoot while they're running away. Wait till the bastard Flemings come back—with all their little Visigoth friends!"

There was a mutter of laughter along the wall. Ash, approaching the edge and leaning out, caught glances from her men: most of them in the exultation that comes immediately after an action, which is nothing more than the joy of having survived it. One or two of the billmen were prodding corpses in obviously European livery, their expressions hard.

Conscious of a wired rapture that is her own response to survival—a hard joy that wishes every man in the Visigoth camp maimed and bleeding—she leans over and looks down at the innocent earth in front of the city. Studies it again for disturbance: sees nothing.

"They must have been countermined; if they'd managed to set off *all* their petards, they'd have breached this wall."

Not particularly aware of her pronouns, she thought *We nearly lost Dijon in one attack!*

The noon sun winked back in sparks from the ground. She realized after a second that she was seeing the caltrops[46] that had been thrown down by the defenders.

"Greek Fire, too. Think they're fucking 'ard," Anselm grunted cynically. "What's the *rush*?"

Ash gave him a breathless, diamond-hard grin.

"Don't be in such a hurry, Roberto. They'll be back."

"You reckon?"

"She wants in here fast. I don't know why. All she has to *do* is sit out there and let starvation do it for her. Christ, she even fired on her own men!" Her facial muscles ached, and she realized the grin had gone. Almost inconsequentially, she added, "Dickon's dead—Dickon Stour."

His gaze was not unaware of other casualties; nonetheless, there was a deep disgust in his voice. "Ah, fuck it. Poor fucking shite."

Ash busied herself in the business of clearing up, seeing her men reassembled, and on their way back to their quarters. Groups of men carried heavy, red-soaked blankets

---

[46] Iron spikes with four points, made so that one spike always projects upwards, no matter how the caltrop falls.

between them: Dickon Stour, his two mates, and seven others dead. And Ludmilla not the only screaming survivor of Greek Fire, but what the wounded list would be, she would not, she supposed, hear from Florian until later.

It was a stranger who found her as she was coming down off the wall at last: a Burgundian knight who rode up to her and her command group in the street, intercepting her as she stepped across the central gutter, still, even in this bitter weather, semiliquid with excrement.

“Demoiselle-Captain—”

“Just ‘Captain’!”

“—the Duke sends word.”

Ash, every muscle aching, and wanting little more than to find Floria’s salve for bruises, dark beer, and pottage—in that order—eyed him wearily. “I’m at the Duke’s command.”

“He told me that you have a more urgent task than the defense of the walls,” the knight said, “and he asks you, when will you begin it?”

THE NOVEMBER DAY died in gray twilight, an hour or more before Vespers.[47] Of the wounded, all survived that long. Those inns within a quarter-mile radius of the company tower became packed with mercenary men-at-arms getting loudly drunk. Riding back

[47] 6 p.m.

through the streets, Ash thought it wise not to see, officially, what might be going on in the way of brawls and sexual encounters in the street, wise to leave ab Morgan to keep it from becoming murder and rape.

The top floor of the company's tower having been reorganized to contain the armory, the war chests, and Ash's own belongings, they were now stacked more or less in order on the open, rush-strewn floor. Ash strode past the armed men at the door, nodding her acknowledgment.

She threw a handful of sketches down on the trestle table in front of Robert Anselm. "There."

"You've been all round the walls."

"Twice." Ash moved over to a brazier, unbuckling and stripping off her gauntlets. A page—one of half a dozen recruited new from the baggage train—ran to take them from her. She huffed, grinned, beating her cold hands together. "Euen Huw's whinging on again. He said *You'll wear the lads out before the ragheads even get* in *here—*."

Her accurate mimicry made Robert Anselm laugh.

"I must have passed six of the Duke's messengers on up to the walls since Nones,[48]" he added, reading the rough charcoal lines and dots that represented enemy dispositions outside the walls, and not her face. "Did any of them happen to find the bit of it you were on?"

"Green Christ! We only got into this fucking town this morning! *And* we've had to fight. Can't the man give me a few *hours*? I'll do it, when I'm ready—" Ash straightened, hearing footsteps and guards' muffled voices. No challenge. The door opened.

Floria del Guiz stepped inside, flushed, her hair disheveled. She shed her cloak as she strode to join Ash at the brazier.

---

[48] 3 p.m.

"Damn, but I love a good row!" Her eyes sparkled, her expression hard. "Free and frank exchange of professional views, I *should* say."

Robert Anselm put the maps down. "Been talking to doctors up at the palace, have you?"

"Half-witted leech-ticklers!"

Ash, her fingers and cheeks prickling with returning warmth, demanded, "So. *Tell me*. How's the Duke?"

Floria's expression lost its anger. She signaled the serving page to add more water to the offered wine cup. "You trust that man. I can see it. That's a new one, for you."

"Do I?" Ash broke off to tell another of the pages, at the hearth, that she should mull the rest of the wine. "Yeah. He's promised me another try at Carthage. That's what I trust. He's in this for survival; and the man knows what to do with an army. So: what's the prognosis? When will he be on his feet again? *Is* it the wound he took at Auxonne?"

"That's what I've been discussing. Ha! Ash, do you know? It was the name of this company that got me through to him. A 'woman-doctor.' " Floria walked across to the window embrasure, peered out into the gloom, and hitched her hip up onto the window ledge. Her hands described the shapes of bodies in the air. "His surgeons finally let me see it—he's taken a wound in the middle of his back. Lance, I'd say."

"Shit!"

Floria's green gaze flickered at the empathic flinch that came from Ash. She pointed at Anselm. "Stand up!"

As the big man stood, she crossed the chamber and seized his left arm, holding it up from his body. Robert Anselm looked gravely at her. The surgeon tapped his armor, under his left arm.

"As far as I can see, a lance strike here—from the front or the side, into the left side of the Duke's body."

"It should have glanced off. That's what the deflective surfaces of armor are for." Ash went to where Anselm stood thoughtfully motionless. She put her fingers on the join of breast and backplate. "Unless the lance hit one of the hinges, here. That would let it bite."

"I've also been able to examine the Duke's armor. It's burst open."

Anselm, not moving except to try and look over his shoulder, speculated, "A lance would hit hard. Bite. Burst the hinges, maybe. The lance tip would penetrate."

"Might slide round the *inside* of the backplate." Ash looked questioningly at the surgeon. "Did the lance deform, maybe? Break off in the wound?"

"I did hear it was a lance," Anselm admitted. "Someone said de la Marche cut the lance shaft with his sword, almost as soon as it struck home."

"Fuck."

"Better than having a full hit. He'd have been dead inside minutes."

Floria waved her hands. "This is what I've been debating with the Duke's physicians! I believe it wasn't the lance that hurt him—it was his armor."

The page approached with wooden cups, serving Ash first, then Anselm—who relaxd his self-imposed immobility—and finally the surgeon; before the girl went back to huddle at the spidery, dirt-crusted hearth with the rest of the children. Smoke gusted into the room with a change of the wind.

"There are fragments of his own armor still in the Duke's wound. I examined the cuirass. The hard outer layers have shattered, and the soft iron underneath has torn." Floria put her free hand on Anselm's waist at the back, above the fauld. Ash noted that he did not flinch.

The surgeon said, "There are two organs, bean-shaped,

that lie under the flesh here. One is crushed; we think the other has fragments of steel in it."

"Oh fuck," Ash said blankly. She shook herself back to concentration. "So, how is he?"

"Oh, he's dying, no argument about *that*."

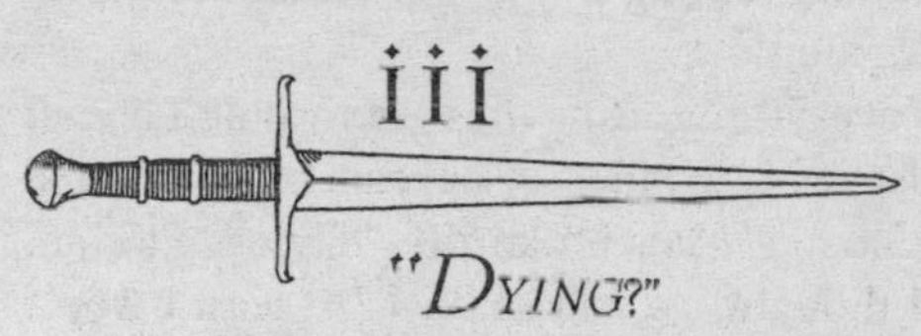

The blank professionalism of Floria's gaze altered as she became cognizant of Ash's appalled stare. The shaggy-haired woman laced her long fingers together.

"His surgeons have been debating cutting him. They won't do it. It won't save him if they do. But it won't harm him much, either. . . . You've seen him. You've talked to him. He's stayed alive for three months, he's nothing but bones. He doesn't eat. It's only his spirit keeping him going. I give him a week or two at the outside."

Anselm rumbled, "Who's his heir?"

Automatic, stunned, Ash said, "Margaret of Burgundy, if she wins at Bruges; de la Marche by default."

"The heart will go out of the defense."

"*Dying*," Ash repeated; ignoring Anselm. "Sweet Christ. A couple of weeks? Florian, are you *sure*?"

Floria del Guiz spoke with a brittle rapidity. "Of course I'm sure. I've seen guys cut up every way you can think of. Barring a miracle, he's dog meat."

Anselm drained his cup and wiped his mouth. "Have to rely on the priests, then."

"His priests' prayers aren't getting any answers. I'm seeing it with our men, here," Floria said. "Bad air from the rivers, maybe. They don't heal well."

"Who knows how bad it is?"

Floria looked at Ash. "For certain? Him, his doctors; the three of us, now. De la Marche. The soeurs, I expect. Rumors? Who knows."

Ash became aware that she was biting at her knuckle, tasting salt sweat, and feeling the tender bruises of blows that have only hit gauntlets.

"This changes everything. If he dies—why didn't he *tell* me? Green Christ . . . I wonder if he can order a force to Africa before he . . ." Ash broke off. "Dying. Florian, you know what I thought, as you said it? 'At least I won't have to talk to the Wild Machines, now.' I've been avoiding it all day. And I won't have to. With Charles dead, the Visigoths are going to come right over those walls out there!"

"Then we find out if your demon-machines are just voices," Robert Anselm stated, pragmatically. "Just farts in the wind. We find out what they can do."

Floria made as if to touch Ash's arm, and stopped herself. "You can't be afraid forever."

Easy for you to say.

Ash said abruptly, "Wake me in an hour, Robert. I'm going to sleep before the food comes."

She was aware that they exchanged glances, but ignored them. The chamber chilled as evening darkened. Noise came up from below, the main hall filling up. She listened to guards patrolling the access corridors, which ran through the twenty-foot-thick walls, and the pages chattering as they stripped her down to her shirt and helped her into her gown, all without noticing much but the shock reaction chilling her body. She lay down on her box bed, close to the hearth, thinking, *Dying? She can't be sure. Only God* knows *a man's last hour—*

But she's been right in the past, about most of the wounded in my company.

Shit.

The flames licked at the wet, smoking logs, charring the damp bark away. Central wood burned away into ash, that still held the shape of the grain until a draft from the chimney stirred it, sparks flying up. Smoke stung her eyes. She wiped at them repeatedly.

What am I *worrying about? It's just one more employer who didn't make it. If I can get him to set a task force up to go from Flanders to North Africa . . . there isn't time.*

Come to think of it, I wonder where John de Vere is, right now? Oxford, I wish you were here; we could do with all the good men we can get.

But if I'm honest, I could do with your companionship as much as your skills.

The ache of fighting eased, now that she lay on the bed, rubbing at one overstrained shoulder, wondering where, exactly, in combat the blue-black bruises on her hands had come from. With practiced ease, she set herself to fall asleep.

On the borders of unconsciousness, the chill draft from the windows turned into a biting gale, and her eyes saw white snow and the light of a blue sky.

She had the impression of a forest, and that she knelt in snow. In front of her, plain to the last winter-thick white hair and gray-brown bristle, a wild boar lay on her side. The earth was scored up by the sow's thrashing hooves.

Ash stared at the beast's fat belly, nipples visible in the thick hair, and the rump that she was facing. Without any warning, the sow writhed, arched and flexed her back, and cocked her leg. A blue-red mass pushed halfway out of her body.

Not here! Ash thought. *Not in the snow!*

The slumped, razor-backed body of the sow rippled. The steaming mass pushed out of her vagina, long blind snout first, teardrop-shaped body after—all in a rush, out into the stinking snow. Mucus smeared the boarlet's body. It flopped, in the snow, wet legs twitching, muzzle blindly turning, seeking the sow's nipple. She groaned, snorting. Ash saw her begin to shift, as if she would get up.

"No . . ." The thickness of her voice as she spoke, aloud, almost brought her back to her bed and the crowded solar, but she deliberately let that go.

As one does in dreams, she fought to move through air as thick as honey. Light sparkled from each snow crystal. She closed her hands around the newborn boar, her fingers slick with mucus and juice, and thrust the thing toward its mother's belly.

Fast as a snake, the sow's jaws clashed.

Ash snatched her bare hands back.

Now that her snout all but rested on it, the sow appeared to notice the boarlet. Her jaw dipped. She chewed through the white birth cord. Her head flopped forward again. She took no more notice of the newborn thing, did not lick it, but by now it had its snout clamped firmly into her belly fur, attached to a nipple.

"Not in the snow," Ash mumbled, anguished. "It can't survive."

—*Stranger things have happened.* Deo gratias.

"Godfrey?"

—*You are hard to reach!*

Robert Anselm's heavy tread vibrated through the floorboards by her head, as he stomped past her toward the mulled wine resting by the hearth. She rolled over, away from him, open-eyed. Muffled under gown and sleeping furs, she whispered, "Only when I want to be. You could be a demon. So tell me something only you would know. Now!"

—In Milano, when you were apprenticed to the armorer, you slept under your master's workbench, not allowed into inns, not allowed to marry without his permission. I used to visit you. You said you wanted to run an arms dealing business.

"God, yes! I remember, now . . ."

—You were eleven, as near as we could judge. You told me you were tired of having to break apprentice-boys' heads. I believe that was with the broom you swept up with.— The voice in her head tinged with amusement.

"Godfrey, you're dead. I saw you. I had my fingers in the wound."

—Yes. I remember dying.

"Where are you?"

—Nowhere. In torment; in purgatory.

"Godfrey . . . what are you?"

Let him say a soul, she thought. Her nails dug painfully into her palms. The life of the company went on around her—she could hear Angelotti's voice, now, in the solar, and Thomas Rochester, and Ludmilla Rostovnaya loudly complaining about burns bandaged and thick with goose grease. Under the noise, she whispered again:

"What are you, now?"

—A messenger.

"Messenger?"

—Here in the dark, I still pray. And answers come to me. They are answers for you, child. I have been trying to speak to you, to give these messages to you. You never relax, except at the edge of sleep.

Hairs shivered on the back of her neck. Although she lay

prone, her body tensed with the alertness of imminent attack.

Ash has a momentary memory, mosaic-like, of a hundred skirmishes, a hundred fields fought, and the same voice always clear in her head: *advise this, advise that, attack, withdraw*. The Stone Golem: the *machina rei militaris*. It is the same voice that she hears now—and yet now it is illuminated by a presence, changed utterly.

"It is you," she said. Water welled in her eyes and she ignored it. "I don't care what this is, demon or miracle, but I'm going to get you back, Godfrey."

—I am not the man you knew.

"I don't care if you're not a saint or a spirit, either. You're coming home." Ash covered her face with her hands, under the edge of blankets and furs. She felt her breath hot against her cold skin. "Do you know, you speak to me where the Stone Golem speaks? Godfrey—can you hear that, too?"

—A voice speaks in me, of war. I have thought, since I became . . . this . . . that such a voice must be your machina rei militaris. *I have tried to speak through it, to the men of Carthage, but they believe my words to be nothing but errors.*

She uncovered her face, if only to see, now that candles were being lit, that she lay on her bed among her company, neither in a snowbound forest, nor in a cell in Carthage. The yellow light swarmed in her vision; she felt hot, then cold.

"My sister? Will *she* speak to you?"

—Not to me. I have tried. Nor, now, will she speak to the machina rei militaris *itself.*

"She won't?"

Is that since I talked to her, last night? Shit! If it is—

"Jesus wept!" Ash said devoutly. "If that's true, she can't have been using it when she attacked the wall—"

—'The wall'?

Vehemently shaking her head, Ash whispered, "Doesn't matter! Not now! Shit, if that was *her* decision—firing on her own men—that was a shit-bad judgment call!"

—*Child, I'm lost on this one.*

"You'd hear, though? You'd hear, if she spoke to it—to you?"

—*I hear everything.*

"Everything?"

The floorboards creaked under her, the noise of a couple of hundred off-duty squaddies coming up from the hall below: belligerent, boisterous, loud. Ash flinched.

She spoke, barely moving her lips:

"Godfrey, I've given my word that I'll speak to the Stone Golem again. I'm afraid of it—no. I'm afraid of what can speak through it. The other machines."

—*The name they have for themselves is 'Wild Machines.' As if your* machina rei militaris *were tame and domestic!*

Fear and amazement washed through her. She thought, *But he shouldn't know about them, he was dead before I found out!* And then: *But it is Godfrey. And he* does *know.*

"How do you know about them?"

—*More than one voice speaks to me. Child, I am among many voices, here. I tried to speak to you, but you put up a wall to keep me out. I have been listening, then, to them. Perhaps this is the rim of Hell, and I hear the great Devils speaking between themselves: these 'Wild Machines.'*

"What . . . what do they say?"

—*They say to me:* WE STUDY YOU . . .

In Godfrey's voice, repeating it, she hears an echo of the voices that blasted her mind wide open.

"Maybe they want to know what people are like," she said, and added painfully, with bracing sarcasm: "Green Christ alone knows why! They've had two hundred years of listening to military reports from the whole Visigoth Empire, they must know everything about court politics and betrayal there is to know!"

—I hear them, voices in the dark. They say WE STUDY THE GRACE OF GOD IN MAN . . . *They say,* LAST SUMMER, THE SUN WENT OUT OVER THE GERMANIES. *I hear them say* THAT WAS ONLY A TRIAL OF OUR STRENGTH.

A long sigh shuddered through her body. "You *do* hear them. That's what they said to me."

—That it served as a demonstration of power? But that it was not done for that, not done to bring darkness to Christendom. It was done only to see if they could draw on such power. If they could use it. But they have not wholly used it yet. That is to come.

"They draw their power from the sun's spirit. I heard them saying they took more from the sun this summer than they had in ten thousand years." Ash licked dry lips. "And that the next time it happened, it would be to use the Faris to make a miracle. What I don't understand is why they haven't done it before now—"

The voice of Godfrey Maximillian in her head whispered on, relentless, with an agonizing determination in its tone:

—They will draw grace from the sun, as we have prayed to the saints for Divine grace. As I have made tiny miracles by the grace of God, so they will make her a channel for their will and their miracle. Soon! It is going to be soon.

"Yes, but, Godfrey—"

A voice that was many and one, loud enough that she bit her tongue at the shock, broke into her mind:

'IT IS SHE!'

Ash sat bolt upright.

"Get me a priest!"

As every face turned toward her, she said, "They found me."

IV

"IT'S TOO DANGEROUS, speaking with Devils!" Robert Anselm protested grimly. "We need you here. Commanding the company. Devils might—break you."

Ash, studying his sweating brow, under the woollen hood pulled low, thought, You *need me commanding the company. Is that it? Is that what you found out, these past three months? Shit, Roberto. I never took you for one of life's natural seconds-in-command.*

What has *it been like here?*

Softly, Antonio Angelotti said, "But it *is* Meister Godfrey. Alive, is it, madonna? Alive, still?"

"No; dead. It's his—" Ash stumbled. "His soul. I know Godfrey's soul as well as I know my own." A crooked smile. "Better."

Floria's hand rested on the shoulder of Ash's gown, her knuckles momentarily warm against the muscles of Ash's neck. Not to Ash, but to Angelotti, she said, "What's the priest to you? It isn't worth losing our girl."

The gunner, ragged curls gold in the candlelight, looked at last as if he had been on campaign, lines drawn down the sides of his mouth, eyes hollow. A thick, stained bandage covered his left arm from shoulder to elbow. "Ash rescued me. Meister Godfrey prayed with me. If I can help him, I will."

"Demon-possessed," Robert Anselm cut in, "what if you end up demon-possessed again?"

"It's too dangerous," the surgeon said.

"I signed a *condotta*. The Duke has a right to demand this. Even if he is dying." Ash held out her arms to her pages. "I'll do it *once*. Guys . . . I might as well talk to the Wild Machines. They know I'm alive now. You can bet *they'll* talk to me!"

One of the pages finished tying the eighteen pairs of aiglettes that fastened her doublet to her hose and handed her a demi-gown. She shrugged into it.

"Now?" Robert Anselm said.

"Now. One of the things we've always known, Roberto. We *have* to have all the information we can get. Otherwise, the company gets fucked. It's my decision." She shook his shoulder. "Digorie; Richard."

The two company priests arrived at the head of the spiral stairs, Digorie Paston somewhat in the lead, his bony face alight with enthusiasm. Richard Faversham trod bearlike in his wake.

"Captain." Digorie Paston's stole lay askew on his shoulders. He gazed around. "Clear this room. The pages should bring clear water, and bread, and then go down below. All to go except Master Anselm, Master Angelotti, and—the surgeon." He flushed pink to the tips of his ears. "Master Anselm, Master Angelotti, will you keep the door, please."

"Just one minute." Ash put her fists on her hips.

"Please, Captain," the priest said. "This is an exorcism."

Ash looked at him for a long minute. "It . . . might turn out to be that, yes."

"Then let me and Father Faversham do what is necessary. We will need all of God's grace that we can get."

The roof of the tower's top floor shifted with shadows, candle flames moving in the drafts. Ash moved to stand with her arms folded, near the fire, and watched as the two priests cleared the room with surprising lack of fuss. While Richard Faversham swung a censer, Digorie Paston followed him, around the corridor in the walls, appearing at the window gaps, disappearing again, their chant echoing up into the vaulted stone.

"You're going to do this," Floria said resignedly, walking to stand beside Ash in the yellow light.

"Somebody has to."

"Do they? Do they have to?"

"To win this—"

"Oh, the *war*!" Floria put her back to the fire's warmth. For a moment, her brother's stone green eyes looked at Ash from her face. "Bloody, pointless, *destructive*—! Won't I ever get it through to you? Most people spend their lives *building* things!"

"Not the people I know," Ash said mildly. "You're maybe the exception."

"I spend my life putting men back together after you get them chopped up. I get sick of it sometimes. Ten people *died* up on that wall!"

"We're all going to die," Ash said. Floria began to turn away. Ash caught her arm and repeated, "We're all going to die someday. Doesn't matter what we do. Till the fields, sell wool, sell your fanny, pray all your life in a nunnery—we're all of us going to die. Four things go over this world like the seasons: hunger, plague, death, and war.[49] They were doing it before I came along, and they'll be doing it long after. People *die*. That's all."

"And you follow the Four Horsemen because you like it, and because it pays well."

"Stop trying to pick a fight, Floria. I'm not going to fight

[49] C.f. The Book of Revelation, Ch. 6.

with you. It isn't just a war here. It isn't just *bad* war. It's complete and entire destruction. . . ."

"Dead is dead," Florian snapped. "I don't suppose your civilian casualties care much whether they died in a 'Just war' or a 'bad war'!"

Paston and Faversham chanted, "*Christus Imperator, Christus Viridianus.*" Their voices swooped, one high, one low. In the light, that is bright only where the candles are, Angelotti and Anselm could be any pair of armed men, standing at the stair entrance. The gunner appeared to be holding an impassioned *sotto voce* conversation. Ash saw Anselm scowl.

Impatience made her shift her footing, stare at the shuttered windows, the stacked crates of the armory.

"Oh yeah—Florian—while I remember. I saw Soeur Simeon in the Tour Philippe le Bon. She wants your Margaret Schmidt back. That was a hell of a shock up on the wall—I never expected I'd see her with the gunners. I thought she'd be one of your surgery assistants."

Floria del Guiz said quietly, "She isn't 'my' Margaret Schmidt."

Conscious of feeling taken aback, Ash said, "Oh."

Floria looked at her with an expression between grimness and bitter amusement. "Whatever I may have been expecting—no. She . . . It seems she's signed on the company books as a gunner's apprentice."

"She'll be all right," Ash offered, somewhat at a loss, still waiting for the blessing to finish. "She was with one of Angelotti's best men; he'll train her."

Florian kept her gaze on Ash. "I can't make you understand it, can I? They're teaching her to kill other men! Not for defense, not even for her lord. For money. And because she'll get to like it. Or if she sickens of it in the end, what is there for her? She can't go back."

Ash said quietly, "I didn't make her join us."

"She's too young to know her own mind!"

Digorie Paston and Richard Faversham reentered the main chamber, a scent of incense with them, singing together a solemn blessing.

"Okay," Ash said authoritatively, "I'll do what I do with very young recruits. I'll put her on guard tonight, up on the east wall, over the Ouche River. No one's going to come in on that side, but it's going to be fucking freezing."

She looked away from the priests, back to Floria.

"Most of the young lads quit after that. They can say they've been at the front, so their pride's okay. If she wants out, I'll let her go. But if she doesn't, Florian, I won't make her. Because we'll need her. Unless we can get supplied up and out of this city, we need everyone we can *get*."

In the sudden silence, Ash realized the blessing had finished.

Faversham and Paston glared at her.

Floria switched her gaze to the waiting priests. "Girl—you haven't got the piety of a *rabbit*. Have you?"

Ash's lips twitched in what would have been a smile if her face had not been stiff with fear. "You'd be surprised."

Digorie Paston said, "The—surgeon—should attend while we do this. It may be dangerous."

"Right." Ash put her hands to her belt, missed it, realized it still lay on her bed, purse and dagger threaded on it, so that she stood without weapons. "Digorie, Richard, I want you to pray for me, while I do this. And, when I ask it—I want you to pray for God's grace to silence the voice between my soul and the Stone Golem."

Floria's dark gaze came up. "You're going to try to cut yourself free of the Wild Machines? The Duke won't like that."

"I'll ask the questions he wants me to ask. If Godfrey's right, and I've scared the Faris off the *machina rei militaris* for now, I'm not going to get any answers about her tactics. And we *know* what Carthage's grand strategy is."

"It may change. If you do this, we won't know."

Ash's voice thinned. "They just—turned me around, Florian. They *made* me walk toward them. Okay, we're a long way from Carthage. But that isn't happening again. It is *not*. I have people depending on me."

"And Godfrey?"

Before Ash answered—the implications of that stark in her mind—Digorie Paston reached out and took her hand in his bony grip and led her to the hearth. Flames leaped, dazzling. The dusty, cluttered chamber was full of cold wind and leaping shadows. At his insistent push, Ash knelt. Ancient carvings glared down from the lintel above the hearth. Shadows moved in the eyes and foliage of *Christi Viridiani*.

Digorie Paston took a loaf of dark bread and broke it. Richard Faversham sprinkled water and salt.

"Fire and salt and candlelight: Christ receive thy soul—"

Ash shut her eyes. She closed out the anxious faces of the two priests, shut out Floria, pacing at the edge of the candlelight, and the voices of Anselm and Angelotti. The floor was painfully hard under her knees, bruised from the assault on the walls of Dijon.

—And you had no business to be leading an attack, child! It is a sin to tempt Death that way.

Salted bread touched her lips. She took it into her mouth. It formed a solid, gelatinous lump.

"How the hell—" she swallowed "—do you know what I was doing up there today, Godfrey?"

—You were praying. To Our Lord, or to the machina rei militaris: *perhaps both. I heard you. 'Keep me alive until*

the rest get here!' I have no knowledge of where you fought, or how; but I am not a fool, and I know you.

"Okay, so I was out in front. Sometimes you have to be. It wasn't suicidal, Godfrey."

—But hardly safe.

She laughed at that, swallowing down the bread and almost choking. With her eyes shut, every sense strained, she listened. In that part of her self which she has been used to sharing, there is a sense of amusement, kindness, love. Tears prick at her eyes: she blinks them back. In the hollow of her mind there is a sense of potential for more voices than this one: Godfrey Maximillian, alone in the dark.

"What comes after death?"

It was not the question she meant to ask. She heard, with her ears, Digorie Paston's sharp, "Blessed be!," and Richard Faversham's "Amen!"

—How can I say? This is Limbo; this is Purgatory. This is pain! Not the Communion of the Blessed!

"Godfrey—"

Anguish flooded through her, with his voice.

—I need to see the face of Our Lord! It was promised to me!

She felt pain, and blinked her eyes open for long enough to see her nails dug into her palms.

"I *will* find you."

—I am . . . nowhere. Not to be found. I have no eyes to see, no hands to touch. I am something that listens, something that hears. Everything is darkness. Voices . . . pry at me. Expose me to them . . . The hours, the days—is it years? Nothing but the voices, here—

"Godfrey!"

—Nothing but the dark, and the Great Devils eating away at me!

Ash reached out. Hands took hers, a man's hands rough

with chilblains and work, and cold with the November chill. She gripped them as if they were the hands of Godfrey Maximillian.

"I won't leave you."

—*Help me!*

"There's nothing we won't do. Trust me. Nothing! I'll get help to you."

She spoke with complete conviction, with the utter determination of combat. That such a rescue might be unknown or impossible is nothing, now, nothing besides the need to reach him.

His voice became gentle laughter.

—*You have said that to us many times before, little one, in the most impossible of fights.*

"Yeah, and I've been right, too."

—*Pray for me.*

"Yes." She listens, inside. In the hollow of her shared soul, listening for voices louder than God.

—*How long it is, since last you spoke to me?*

"Minutes . . . Not even an hour."

—*I cannot tell, child. Time is nothing where I am. I read once in Aquinas that the duration of the soul in Hell may be only a heartbeat, but to the damned it is eternity.*

Momentarily, she lets herself feel his desolation. Then, harshly: "You hear my sister. Has she spoken to the Stone Golem again, yet?"

—*Once more. I thought at first that it was you. She spoke to it, to Carthage, saying that you live. Saying that whatever she asks the* machina rei militaris, *you can ask, and be told. She tells her master the King-Caliph that they are overheard, now.*

In her ears, her own heartbeats sound, and the whispered addendum of the voice in her head:

—*You are very different, you and she.*

"How? No: tell me later."

The boards beneath her knees brought pain, focusing her. "Tell me what troops she's got deployed here. What recent messengers she's had from the armies in Iberia and Venice. And how strong she is in the north—I know she had another two legions with her when we were at Basle: they *must* be in Flanders!"

—I . . . can tell you what reports have been made to the machina rei militaris, *I think.*

Ash bowed her head, her hands still tightly gripping the hands of the man in front of her, her eyes closed.

"And . . . I have to speak with the Wild Machines, if I can. Will you stand by me?"

There was, for the first time, a hiatus in her mind. His sadness suffused her. Godfrey Maximillian's voice sounded, soft as thistledown:

—When I was a boy, I loved the forests. My mother vowed me to the Church. I would have stayed under the sky, with the animals. I loved my monastery no better than you loved St. Herlaine, Ash, and they beat me as they beat you, brutally. I still do not believe God intended me for a priest, but he gave me the grace to perform small miracles, and the gift of being in your company. It was worth it. On earth, or here, I stand with you. If I regret anything, it is only that I could not gain your trust.

The *it was worth it* she shoved into a dark part of her mind, wiped out, ignored. A tight, cold ball of muscle knotted under her breastbone. Before she could lose the courage and the warmth of him, she said, "Visigoth troop dispositions, siege of Dijon, main units, give position."

The *machina rei militaris*, in Godfrey's voice, began to speak:

—Legio VI Leptis Parva, northeast quadrant: serf-troops to the number of—

'IT IS SHE . . .'

The same silence that had blanketed her mind among the pyramids of the desert numbed her. For a second, she lost the feel of the boards under her shins and the grip she had on Digorie Paston's hands.

"Son of a bitch—" Ash opened her eyes, screwing up her face. Richard Faversham held her shoulders, Digorie Paston her hands. As far away as if they had been at the other end of a field of combat, faces surrounded her: Anselm, Angelotti, Floria.

She gripped Digorie's bony hands. "Godfrey!"

Nothing answered. A chill inside her mind began to spread. She reached into herself, meeting only numbness, deafness. *They can reach this far, then.*

Christ, all the way over the seas from Carthage, across half of Christendom . . . ! But the Stone Golem can, so why shouldn't they?

"Godfrey!"

Faint as a dream, Godfrey's voice whispered:

—I am here, always.

'IT IS SHE. IT IS YOU, LITTLE ONE . . .'

It is not enough, now, that there are men and women—Thomas Rochester; Ludmilla Rostovnaya; Carracci; Margaret Schmidt—whose lives may be rescued or ruined by her decisions.

She thinks, *No one is indispensable.*

Now it is Ash, a woman, alone, after nineteen years; kneeling on hard wood in a cold wind, with the searing flicker of the hearth-fire hot on the sleeve of her doublet. A woman who prays, suddenly and separately, as she has not done since she was a child: *Lion protect me!*

She recalls painted plaster crunching under the hooves of a brown mare, in snow, in the south, riding between the great pyramids. If she is numbed, now, it may be with silence or with cold. The voices in her head—and they are plural, multiple, legion—whisper as one:

'WE KNOW THAT YOU HEAR US.'

"No shit?" Ash said, mildly acid. She let go of the priest's hands, her eyes still shut, and heard his gasp of pain released. She sat back on her heels. There is no compulsion to stop performing any of these acts. In utter relief, she says, "But you can't reach me. I could be anywhere."

'YES. YOU COULD BE. BUT YOU ARE IN DIJON. GUNDOBAD'S CHILD TELLS US SO.'

"I don't think so. Told the Stone Golem and House Leofric, maybe. But not you. She won't listen to you."

'THAT IS NOTHING. SHE WILL *HEAR*, WHEN THE TIME COMES. LITTLE ONE, LITTLE ONE; STOP FIGHTING US.'

"In a fucking pig's ear!"

It is pure mercenary, mercenary as she has always wanted to be seen: foul-mouthed, cheerful, brutal, indestructible. If anything else is under the surface, it is hidden even from her, now, in this adrenaline rush.

"You're not Wild." Tears dripped down her face: and she could not have said whether it was pain or painful humor that put them there. "We *made* you. Long, long ago—by accident—but it was us, we made you. Why do you hate us? Why do you hate Burgundy?"

'SHE HAS HEARD.'

'SHE HAS SHARED.'

'KNOWN WHAT WE KNOW.'

'LITTLE AS WE KNOW.'

'KNOWN THE BEGINNING. BUT WHO KNOWS THE END?'

What had been chorus became, with the last voice, a braided sound. Sorrow keened in it. Ash blinked under the power of it, momentarily saw the flames in the hearth and the blackened stone chimney behind, burned with the fires of centuries. Where the fire had been fierce, a piece of stone had cracked and fallen away. The pattern of fracture remained.

In her memory, Ash sees the dome of the King-Caliph's palace fracture and fall, the weight of stone hurtling down.

'WE KNOW THE END. . . .'

'THE VILENESS OF FLESH!'

'LITTLE VILE THINGS, NOT WORTHY TO LIVE—'

'—BECAUSE OF YOUR EVIL—'

Pressing her fingers into her palms so hard that her nails penetrated the skin, Ash gasped, sardonically, "Don't let two hundred years of listening to Carthage prejudice you!"

There is something that may be rueful amusement—Godfrey? And a soul-deafening, icy babble in her mind:

'CARTHAGE IS NOTHING—'

'—THE VISIGOTHS, *NOTHING*—'

'GUNDOBAD SPOKE WITH US, LONG BEFORE THEM—'

'VILEST OF MEN!'

'WE REMEMBER!'

'WE REMEMBER . . .'

'WE WILL BURY YOU, LITTLE THING OF FLESH.'

The last reverberation in her head made her wince, taste blood where she bit her tongue. She said aloud, not seeing the people around her, "Don't worry. If they *could* move the earth here, they would. If they're not doing it, they can't."

'ARE YOU SO SURE, LITTLE ONE?'

Chills ran down the skin under her clothing; she thought, with appalled disgust, *'Little one': that's what Godfrey calls me; they've taken that from* him.

"Something's stopping you," she said aloud. With a fierce sarcasm, she spat, "According to you, the Faris doesn't *need* an army! She's Gundobad's child, she's a Wonder-Worker; she can make Burgundy into a desert just like that. All you have to do is pray to the sun, and *bang!* there you are. One miracle. *So why haven't you done it*?"

With that vehemence, she instantly focused herself—finding the same interior state that she finds when she handles a sword—and *listened.*

Instantly, she grunted with a soundless impact. Her mouth stung. She put her hands up, opened her eyes, saw blood, realized she had bitten her lip. Someone said something abrupt, beside her. She could say nothing, only jerk her hand, wave them back. She felt at once winded, and numb, as she felt when she first learned to ride. It is that split second between hitting the ground, and pain. She froze.

Physical pain did not come.

'YOU CANNOT HEAR US. NOT IF WE CHOOSE. YOU WILL NOT SURPRISE US AGAIN.'

"Shit, no." Ash rubbed her hand across her mouth, feeling blood slick on her skin. "No, *sir.*"

'WE DO NOT UNDERSTAND YOU.'

"No. You don't. Join the fucking club," Ash said bitterly.

There was no feeling in her of their puzzlement or confusion. Only the interior sound of the voices. Her blood dried cold, pulling on her skin. She probed it tenderly with her tongue, thought *That's going to hurt*, and swallowed blood and saliva before she said, "You can't keep me out forever."

Nothing.

"What does it matter if you tell me? It's *already* getting cold. You're drawing down the sun, and it's getting cold, where you are. Pretty soon you won't need the Faris here. Or a miracle! The winter will kill us all."

Again, voices in unison:

'WINTER WILL NOT COVER ALL.'

"Goddammit!" Ash hit her fist against her thigh, exasperated. "Why is Burgundy so *important* to you?"

'WE CAN DRAW DOWN THE SUN'S SPIRIT[50]—'

'USE ITS POWER, WEAKEN, BRING DARKNESS—'

'DARK, COLD, AND WINTER—'

'—BUT—'

'WINTER WILL NOT COVER ALL THE WORLD.'

Ash opened her eyes.

Robert Anselm knelt in front of her, one hand steadying his hilt. Behind him, Angelotti had his hand on Anselm's mailed shoulder. Both of them stared at her. Floria squatted between the two priests, resting her arms on her thighs, her long fingers almost touching the floorboards.

'WINTER WILL NOT COVER—'

'—ALL!—'

'DARKNESS WILL NOT COVER ALL THE WORLD.'

"*In nomine Patri, Filii, et Spiritus Sancti,*" Richard Faversham said in a hoarse, bass whisper.

Ash repeated, " 'Darkness will not cover *all the world*' . . . ?"

She did not shut her eyes, could still see them all, but the sound of great voices in her head blasted her attention away from the tower room. A vast, cold sorrow almost drowned her:

'—WINTER MAY KILL ALL THE WORLD, BUT FOR HIM.'

'DARKNESS MAY COVER ALL THE WORLD—BUT FOR HIM.'

'WE CANNOT REACH—'

'—BURGUNDY DIES AT HER COMMAND, ONLY—'

'SHE WILL DESTROY BURGUNDY. OUR DARK MIRACLE. AS SOON AS THE DUKE DIES.'

---

[50] I wonder if this phrase might better be translated as 'energy,' or even—to a modern reader—as 'solar power'? Perhaps even as 'electromagnetic force'?—PR

"All the world," Ash said. "All the world!"

'WHEN IT IS GONE—'

'—MADE DESOLATE, MADE A DESERT—'

'WHEN IT IS NOTHING: BURGUNDY DESTROYED, AS IF IT HAD NEVER BEEN—'

'THEN EVERYTHING—'

'ALL THE WORLD—'

'—CAN BE CLEANSED AND PURE, ALL THE WORLD—'

'—FREE OF FLESH, VILE, DESTRUCTIVE FLESH, FREE—'

'AS IF YOU HAD NEVER BEEN.'

The surge and ebb of the great voices drained away. The floorboards shifted under her feet—no, were solid, but she lost balance and fell back and sat on her rump, Richard Faversham catching her, so that she sprawled up against him, his blacksmith's arm around her shoulders.

A numb, desolate silence filled her soul. Into it, no voice came. No Godfrey. A white and deathly tiredness filled her.

"Did you pray?" she asked.

"To cast out the voices." Faversham's body shifted as he nodded his head. "To cast the demons out of you."

"It may just have worked . . ." She snuffled, not knowing quite whether she would laugh or cry. "Godfrey, Godfrey."

Softly, in her mind, his voice spoke:

—I am with you.

"Son of a bitch." She reached up to thump Digorie Paston on the arm. "Exorcism isn't going to do it. No. And I don't even know if it matters, now—"

She found her gaze fixed on Floria's face.

"What?" the surgeon demanded. "*What?*"

"Burgundy isn't an objective," Ash said. "Burgundy is an obstacle."

Robert Anselm growled, "What the fuck, girl?"

She stayed resting against Faversham's solidness

because she doubted her ability to sit up on her own. A fever ran through her body, all her muscles weak.

"Burgundy isn't the objective. Burgundy is the *obstacle*." She looked up at Robert Anselm's sweating face. "And I don't know why! They've kept saying they must destroy Burgundy—but it isn't because they just want *Burgundy* wiped out. After Burgundy's gone . . ."

A shudder went through her flesh, weakness at some deep level better not examined, better ignored. To her own surprise, her voice came out harsh and amused:

"It's *us* they want to be rid of. Men. All men. Burgundy—Carthage, too. They're . . . farmers who'd set fire to a barn to get rid of the rats. It's why they want their 'evil miracle.' After Burgundy's gone—they say, *then* they can make their Darkness cover the whole world."

V

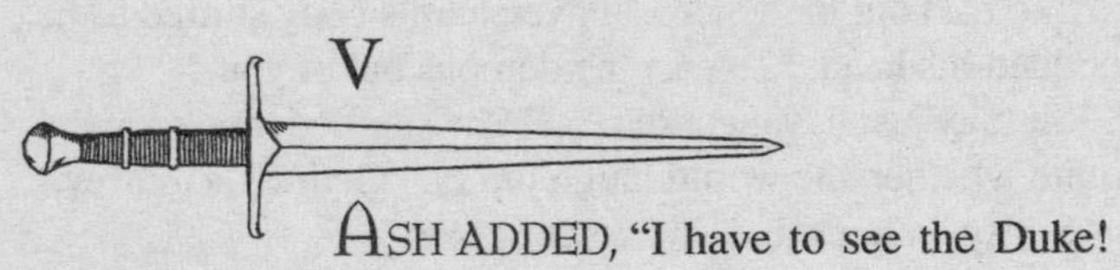

ASH ADDED, "I have to see the Duke! Right now!"

Floria, holding a candle up uncomfortably close to Ash's face, ceased peering into her eyes and focused instead on her. "Yes. You do. I'll go ahead and clear it with his physicians."

The disguised woman stood abruptly, shoved the wooden candlestick into Digorie Paston's hand, and strode toward the dark stairwell. Her footsteps clattered down the stone steps.

"I'll get you an escort." Robert Anselm stood and bellowed. Ash heard the sound of men in mail running.

"But, madam, you should rest," Digorie Paston protested. The English priest took her hands and turned them over, studying her palms in a businesslike way. "God's grace has failed to rescue you. It were better you should fast and pray, humble yourself, and pray to him again."

"Later. I'll come to Compline.[51] The Duke has to know about this!" Ash probed for voices, as a tongue probes an aching tooth. "Godfrey—"

A weak warmth. Godfrey's voice faint, all but inaudible:

—Blessed be!

A sound like wind through trees filled her soul. Creaking and whispering at first, and then loud, until her eyes watered, and she rubbed with the heel of her hands at her temples. "Okay—"

As she withdrew the impulse of her mind, the deafening interior sound sank to a keening mutter.

The Wild Machines, choral, keening, their language old, now, and incomprehensible. The language in which they spoke to Gundobad, so many centuries ago: an ancient, impenetrable Gothic tongue.

Richard Faversham remarked, "Don't tell God 'later,' madam. He wouldn't like it."

Ash stared at him for a second, and chuckled. "Then don't tell Him I said it, Master priest. Come with me to the Duke. I may need you to explain that your prayers failed. That I can't be cut free of the Stone Golem."

And I'll ask him again. Why is Burgundy so important? Why is Burgundy an obstacle *to the Wild Machines? And this time I'm going to* have *to have an answer out of him.*

With the reappearance of Rickard and her younger

---

[51] Final service of the day, 9 p.m.

pages, she was fully dressed in minutes, borrowed sword belted on under a thick campaigning cloak and the edge of her hood pulled down over her helmet.

Anselm and the escort surrounded her through Dijon's pitch-black streets, under the stars. The deep boom of cannon shattered the silence, and from somewhere far off, toward the northern wall, came the crackle of fire. Men and women slid through the shadows, civilians running from the bombardment, or thieving; Ash did not stop to investigate. A company of Burgundian men-at-arms passed them in one square, a hundred men, feet slapping the frozen earth, running in order for the wall. Her hand went to her sword hilt, but she kept on going.

The palace was a flare of light: candles brilliant through the glass of ogee windows, torches flaring among the guards at the gates. In the light, Ash caught sight of a flaxn head of hair.

Floria, her hood pushed back and her face red, stood gesticulating at a large Burgundian sergeant. As Ash arrived at her side, she broke off.

"They won't let me in. I'm a bloody *doctor*, and they won't let me in!"

Ash pushed to the front, standing between men-at-arms in Lion livery. Smuts from torches stung her eyes. Bitter wind snapped at her mittened hands; her exposed face. Her stomach thumped, cold.

"Ash, mercenary, Duke's man," she explained rapidly to the sergeant in charge of the cordon of guards. "I must speak with His Grace. Send word to him that I'm here."

"I 'aven't got time for this—" The Burgundian sergeant's harassed expression faded as he turned. He gave her a nod. "Demoiselle *Ash!* You came in last night; I was on the gate. They say you razed Carthage. That right?"

"I wish it was," she said, putting all the frankness she

could into her tone. Seeing that she had his momentary respect and attention, she said quietly, "Pass me through. I have important information for Duke Charles. *Whatever* crisis you've got here, this is more important."

She had time to think *But I don't need to fool him, this* is *more important*, and to see that it was her conviction of that, rather than her faked sincerity, that convinced the man.

"I'm sorry, Captain. We've just cleared all the physicians out. I can't let you in. There's only priests in there now." The Burgundian sergeant jerked his head, and as she stepped aside with him from the front of the crowd, lowered his voice:

"No point, ma'am. There's a dozen abbots and bishops up in His Grace's chamber, all wearing their knees out on the stone, and it isn't going to do one damn bit of good. God lays His heaviest burden on His most faithful servant."

"What's happened?"

"You've seen wounded men when they're in the balance, and it suddenly goes one way or the other." The sergeant reached up, tilting his sallet, his bloodshot eyes weary in his lined face. "Keep it quiet, ma'am, please. There'll be upset soon enough. Whatever your business, you'll have to keep it for whoever succeeds him. His Grace the Duke is on his deathbed now."

Floria came back into the upper floor of the tower. "It's true."

She walked across the chamber to the hearth, ignoring Anselm and Angelotti, spoke directly to Ash, and sank down in a huddle by the fire, holding her hands out to the flames.

"I managed to get as far as his chamber door. One of his physicians is still there: a German. Charles of Burgundy is dying. It started two hours ago, with fever, sweats. He became unconscious. It seems he hasn't passed water or fecal matter for days. His body has begun to stink. He isn't conscious for the prayers."[52]

Ash stood, gazing down at the company surgeon. "How long, Florian?"

"Before he dies? He's not a lucky man." Floria's eyes reflected flames. She continued to stare into the hearth. "Tonight, tomorrow; the day after, at the latest. The pain will be bad."

Robert Anselm said, "Girl, if he were one of your men, you'd be up there with a misericord right now."[53]

An air of unease had spread up and down through the tower's floors, from the cooks and pages in the kitchens, to the troops, to the guard on Ash's door. Knowing that the surgeon would be overheard, Ash made no attempt to stop her speaking. *If there's going to be a morale problem, I want it out in the open where I can see it.*

"Well, we're fucked," Robert Anselm remarked. "No second try at Carthage. And watch this fucking siege collapse!"

His tread was heavy as he clattered, still fully armored, across the floor. Outside the slit-windows, the sound of a night bombardment echoed, golem-machines, which require neither sleep nor rest, throwing missiles, battering ceaselessly at Dijon's walls. She saw him flinch at the nearer strikes. "What does happen 'when the Duke dies'? What will these Wild Machines be able to do?"

"We are about to find out." Antonio Angelotti came for-

---

[52] This description in the original text resembles death by renal failure, after prolonged illness. Confusingly, in our history Charles the Bold is not reported as dying until two months later, 5 January 1477, and in this case from fatal wounds, on the battlefield at Nancy, fighting the Swiss.

[53] A dagger used to give the *coup de grâce*, so called from the religious aspect, granting the final mercy.

ward into the fire's light from the door. "Madonna, Father Paston sends word he is about to begin the service of Compline."

Ash gestured irritably. "I'll do Matins.[54] Angeli, we don't just *sit* here. If that's 'Gundobad's child' out there . . . If the Wild Machines say the Faris can do a miracle, like Gundobad did when he made Africa into a desert—are you going to sit there and wait to find out if they're right?"

The gunner came to squat beside Floria del Guiz, two golden heads together. Angelotti had the air of a man who knows that, as soon as the bombardment stops, he will have to be ready to deal with the follow-up assault. From time to time he experimentally flexed his bandaged, gut-sewn arm. "What is there to do but wait, madonna? Sally out and see if you can kill her in battle?"

There was a small silence. Angelotti cocked his head. She saw him recognize that the Visigoth guns had ceased firing.

"He promised another raid on Carthage. I was counting on it." Ash calculated as she spoke. "With him dead—no chance. So: we don't get to take out the Stone Golem. There's only one answer left. Angeli is right. We take out the Faris. And then it doesn't *matter* what the Wild Machines planned, or what they bred her for, or any of that. Dead is dead. You don't do miracles of any kind when you're dead."

Robert Anselm shook his head, grinning. "You're mad. She's in the middle of a fucking army, out there!" He paused. "So—what's our plan?"

Ash shook his shoulder as she passed him, walking to study the papers on the trestle table, maps and calculations drawn spider-thin in the candlelight. " 'Plan'? Who said anything about a plan? Damn good idea if we *had* a plan. . . ."

[54] First service of the day, held at midnight.

Between Anselm's deep laugh and Angelotti's more subdued amusement, Ash heard a commotion on the stairs. Deep voices boomed. She was instantly and instinctively shoulder to shoulder with Anselm and Angelotti, a glance checking that Floria was safely behind them, all three facing the stair entrance, hands gripping sword hilts.

Rickard stumbled as he came in, falling to his knees on the floorboards. He dropped what he was carrying in both arms.

The blanket-wrapped bundle dropped with a muffled, sharp clatter.

"What the fuck?" Ash began.

Still kneeling, the black-haired boy flipped the blanket open.

The shifting candles reflected from a mass of curved, banded, and shining metal. Ash glimpsed confusion on Floria's face as the surgeon stared, while the two men already began to laugh, Robert Anselm swearing in an amazed, cheerful stream of filth.

Ash walked across the floor to the blanket. She leaned down and picked her cuirass up by its shoulder straps. The hollow cuirass sat in the concertina'd skirts; and the fauld clicked down as she lifted the empty armor up, the tasset plates swinging on their leathers.

"She's sent my fucking armor back!"

Two complete metal legs lay in the blanket, together with a tangle of shoulder defenses: pauldrons, spaulders, and a gorget. One arm defense was unpointed, the butterfly-shape of the couter taking the light and splintering it. Ash put her cuirass down and picked up a gauntlet, flexing it, letting the laminations slide over each other. A few spots of rust, and some scratches, were new.

Incredulous, Ash said, "Shit! She *must* have been

impressed by us holding the wall! If I'm worth bribing—Does she still think we'll betray Dijon? Open a gate?"

Half of her furiously thinking *What does this mean?*, the other half can only stroke metal, examine linings for tears, remember each field that earned her the money to say to an armorer *Make me this.*

"Why *now*? If she's thought better of direct assault—"

What has she—heard?

Turning her head, Ash confronted Rickard's immense, utter pride. "Uh—right. Better get it cleaned up, hadn't you? Finish the job."

"Yes, boss!"

Under the curved plates, with its long belt wrapped up neatly around the hilt, a wheel-pommel single-handed sword lay in its scabbard, her own sweat-marks still dark on the leather grip.

"Son of a bitch." Ash's fingers continued to slide over the gauntlet. She squatted, touching cold metal: sword, breastplate, backplate, visored sallet, checking leathers and buckles, as if only touch and not sight could confirm its reality. "She sent my sword and harness back. . . ."

And Carthage didn't tell her to do this—if what Godfrey says is true, she's not talking via the Stone Golem!

Rickard sat back on his heels and wiped his running nose. "Sent a message, too." He waited, a little self-importantly, until Ash's attention focused solely on him.

"A message from the Faris?"

"Yeah. Her herald told it to me. Boss, she says she wants to see you. She says she'll give you a truce, if you come out to the northside camp at dawn."

"A *truce!*" Robert Anselm guffawed coarsely.

"Tomorrow morning, boss." Rickard himself looked sceptical. "She says."

"Does she, by God?" Ash straightened up, one gauntlet still in her hand. She stared thoughtfully at the knuckle-plates. "Florian, the Duke—you said it could be as early as tonight?"

The surgeon, behind her, said, "It could be anytime. I wouldn't be surprised to hear the mourning bells right now, if it comes to it."

"So we don't have any argument." Ash turned to her command group. "And we don't get the idea that this is a democracy. Rickard, send a page to find the herald again. Roberto, get me an escort for dawn—I want people who aren't trigger-happy. You're in command until I get back into the city."

Robert Anselm said, "Yes."

Floria del Guiz opened her mouth, shut it, stared at Ash's expression for a moment, and snapped, "*If* you get back."

"I'll come with you, madonna." Antonio Angelotti stood up lithely. "Ludmilla's burned, but she can walk, now: she'll command the guns. You may need me. I know their scientist-magi. I may see things that you won't."

"True." Ash rubbed the heel of her hand against her gauntlet. "Rickard, let's armor me up, shall we? Just for practice, before morning. . . ."

Robert Anselm said, "You'll get stopped at the city wall. Mercenary captain, off to see the enemy as soon as she hears the Duke's dying? They won't like it."

"Then I'll get a written pass from Olivier de la Marche. I'm the hero of Carthage! He knows Duke Charles trusts me. More to the point, he knows I wouldn't be leaving my movable valuables—that is, you lot!—unless I was coming back. You can work out a sally-and-rescue with him, if the Visigoths turn treacherous."

" 'If'?" Floria spit. "Have some sense in that pointy

head of yours, woman! If you're on the other side of these walls, she'll kill you!"

"That must be why I'm shitting myself," Ash said dryly, and saw the creases at the corners of Floria's eyes as she unwillingly smiled.

As Ash began to strip off, and Rickard dug her arming doublet and hose out of one of the oak chests, she said quietly, "Robert, Florian, Angeli. Remember—it's different now Charles is dying. *Don't lose sight of the objective.* We're not here now to defend Dijon. We're not here to fight Visigoths. We're here to survive—and, since we can't get away from here, right now that means we're here to stop the Faris."

Robert Anselm gave her one keen glance. "Got it."

"We mustn't get caught up in fighting to the point where we forget that."

Floria del Guiz bent down and heaved the cuirass clumsily into the air. As Rickard rushed to help her support it, and hinge it open for Ash to put it on, Floria said, "Will you kill her, tomorrow?"

"It's under truce!" Rickard protested, scandalized.

Ash, grimly amused, said, "Never mind the moral question. She's not going to give me the chance, not on this one. Maybe, if I can set it up for more negotiations, at a second meeting . . ." She caught the boy's gaze. "*She* obviously thinks we have an unfinished conversation. I might stand a better chance when her guard's—down—oof!"

The familiar heave clicked the cuirass shut around her body. Rickard cinched the straps tight on its right-hand side.

"Don't *you* forget," Floria said, standing close by her side, touching Ash's cheek, her eyes bright. "What you call 'stopping' her—I've spent five years watching you kill people. This one is your sister."

"I don't forget anything," Ash said. "Robert? Get Digorie and Richard Faversham back up here. I want my lance leaders, and their sergeants, and the rest of the command group. Here. *Now*."

"So how's it look, boss?" Rochester asked.

"Shite, thanks!"

Ash shot a quick glance across the map-strewn table at Digorie Paston, his chewed goose-quill pen, and the oak-gall ink blackening both his hands and bony features.

"—Hold on, Tom—Father, repeat that back."

Digorie Paston held up his scribbled page slantwise to the candle, reading with some difficulty in the golden light. " 'Thus fifteen legions were committed in the first phase—' "

On the tail of his words, stumbling to echo him phrase by phrase, Ash repeated: " 'Fifteen legions, committed in the first phase...' "

—*Yes.*

The voice is mild. She shook her head, cropped hair shifting, as if a fly bothered her.

" 'With ten remaining, deployed now as I have said—' "

" ' . . . ten remaining, now deployed . . .' "

The voice of Godfrey, in her head, is not weary—has, in fact, the tireless ability that the *machina rei militaris* has always had, to speak when any human soul would be dropping from exhaustion.

Her own voice is rasping, after bellowing on the walls of Dijon. After so much rapid dictation, her throat croaks. " ' . . . Report made this feast day of St. Benignus.' "[55]

—*Yes.*

"Here, boss."

---

[55] 1st November. Second century; martyred, coincidentally enough, at Dijon.

She took a wooden cup of (admittedly sour) wine from Rickard, and drained it. "Thanks."

"The others are on their way up, boss." He turned to serve Rochester.

Ash stretched her arms, under asymmetric steel plates, feeling the sensation of each leather strap pulling against cloth and the flesh beneath—all of it grown unfamiliar in the space of three months. Her armor shells snug around her body, clattering at her thighs. Weight is nothing, but she finds herself almost forgetting how to breathe, sheathed so close in metal.

The warmth is welcome.

"Godfrey—the Wild Machines?"

—Nothing.

Shit. Oh, fuck, maybe from their point of view, it doesn't matter *what I know? No: that can't be right!*

Digorie Paston straightened up from his writing, flicking a sideways glance at her from cherry-rimmed eyes. He held himself upright on the joint stool, ready to read, and said nothing. He licked his lips.

"Okay, that'll do it for now." Ash placed her palms flat on the trestle table and leaned her weight on her arms.

As she stood, momentarily weary, the rest of the lance leaders and sergeants shoved through the stone doorway into the tower's upper floor. Their voices rose over the noise of the wind banging at the wooden shutters, and the desultory crash of bombardment from the darkness outside.

"Shit. Another night when I ain't gonna get more than two hours' sleep!"

"You're young." Robert Anselm grinned at her, demonic in the smoky light of the tapers. "*You* can do it. Think of us poor old men. Right, Raimon?"

The white-haired siege engineer acknowledged that, briefly; walking in beside Dickon Stour's apprentice—promoted to chief armorer—and behind him Euen Huw and Geraint ab Morgan in close talk, and Ludmilla Rostovnaya, with black-singed hair still not cropped off, but her body and shoulder bound up bulky in linen rags and grease and moving painfully.

"You been talking to your old machine, boss?" Ludmilla asked huskily. "Thought you didn't want it knowing where you are?"

"Bit late to worry about that, now. . . ." Ash grinned ruefully at her. "The ragheads have already told Carthage I'm right here."

Forty or so men and women came in, enough to make the bleak stone-walled upper chamber seem crowded. They brought welcome body heat. Ash paced around the trestle table where Digorie Paston and Richard Faversham sat among piles of paper.

"Okay, what we got here is some . . . intelligence, on Visigoth troop deployment in Christendom. I have to say, it ain't gonna cheer us up any. As we thought, they've got things sewn up tight—with some interesting exceptions," she added thoughtfully, leaning between the clerks to spread out the spider-scrawled map of Christendom, as the men-at-arms crowded at her shoulder.

"For example—I can see how we got in from Marseilles the way we just did. . . . When they first landed, the Faris put three legions directly into Marseilles—but they ended up fighting their way up to Lyons, and then Auxonne. I reckon the Legio XXIX Cartenna must be that garrison we were avoiding on the coast. . . . They took heavy casualties. She's got the remnants of the Legio VIII Tingis and the X Sabratha in Avignon and Lyons, but apart from that, almost *nobody* holding down the Langue D'Oc."

"Then that's why we could eat," Henri Brant offered.

"There wasn't half the number of enemy supply parties out that I expected to see."

"We were fucking lucky."

"Oh yeah, boss." Pieter Tyrrell said alcoholically, his arm around Jan-Jacob Clovet's shoulder—it must, Ash realized, have been pretty much the first time he'd seen his fellow crossbowman since he got back from Carthage. He looked up from puzzling over the maps. "Got us here. *Real* lucky!"

"You ain't got no gratitude, Tyrrell! If I'd taken us up here, where the Venetian captains wanted—" Ash tapped the eastern coast of Italy "—we'd be currently enjoying the hospitality of the two fresh legions that are sitting there watching the Dalmatian coast!"

Tyrrell grinned. Antonio Angelotti, putting wooden plates and an eating knife down to trap the edges of his map of Christendom flat, murmured, "I make it fifteen Carthaginian legions in the first invasion, another ten for reinforcement of ports like Pescara, madonna—and five more in reserve. Say perhaps a hundred and eighty thousand troops."

In the silence that followed, Robert Anselm gave a low whistle.

Thomas Rochester prodded Angelotti's map, and the rough sketches that Digorie Paston and Richard Faversham spread out beside it. "This their deployment? How old's this news, boss?"

"Beginning of this month. It's the most recent overall sit. rep.[56] from the Faris back to Carthage. Some of *her* news is going to be out-of-date, given the problems traveling through the Dark—especially the legions in northern France and the Germanies. . . . But what we've got—"

56 'Situation report.'

Ash stopped, took a breath; walked a pace or two forward and back, in the light from the blazing hearth-fire. A brush-haired younger page, at Rickard's direction, squatted there in case of embers falling onto the timber floor. His eyes reflected silver as she walked past him, the fit of greaves to her calf muscles not *quite* right—too much walking, too little riding, in the last few weeks—and the fit of cuisses to thigh muscles a little clip for the same reason, but all in all (and this, also, she sees in the boy's eyes) beginning to move with her as if the metal plates are part of her body. Part of her self.

"What we've *got*," she said, turning to face them, "is what happened during the initial deployment of the invasion—and what happened in phase two: the resupply and redeployment of fresh troops. We know where we are now."

Simon Tydder, promoted sergeant, and with stubble on the angular bones of his face that are growing out of plump adolescence, squeaked, "We *know* where we are now, boss. In deep doo-doo . . . ," and then blushed at his change of register.

"Too fucking right!" Ash slapped his shoulder in passing. "But now we know it in detail!"

There was a strong smell of horse in the room, as is inevitable with knights. Despite lack of sleep, most of the faces watching her as men crowded around the trestle table, or leaned over the shoulders of the men in front, were aggressive, sharp, keyed-up. Ash blinked against the eye-stinging smell of mold on cold stonework, urine, and woodsmoke. She drew her bollock dagger and plonked it down on the center of the map.

"There," she said. "That was their main thrust. In at Marseilles, and Genoa—where we were lucky enough to meet them—"

"Lucky, my fucking arsehole!" John Price rumbled.

Antonio Angelotti murmured, "What you do with your arsehole is entirely up to you. . . ."

Ash glared at the innocent expression of her master gunner. "*Okay*. The main force, under the Faris, made two landings: the one I mentioned at Marseilles, and seven additional legions at Genoa."

Ludmilla, moving stiffly, leaned past her sergeant, Katherine Hammell, and studied Paston's sketch. "Agnes was right, then, boss? Thirty thousand men?"

"Yup." Ash drew her finger across the map. "The Faris sent three of those legions to raze Milan, Florence, and Italy, while she took her own four legions over the Gotthard into Switzerland. As far as I can make out, she devastated the Swiss somewhere near Lake Lucerne, over several days, and then moved on into Basle. At that point, with the Germanies surrendered, she moved west, met up with the other legions marching north from Lyons, and advanced toward the southern border of Burgundy."

"Fuck me, boss, don't tell me we were facing seven legions at Auxonne!"

"Oh, we were—but it looks like the scouts were pretty shit-hot on the figures. The ragheads took heavy casualties getting to Auxonne. By the time we were facing them, we *did* outnumber them."

"Shoulda fucked 'em," Katherine Hammell growled.

"Yeah, well, we didn't. . . ."

"Fucking nancy Burgundians," John Price added.

"Fucking war-golems! We've held this place, though!" one of the remaining Flemish lance leaders said: Henri van Veen, his breath thick with wine. At his shoulder, his sergeants nodded enthusiastically.

"You should have seen us, boss!" Adriaen Campin

blurted. The big Flemish sergeant glanced around, hit the table with his clenched fist. "You shoulda been here! It's been fucking hot, but they haven't shifted us yet!"

"We're not all like that motherfucker van Mander," the lance leader beside him said; Willem Verhaecht, another of the Flemings who had stayed with the Lion Azure. His pale face, in firelight and candlelight, was stubbled and scarred, black in places with small crusts of old blood.

"We're the Lion; he's not," Ash said brusquely. "Okay, as far as I can work it out from the Faris's casualty reports, the legions coming up from Marseilles took forty percent casualties against the southern French lords, and the legions she brought up from Genoa lost fifty percent of their men to the Swiss. Most of their legions are amalgamated now. Same goes for the Langue D'Oc. The legions over in France took casualties; most of the German ones didn't."

"*Fifty* percent?" Thomas Rochester blinked.

"I'd say by the time she was at Auxonne, she had not much more than two and a half legions, total. Fifteen thousand men. They took another twenty-five percent casualties there—some of them from us." Ash shook her head. "She doesn't care how many men she loses. . . . That legion and a half outside here, now, is the Legio XIV Utica in shit-hot shape, and the remnants of the XX Solunto and XXI Selinunte in with the tag end of the VI Leptis Parva. Nearly seven thousand men. Price, tell your lads they got it absolutely right."

Most of the men-at-arms grinned. John Price merely grunted a small acknowledgment.

"Other than that . . . there's the French deployment, and the Legio XVII Lixus garrisoning Sicily, holding the naval base, and keeping the entire west of the Mediterranean Carthaginian. She won't move *them*. That was the situation toward the middle of August. She brought the second wave in shortly after Louis XI and Frederick III surrendered. One extra legion into middle Italy, so that Abbot Muthari could get his bum on the Empty Chair—the XVI Elissa."

"Them? Hard-core nutters, boss," Giovanni Petro offered. "I met them before, in Alexandria."

Ash nodded acknowledgment. "Two more legions into north Italy, around Venice, and Pescara, watching the Turk and the Turkish fleet. Another two to reinforce Basle and Innsbruck: that's the Cantons nailed down, I guess. And two more to keep order in the Holy Roman Empire—one's stationed in Auchen, with Daniel de Quesada, but the other's been given orders to march to Vienna: it should be there by now. And then three more legions were sent in to reinforce the Faris."

"Shit. *Three?*" Robert Anselm queried.

Ash scrabbled among the papers, settled at last for Rickard reading one of the lists to her, *sotto voce*. "—the V Alalia, IX Himera, and XXIII Rusucurru. She ordered them to divert around Dijon, fight their way up through Lorraine, and take Flanders. They're up in the Antwerp-Ghent area; *those* are the ones we hope Margaret of Burgundy's army is knocking seven kinds of shite out of."

Antonio Angelotti kissed his St. Barbara medal. "God send us such grace. I wonder how many cannon they have?"

"Rickard's got an artillery list here somewhere. . . ." Ash straightened up from the map. "Their *overall* losses in the first wave of the invasion amount to almost seven legions. Out of thirty, in total. That's under twenty-five percent, that is," she echoed the *machina rei militaris*'s even tone, "acceptable. It's getting her people killed trying to break Dijon in a hurry that's her problem."

"Look at this." Angelotti, scanning the papers as quickly as Father Faversham or Father Paston, put his finger down blindly on the map, then moved it to Carthage. "Gelimer's got two more legions in Carthage, but he won't plan to move them with the Turkish fleet still untouched, even if they do hold Sicily and the western Med."

Ash moved aside as Robert Anselm leaned in over the table, unself-consciously scratched red fleabites, and then traced with his blunt, dirt-ingrained finger the coast of North Africa.

"Egypt. *That's* the spike up Gelimer's ass," he grunted. "Look at that! He's got three whole legions in Egypt—fresh—and he can't move them. Not if he don't want the Turks across the Sinai faster than you can say *Great Mother*! But he fucking needs them in Europe, because if this is right, he's spread *way* thin. . . . He can't even reinforce southern France."

Angelotti remarked, "Don't get excited. Right now, the Faris thinks she can keep three legions fighting up in Flanders. She can always move those men south to here. Throw three legions against this city, and it'll fall over pretty quick."

"Maybe. She'd have to stop using the French and Saxon ports to feed them. Try resupplying with riverboats."

"Depends if the Rhine or the Danube's frozen."

"That's another reason they can't let go of Egypt; with Iberia going under the Dark, they need to get corn from *somewhere*—"

Ash, grimly interrupting, said, "There isn't a peep out of King Louis—or his nobles, which is far more remarkable. And even the Electors are holding to the Emperor's surrender in the Germanies. I think it's what happened at Venice, and Florence, and Milan—and to the Swiss. They don't dare move—and they don't know the Visigoths are running at full stretch and then some."

A glance went between Anselm, Angelotti, and Rochester.

Geraint ab Morgan threw down the piece of paper he had been attempting to decipher, with a look of disgust at Richard Faversham. "Too many fucking clerks in this!—no offense, Father. Boss, how do you know that what your demon-voice says about all this is true? How do we know they ain't got a few more legions tucked away?"

Other faces turned to hers, at that—Geraint's old sergeants, now Ludmilla's: Savaric and Folquet, Biciris, Guillelma, and Alienor. John Price, John Burren. Henry Wrattan broke off a low-voiced conversation with Giovanni Petro.

"It isn't a demon-voice," Ash said, "it's Father Godfrey now."

She has a moment of doubt: must she explain it all, examine rumors that have spread through the company in the last forty-eight hours, go back in her mind to the shattering collapse of Carthage? Two or three men cross themselves; most of the others touch Briar Crosses, or saint's medals, to their lips.

"Yeah, well," Jan-Jacob Clovet grinned, showing yellow-and-black teeth. "Father Godfrey always did manage a shit-hot intelligence service. Don't suppose that's changed since he's dead."

There was a subdued chuckle in the room: Henri van Veen muttering something to Tyrrell, who punched his arm and cheerfully said, "Motherfucker!" John Price and Jean the Breton palmed and drank from a stoppered wineskin with practiced ease.

Thomas Rochester held up a fistful of illustrative paper. "Are we giving this information to the Burgundians, boss?"

"I'm getting Digorie to make a copy for the Sieur de la Marche. We haven't broken a *condotta*[57] yet. . . ."

She waits, gaze flicking across lined, filthy faces, to see if anyone will say *Always a first time.*

"We've held that fucking north wall!" Campin muttered again. "I'm losing too many of my people to Greek Fire, boss. Mind you, so are the nancy-boy Burgundians. . . ."

"I know you reckon we can't get out of here with you, boss, but how would we manage, if we were still heading for England, then?" Euen Huw bent down over the table, his expression hidden as he studied the sketched map. "They ain't going to take those northern legions across the Channel while Duchess Margaret's still fighting. Say we didn't go north or east, suppose we went back west, and then into Louis's lands? Calais, maybe?"

"Under the Dark? When we still need to eat?" Ash put her finger on the map. "Even if we tried . . . initially, back in July, the Faris landed three legions here, at St. Nazaire; they've moved up the Loire valley. The II Oea and the XVIII Rusicade are occupying Paris. We're not going to make Calais if they want to stop us. . . . As for the far west, the Legio IV Girba are sitting *here*, at Bayonne—either to be shipped up the west coast of the French king's territories, or to be moved back into Iberia if the unrest there gets worse—they didn't expect the Dark to cover half of Iberia, it's playing merry hell with their logistics. That's one she *could* bring west."

"Has she?"

"Jeez, Euen, how the fuck do *I* know! She reports back to Carthage every fucking day!" Ash took a breath. "Godfrey's been taking me through her sit. reps. for the past

---

[57] The *condotta* or contract from which the *condottiere*, or mercenaries, take their name.

three weeks. I don't think she's recalled the IV Girba to here."

She paused, shifting her body in her Milanese armor, still less than comfortable, retraining muscles and balance at a level below the conscious. Because it is only a few hours to morning.

"It isn't likely," Ash said, at last. "Not with those huge logistics problems. But . . . if she was stupid enough to send an order—and didn't report it through to Carthage—we wouldn't know."

"So if we go west, we'll meet legions." Overt, now, Geraint ab Morgan shouldered in beside Euen Huw, and asked, "What if we went back down south, boss? To Marseilles? I know it was 'ell, but we might get a ship, get out of the Med, sail up the west coast of Iberia—"

"Good God, no, Geraint—if you think I'm going to spend five hundred miles watching you puke over the side of a ship—!"

A gust of laughter. Simon Tydder, shouldering his way in beside Rickard, gave a guffaw that ended in a squeak, which started the snorts and chuckles off again.

"If we ain't thinking of breaking out for England, boss, what's this truce about?"

Ash gave him a rather old-fashioned look. "Defeating the enemy might be a start!"

"But, *boss*—"

"They're not chucking rocks at us for fun, Tydder! We're signed on with Burgundy: that lot out there is the *enemy*. Look, these legions don't matter a toss. Except that the Faris is pretty damn safe sitting in the middle of them."

"Man, do we need backup!" Adriaen Campin sighed.

"Maybe *we* could go ask the Turks for help." Florian, who had been silently checking Ludmilla's burns, Angelotti's bandages, and the assorted minor wounds of the other knights and sergeants, plonked a filthy hand down on the table. "What's it like in the east?"

Anselm consulted the annotated map. "Thin, if Father Godfrey's right. She's trying to hold down the Germanies with a couple of legions."

"So maybe . . . ?"

"If we had some eggs, we could have some eggs and ham—if we had any ham."

Geraint ab Morgan snorted. "Never thought I'd say this, but England's looking better all the time. . . ."

Katherine Hammell, still moving stiffly from her wound at Carthage, looked across at Ludmilla Rostovnaya. "What about your lot, Lud? We could try the Rus lands. How would we do in St. Petersburg? Any good wars?"

The commander of archers scowled. "All the time. Too fucking cold for me. Why d'you think I'm here?"

"Cold everywhere, now."

"Yeah. Fucking raghead cunt. Why'd she have to bring her lousy weather with her?"

Ash let the discussion ramble, apparently studying the map, studying instead the maps of faces, chiaroscuro in the firelight.

"We're here for the moment," she said flatly, at last. "We'll keep the Burgundians up-to-date with this. For one thing, our contract obliges us to do it."

The Wild Machines can't think I'll keep quiet—can they?

"And for another—who's going to know that we told?" Ash grinned briefly at her men. "At best, it'll be just one of a whole set of confused rumors—*won't* it?"

"Oh yes, boss." Euen Huw looked pious. "You can rely on us."

Morgan grunted, "We got a rep for breaking contracts after Basle, does it matter now?"

"Yes."

His gaze slid away from hers. More importantly, she let her flat gaze take in the faces of the men near him—Campin, Raimon, Savaric—to see if he had any support.

"Fuck it, they think we're oath-breakers already," Morgan grumbled.

"I won't argue with you there. But we're not. We're professionals."

The Welshman said, "Screw the Burgundians! Who cares?"

"He's got a point, madonna," Angelotti said. She looked at him in surprise. He said, "Screw the Burgundians. Why is it *our* responsibility to kill the Faris?"

Not a flicker of her expression, or his, either thanked him for putting the question where it could be answered, or acknowledged that that had happened.

"We need a debrief on all this info," Ash said, as a page brought her a joint stool, and she took her place behind the trestle table. "We're going to go through this in detail, now. I want to know if anybody's fought against any of these legions before, what you know about them, what the commanders are like, anything. I want to know if anybody's got any suggestions, ideas. But first I'll give you the answer to your question."

Geraint ab Morgan pushed forward to the table's edge. "Which is?" he demanded.

Ash looked up at him calmly.

"Which is—Screw the Burgundians, all right—we might as well be behind these walls, trying to work out a way to kill my sister. Because where do you suggest we go, Geraint? When the Wild Machines kill the world, it won't help us to be in England, four hundred miles away from Dijon—not one little bit."

VI

THE TOING AND froing of interminable messages at last over, Ash discovered the long November night to be almost past: Lauds[58] sung three hours earlier by Dijon's striking town clock, and the office of Prime[59] about to begin. Sleeplessness gritted in her eyes.

Striding through Dijon's cold streets, she berated herself: Come on girl, think! I may not have long. Is there anything else?

Under her breath, she whispered: "Current position of Gothic forces' overall commander?"

In her head, the *machina rei militaris*, in Godfrey's voice, said—*Dijon siege camp, northwest quadrant, four hours past midnight; no further reports.*

Still, nothing drowned out that interior voice.

Why not? Is it the Faris—the Wild Machines don't want to scare her? Or is this something else?

De la Marche's clerk hurried at her side, between squat masonry houses with deep shadowed doorways, in the filth of the winding streets, as light faintly sifted down from the presunrise gray east. There were men and women, their children bundled at their sides, sleeping tucked against walls, and against ironbound oak doors. Horses and pack mules neighed, tethered outside stables turned over to refugees.

---

[58] 3 a.m.

[59] Sunrise: 6 a.m.

"We have everything," the clerk gasped. His stoppered ink bottle bounced at his belt; his woollen cloak was blackened with earlier attempts to stop and write. His face was white with lack of sleep. "Captain—I shall report to the Duke's deputy—their forces' positions—"

"Tell him I don't expect to be able to do this again. Not now they know their communications are compromised."

A church bell rang a few streets away. All of them—Ash, the clerk, her escort—simultaneously halted and listened. Ash gave a sigh of relief. The normal call to mass: no slow, funereal bells.

"God preserve the Duke," the clerk murmured.

"Report back to de la Marche," Ash ordered. She started off again, boot soles slipping on the frozen filth underfoot. The leaning buildings closed out all but the slightest dawnlight. Thomas Rochester thrust to the front of his lance with a pitch torch. Serfs and villeins come into the city for refuge half woke, moved out of the way; one or two recognized the banner, and Ash heard a "hero of Carthage!" float across the cold air.

Rochester said, "You sure this is a good idea, boss?"

"Piece of piss," Ash said, between the grunts that trotting through Dijon's streets in unaccustomed full armor forced out of her. "The Duke's on his last legs, we're going into the enemy camp under a supposed truce, and they have every reason I can think of to kill us out of hand—yeah, sure, Thomas: this is a brilliant idea!"

"Oh. Good. Glad you said that, boss. Otherwise, I might have started to worry."

"Just worry enough to stay alert," Ash said sardonically. "And ask yourself if they'd rather have the 'hero of Carthage' and the Faris's bastard sister alive or dead?"

The dark Englishman, at the head of the escort, gave her a completely careless grin. "You can hear what she says privately to her War-Machine? My money's on them using crossbows the second we're in range! *I* wouldn't take chances, boss. Why assume they're stupider than I am?"

"That would be almost impossible."

Thomas Rochester and the men behind him guffawed.

"She won't kill me. Yet." *I hope. Not when I'm the only other person who hears the Wild Machines.*

Of course, she may not give that the importance that I do.

Rochester was aware, she saw, of the likelihood of his own death, and no more bothered about it than he would have been before the field of battle. She thought, *It is the hardest thing in the world, to give orders that will mean other people may die.*

"The Faris wants to talk to me," Ash said. "So look on the bright side. They maybe won't kill us until she has."

"That's all right, boss," one of Rochester's sergeants said: a fair-haired English man-at-arms carrying her personal banner. "You can talk the hind leg off a donkey . . . !"

Her armor, tied, strapped, and buckled about her, gave the usual feelings of invulnerability. She began to move with it as if it had never been gone. She had tied down her scabbard to her leg, with a leather thong, so that she could draw her sword single-handed if necessary: one of Rochester's lance carried her ax.

A thread of coldness tickled in her gut.

"Nice kit." She rapped the knuckles of her gauntlets against the sergeant's cuirass. All twenty of Rochester's men had armored up, borrowing what fitted from other men.

"Showing the ragheads what we got," the sergeant grunted.

Walking between them, surrounded by men mostly taller, and all in armor, Ash felt a fallacious sense of complete security. She smiled to herself and shook her head. "All this metalware, and what happens? Some little oik shoves a pointy stick up your backside. Never mind, lads. All wearing our mail braies,[60] are we?"

"Don't plan to turn our backs on them!" Rochester snorted.

The atmosphere of expectancy was electric: an exhilaration born out of the certainty of risk. Ash found herself striding energetically forward across the narrow square leading to the northern sally gate. Black rats, and one stray dog, scuttled away into the dimness at the clatter of armor.

"Godfrey, *has* she spoken to the Stone Golem again?"

This time the voice of Godfrey Maximillian sounded quietly inside her head. *—Once, only. She ignores Carthage: their words to the* machina rei militaris *grow frantic. She has asked only if* you *speak to it . . . where you are, what your men are doing, if there is to be an attack.*

"What does it—do you—tell her?"

—Nothing but what I must, what I can know, from the words you speak to me. That you are on your way to her. For the rest, I know nothing of it; you have not told the machina *your forces, nor asked for tactics.*

"Yeah, and I'm keeping it that way."

She spoke quietly, aware that the men closest around her would be hearing what she said over the clatter of armor and scabbards.

"The Wild Machines?"

—They are silent. Perhaps their will is to let her think they are a dream, an error, a story.

Ash's personal banner hung from its striped staff, a chill breeze not enough to stir the blue-and-gold cloth. The Burgundian troops at the sally port recognized it, coming forward with their own torches.

"Madonna." Antonio Angelotti walked out of the gloom

---

[60] Underwear. A cloth-lined mail covering for this vital area.

by the wall, noise announcing a cluster of grooms and beasts behind him in the dimness. "I've arranged horses."

Ash surveyed the riding horses—most ill conditioned from the long siege and with their ribs visible to count. "Well done, Angeli."

While Rochester confirmed passwords and signals, she remained silent, hands cupping the points of elbow couters, her eyes fixed on the eastern sky. Gray clouds lightened above the pitched roofs, and the merlons of the city wall above. One of the nearer buildings—a Guild-house—still smoked, blackened, and burned-out, from the alarm that had turned out most of the Burgundians in this quarter to fight the fire. The weather had warmed from frost to bitter-cold rain, in the night; it began to freeze again.

"Thank Christ for bad weather!"

Angelotti nodded. "If this were summer, we would be burned-out, and have pestilence besides."

"Godfrey, is there any later report of where she is?"

—She has not told me where she is since Lauds.

"This is a dumb thing to do, isn't it?"

—If this were merely a war, child, you would not do it. In eight years I have known you be reckless, bold, and adventurous; but I have not known you waste lives.

Another one of Rochester's men-at-arms glanced sideways at her, and she gave him a reassuring grin. "Boss talking to her voices. That's all."

The young man-at-arms had a white face under his visor, but he gave her a sharp, efficient nod. "Yes, boss. Boss, what have they got for us out there? What should we watch out for?"

Fuck only knows! About ten thousand Visigoths, I should think. . . .

"Those recurved bows. They don't look like much, but

they're as fast as a longbow, even if they don't have the penetrating power. So. Bevors up, visors down."

"Yes, boss!"

"Now they feel safer," Angelotti observed in an undertone. "It isn't weapons, madonna. It's sheer numbers."

"I know."

The thread of disquiet in her belly turned into a distinct twinge.

"That's the problem with armor," she said musingly. "Strapped in. You can't take a shit in a hurry when you need to."

—*Ah. Dysentery: the warrior's excuse.*

"*God*frey!" Ash spluttered, amused and appalled.

—*Child, are you forgetting? I've followed you around military camps for eight years. I minister to the baggage train. I know who does the laundry, after a battle. You can't hide anything from the washerwomen. Courage is brown.*

"For a priest, Godfrey, you're a deeply disgusting man!"

—*If I were a man still, I would be at your side.*

It jolted her, not out of the warm feeling of comradeship, but into a keener grief for him. She said, "I *will* come for you. First: this." She raised her voice. "Okay, let's do it!"

As the units of armed men passed into the tunnel-like gate below one of Dijon's watchtowers, Thomas Rochester's sergeant bent down and muttered in her ear, over the noise. "What does he say?"

"What does who say?"

The Englishman looked uncomfortable. "Him. Your voice. Saint Godfrey. Do we have God's grace in this?"

"Yes," Ash replied, automatically and with complete conviction, while her mind murmured *Saint Godfrey!* in something between appalled amusement and awe. *I suppose it was inevitable . . .*

"Troop movements, Visigoth camp, central north section?"

—No movement reported.

And that means fuck-all, Ash thought grimly, hearing her boots echo off the raw masonry walls of the sally port, hearing, in her soul, an incursion of ancient, inhuman muttering. *Right now,* she's *not talking to the Stone Golem either.*

The Lion grooms brought the horses forward; Ash's new mount a pale gelding some yellow-tinged color between chestnut and bay, points barely dark enough to be distinguished; Orgueil returned to Anselm. She mounted up. Angelotti reined his own scrawny white-socked chestnut in beside her, still favoring his wounded arm. Ash glimped the bulk of linen bandages under the straps of his vambrace and his arming doublet.

Ahead, Burgundian soldiers yanked iron bars down from the gates as quickly as possible, passing her and her men through and out with indecent haste. The gates slammed behind them. She looked up, as they came into the open air, but her helmet and bevor prevented her turning her head enough to see the top of the wall, and the Burgundian archers and hackbutters she hoped would be up there.

The high saddle kept her extremely upright, legs extended almost straight. She shifted her weight, moving forward in the gray light, anxious to traverse the uncertain sloping ground before the walls. One of the men-at-arms on foot beside her grunted and efficiently kicked a caltrop out of the way.

A quick glance to the east showed her Dijon's city walls emerging from white mist, and, at their foot, a moat three-quarters choked with faggots of wood thrown down by assaulting troops. Beyond the churned earth, trenches and ranks of mantlets covered the ground between her and the Visigoth main camp.

"Okay: move out."

Once out of the gateway, Rochester's sergeant raised Ash's personal banner.

"*Ash!*"

The shout came from the walls above: a deep roar of voices, that broke into "Hero of Carthage!" and "Demoiselle-Captain!," and ended in a ragged cheer, extremely loud in the early morning. She wheeled the gelding, leaning back in the saddle to look up.

Men chanted: "Scar-face! Scar-face!"

The battlements were lined with men. Every embrasure thick with them; men climbing onto merlons; adolescent youths hanging from the wooden brattices. She lifted her hand, the gauntlet dull with freezing cold dew. The cheerful noise went up again—raucous, bold, and disrespectful—the same noise that men make before, unwillingly trusting, they commit themselves to the line-fight.

"Kick the bitch's ass!" a woman's contralto voice yelled.

"There you are, madonna," Antonio Angelotti, at Ash's side, said. "We have a doctor's advice!"

Ash waved up at Floria del Guiz, tiny face almost invisible on the high walls. There was a cluster of Lion livery jackets with her; they made up a sizable proportion of the crowd.

"You can't keep anything a secret overnight." Ash turned the gelding. "Just as well, really. We may need someone to haul our asses out of this fire."

Ahead, east of the river, lateral banks of white mist clung to the Visigoth barrack-tents and turf huts. Droplets of water illuminated the guy ropes, and the tethers of the horse-lines, in the weak rising sun. A freezing wind flapped one tent, its canvas side bellying out.

A long, black line of Visigoth men-at-arms stood along the palisade. A thin shout went up, in the distance.

There's bold, and there's stupid, Ash reflected. *This is stupid. There's no way we're going to be allowed back out of there.*

She tapped one long rowel spur back, just touching the gelding's flank. It plodded forward. Not a fighting horse.

No, Ash thought, squinting against the first rays of the sun. *Not stupid. What did I say to Roberto? Don't lose sight of the mission objective. I'm not here to fight the Visigoth army.*

Faintly, in her shared soul, the clamor of the Wild Machines begins to grow again. Nothing intelligible to a human mind.

Does she hear it too?

I'm not even here to get out of their camp alive, if there's a chance to take out the Faris.

What do I know about sisters, anyway?

"Doesn't look good, boss," Thomas Rochester said quietly.

"You have my orders. If we're attacked, and the Faris is there, kill her. We can worry about getting us out *after* she's down. If we're attacked, and the Faris isn't present, we bang out. Make for the northwest gate, behind us. Sound the retreat loud and clear, and pray for some Burgundian help. Got it?"

She spared a glance for the Englishman, his stubbled face visible between visor and bevor, his expression alert. Lines of strain showed he understood that they might be dead before the end of the morning. He was, nonetheless, unexpectedly cheerful.

"Got it, boss."

"But if it looks like sheer suicide for no result—we don't attack: we *wait*."

Antonio Angelotti turned in his saddle, pointing into the early-morning mist. "Here they come."

The long clarion call of a truce rang out. White standards went up, five hundred yards away.

"Let's go," Ash said.

Rochester and the escort formed up and moved forward.

Ash became aware of the way they closed around her, horse and foot, not protectively, but prideful, as if to show their own efficiency as guards. Men who would let no fear show.

She rocked gently to the pace of the gelding, riding on, in among the tents, staring down from the saddle at Visigoth soldiers. Not a barefoot woman, now, prisoned in Carthage; nor a lone woman walking through their camp; but a captain who is surrounded by well-armed men, who has—for good or ill—the responsibility of ordering them to fight and live or die.

The Faris, illuminated by the lemon yellow low light of dawn, stepped out onto the beaten earth. She wore armor but no helm. From fifty yards, there is no reading her expression.

I could kill her now. If I could get to her.

Companies of the XIV Utica lined the way through the camp; men in mail and white robes, dank in the dawn, the light flashing from the leaf-shaped points of their spears. Somewhere between two and two and a half thousand men, she guessed. All eyes on her and her men.

"God damn you," Ash said quietly. "*Fuck Carthage!*"

A voice in her head, that was both the *machina rei militaris* and Godfrey Maximillian, said, —'*Before you take vengeance, go and dig your own grave.*'

A smile moved her lips. It did not reach the taut, controlled fury that she would not let show. "Yes . . . I was never sure how you used to mean that one."

—It means no vengeance is worth such anger, such hatred. You may lose your own life in the attempt.

She feels the rocking of her hips, as she rides, lays one hand on the fauld of her armor, over her belly. A chill, controlled shudder goes through her. A memory of the smell of blood, in a cold cell like this same cold morning, passes through her mind. She is suddenly aware of the razor-sharp edge of her sword in its scabbard, of the balanced weight of metal at her thigh.

"I'll give you another version of your proverb," she murmured. "It means, the only way that you can be sure to achieve vengeance is to count yourself already dead. Because there's no defense against an attacker who isn't afraid of dying. 'Before you take vengeance, go and dig your own grave.' "

—Be very sure that you are right, child.

"Oh, I'm *sure* of nothing. That's why I have to talk to this woman."

Angelotti, quietly, said, "Have you forgiven them the Lord Fernando's child? Carracci, Dickon; those who died in House Leofric, that's war—but have you forgiven them your child?"

"It didn't have a soul. Isobel used to lose two out of every three, when I was living with her on the wagons. Every year, regular as a clock." Ash squinted into the light, growing as the mist lifted. "I wonder if Fernando's dead as well?"

"Who is to know?"

"What I *won't* forgive her is, she should have thought this through years ago. She's known for years that she's hearing a machine. Sweet Green Christ! She's just followed it blindly, she's never thought, why *this* war?"

Angelotti smiled with enigmatic calm. "Madonna, when you untied me from a gun carriage outside Milano and told me, 'Join my company because I hear the Lion telling me to win battles,' I might have said much the same thing. Did you ever ask the Lion, why any particular war?"

"I never asked the Lion which battles I should fight," Ash growled. "I just asked Him how to win them once we were on the field. Getting me the job in the first place isn't His business!"

Angelotti's pale throat showed, under his helm, where he had left off his bevor, and now threw his head back and laughed. Several of the Visigoths they passed stared curiously. Rochester's escort had the expressions of men thinking *he's a gunner.*

"Madonna Ash, you are the best woman of any in the world!" Angelotti sobered; his eyes still bright with affection. "And the most dangerous. Thank God you are our commander. I shudder to think how it would have been, otherwise."

"Well, you'd still be ass-upwards on a gun carriage, for one thing, and the world would have been spared one more mad gun captain. . . ."

"I will see who I may speak with among the Visigoth gunners, during this truce. Meantime, madonna—" Angelotti's gold curls, clamped down by his sallet, were dulled by the dank morning. He lifted his steel-covered arm, pointing: "There, madonna. See. That is where she expects you."

In a rattle of scabbards on armor, they rode forward. Ash saw the Visigoth woman turn away from her commanders and walk out to a little awning, set up in a space in the middle of the camp. A table, two ornate chairs, and a plain canvas awning: set in the middle of thirty yards of bare earth. No room for anything to be concealed, and anything done there would be public.

Public, but not overheard, she reflected, judging the distance to the surrounding Visigoth *qa'ids*, *'arifs*, *nazirs*, and troops.

The *'arif* Alderic, as she expected, stepped forward from among the units of soldiers.

"Please you to join the Captain-General," he said, formally.

Ash dismounted, slinging her reins to Rochester's page. She kept one hand automatically on the hilt of her sword, palm flat against the cold metal of the cross.

"I accept the truce," she replied, equally formally. Surveying thirty yards of unoccupied, trodden earth, with the table in the middle of it, she thought, *What a target for the archers*.

"Your weapons, *jund* Ash."

Regretfully, she unbuckled her sword belt, handing him sword, scabbard, and dagger together in a tangle of leather straps. With a nod of acknowledgment, she went forward.

Under the laminated plates of her backplate, under the pinked silk arming doublet, sweat dampened the skin between her shoulder blades as she walked out across the open space.

The Faris, seated at the small table under the awning, stood up as Ash came within ten yards of her, holding her hands out from her sides. Her hands were bare, and empty. The white robes over her coat of plates and mail hauberk might easily conceal a dagger. Ash contented herself with leaving her bevor up and tilting her sallet for a clearer view of the Visigoth woman, leaving steel plate and riveted mail to cope with any theoretical stiletto.

"I would have had wine set out for us," the Faris said, as soon as Ash came within speaking distance, "but I thought you would not drink it."

"Damn right." Ash stopped for a moment, resting her

gauntleted palms on the back of the carved white-oaken chair. Through the linen, she felt the shapes of the ornamental carved pomegranates. She looked down at the Faris, seating herself again on the opposite chair. The remarkable face—familiar to her only from scratched, polished-metal mirrors, and the dark, glassy pools of river backwaters—still shocked her: a churning sensation somewhere in her gut.

"But in that case," Ash added, "we get to sit here and freeze our asses off, and be thirsty."

She managed a pragmatic, confident grin, walking round and hitching up back tasset plate and fauld to sit down on the ornate chair. The seated Visigoth woman signaled without looking behind her. After a few seconds, a child-slave approached with a wine jug.

The bitter wind that now shifted the morning mist blew filaments of silver hair across the Faris's face. Her cheeks were white, the flesh drawn; and faint purple shadows lay under her eyes.

Hunger? Ash thought. *No. More than that.*

"You were in the forefront of the defense of the walls, yesterday," the Faris said abruptly. "My men tell me."

Ash sprang the bevor pin, pushing the laminated plate down, and reached for the silver wine goblet offered by the slave. The wine smelled, to her chilled nose, merely like wine. She clamped her mouth over the edge of the goblet, tilted it, from long practice appearing to drink deeply, put it down, and wiped the wine from her lips with the gauntleted heel of her hand. No liquid entered her mouth.

"You won't take this place by assault." She looked from the flat area, toward Dijon. From the ground, the gray-and-white walls and towers appeared satisfactorily solid and appallingly tall. She noted the interview was being conducted well away from the remaining saps, creeping ever closer under the earth. "Hell. It really does look nasty from out here. Glad I'm not on the outside! Golem siege towers or not . . ."

The Faris, ignoring her, persisted: "You were fighting!"

The Visigoth woman's tone told her much. Ash kept her expression calm, friendly, and confident, and listened to the note of extreme strain.

"Of course I was fighting."

"But you were silent! You asked the Stone Golem nothing! I know you asked for nothing, no tactics; I asked it!"

The lemon yellow of the rising sun paled to white. With the mist dispersed, Ash risked a quick glance around the nearer part of the Visigoth camp. Deep mud ruts, some tents ragged; fewer horses than she had expected. Behind the troops drawn up in ranks—obviously the best, for show purposes—she could see many men sprawled on the freezing-wet earth in front of some of the turf huts. At this distance, hard to see if they were wounded or whole, but possibly whole, and just short of tents in winter. Faces in the ranks showed hunger, were thin—but not yet gaunt. A whole cluster of stone self-moving siege machines appeared to be parked toward the Suzon bridge, either in waiting, or broken-down.

The Faris burst out: "How can you risk fighting, without the voice of the machine!"

"Oh, I get it." The armor would not let her lean back, but Ash carefully spread her arms onto the arms of the chair, giving the impression of relaxed expansiveness. "Let me tell you something, Faris."

While her gaze avidly totted up the number of spears and bows, the numbers of barrel-laden wagons in the background, Ash said aloud, "I could already fight when I was five. They had us in training, the kids on the wagons. I could already kill a man with a stone from a sling. By the time I was ten, I could use a half pike. The women on the baggage train weren't there for ornament. Big Isobel taught me how to use a light crossbow."

Ash flicked her gaze back to the Visigoth woman. The Faris stared, opening her mouth to interrupt.

"No. You asked me a question. This is the answer. I killed two men when I was eight. They'd raped me. I was in sword-training with the other pages by the time I was nine, with somebody's broken, reground blade. I wasn't strong enough, the camp *dog* could have bowled me over—but it was still training, you understand?"

Silent, her dark eyes fixed on Ash, the Visigoth woman nodded.

"They kept knocking me down, and I kept getting up. I was ten or eleven, and a woman, before the Lion ever spoke to me. The Stone Golem," Ash corrected herself. A dry wind blew across the camp. Prickles of cold touched the small amount of skin she had exposed: snow crystals stinging her scarred cheeks. "In the year or so before I could get back to our company, I made my mind up that I would never come to rely on anything—not a saint, not Our Lord, not the Lion: nothing and nobody. So I taught myself to fight with and without my voices."

The Faris stared at her. "Father told me it came to you with your first woman's blood. With me—I have never *not* heard it. All my games as a child, with Father, were playing how to speak with the *machina rei militaris*. I could not have fought in Iberia without it."

Both her face and her voice remained calm. Ash saw that on her lap, almost concealed by the edge of the table, the Faris's bare hands were clenched into white-knuckled fists.

"We have a conversation to finish. When I came into your camp, two nights ago, you asked me about my priest,"

Ash said harshly. "Godfrey Maximillian. You were hearing him then, weren't you? He speaks to you as the machine."

"No! There is only one voice, the Stone Golem—"

"*No*."

Ash's impatient contradiction cracked out, loud enough to be heard across the open square of earth. One of the Visigoth *qa'ids* moved forward. The Faris signaled him back, without taking her eyes off Ash's face.

"God damn it, woman," Ash said softly. "You know the other voices are real. Otherwise, you wouldn't have stopped talking to the Stone Golem. You're afraid they're listening to you! It's *their* voices you've been following, for the last twenty years. You can't ignore this."

The Visigoth woman unclenched her hands, rubbing them together. She reached for her goblet and drank.

"I can," she said briefly. "I could. Not now. Every time I fall asleep, I have nightmares. They speak to me on the borders of sleep—the Stone Golem, the Wild Machines—your Father Godfrey, he speaks to me, in the place where the *machina* should be. And how can *that* be?"

Ash moved her shoulders, restrained by cuirass and pauldrons from a shrug. "He's a priest. When he died, the machine was speaking through me. I can only suppose God's grace saved him by a miracle and put his soul into the machine. Maybe not God—maybe the Devil. The hours don't pass the same for him. It's more like Hell than it is like Heaven!"

"It's strange. To hear a man speak, here." The Faris touched her bare temple. "Another reason for doubt. How can I be sure anything the *machina rei militaris* tells me is trustworthy now, if it carries the soul of a man—and an enemy?"

"Godfrey wasn't anyone's enemy. He died trying to rescue a physician who'd been treating your King-Caliph."

Somewhat to Ash's surprise, the Visigoth woman nodded. "Messire Valzacchi. He is one of the men treating Father, under Cousin Sisnandus's care."

The morning sun made Ash squint. A growing bitter cold froze the dank morning. The wind blew a flurry of white snow powder across the earth, from the thin clouds massing in the north. Momentarily diverted, she said, "What *did* happen to Leofric?"

She was not expecting an answer. The Faris, leaning forward, said earnestly, "He returned from the Citadel in time to take refuge in the room of the *machina rei militaris*."

"Ah. So he was down there while we were trying to blow the place."

As if Ash's mild, sardonic amusement didn't exist, the Visigoth woman went on:

"He was there when the Stone Golem . . . spoke. When it repeated what the—other voices—said." Her gaze flicked away from Ash's face, but not before Ash filled in the missing phrase: "what the other voices said *to you*."

"I am not a fool," the Faris said abruptly. "If Cousin Sisnandus believed that what my father heard was more than a product of his mental breakdown, he still would not tell the King-Caliph and rob House Leofric of what political influence we have left. I know that. But I know that Father *is* ill. They found him the next day, among the pyramids, under God's Fire, surrounded by dead slaves. His clothes were torn. He had scratched away part of the side of a tomb, with nothing but his hands."

The thought of those hands, that have examined her body with steel instruments, being torn and bleeding; of the man's mind shattered—Ash kept herself from showing her teeth. *How sad.*

"Faris, if you've heard Godfrey," she persisted, pressing her point, "then you've heard the Wild Machines."

"Yes." The Visigoth woman looked away. "Finally, this past night, I could do nothing else but listen. I have heard."

Ash followed her gaze. Hundreds of surrounding faces stared back at the two of them: at the fate of Dijon being negotiated under truce, in the mud of a camp with winter coming on.

"They follow you, Faris."

"Yes."

"Many of them men from your Iberian campaigns? And from fighting the Turk, over by Alexandria?"

"Yes."

"Well, you're right," Ash said, and when the woman looked back at her, went on: "Your own men *are* in danger. The Wild Machines don't care how they win this war. For one thing, they're telling you to assault the city, take it in a hurry, kill the Duke by sheer force of numbers; and that's bad tactics, you could lose half an army of men here for nothing. That's lives wasted, lives of men you know."

"And secondly?" the Faris said sharply.

"And, secondly—'We have bred the Faris to make a dark miracle, as Gundobad made one. We shall use her, our general, our Faris, our miracle-maker—to make Burgundy as if it has never been.' "

Ash, speaking the words seared into her memory, watched the woman's face start to seem gray, sunk-in, desperate.

"Yes," the Faris said. "Yes, I have heard those words. They say it is they who made the long darkness over Carthage. They *say*."

"They want the Duke dead and Burgundy gone so that they can make a miracle that makes the world into a desolation. Faris, will the Wild Machines care if the Visigoth army is still inside the borders of Burgundy when that happens? When there's nothing but ice, darkness, and decay—

the same way it's starting to be around Carthage. And do you think anyone's going to survive it?"

The Faris leaned back in her chair, her coat of plates creaking slightly. Aware of every movement—any signal that might be an attack, a hand that might be going for a stiletto—Ash found herself mirroring the Visigoth woman, sitting back and away from her.

Another flurry of snow particles dust-deviled across the earth, beyond the guy ropes and tent pegs of the awning.

"Winter," the Faris said, and looked straight at Ash. " 'Winter will not cover all the world.' "

"You heard that, too." A tension that she had not been conscious of relaxed.

It's me telling Roberto and Angeli and Florian these things, it's me staking the company, and Dijon, and a whole lot of lives on being right—and whether it's true, or a lie, at least someone else has heard it.

"*If* this is true," the Faris said, "where do you suggest I take my men—or you take your men, if it comes to that—to be safe? If they want the whole world made into a desert, burned, sown with salt. . . . Tell me, Frankish woman, where we may go to be *safe*?"

Ash hit the wooden table with her gauntleted fist. "*You're* Gundobad's descendant! *I* can't even miraculously light a bloody altar candle! You're the one that's going to make this miracle for them!"

The Faris's gaze slid away. Almost inaudibly, she said, "I do not know this to be true."

"Don't you? Fucking don't you? Well, I'll tell you what's true. When I was outside Carthage, the bloody machines just turned me round and walked me toward them, and there wasn't a Christ-damned thing I could do about it! I didn't have a *choice!* If Duke Charles dies, we're all going to find out if *you've* got a choice, but by then it's going to be far too late!"

"And so the answer is that you kill me."

It stopped Ash as if she had walked into a wall: the Visigoth woman's abrupt shifts from fear to concentration and back again. Now the Faris, without moving, added:

"I can think for myself. You reason thus: if am I dead, the Wild Machines can do nothing. If you make a move, there are twelve of my sharpshooters who will put bodkin-head arrows through your armor before you get out of that chair."

An arrow shaft as thick as a finger; an arrowhead four inches long, four-sided, sharp: able to punch through metal. Ash pushed the image out of her mind's eye.

"Of course there are archers," she said equably. "If nothing else, I overhear your communications with Carthage. You'd have shot me before now, except that Dijon will be even harder to take if you go around killing their current heroes. And you still think I might betray the city to you."

"You are my sister. I will not kill you unless it is necessary."

In the face of the woman's intent seriousness, Ash felt nothing but a sudden impulse of pity. *She's young. She still thinks you can do that.*

"I'll kill you without a second thought," Ash said. "If I have to."

"Oh yes." The woman's gaze wandered to the child-slave, standing a few paces off with the wine jug; a boy with thistledown white hair. Ash saw her glance around at other slave, at Ash herself.

The Faris said, "There is nothing they can make me do. Not a miracle, nothing. I will no longer speak to the *machina rei militaris*, I will not listen! Surely they can do nothing unless I speak with them, and I will not, I will not!"

"Maybe. It's a hell of a chance to take."

"What would you have me do?" Her keen expression sharpened. "Kill myself, because voices in my head tell me I'm going to do a hellish miracle? I'm like you, *jund* Ash, I'm a soldier. I've never done miracles! I pray, I go to mass, I sacrifice where it's proper, but I'm not a priest! I'm a *woman*. I'll wait until we kill this Burgundian Duke, and see if I—"

"It's too late then!" Ash's interruption silenced the Faris. "These are creatures who have the power to put out the sun. They did that. When they draw on the sun's spirit again, when they force it on you, the same way God's grace comes to a priest, do you think you can refuse it?"

The woman licked her lips. When she spoke, it was without the rising note of hysteria.

"But what would you have me do? Fall on my sword?"

Ash said instantly, "Persuade Lord-*Amir* Leofric to destroy the Stone Golem."

The Visigoth woman stared, completely silenced, while a man might have counted a hundred. The sound of a warhorse, neighing from the lines, broke the silence. The eagles of the Visigoth legions glinted in the sunlight.

I can't get to her and kill her before they kill me.

Maybe I won't have to.

"*Do* it," Ash urged. "Then they can't reach you. The Stone Golem is their only voice."

"My God." The Faris shook her head in amazement.

"They spoke once to your Prophet Gundobad, and once to Roger Bacon," Ash said steadily, "and then with the *machina rei militaris*, to us. It's their only voice. You've got an army here. Leofric's your 'father,' even if he's sick. You've got the authority. No one can stop you going back to Carthage and breaking the Stone Golem into rubble!"

The woman in Visigoth mail, with a quick apprehension

that Ash read as long, if unconscious, consideration of the subject, said, "Cut these 'Wild Machines' off—at the cost of my never taking the field again."

"It's you or the machine." A ghost of humor pulled Ash's mouth up at the corners. "So: you're right, finally—here I am with the general of the Visigoth army, asking her to destroy the tactical engine that makes her win wars."

"I wish, truly, that this was such a ruse of war." The Faris linked her fingers, rested her elbows on the table, and her lips against her joined hands.

There is no sound in Ash's mind of the Faris's voice speaking to the *machina rei militaris*, appealing to Leofric or Sisnandus. Nothing speaks.

After a moment's silence, the Faris lifted her head to say, "I could pray, now, for your Duke to stay alive."

"He's—" *not my Duke*, Ash had been about to protest. She cut herself short. "He's my current employer, so I'm supposed to want him to stay alive! Even if there wasn't so much at stake."

The Faris chuckled briefly. She reached out for the goblet and drank again, the wine staining her upper lip purple. "Why Burgundy's Duke?"

"I don't know. You don't know either?"

"No. I dare not ask." The Faris squinted at the sky, and the gathering yellow-gray cloud cover. "My father—Leofric will never destroy the Stone Golem. Even now. He gave his life to it, and to breeding us. And he is sick, and I cannot talk with Cousin Sisnandus unless I use the *machina rei militaris* to do it, and am . . . overheard. Or unless I travel back, over land and sea, to speak face-to-face."

"Then do that!"

"It—would not be so easy?"

Ash felt the lessening of tension, heard it in the Visigoth woman's questioning voice. They sat, either side of the table, staring at each other: a woman in Milanese harness, a woman in a bright cloth-covered coat of plates, scarred and unscarred faces suddenly still.

"Why not? *Extend the truce*." Ash tapped a finger on the table, the gauntlet's laminations sliding one over the other. "Your officers would rather hold siege and try to starve us out. They know they're going to lose a lot of men with constant assaults. Extend the truce!"

"And go south, to Carthage?"

"Why not?"

"I would be ordered back here. Ordered not to leave."

Ash heaved a great breath of air in, feeling a tension relax, feeling an excitement and expectation. "Shit, think about it! You're the Faris, no one here has the authority to argue with you. You'd get to Carthage. This siege is good for months."

The unexpected feeling, Ash realized, was hope.

"But, sister," the other woman said.

"Better go back to Carthage and have the Stone Golem destroyed, whether Leofric wants it to happen or not. Better that, than sit here knowing you're the one person that has to be killed to stop this." Ash jabbed her finger in the air. "This isn't about war anymore! It's about being wiped out. Hell, take the Visigoth army home and take out House Leofric if you have to!"

A smile curved the other woman's lips. "That, I think, these men would *not* do. Even for me. The Empire takes certain precautions against that. But . . . Father might listen to me. Ash, if I leave, and if I fail, then perhaps we are still safe. Perhaps, if I am not in Burgundy, then nothing can happen."

"We don't know that, either."

If you leave here, Ash thought suddenly, *there'll be no one with you who knows that you have to be killed. Shit: I should have realized that. But the chance, the chance that this could work and take out the Stone Golem—*

"They are great Devils," the Faris said soberly. "Princes and Thrones and Dominions of Hell, set loose in the world and given power over us."

"Will you extend the truce?"

The Faris looked up, as if her thoughts had been elsewhere. "For a day, at least. I must think, must carefully consider this."

To stop the assaults, the fucking bombardment, for a whole day; is it this easy?

Such a phenomenal concession made Ash dry-mouthed with the fear that it might be retracted. She made herself sit with the confident expression of a mercenary who is used to negotiating the rules of engagement in war, tried to keep the strain and the sudden hope off her face.

"But Duke Charles," the Faris said. "There have been rumors that he is sick? That he was wounded mortally, at Auxonne?"

Startled, Ash realized from the woman's expression that she asked the question in all seriousness. *She really thinks I'm going to tell her?*

"There'll be rumors that he's sick, wounded, and dead," Ash said caustically. "You know what soldiers are like."

"*Jund* Ash, I am asking you—how much time do we have?"

It was the first time that Ash truly heard the *we*.

"Faris . . . I can't tell you things about my employer."

"You said it yourself: this is not about war. Ash, *how much time?*"

I wish I could talk to Godfrey, Ash thought. *He'd know whether I should trust her. He could tell me. . . . But I can't ask him. Not now.*

She keeps the part of her that listens passive, silent,

absorbed, offering no chink for a voice to come through. The fear of the ancient voices gnaws at the back of her mind, like a rat.

No one can make this decision but me, on my own.

"You call me your sister," Ash said, "but we're not, we're nothing to each other, except by blood. I know nothing about whether I can trust your word. You're sitting out here with an army—and I have men who will die if I make a bad decision."

The Faris said steadily, "And I am Gundobad's child."

Now, as she sat back in her chair, the scarlet cloth covering riveted over the metal plates of her armor could be seen to be rubbed, worn, black with dirt under the cuffs. The Visigoth woman's long hair shone silver-gray with grease. Ingrained mud penciled fine lines in the skin at the corners of her eyes. She smelled of woodsmoke, of the camp; and Ash, feeling it hit home under her breastbone, leaving her without breath, was overcome with an utter familiar closeness nothing to do with blood kinship.

The woman added, "We neither of us can say for certain what that means, but will you risk waiting to find out? Ash, how much *time* do we have? Is the Duke well and whole?"

Ash remembers a dream of boar in the snow, Godfrey's whisper of *you are one of the beasts of the world with tusks*, and *it took me so long to gain your trust*.

The Faris got to her feet. Ash's own face looks back at her from between wind-strewn tendrils of white hair, hair that falls in ripples over the rose-head rivets of a coat of plates, down past the waist and the sword belt with its empty scabbards.

Ash shut her eyes briefly, to blot such a strong resemblance out of her mind.

"More than sisters," she said, opening her eyes to cold wind and the surrounding ranks of troops, and armed men moving and talking quietly while discussion goes on out of their earshot: strategy, tactics, decisions. "Never mind what we are by birth. *This*. We both do this. We both understand it. . . . Faris, don't take long to consider your decision. The Duke is dying as we speak."

The woman's gaze became fixed: no other change of expression gave away her shock.

Now we shall find out, Ash thought. *Now we shall find out how much she really believes of all this, how much she's actually heard the voices of the Wild Machines talking to her. How much this is just another war to her—and if I've given her Dijon. Because she can hit the city now it doesn't have a leader. And she may just get in.*

Ash watched the Faris's expression, and missed having her sword ready for use.

The young woman in Visigoth armor put her hands out. The gesture was made slowly, so that watching men might not mistake it. Bare hands held out to Ash, palm-upward.

"Don't be afraid," the Faris said.

Ash looked at the woman's hands. Dirt was ingrained in the lines of her palms. Small white scars, from old cuts, were visible through the dirt: a peasant's hands, or a smith's, or the hands of someone who trains for the line-fight.

"Ash, I will extend the truce," she said steadily. "A day: until dawn tomorrow. I swear this, here and now, before God. And God send we find an answer before then!"

Slowly, without a page, Ash undid the buckles on her right gauntlet with her gauntleted left hand and stripped the armor off. She reached out and gripped the Faris's bare hand in her own. She held warm, dry human flesh.

The cheer that went up from the walls of Dijon shook the snow out of the clouds.

"I don't have any authority to do this!" Ash grinned.

"But if I've got a truce, those motherfuckers on the council will ratify it! Can you hold your *qa'ids* to a truce?"

"My God, yes!"

As the noise died down, as the ranked, bored troops of the Visigoth army began to stir and talk among themselves, a shrill bell suddenly cut through the air. About to speak again to the Faris, Ash momentarily did not realize what she was hearing. Loud, hard, bitter, grieving—

A single bell rang out from the double spire of Dijon's great abbey, within the city walls. Heart in her mouth, Ash waited for the second spire bell to join in.

Only the single bell continued to toll.

Solemn, urgent, once every ten heartbeats.

Each harsh clash of metal shook the still camp outside the walls, all men gradually falling silent in the cold air as they heard it, and realized what they were hearing.

"The passing bell." The Faris turned her head back to Ash, staring at her. "You have the same custom here? A first bell for the beginning of the last few hours. The second bell for the moment of death?"

The repetitive single strokes of the bell went on.

"The Duke," Ash said. "Charles the Bold has begun to die."

The Faris's hand, still clasped in her own, tightened. "If it *is* true, if I have no choice, now -!"

Ash winced at the strength of her grip, grinding the small bones of Ash's hand together.

A complete calm came to her. As in the line of battle, when times seems to slow, she made her decision and began to move her body: clenching her left hand still in its reinforced metal gauntlet, choosing the unprotected throat of the Visigoth woman as her target, tensing arm muscles to punch the sharp edge of the knuckleplate straight through the carotid artery.

Will I make it before the arrows? Yes. Needs to be first blow; no second chance, I'll be skewered—

"The Burgundy Duke's standard!" a Visigoth *nazir* bellowed, his deep voice cracking shrill with shock.

As if she were in no danger, the Faris dropped Ash's hand and stepped forward, away from the table and awning. Ash thought *why am I doing nothing?* and, appalled, looked to where the *nazir* was pointing.

Her heart jolted.

The port in the northwest gate of Dijon stood open.

Opened while all were transfixed by the abbey bell, Ash guessed: portcullis hauled up, the great bars taken down—*Shit! can they close it before there's an assault—?*

The Faris's shouted orders dinned in her ears. No Visigoth soldier moved. Ash strained her gaze to see who it was riding out. She saw a man on horseback, carrying the great blue-and-red standard of the Valois Dukes, and nobody with him: no noble, no Duke miraculously raised from his deathbed, nobody. Only a man on foot, and a dog.

At the Faris's bemused order, the Visigoth troops parted to let the rider and footman through.

Ash began to put her right-hand gauntlet on, fumbling the buckles; glancing quickly toward Rochester and her escort, thirty yards away, pitifully outnumbered among the Visigoth legions.

The standard-bearer rode across the trodden earth. He reined in a few yards in front of the Faris. Ash did not recognize the man, from the small part of his face she could see under his raised visor, wondered *Olivier de la Marche*? and read from the livery that it was not, was no great Burgundian noble at all. Only a mounted archer.

While she and the Faris continued to stare, the man on foot walked forward. He pulled off his hat.

His leashed hound, a great square-muzzled dog with a

head that seemed too big for its body, gave Ash's leg a cursory sniff.

"It's a lymer,"[61] she said, startled into speech.

The man—white-haired, elderly, his cheeks red with the broken veins of a man who has been outdoors much of his life—smiled with a slow pleasure. "He is, Demoiselle-Captain Ash, and one of the best. He can find you any day a hart of ten, or a great-toothed boar, or even the unicorn, I swear it by Christ and all His saints."

A glance at the Faris showed Ash the Visigoth woman staring in total bewilderment.

"Demoiselle Captain-General Faris?" The man bowed. He spoke respectfully, and a little slowly. "I have come to ask you permission for the hunt to pass, undisturbed."

"The hunt?" The Faris turned an expression of complete bewilderment first to Ash, and then to the thirty or more of her *qa'ids* who now walked up to surround her. "The *hunt*?"

This is lunacy! Ash, openmouthed, could only stare. *If I give the order now and we go straight for the gate, will we make it?*

The elderly, bearded man lowered his gaze and mumbled something, abashed at seeing the commanders of all the Visigoth legions as well as their army commander. The lymer shook its head, drooping round ears flapping, and wagged a ratlike tail with urgent excitement.

The Faris's dark gaze flicked once to Ash as she said gently, "Grandfather, you are in no danger. We are taught to revere the old and wise. Tell me what message you bring from the Duke."

The red-cheeked man looked up. More loudly, he said, "No message, missy. Nor there won't be one, neither. Duke

[61] A variety of hunting dog.

Charles will be dead before noon, the priests say. I am sent to ask you, will you let the hunt pass?"

"What hunt?"

Yeah, you and me both! Ash thought, not about to interrupt the Visigoth woman. *What hunt!*

"It's custom," the man said. "The Dukes of Burgundy are chosen by the hunt, the hunting of the hart."

When the Faris merely stared at him, in complete silence, he said gently, "It's always been so, Demoiselle Captain-General. Now that Duke Charles is near death, the hart must be hunted to find his successor. The one who takes the quarry takes the Duke's title. I'm bidden to ask you free passage through your camp. If you give it, then me and Jombart here will go and quest for quarry."

The Faris held up her hands to quiet her officers. "*Qa'ids!*"

"But this is insanity—" A man whom Ash recognized, now, to be Sancho Lebrija, subsided at the Faris's look.

The Visigoth woman said, "Captain Ash, have you knowledge of this?"

Ash regarded the white-haired hunter. If the Visigoth commanders intimidated him, he was still standing with a serene confidence in his trade.

"I don't know a damn thing about it!" she confessed. "It's not even the season now for hunting the hart. That ended on the last feast of the Holy Cross."[62]

"Demoiselle, it must happen when it happens, when the old Duke dies."

"It is a trick, to remove their nobles from the besieged city!" Sancho Lebrija burst out.

"And go where?" the Faris challenged. "War has passed over this land. The castles and towns are sacked. Unless

---

[62] 14 September.

you think they will cut through our forces, march hundreds of miles to the north and famine, and to Flanders—and then there is nothing for them there but more war. *Qa'id* Lebrija, with their Duke dead, they will be leaderless; what can they do?"

The hunter interrupted an exchange that, in Carthaginian Gothic, it was doubtful he understood. "Demoiselle, there isn't much time. Will you let the hunt pass out, and then back into the city, unmolested?"

Ash's gaze went absently, and automatically, to the sky. In the southeast, the white sun hung above the horizon. Veils of cloud covered and uncovered it, and a thin powder of snow flurried in the air. The stench of woodsmoke was strong in her nostrils. She thought, *The weakness of the light may be nothing more than autumn.*

"Perhaps," Ash said urgently to the Faris, on the heels of the elderly man's words, "perhaps *one Duke is as good as another.*"

The *qa'ids* and *'arifs* surrounding the Faris glanced at Ash with minor irritation, as if what she said were a frivolous comment. Only the Faris, holding Ash's gaze, inclined her head a fraction of an inch.

"I give my authority to this," she said, and swung around at the outburst from her officers. "*Silence!*"

The Visigoth commanders quieted. Ash watched them exchanging glances. She became aware that she had, unconsciously, started to hold her breath.

The Faris said, "I will let them follow their custom. We are here to conquer this land. I will not have it again as it was in Iberia, a thousand little quarreling noblemen, and no one man able to give word to control them!"

Some of her officers nodded approvingly.

"If we are to impose an administration on a conquered country, it were better they had their Duke to obey, and we had him to obey us. Otherwise, there is nothing but chaos, mob rule, and a hundred tiny wars to tie us down here, when we should be fighting the Turk."

More nods, and comments in low voices.

It even sounds convincing to me! Ash reflected, in grim, amazed humor. *And it's at least half-true. . . . Obviously I'm not the only good bullshitter in this family.*

"Tell your masters, I will let the hunt pass," the Faris said to the hunter. "Upon one condition. A company of my men will ride behind you, to see that you and your new Duke *do* return to the city."

She raised her voice so that the group of officers could all hear:

"While you hunt, this day let God's truce operate in this camp, and in Dijon, as if it were a holy day, with no man raising his hand to another. All fighting shall cease. Captain Ash, will you answer for that?"

Ash, her expression completely controlled, let herself look briefly at the serf-army, the low-ranking officers. *They don't like this. I wonder how long before they'll do something about it—mutiny? Hours? Minutes*?

The Faris may have lost it, right here.

Better do something while she still has command.

The single bell rang out across the wet, cold air.

If one Duke isn't as good as another, Ash thought grimly, *we shall soon know.*

"Yes," Ash said aloud. "If Olivier de la Marche isn't a complete fool, yes, I guarantee the fighting will stop, the truce will be observed today. Until Prime tomorrow?"

"Very well." Briskly, with a sheen of sweat on her temples, the Faris turned back to the huntsman. "Go. Ride out, hunt. Choose yourselves a new Duke of Burgundy. *Waste no time.*"

[Original e-mail documents found inserted, folded, in British Library copy of 3rd Edition, Ash: The Lost History of Burgundy, (2001) — possibly in chronological order of editing original typescript?]

Message: #162 (Pierce Ratcliff)
Subject: Ash
Date: 11/12/00 at 07.02 a.m.
From: Longman@

format address deleted
other details encrypted
and non-recoverably deleted

Pierce--

This is amazing. I need more!

Do I get a credit for finding it? :-)

We _must_ have the rest of your translation of the Sible Hedingham manuscript as soon as possible. You'll need to write at least a preface, connecting it with 'Fraxinus'. Pierce, our publication date is only four months away!

So—we have to take some decisions. Go ahead and publish 'Fraxinus', and then 'Sible Hedingham' later? Delay publication of _both_ for a few months? I'm in favour of the latter, and I'll tell you why.

If we can bring out your translation of these manuscripts _simultaneously_ with the release of Dr Napier-Grant's initial findings at the Carthage sea site, and with the possible tv documentary that we've discussed, then I think we're going to have the kind of academic success that only comes once in a generation.

Academic and _popular_, Pierce. You could be famous! ;-)

I've got to have your OK to tell my MD about the Sible Hedingham ms. He knows about academic confidentiality! This is so frustrating—he's already desperate to continue negotiations with Dr Napier-Grant's university board, or with her, direct; and I'm having to fudge. I don't want office politics to take this away from me! How soon do you think Doctor Isobel will be ready to release details of the

Carthage sea site? When can I tell Jon that we've got a new manuscript?? When can I tell _anyone_ about the Stone Golem??

I cannot tell you how excited I am!

--Anna

Message: #304 (Anna Longman)
Subject: Ash/Sib. Hed.
Date: 11/12/00 at 04.23 p.m.
From: Ngrant@

format address deleted
other details encrypted by non-discoverable personal key

Anna--

I can only do a translation just so fast! Mediaeval Latin is notoriously difficult, and if it weren't for the fact that I'm used to this hand and this author, you could expect to wait for years!

From a quick-and-dirty read-through of the whole ms., I can state now that the Sible Hedingham document is definitely a continuation of the 'Fraxinus' text, by the same hand. But it differs in almost all of its particulars from our conventional history of the events of the winter of 1476/77. I don't recognise this history! And some of the passages towards the end of the ms. are impenetrably resistant to translation!

Even towards the end of this section that I'm about to forward to you, the text becomes very difficult. The language is obscure, metaphoric: I may be mistaken—a tense, a case, an unfamiliar word-usage, can alter so many meanings! Bear in mind this is a *first* draft!

Let's reserve our opinions. The first part of this very document—'Fraxinus'—gave us a street-map accurate description of the city that we have since discovered on the bed of the Mediterranean Sea. And it may be that, reading and translating late at night, I'm getting confused. I haven't worked at quite *this* intensity since Finals, and coffee and amphetamines will only take one so far!

I've been told to take a short break today, before getting back down to it. Isobel wants me to meet some of her old Cambridge friends (as a post-grad, she was apparently very friendly with the physics people)—and the helicopter's due in an hour.

And the ROV team have got the Stone Golem as cleaned up _in situ_ as is desirable with our equipment, and I want to see the new images as they come through. If the new equipment passes its checks, the first divers will be going down later today. What I really want, of course, is to get my hands on the physical object. That won't be for weeks—I'm no diver! Even if it can be lifted from the seabed; I'm considerably far down the queue. I'll have to be content at the moment with the images coming in as the settlement is mapped.

Between this and the new manuscript, I don't know which way to turn! I have, of course, tried to bring this new information to Isobel's attention. Surprisingly, I found her abstracted, abrupt.

It's useless to tell her that she's working too hard—she has always worked far too hard, all the years that I have known her, and she is, understandably, spending all twenty-four hours of the day on this site—and as much of the time as is physiologically possible under the Mediterranean! Perhaps that's why, when I asked her on your behalf about releasing more details of the archaeological finds, she 'bit my head off', as they say. Perhaps it isn't surprising at all!

I'll show her more when I have more translated.

–Pierce

- -

Message: #310 (Anna Longman)
Subject: Ash/golems
Date: 12/12/00 at 06.48 p.m.
From: Ngrant@

format address deleted
other details encrypted
by non-discoverable
personal key

Anna--

I just thought I would let you know: Isobel has given me the new report on the 'messenger golem' that we found at the Carthage land site.

Apparently, the metallurgy department are _now_ stating that materials incorporated into the bronze-work during the smelting process indicate a time period of *five to six hundred years ago*!

Isn't it nice of them to admit their error like that?

(Yes, I do feel smug.)

When I've had time to read the full text of the report, I'll ask Isobel—if I can get hold of the woman!—if I can have it to incorporate in an appendix to our book.

Back to translation and the Sible Hedingham document–

--Pierce

- -

Message: #180 (Pierce Ratcliff)
Subject: Ash
Date: 12/12/00 at 11.00 p.m.
From: Longman@

format address deleted
other details encrypted and
non-recoverably deleted

Pierce--

I'm so pleased, Pierce! How in the world did they come to make such an error in the first place? Dr Isobel needs to use a far better metallurgy department. All that unnecessary worry!

I think we have to think about moving fast. Jon Stanley's started to mention rumblings on the American academic publishing grape vine: apparently someone knows that you're translating 'something'. 'Fraxinus', I'd guess—I've kept the existence of anything else utterly confidential. But Pierce, I can't tell William Davies what to do with the original Sible Hedingham manuscript, can I?

I expect there's an archaeological grape vine, too, and that it's working overtime. Can you suggest to Dr Isobel that some sort of controlled press release might be _really_ _useful_ about now?

Isn't this exciting? I'm so happy to be involved, even if it is only long-distance!

Love,
Anna

Message: #187 (Pierce Ratcliff)
Subject: Ash
Date: 13/12/00 at 06.59 p.m
From: Longman@

format address deleted
other details encrypted and non-recoverably deleted

Pierce–

I NEED THE REST OF THE TRANSLATION.

Theories are all very well, Pierce, but

No. It doesn't matter. Something did happen, IS happening. Isn't it? I'll tell you why I know—

I came home tonight, about half an hour ago, and flaked out in front of the tv, which happened to be on local news. I get London local, or East Anglian. By sheer chance I was on East Anglian news. The lead story was a human interest piece on a war veteran reunited with his long-lost brother after sixty years.

I heard half of it—no names—sat up and stared—picked up the

phone, thought who can I call, and realised: there was a message waiting for me.

I've just played it. It's William Davies. Such a kind, formal voice, speaking to the empty air of an answering machine. He wants to know if I would like to speak to his brother, Vaughan. Vaughan has 'been away'. Now he's back.

No, I don't want to, I want YOU to fly back to England and talk to him, Pierce. This isn't me, this isn't what I do. I'm an editor, not a journalist or historian, and I don't think I even want to go near him. He's YOUR baby. YOU do it.

--Anna

Message: #188 (Pierce Ratcliff)
Subject: Ash
Date: 13/12/00 at 07.29 p.m.
From: Longman@

format address deleted
other details encrypted and non-recoverably deleted

Pierce--

Answer my message!

--Anna

Message: #189 (Pierce Ratcliff)
Subject: Ash
Date: 13/12/00 at 09.20 p.m.
From: Longman@

format address deleted
other details encrypted and non-recoverably deleted

Pierce--

Read your bloody mail!!!

--Anna

Message: #192 (Pierce Ratcliff)
Subject: Ash
Date: 14/12/00 at 10.31 p.m.
From: Longman@

format address deleted
other details encrypted and non-recoverably deleted

Pierce--

Where the hell are you?

Well, I did it. I drove out to the old people's home this evening, and I saw William Davies and his brother Vaughan. Two very elderly gentlemen, with nothing much to say to each other. That's sad, don't you think?

Vaughan Davies isn't frightening. Just elderly. And senile. He's lost his memory—as the result of a war-time trauma, bombed in the Blitz. He's not a distinguished academic any more.

It seems the amnesia is genuine. William is a surgeon, and of course he has all his old medical contacts, even though he is retired, so Vaughan has been checked up in the best hospital in England, by the best neurosurgeons. Amnesia after traumatic shock. Basically, he got blown up, got picked out of the rubble, didn't know who he was, was put in a home after the Second World War, forgotten, and then chucked out on the streets a few years back for 'care in the community'.

The police eventually picked him up when he appeared in Sible Hedingham and tried to get into his old house. He's pretty gaga, and no one would have known who he was, except one of the family who own Hedingham Castle was there the third or fourth time he tried this, and finally recognised him.

This is a dead end, Pierce. He doesn't remember editing the second edition of ASH. He doesn't remember being an academic. When he talks to William, he thinks they are still fifteen and living with their parents in Wiltshire. He doesn't understand why William is 'old'. His own face in a mirror distresses him. William just pats his brother's hand, and tells him he'll be all right now. It made me cry to listen to him.

Sometimes I don't like myself much. I don't like myself because he's a real person, who has suffered appallingly; and his brother is a sweet old man who I'm fond of.

FFS, Pierce, why aren't you checking your mail!

--Anna

Message: #322 (Anna Longman)
Subject: Ash
Date: 14/12/00 at 10.51 p.m.
From: Ngrant@

format address deleted other details encrypted by non-discoverable personal key

Anna--

I can't leave here now. I can't take the time away from this translation! You will see why. Am sending the next section.

Talk to Vaughan Davies again, for me. _Please._ If he is *at all* coherent, ask him: what was his theory about a 'connection' between the ASH documents and the history—our history—that superseded it? Ask him what it was that he was going to publish after his Second Edition!

--Pierce

Message: #196 (Pierce Ratcliff)
Subject: Ash
Date: 14/12/00 at 11.03 p.m.
From: Longman@

format address deleted
other details encrypted and non-recoverably deleted

Pierce--

ARE YOU MAD?

--Anna

Message: #333(Anna Longman)
Subject: Ash
Date: 14/12/00 at 11.32 p.m.
From: Ngrant@

format address deleted
other details encrypted by non-discoverable personal key

Anna--

No, I'm not mad.

It's late, here. Too late to do any more translation tonight, and besides, I am too tired to think in English, never mind in dog-Latin. I'm sending you what I have complete. Dawn tomorrow I'll carry on, but for now, I owe you an explanation of why I'm not flying back to Gatwick, and here it is.

I have at last been shown the Admiralty charts of this area of the Mediterranean. As you might expect, given the sheer amount of submarine activity during the last war, their charts of the seabed are extensively-detailed, and accurate.

None of them show any kind of a 'trench' on the sea-floor in this location.

--Pierce

PART FOUR

16 November AD 1476

THE HUNTING OF THE HART[63]

[63] 'Sible Hedingham' mss., #2

I

"THERE'S A FUCKING *army* outside the walls," Ash yelled, "and you think you're just going to go out and hunt some *animal*?"

Olivier de la Marche brought his big chestnut stallion around, avoiding rubble, and answered her question between orders to the throng of huntsmen. "Demoiselle-Captain, we ride *now*. We must have a Duke."

Ash, looking at his weather-beaten features under his visor, recognized a capable man with much to organize, and also something else, some quality of abstraction that she realized to be present everywhere in these ravaged streets.

The blitzed great square behind Dijon's north wall must have three thousand people in it, to her quick calculation: and more coming in every minute. Knights mounted on horseback, archers running with messages, huntsmen and their varlets, and couple upon couple of running hounds. But most—she squinted her eyes against the morning sun falling between the burned-out timbers of buildings—wet, and blackened from fire—mostly women and men in drab clothes. Shopkeepers. Apprentices. Farming families: peasants taking refuge from the devastated countryside. Wine-makers and cheese-sellers, shepherds and small girl-children. All of them bundled up in their layers of neatly mended muddy woollen tunics, gowns, and cloaks, faces bitten red and white by the wind. Most of them solemn, or abstracted. For the first time in months, not flinching in anticipation of falling stone or iron.

And quiet. The noise of her own men walking and riding back in was the loudest noise, audible over the whining of the hounds. Her rough voice, and the single passing-bell, were all that broke the almost complete silence.

"If there are Burgundians among your mercenaries," Olivier de la Marche concluded, "they may hunt with us."

Ash shook her head. The pale bay gelding, abruptly alert to her movement, skittered a step sideways in the mud and broken cobbles. She brought him under control. "But *who* inherits the Dukedom?"

"One of the royal ducal bloodline."

"*Which one?*"

"We will not know, until they are chosen by means of the hunting of the hart. Demoiselle-Captain, come if you will; if not, keep the walls and watch the truce!"

Ash exchanged glances with Antonio Angelotti as the Duke's deputy rode off toward the houndsmen. " 'The hunting of the hart'. . . . Am I crazy, or are they?"

Before Angelotti could answer, a tall scarecrow figure approached, pushing its hood back. Floria del Guiz beat her sheepskin mittens together against the bitter wind.

"Ash!" she called cheerfully, "Robert has a dozen men who need to speak to you about the hunt. Should he bring them from the tower, or will you go to him?"

"Here." Ash dismounted, the steel and leather war-saddle creaking. The tension of the Faris's camp released itself, momentarily, in aching muscles, under her armor.

Down at ground level, she became more aware of the men and women packing into the square. They walked quietly, most not speaking, a few with expressions of grief. Where they were forced by the devastation of the narrow winding streets to crowd together, she saw how they courteously stepped aside, or gave a nod of apology. The Burgundian men-at-arms, which she expected to see using their bills to hold the crowd back under control, were standing in small clusters watching the flood of humanity go past them. Some of them exchanged brief comments with the peasants.

Many of the women held lit tapers carefully between their cupped hands.

"This silence . . . I've never heard anything like it."

There were two women behind Floria, Ash now saw; one in the green robes of a soeur, and one in a stained, grubby white hennin. As the press lessened around her and the bay gelding, she could see their faces. Soeur Maîtresse Simeon, and Jeanne Châlon.

"Florian . . ." Bewildered, she turned back to her surgeon.

Floria looked up from sending a baggage-train child back with a message. "Robert says the dozen or so Flemings who stayed with us after the split, they want permission to ride in the hunt. I'm riding, too."

Ash said sceptically, "And when was the last time you thought of yourself as Burgundian?"

"This does not matter." The Soeur Maîtresse's fat white face did not look disapprovingly at Ash; rather, sadly, and with no condemnation. "Your doctor has been ill treated by her homeland; but this draws all of us together."

Ash caught Jeanne Châlon looking at her without bitterness. Tears had reddened the rims of her eyes. That or the cold wind kept her sniffling. Amazingly, she had her arm linked in Floria's.

"I can't believe he's dying," she croaked. Ash felt her throat tighten in involuntary sympathy with the woman's plain grief. Jeanne Châlon added, "He was our heart. God lays His sternest burdens on His most faithful servant. . . . God in His mercy knows how we shall miss him!"

Apart from the Soeur Maîtresse, Ash suddenly realized,

she was seeing no priests out on the streets. The single bell continued to toll. Every ordained priest must be in the palace, with the dying Charles; and she felt a curious impulse to ride there and wait for the news of his final passing.

"I was born here," Floria said. "Yes, I've lived away. Yes, I'm outcast. All the same, Ash, I want to see the new Duke chosen. I wasn't in Burgundy; I was abroad when Philip died and Charles hunted. I'm going to do it now, whether—" and her eyes became small with the constriction of reckless, bitter humor on her face: "—whether I think it's rubbish, or not. I'm still going!"

Ash felt the cold wind redden her nose. A drop of clear liquid ran down. She unbuckled her purse to take out her kerchief, and, having given herself time to think—time to look at the hunters, the archers in the liveries of Hainault and Picardy mounting up; even the refugee French knight Armand de Lannoy standing ready with grooms and a group of Burgundian nobles—Ash wiped her nose vigorously and said, "I'm coming with you. Robert and Geraint can look after the shop."

Antonio Angelotti spoke down from the saddle of his scraggy gray. "But if the Visigoths don't keep the truce, madonna!"

"The Faris has her own reasons for keeping this truce. I'll brief you after this." Her tone lightened. "Come on, Angeli. The lads are getting bored. I'm going to show them we don't have to sit inside Dijon like we're terrified. Good for morale!"

"Not if they stick your head on a spear, madonna."

"I don't suppose that would improve my morale, no." Ash turned as the child-messenger threaded her way back through the polite crowd, Robert Anselm and a number of men-at-arms behind her. "What's the request here?"

Pieter Tyrrell stood behind Anselm, his maimed hand in

its specially sewn leather glove tucked behind his belt. His face under his archer's sallet looked white. With him, Willem Verhaecht and his lance second, Adrian Campin, seemed equally stunned.

"We didn't think he was going to *die*, boss," Tyrrell said, not needing to explain who he referred to. "We'd like to ride the hunt in memory. I know it's a siege, but . . ."

The older Willem Verhaecht said, "A dozen of my men are Burgundian by birth, boss. It's respect."

"He was a good employer," the lance second added.

Ash surveyed the men. A pragmatic part of her mind said *A dozen men either way won't save us if the Visigoths turn treacherous*, and the rest of her responded, in the weak morning sunlight, to the effect of the immense press of people and the almost total silence.

"If you put it that way," she said, "yes, it's respect. He knew what he was doing. Which is more than you can say for most of the sad bastards who pay us. Okay: permission granted. Captain Anselm, you and Morgan and Angelotti will hold the tower. If there's treachery, stand ready to have the city gates open—we'll be coming back in a hurry!"

A quiet appreciative chuckle went round the group. Willem Verhaecht turned to organizing his men. Robert Anselm's mouth shut in a firm line. Ash caught his eye.

"Listen."

"I don't hear anything."

"Yes, you do. You hear grief." Instinctively, Ash kept her voice at a low conversational tone. She pointed to where, among the huntsmen and hounds, Philippe de Poitiers and Ferry de Cuisance stood with Olivier de la Marche, all of them surrounded by their men, all of them bareheaded in the autumn day. "If this city's going to stand, they *need* a successor to Charles. If he dies, and there's no one—then this is over: Dijon will fall tomorrow."

Over the slight susurrus of the crowd, the noise of the single bell came clearly. Ash glanced up at the peaked roofs. She could not see the twin spires of the abbey. *They'll be anointing him, giving him the last sacrament.*

The back of her neck prickled with anticipation, waiting for the second and final peal to begin. *Dead before midday, the huntsman thinks. And it's got to be past the fourth hour of the morning now. . . .*

"What about the Faris?" Robert Anselm rumbled.

"Oh. She's sending an escort with the hunt," Ash said wryly.

"An *escort*?" Anselm's bullish, stubbled face looked bewildered. He shook his head dismissively. "That's not what I meant. When he dies—is she Gundobad's child? Can she do a miracle?"

"I don't think even she knows."

"And do you know, girl?"

The pale gelding butted Ash's pauldron. She reached up absently and firmly stroked its muzzle. It lipped at her gauntlet.

"Roberto . . . I don't know. She hears the Wild Machines. They speak to her. And if they speak to her—" She switched her gaze to Robert Anselm's brown gaze, under pinched, frowning brows. "If they made me turn around and walk to them—then, whatever she's capable of, they can make her do that, too."

There are no last hedgerow flowers in this ravaged autumn, but she can smell evergreen branches, and pine sap: half the men and women in the crowd are wearing homemade green garlands. Ash stands where she has stood so often before: among a group of her officers, familiar faces, horses being held by the company's grooms, men-at-arms in Lion livery sorting themselves out and swapping kit among them.

Everything's different now.

They watch her with more seriousness than they would give to the morning of battle.

"The Faris is frightened. I *may* have frightened her all the way back to Carthage—but I don't know," Ash said thoughtfully. "She's heard the Wild Machines say *winter will not cover all the world, unless Burgundy falls.* But what she's lived under is the Eternal Twilight—I don't know if she really understands that they want everything black and freezing and *dead.*"

Her gaze went above the silent crowd and the ruined roofs, toward the sun, for reassurance.

"I've been forced by them. She hasn't. She thinks it can't happen to her. So I don't know if she can bring herself to harm the Stone Golem. Even now that she knows it's the only way the Wild Machines can get at her."

Robert Anselm completed her thought: "It's what she's depended on, in the field, for ten years."

"It's her life." Ash's scarred face twisted in a grin. "And it isn't mine. I'd blow the Golem sky-high—but I'm not there. So that doesn't leave me much of an option."

Her mind recovering itself, she found herself with a plan rapidly falling together under the stimulus of that demand. "Robert, Angeli, Florian. I said to the Faris, one Duke's as good as another. But I can be wrong. If the Wild Machines only need *Charles* dead—then we're about to find out what that means."

Ash made an effort, ignored the silent crowd.

"Let's hope the Visigoths have got all their attention on this hunt. Damn us riding *with* it—I'm going to lead a snatch-squad. Once we're outside the area, we're going to slip away from the hunt, come back to the Goth camp, and make an attempt to kill the Faris."

"We're dead," Anselm said brutally. "If you took the

whole company, you wouldn't get through thousands of men!"

Ash, not at all contradicting him, said authoritatively, "Okay: we'll *take* the whole company—all those with mounts, anyway. Roberto, the Faris can declare a truce, but there could be an armed mutiny going on out there before midday. The hunt could turn into a slaughter. If we want to kill the Faris—this is going to be the only chance to get outside the walls and try."

Anselm shook his bull head. "Truce be buggered. *I'd* kill any Burgundian noble who stuck his head outside, if I was Goth commander. De la Marche thinks he can be in and out of here like a rat up a drainpipe!"

"This whole hunt is mad," Ash said, lowering her voice, under the noise of the single bell. "That's *good*. The confusion will work for us. But I should start praying, if I were you." A brief grin. "Roberto, I'll take picked men, volunteers only."

"Poor bastards!" Robert Anselm gave a glance at the Lion captains sorting their men out into units, in the square. "The ones you took to Carthage. They *believe* they're 'heroes' now. They forget they got their asses kicked. And the ones that stayed here, they think they missed out, so they can't wait to get stuck in. They'll think you've got a plan."

Alert to nuance, Ash said, "I'd planned to leave Angelotti in charge here, the gunners need keeping under control. I think the foot needs an officer, too—maybe you *should* stay in Dijon, not volunteer to come with me now."

She expected a protest, along the lines of *let Geraint Morgan do it!* Anselm only glanced at the city gates and nodded acknowledgment.

"I'll put a watch up on the walls," he grunted. "Soon as I

see you attack the camp, we'll shoot from here, add to the confusion. Sod the truce. Anything else, girl?"

His gaze slid away from hers.

"No. Sort out all the mounts you can for the men who're coming with me on this."

Ash stood in the weak sun, watching him walk away; a broad-shouldered man in English plate, his scabbard tapping against his leg armor as he walked.

"Robert's turning down a fight?" Floria said incredulously, at her elbow.

"I need someone smart to stay in the city."

The surgeon looked at her with a brief, cynical expression. She did not say *his nerve's gone*, but Ash read it on her face.

"He'll be okay," Ash said gently. "We all get like that. *My* nerve isn't brilliant right now. Maybe it's something about sieges. Give him a day or two."

"We may not *have* a day." Floria bit her lip. "I've seen you talk to Godfrey. I've seen you turned around by the Machines—we all have. I know it as well as the rest of this sorry lot: we may only have an hour, now. We don't *know* how long until it happens."

A familiar coldness insulated Ash. "I'll do this without Robert. He knows what I'm planning here could be a one-way trip. I need people with me who know that—and still come."

On the far side of the square, the town clock struck ten. Its chimes battered the silence. Ash saw people unwrapping bread from dirty kerchiefs, sitting and eating on heaps of fallen bricks and furniture, all of it done in a contained, reverent practicality.

Floria closed her fingers around Ash's hand in its chill metal gauntlet. She said, as if the effort were suddenly too great, "Don't do this. Please. You don't need to. Leave your sister alive. There'll be another Duke in an hour or two. You're going to get yourself killed for no reason."

Ash turned her hand so that she could clasp the woman's hand, carefully, between metal and linen. "Hey. I spend my life risking getting killed for no reason! It's my job."

"And I get sick of stitching you back together!" Floria scowled. She looked, despite the dirt lining her face, very young: a youth wrapped in doublet and demi-gown, candlewax drippings white down the front of her cloak. She smelled of herbs and old blood. "I know you need to do this. And you're scared. I know it. You're not talking with Godfrey, either."

"No." The thought of speaking, or listening, brought a dryness to Ash's mouth. In that part of herself that she has shared for a decade, there is a growing tension, an oppression, like the pressure before a storm. The silent presence of the Wild Machines.

"At least see the Duke chosen, before you try military suicide!" Floria's voice was gruff, with a raw dark humor. "There'll be as much confusion in their camp after that as before. Maybe more. They might even be more off guard. Come on, you're telling me you don't want to see de la Marche become Duke?"

Responding to the humor, to the woman's plain attempt to control her own emotion, Ash said lightly, "I thought no one knew who gets chosen?"

Floria squeezed her hand hard and released it. Thickly, she said, "Technically, no. *Technically*, anyone with Burgundian ducal blood's eligible. Hell, with the way the noble families intermarry, that's about every arms-bearing family between here and Ghent!"

Ash flicked a glance toward Adriaen Campin, where he did a last kit-check for Verhaecht's other Flemish men.

"Hey, maybe we've got the next Duke of Burgundy riding with the company!"

That made Floria wipe her eyes, and grin cynically. "And maybe Olivier de la Marche isn't the experienced noble military candidate. Come on. Who do you think they're going to pick?"

"You mean when they open up the deer and look at the entrails, or whatever it is they do here, it's going to say 'Sieur de la Marche' in illuminated capitals all over it?"

"That's about the size of it, I guess."

"Makes life easier." Ash shook her head. "Why go to the bother of hunting the fucking thing! *Christus.* I'll never understand Burgundians—present company excepted, of course."

When she looked at Floria, it was to see the young woman smiling at her, eyes warm, wiping her nose with a dirty rag.

"You don't understand a damn thing." Floria's voice shook. "For the first time in my life, I wish I knew how to hack someone up with your bloody meat cleavers. I want to ride with you, Ash. I don't want to see you ride off on this suicidal, stupid idea and not *be* there—"

"I'd sooner throw a mouse into a millwheel. You'd stand about as much chance."

"And what chance do *you* stand!"

That this morning—the clouds thinning in the north, no more flurries of snow; the sun harsh and white in the south; the air full of the scent of broken evergreen—that this may be the last morning she sees: it is not new to her. But it is never old, never something which one becomes used to. Ash took a deep breath, into lungs that seemed dry and cold and constricted with fear.

"If we do take out the Faris, all hell will break loose. Then I'll get the guys out in the confusion. Listen, you're right, this is suicidally stupid, but it won't be the first thing to succeed simply because it is. No one out there is expecting anyone actually to *do* this."

She reached out quickly as Floria turned on her heel to stalk off, and grabbed her arm.

"No. This is the hard bit. You don't go off and cry in a corner. You get to stand here with me and look like we *know* it's going to work."

"Christ, you're a hard bitch!"

"You can talk, surgeon. You feed my guys up with opium and hemlock,[64] and chop their arms and legs off without a second thought."

"Hardly that."

"But you do it. You sew them up—knowing they're coming back to this."

After a silence, Floria muttered, "And you lead them, knowing they wouldn't do this for anyone else."

A flurry of activity among the Burgundian nobles made Ash turn her head. She saw lords and their escorts mounting up, on what nags and palfreys three months' siege had left in the city; a clarion rang out, and a hunting horn over that shrillness. All across the square, people began getting to their feet.

In the part of her soul that listens, ancient voices mutter, just below the threshold of hearing.

Ash said briskly. "All right—but stay with the hunt, Florian, where it's safe. I'll break off immediately the full cry sounds. I can't wait until the hunt's over to attack. We can't wait for anything, now."

---

[64] Together with black henbane, the ingredients of an anaesthetic recently uncovered by a dig at the fourteenth-century Augustinian hospital at Soufra, near Edinburgh. Oak-gall solution served to revive the patient after surgery.

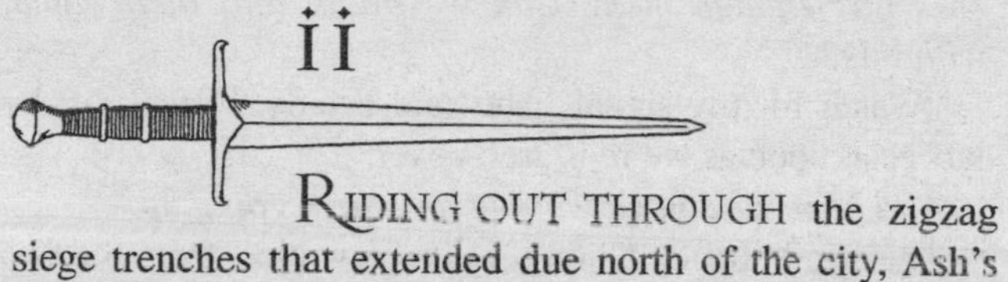

ii

RIDING OUT THROUGH the zigzag siege trenches that extended due north of the city, Ash's neck prickled. Silent Visigoth detachments stood and watched them pass.

She swiveled in her war-saddle. Black and massed as ants, a Visigoth spear-company fell in behind the cavalcade.

"Lousy bloody hunt, *this* is," Euen Huw complained.

Ash has an immediate tactile memory: six months ago, riding from Cologne at the Holy Roman Emperor's own lackadaisical pace toward the siege at Neuss, and stopping for a day's hunting. Frederick III had had the regulation trestle tables spread with white linen set up in the forest, for his noblemen to have their dawn breakfast at. Ash crammed her mouth full with white bread while lymerers returned from their various quests and unfolded, from the hems of their doublets, fumays, which they spread on the cloth, each debating the merits of his own particular beast.

The hot June sun and German forests faded in her memory.

"They don't find a hart soon, see," the Welsh captain added, "and there won't be a hunt at all. We'll have scared off the game for leagues around!"

His gaze was febrile. Ash, without appearing to watch, took in Euen Huw, Thomas Rochester, and Willem Verhaecht, the armored escort that rode with her and her banner, and her fifty men riding behind.

It has been a scramble to raise even fifty battle-trained horses.

Is this enough men? Can we break into their camp, with this?

"Watch for my signal," she said briefly. "Break off by lances as soon as we're in tree-cover."

And hope we can go without an alarm going up.

The wind outside Dijon's walls blew chill from the two rivers. Sun winked from Visigoth helmets—the amazing, still-new, still-welcome sun. Ash wore her demi-gown over her harness, the thick wool belted at the waist so that her arms would be unencumbered. The pale sun shone back also from the armor of her men, and from the rich, dirty reds and blues of the Burgundian liveries a few yards ahead.

Thin, across the cold air, the noise of clapper against bell struck, singly.

"I can hear the abbey bell, boss," Thomas Rochester said. "Charlie's still with us."

"Not for long. Our surgeon had a word with his—he's in a coma; has been since Matins—" Seeing de la Marche stopping, on the verge of the trees, Ash reined in, checking the pale bay with a curse. Silent people on foot crowded the horses: peasants, townsmen, huntsmen. An anxious whining rose from the hounds.

"Wait here." She shouldered the gelding forward with only Thomas Rochester and a lance escort. The Duke's deputy had dismounted. He stood, surrounded by a dozen men with silent square-muzzled lymers.

"Bloody Burgundians. Ought to have my old granddad here," Thomas Rochester muttered. "Used to reckon, boss, if you showed him a fumay, he could tell you if the beast was an old or a young one, a male or a female. Just from a turd. 'A fat long and black 'un's a hart of ten.' That's what he used to say."

Fifty men's nowhere near enough. But the foot troops couldn't keep up. Fifty cavalry, medium and heavy; we need to smash our way into the camp—I need to know how she's deployed her troops, where she is—

She bit down on her lip, within a split second of automatically speaking aloud to the *machina rei militaris.*

No! Not to the Stone Golem, not to Godfrey: because the Wild Machines are there, I can feel *them*—

A swelling pressure in her soul.

The Faris won't have reported through the Stone Golem anyway.

"Is that the word of you all?" Olivier de la Marche asked. The bluff, armored man had the look of someone who would far rather be organizing a tournament or a war. Ash wondered briefly if the Duke's deputy would be a Duke who could keep control of an invaded country: war there, war in Lorraine, war in Flanders . . .

The white-bearded lymerer looked around for confirmation at his fellows. "True, my lord. We've been out on foot since before dawn. Downriver, to the plains, and east and west to the hills. West and north, to the forests. All the hollows are cold. All the fumays are old. There are no beasts."

"Oh, *what!*" Ash exclaimed under her breath. She risked a glance back. No more than quarter of a mile outside the Visigoth camp: too soon to break off.

But if there's not going to be a hunt—

Olivier de la Marche stomped around and held up both hands, in an unnecessary demand for silence. He bellowed: "The quest has found no beasts! The land is empty!"

" 'Course it's bloody empty!" Thomas Rochester snorted with self-disgust. "Shit, boss, think about it!

They've got a bloody army camped here. The ragheads probably ate everything in sight months ago! Boss, you can forget this, it ain't gonna happen."

From the men and women around them, like the mumbled response of a mass, many voices echoed: "The land is empty."

Olivier de la Marche swung himself back up into his saddle in a clatter of armor. Ash heard him order the huntsmen.

"Send the lymers back. We will have no scent to follow. Bring the running hounds. Send the greyhound relays to the north." He raised his voice: "North, to the wildwood!"

A swirl of people went past Ash. The pale bay gelding whickered, half kicking out; and she brought him back under control in time to see all the men, women, and children on foot streaming past, in the wake of the mounted Burgundian nobles. The black standard of the Visigoth company bobbed at their rear. She saw a number of cavalry with the spearmen: mounted archers.

Archers. Shit.

"Let's go!" She raised her arm and jerked it forward. The bay wheeled, and she brought it up with the mounted men-at-arms and archers of the Lion, falling in beside her banner and Euen Huw.

"Go where, boss?" Thomas Rochester demanded.

Ash rapped out crisp orders. "North. Ride for the trees. Once in cover, break off; then rendezvous at the ford on the west river."

Verhaecht's Flemings pushed ahead, so that she rode toward the rear of the company, among faces she knew. A thin youth turned his head away: she recognized Rickard, forbidden to ride on this assault, and said nothing—too late, now.

"This is stupid!" Rochester fumed, riding by her side. "How can he send the hounds out, when he doesn't know which way the beast is likely to run? And there isn't a beast! How can they hunt when there isn't a quarry, boss?"

With automatic cheerfulness, Ash said, "That's Burgundians for you."

A low chuckle went around the riders. She sensed their apprehension, the immediate excitement of daring oozing away. She glanced up at her banner. *There's a reasonable chance they won't follow me for this. It's murder. Can I get to the Faris on my own? Ride back, give myself up, smuggle a dagger in—no. No. She knows she's the target.*

Pushing the gelding across, she rode out to the edge of her company, to where ladies in padded headdresses and veils rode sidesaddle on underfed palfreys. Floria's big-boned scrawny gray stood out like a mercenary in church. The surgeon spurred across to her from Jeanne Châlon's side.

"What are we doing?" Ash called.

"Fuck knows!" Coming closer, ignoring the appalled stares of the crowd on foot, Floria lowered her voice. "Don't ask me, ask de la Marche, he's Master of Game for this one! Girl, it's November. We won't find so much as a wren out here. This is mad!"

"Where's he taking us?"

"Northeast, upriver. Into the wildwood." Floria pointed from the saddle. "Up ahead, there."

The head of the column was already in the edge of it, Ash saw. Riding among leafless trees, brown branches stark against the pale sky. She slowed the gelding's pace as they began to come among tree stumps. Chopped bark displayed weeping pale wood. The scent of woodsmoke went up from a number of campfires; one stump had a rusting ax left sticking in it. Of the wood gatherers and charcoal burners and swineherds she would have expected to see, in peacetime, there was no sign. Gone, weeks before, as refugees.

"There," Floria said, as if she realized what Ash had been looking for.

Where she pointed, men in black coifs and sodden wool tunics and bare legs walked with the hunters, talking animatedly to the men with their leashed couples of hounds. One elderly, stout man carried a taper, its flame all but invisible in the sunlight.

This cultivated edge of the forest was all hornbeam, coppiced down to thin thumb-width growth, and ash, for staves, and hazel, for nuts in season. All the winter-dark branches stood equally bare. The last chestnuts and leaves hung from bigger trees. Ash glanced down to bring the gelding around a stump, lifted her gaze, and found that she had lost the walkers and riders at the edges of the cavalcade in the multiple thin thickets. The horses' hooves sounded softer on leaf mulch and muddy moss.

Ahead, with de la Marche's banner, the bearded huntsman lifted his horn to his lips. A shattering call split the silent, crowded wood. Handlers bent down to the leashes of the running hounds, uncoupled them; and a bellow went up: "Ho moy, ho moy!"

Another handler shouted at his hounds by name: "Marteau! Clerre! Ribanie! Bauderon!"

The Soeur Maîtresse of the *filles de pénitence* dug her heels into her palfrey and shot past Ash. "*Cy va! Cy va!*"

"Ho moy!" Jeanne Châlon wheezed. Her little wheat-colored mare dug in its heels, among the fallen sticks under the chestnut trees and oaks. She gestured energetically at Floria. "Ride for us! Be my witness!"

"Yes, Tante!"

A surge of men running pushed them apart from the women riders, Ash with Floria's rangy beast shoving close to her gelding's rump. Heart thumping, she all but gave in and spurred over the cut trees and rough ground in the wake of the Burgundians, caught up in the chase. She leaned her weight in, turning back toward Thomas Rochester and Willem Verhaecht and the men.

"Get in among the trees!" she yelled. A glance back south showed her more riders, more men running on foot, and the Visigoth banner just entering the line of the wood.

Floria yelped, "Ho moy!" at the hounds, streaming away through bush and briar, and reluctantly reined in back beside Ash, cheeks flushed. Bare branches rubbed together over their heads, creaking audibly over the clink of tack and the rapid footsteps. The hounds' shrill baying ran ahead. The press of men and women running up from behind forced Ash into a trot, ducking low branches, careful on the broken earth.

Floria, behind her, called, "What the hell do they think they've found?"

"This late in the day?" Ash jerked her thumb at the sun, low through the trees behind them, close on midmorning. "Nothing! There isn't a bloody rabbit left between here and Bruges. Get up ahead with your aunt."

"I'll ride with you—go ahead in a minute—"

"Thomas." Ash signaled. "Start sending them off. Lance at a time. North first, then west through the woods."

The man-at-arms nodded, turning his mount awkwardly among wilted banks of briar and dead goldenrod, and spurred back into the company cavalry. She watched the few seconds necessary to see him approach the lance leaders.

"Florian." She checked position of her banner, the tag end of the running crowd among holly, hornbeam, and oak wood, the standard of the Visigoths—out of sight, somewhere back at the edge of the wood. "Get your ass up there with the hunters. When you get back to the city, have everything ready for wounded."

The surgeon ignored her. "They're coming back!"

A throng of men on foot and on horse went past, couples of hounds tugging away from their handlers, moving too fast for the rough ground underfoot. Swept back toward a holly thicket, Ash shifted her weight forward and hauled on the rein.

The pale gelding turned. Ash shifted her weight back, tassets sliding over cuisses, and brought the horse around. Apart from Rochester's sergeant with her banner, a yard or two off her flank, all the riders and people on foot around her now were strangers. She risked a glance off to the far right—to see the backs of men in Lion livery riding out into thicker woods that way—and another look behind her.

Two heavy cataphracts in scale armor, that flashed in the slanting light under the trees, were riding up close behind; the Visigoth company standard caught up somewhere in branches behind them, and fifty or more serf-troops with spears running on foot with the riders.

"It is not their business to be here!" a tight-lipped voice said, at her right side. Ash, turning in her saddle, found herself right beside Jeanne Châlon's palfrey.

"It is not yours, either!" the woman added, her tone not hostile, but disapproving.

Ash could not now see Soeur Maîtresse Simeon, or Floria, in the mob. She kept the gelding tightly reined in as he rolled his eye, shifting his hooves on the bank that sloped down ahead of them.

"Better hope the chase doesn't come back this way!" Ash grinned at Mistress Châlon and jerked her thumb at the serf-troops running past them through briar and tree stumps. "What happens to Burgundy if a Visigoth kills the hart?"

Jeanne Châlon's pursed mouth closed even tighter. "They are not eligible. Nor you, you have not a drop of

Burgundian blood in your veins! It would mean nothing: no Duke!"

Ash halted the pale gelding. Water ran black under the leafless trees. A pale sun, above, put white light down through the tall branches. Ahead, men with hose muddy to the thigh, and women with their kirtles kilted up and black at the hem, waited patiently to cross a small stream. Ash thumbed the visor of her sallet farther up.

A strong smell hit her. Made up of horse—the pale gelding sweating, as it fretted in the moving crowds of peasants—and of woodsmoke, from distant bonfires, and of the smell of people who do not bathe often and who work out in the air: a ripe and unobjectionable sweat. Tears stung her eyes, and she shook her head, her vision blurring, thinking *Why? What does—*

What does this remind me of?

The picture in her head is of old wood, that has been faded to silver and cracked dry by summer upon summer in the field. A wooden rail, by a step.

One of the big roofed wagons, with steps set down into grass; the earth trodden flat in front of it, and grass growing up between the spokes of the wheels.

A camp, somewhere. Ash has a brief associational flavor in her mouth: fermented dandelion, elder flower, watered down to infinitesimal strength, but enough to make the water safe for a child to drink. She remembers sitting on the wagon steps, Big Isobel—who could only have been a child herself, but an older child—holding her on her knee, and the child Ash wriggling to be set down, to run with the wind that ruffled the grasses between lines of tents.

The smell of cooking, from campfires; the smell of men sweating from weapons practice; the smell that wool and linen get when they have been beaten at a riverbank and hung out to dry in the open air.

Let me go back to that, she thought. *I don't want to be in charge of it; I just want to live like that again. Waiting for the day when the practice becomes real war, and all fear vanishes.*

"*Cy va!*"

Hounds gave tongue, somewhere far ahead in the wood. The crowd at the stream surged forward, water spraying up. Both her sergeant and banner were gone. Ash swore, unbuckled the strap under her chin, and wrenched her sallet off. She pushed the cropped hair back from her ears, tilted her head, and listened.

A confused noise of hounds echoed between the trees.

"*That's* not a scent—or they've lost it again." Ash found that she was speaking to the empty air: the Châlon woman had vanished into the throng.

Visigoth serf-troops pounded past on foot, either side of her; most of them with nothing but a helmet and a dark linen tunic, running bloody and barefoot on the forest floor. Skin prickled down the whole length of her spine. She dared not put her hand to her riding sword. She sat poised, bareheaded, waiting, ears alert in the cold wind for the sound of a bow—

"Green Christ!" a voice said at her stirrup.

Ash looked down. A Visigoth in a round steel helm with a nasal bar, arquebus clutched loosely in a dirty hand, had stopped and was staring up at her. Boots, and a mail shirt, marked him out as a freeman; what she could see of his face was weather-beaten, middle-aged, and thin.

"Ash," he said. "Christ, girlie, they did mean you."

In the rush of people, the two of them went unnoticed: Ash's gelding sidling back into the shelter of a beech tree with a few last brown leaves still curled like chrysalides on its twigs; the Visigoth's mounted officer too busy yelling his men back into some kind of order and off the trail of the hounds.

Alert, safe in her armor, she tucked her sallet under her arm and looked down from the high saddle. "Are you one of Leofric's slaves? Did I meet you in Carthage? Are you a friend of Leovigild or Violante?"

"Do I sound like a bloody Carthaginian?" The man's raw voice held offense, and amusement. He cradled the arquebus under one arm and reached up, pulling his helmet off. Long curls of white hair fell down around his face, fringing a bald patch that took up almost all his scalp, and he pushed the yellow-white hair back with a veined hand. "Christ, girl! You don't remember me."

The belling of the hounds faded. The hundreds of people might as well have not been present. Ash stared at black eyes, under stained yellow eyebrows. An utter familiarity, coupled with a complete lack of knowledge, silenced her. *I do know you, but how can I know anyone from Carthage?*

The man said rawly, "The Goths hire mercenaries, too, girlie; don't let the livery fool you."

Deep lines cut down the side of his mouth, ridged his forehead; the man might have been in his fifties or sixties, paunchy under the mail, with bad teeth, and white stubble showing on his cheeks.

The gulf that she felt opening around her was, she realized, nothing but the past; the long fall back to childhood, when everything was different, and everything was for the first time. "Guillaume," she said. "Guillaume Arnisout."

He had shrunk, and not just by the fact that she sat so high above him. There would be scars and wounds she knew nothing of, but he was so much the same—even white-haired, even older—so much the gunner that she had known in the Griffin-in-Gold that it took her breath: she sat and stared while the hunt raged past, silenced.

"I thought it had to be you." Guillaume Arnisout nodded to himself. He still wore a falchion; a filthy great curved blade in a scabbard at his waist, for all he carried a Visigoth copy of a European gun.

"I thought you died. When they executed everybody, I thought you died."

"I went south again. Healthier overseas." His eyes squinted, looking up at her, as if he looked into a light. "We found *you* in the south."

"In Africa." And, at his nod, she leaned down from the saddle and extended her hand, grasping his as he offered it, forearm and forearm; his covered in mail, hers in plate. A great smile spluttered out of her, into a laugh. "Shit! Neither of us has changed!"

Guillaume Arnisout looked quickly over his shoulder, moving back into the scant concealment of the branches. Thirty feet away, a Visigoth cataphract bawled furiously and obscenely at the standard-bearer, the eagle still tangled between hornbeam clumps.

"Does it matter to you, girlie? Do you want to know?"

There was no malice, no taunt, in his tone, nothing but a serious question, and the rueful acknowledgment of a nearby sergeant likely to exercise proper discipline for this infringement.

"Do I?" Ash straightened, looking down at him. She abruptly put her sallet back on, unbuckled, and swung down from the saddle. She looped the gelding's reins around a low branch. Safe, unnoticeable among the passing heads, she turned back to the middle-aged man. "Tell me. It makes no difference now, but I want to know."

"We were in Carthage. Must be twenty years ago." He shrugged. "The Griffin-in-Gold. A dozen of us were out in the harbor, one night, drunk, on somebody's stolen boat. Yolande—you never met her, an archer; she's dead now—heard a baby crying on one of their honeyboats, so she made us row over there and rescue it."

"The refuse barges?" Ash said.

"Whatever. We called them honeyboats."

A shrill horn sounded close by. Both she and the white-haired man looked up with identical alertness, registered a Burgundian noble carrying a lymer across his saddlebow; and then the rider and hound were past, gone into the people still massing to cross the stream.

"*Tell me!*" Ash urged.

He looked at her with a pragmatic sadness. "There isn't much more to tell. You had this big cut on your throat, bleeding, so Yolande took you to one of the raghead doctors and got you sewn up. Hired you a wet nurse. We were going to leave you there, but she wanted to bring you back with us, so I had the charge of you in the ship all the way over to Salerno."

Guillaume Arnisout's creased, dirty face creased still further. He wiped at his shiny forehead.

"You cried. A lot. The wet nurse died of a fever in Salerno, but Yolande took you on into camp. Then she lost interest. I heard she got raped, and killed in a knife fight later on. I lost track of you after that."

Openmouthed, Ash stood for a short time. She felt stunned, conscious of the leaf mulch under her feet, and the warmth of the gelding's flank at her shoulder; for the rest, was numb.

"You're saying you saved my life casually and then got bored."

"Probably wouldn't have done it if we hadn't been drunk." The man's worn, livid face colored slightly. "A few years later, I was pretty sure you were the same kid, no one else had that thistledown-color hair, so I tried to make up for it, a bit."

"Sweet Christ."

There's nothing in this I didn't know or couldn't have guessed. Why are my hands and feet numb; why am I dizzy with this?

"You're the big boss, nowadays." Guillaume's rasping voice held scepticism, and a hint of flattery. "Not that I wouldn't have expected it. You were always keen."

"Do you expect me to be grateful?"

"I tried to show you how to look after yourself. Stay sharp. Guess it worked. And now you're this general's sister, and a big shot on your own account, from what I hear." His lined cheeks twisted into a smile. "Want to take an old soldier into your company, girlie?"

She wears a fortune on her back, strapped around her body: forged and hardened metal that it would take Guillaume Arnisout decades to buy—if, indeed, he could buy a whole harness in his lifetime. Hers comes from third-share enemy ransoms: one-third for the man who makes the capture, one-third for his captain, and one-third for the company commander. At this second, it is nothing but a prison of metal that she would like to shuck off, run through the woods as freely as she did as a child.

"You don't know the half of it, Guillaume," Ash says. And then: "I *am* grateful. There was no reason for you to do any of it. Even casual interest, at the right second—believe me, I'm thankful."

"So get me out of this bloody serf-army!"

So much for disinterested information.

The wind rubs bare branches together above their heads. The ammoniac stench of disturbed leaf mulch comes up from the bed of the stream, the black water churned into gray mud by passing men. Ash's gelding whickers. The flow of people is becoming thinner; the Visigoth eagle glints under the thickets of evergreen holly.

I would do it for any man—any mercenary—if he asked me at this moment.

"Lose the kit." She scrabbled with gauntlet fingers at the ties of her livery tabard, and gown, that she wears over her armor. By the time the ties loosened, she looked up to see the Carthage-manufactured gun gone who-knows-where, the helmet slung overarm into the stream, and Guillaume with his dirty linen coif tied tight down over his balding head.

She thrust her demi-gown and the crumpled blue-and-gold cloth at him, turned, and sprang herself up into the saddle, the weight of the armor ignored.

"Burgundian!" a harsh voice bawled.

Ash spurred the gelding out of the low-hanging branches and twigs under the beech tree. At her stirrup, an anonymous man in a demi-gown and Lion livery ran beside her, limping from an ancient wound. Mail and falchion: plainly just another European mercenary.

"Which way rides the hunt?"

"*Every* way!" the Visigoth *nazir* yelled, in the Carthaginian camp patois. Ash couldn't help a grin at his frustration. He threw his arms wide in a gesture of despair. "Lady warrior, what in Christ's sweet name are we doing in this wood!"

"Don't ask me, I only work here. You!" Ash sharply ordered Guillaume Arnisout. "Let's find the Burgundians, sharpish!"

Burgundians, hell: let's find the Lion Azure!

The ground was too bad to push the gelding to more than a walk. She spurred across the stream, Guillaume Arnisout splashing after her, and slowed again, riding forward. The sun through the tree cover let her see roughly where south might be. *Another couple of furlongs, and turn west, try and find the edge of the forest, and the river ford. . . .*

"Fuck of a hunt *this* is," Guillaume remarked, from beside her stirrup. "Bloody Burgundians. Couldn't organize a piss-up in an English brewery."

"Fucking waste of time," she agreed. She has enjoyed hunting, when the opportunity has presented itself: a noisy organized riot of a rush through bad countryside, not unlike war. This . . .

Ash removed her sallet again. She rode bareheaded in the chill wind, that the trees robbed of an edge. Too far, by many leagues now, to hear the bell tolling from the Dijon Abbey, and if there are two bells: if Charles the Bold has breathed his last. A brief solemnity touched her.

And too confusing to be able to tell which of the baying hounds, hunting horns, voices shouting "Ho moy!" and horses neighing—all glimpsed a hundred yards away, between tree trunks—which might be the main body of the hunt.

"Sod this for a game of soldiers." Ash checked the position of the Visigoth troops behind her. "Ease off to the west."

With Guillaume beside her, and the pale gelding picking a careful way between tree roots and badger setts, Ash rode across the trampled woodland floor. Briars held tags of cloth on long thorns, witness to men passing.

The white flash of a hound showed a furlong ahead, for a moment, questing busily.

Guillaume Arnisout, and a rider on a scrawny horse emerging from a holly thicket, bawled "*Gone away!*" at the same moment.

"There it is!" The rider—flushed, standing in her stirrups, hood down and hair thick with twigs—was Floria del Guiz. She spurred in a circle and pointed. "Ash! The *hart!*"

Within seconds, they were the center of attention: a slew of riders cantering up, with the red X's of Burgundian livery on their jackets; two *'arifs* and the eagle and a flood of serfs in munition-quality helmets pouring into the clearing; twenty huntsmen with leashed couples of hounds pounding between tree trunks, over fallen branches and briars, sounding horns. The hounds, freed, quested busily, bayed, and shot off in a long trailing column into the forest ahead.

Shit! So much for sneaking off—

A pale flash of color, ahead. Ash stood in her stirrups. Floria pointed again, shouting something, the horns blowing to let other huntsmen ahead know the hounds had been released drowned her out.

"*There it goes!*"

Two greyhounds tore past, under the gelding's hooves. The reins jerked through her fingers. Ash swore, blood thumping in her veins, pulled back, and felt the gelding gripping the bit between its teeth. He thrust forward into the crowd of Burgundian noblemen, shouldering aside a gray, and cantered beside a chestnut, partnering it, ignored Ash's attempt to bring him back by wrenching her weight back.

"*Ho moy!*" Floria bawled to the running hounds, riding stirrup by stirrup with Ash. Her face flushed puce in the cold air. Ash saw her dig her spurs into the scrawny gray's flanks, all caution forgotten, everything else lost in the wild excitement of the hunt. "The hart! The hart!"

With her legs almost at full extension from war-saddle to stirrups, Ash could do nothing but grab the pommel and cling. She flew ahead of Guillaume Arnisout. The rough, broken canter jolted her up and down in the saddle. Armour clattered. The gelding, trained for war, chose to forget his training, stretched out to a full gallop. Ash threw herself facedown as a branch whipped across her face.

Pain blinded her momentarily. She spit out blood. Her sallet was gone, fallen from the pommel of the saddle. She straightened up, yanked the reins, felt the bit bite, and prepared to haul the gelding's mouth bloody.

His ears came erect again, the noise of the hunt lost; and he slowed.

"God *damn* you," Ash said feelingly. She looked back, without hope, for her helmet. Nothing.

The wood's full of soldiers. I've seen the last of *that*.

The pale gelding lathered up, under his caparisons. Dark patches stained the dyed blue linen cloth. Ash let him place his hooves delicately, picking a way down the winding track. Pebbles bounced down ahead, into the chine. A crumbling chalk bluff rose up, out of the trees, raggedly topped by thornbushes and scrub. It was no higher than the tops of the trees beyond it.

The sun shone weakly. Ash lifted her gaze, expecting to glimpse cloud cover through the treetops. Beyond the bare branches, she saw nothing, only clear autumn sky and the white sun at treetop height. The myriad bare twigs and branches swaying in the wind blurred her vision. She reached up carefully with metal-shod fingers to rub at her eyes.

The sunlight lessened again: not its light, but its quality.

Fear constricted her heart. Alone, the rest of the hunt gone Christ-knows-where, she rode on down the slope. The high war-saddle creaked as she let herself rest back, pelvis swaying to the horse's gait. A faint haze of rust already browned the cuisses covering her thighs, and the backs of her gauntlets; and she smiled, thinking of how Rickard would round up half a dozen of the youngest pages to do the cleaning, back in Dijon.

If I get back to Dijon. If there is any of Burgundy left.

"Halloo!" Ash bellowed, bringing her voice up from deep in her belly. It did not crack, despite the dread she felt. "Halloo, a Lion! *A moi!* A Lion!"

Her voice fell flat in the wood: no echo.

The quality of the light changed again.

We're too late. He's dying; the last breaths—

Now, the wind blowing cold between the trees, all the high bare branches swayed, rubbing bark against bark, creaking and surging like the sea. The face of the chalk bluff glowed, as clouds do before a storm, when there is still some sunlight to gleam off their white ramparts.

"*A moi!*" she shouted.

Faintly, far off, a woman's voice called, "*Cy va!*"

Hounds clamored. Ash sat up and stared around, searching as far as she could see in any direction. No way to tell where the barking, yelping, and belling came from. The gelding, reading her hesitation, lowered his teeth to a clump of grass at the foot of the bluff.

"Halloo!" Cords rasped in Ash's throat. She swallowed, in pain, too scared to project her voice properly. "The Lion!"

"Here!"

The rip of the gelding tearing grass distracted her. She could not tell which direction the voice came from. Hesitant, she touched spurs to flank and moved off down into the chine. The shifting perspective of tree trunks as she rode hid any movement from her.

Above, a bird shrilled out a long call. Wings whirred. The gelding tossed his head.

"*A Lion!*"

Silence followed her shout.

The long slope ran down under beech trees to another stream. Briars overgrew the water. The gelding caught the scent. Ash let him drink, briefly. No hoofmarks dinted the banks, no footsteps, no muddied water from upstream, nothing to show any man had ever passed this way.

The air around Ash took on the quality that it has before rain: a luminous sepia darkness. By instinct, she crossed the streamlet and turned the gelding's head uphill, riding toward the brightest light.

A silent whiteness floated between her and the turf-crowned bluff. The owl vanished almost as soon as she saw it. She leaned forward, urging the warhorse on up and around the rise.

Coming up onto the shoulder of the bluff, she could look behind her, and to the west, and ahead. A faint mist of gray-black twigs met her gaze, interrupted here and there by the solidity of holly and evergreens. Nothing but forest top, nothing for leagues in every direction—and now, as she mounted the bluff, and could see over it to the east, nothing there either but trees: the ancient wildwood of Christendom.

No voices: no hounds.

Something white moved at the foot of the bluff, where it sloped down shallowly into the forest. *Another owl?* she thought. It was gone before she could be sure. Searching the line of trees, her eye caught a flash of another color—straw-pale, gold—and she was spurring forward before she thought, reacting to what had to be a man's or woman's uncovered hair.

The air tingled.

Riding bareheaded, helmet gone, chilled in the cold east wind, and alone, she could have wept to see even Visigoth soldiers. The small open space gave way to trees as she entered the wood again. She searched for the red and blue of Burgundian liveries, for the flash of light from a hunting horn, strained her ears to hear them blow the mote and rechase. *Someone, somewhere,* she thought, *must be working the main pack.* If they had a hart, they might have released the back relay of hounds, to bring it to bay.

The wind creaked in the branches.

"Haro!" she called.

Movement registered in the corner of her eye.

Liquid brown eyes looked into hers. The gelding snuffled. Ash froze.

Brown-gold animal eyes watched her, looking out of the lean face of a hart. Ivory-brown tines climbed the air above its brow—a hart of twelve, poised with one hoof raised, and its coat the color of milk fresh from a cow's teat.

Ash's knuckles tightened. The gelding responded, rearing up, lifting both front hooves from the leaf carpet. She swore, slapped his neck, and without her taking her eyes from the forest floor ahead of her, the white hart had gone.

"*Haro!*" she bawled, spurring forward. A spray of twigs lashed her, scratching pauldrons, breastplate, and her bare chin. A drop of blood stained her breastplate. Knowing only that the one hart in this whole forest must, if the hunters served the hounds right, bring the hunt down on it, Ash spurred hard through the trees—the ground open, the spoil heaps of charcoal burners scarring the earth—after the fleeing beast.

A screen of dark holly blocked her way. By the time she found a way around it, the hart was gone. She sat still in the saddle, listening intently; and could hear nothing; might—she thought in a sudden panic—be the last living soul in Burgundy.

A greyhound bayed. Ash's head jerked round, in time to see a dog sprinting down what must be a cart track from the charcoal burners' camp, its pads kicking up dirt from the deep ruts. In a split second, it vanished down the track. The deep thump of hooves on mud sounded, where it went: Ash had one glimpse of a rider—hooded head down, riding neck-or-nothing—and six or seven more hounds, strung out in a long line, and a huntsman in a dagged hood, his curved horn to his mouth; and all the small group were gone.

"God *damn* it!" She jabbed the gelding's flanks and shot off down the cart track.

There were no tracks.

Several minutes of casting up and down gave her nothing. She reined in and dismounted, leading the pale gelding, but nothing met her searching gaze except the hoofmarks of her own mount.

"They crossed this fucking path!" She glared at the gelding. It flickered long pale lashes, in disinterest and weariness. "Christ and all His saints help me!"

A few hundred yards down the cart track, the ruts became overgrown with brown grass. She led her horse, the noise of its hooves and the noise of her armor as she walked breaking the silence. Another hundred yards, and the track itself trailed off into bushes, briar, and fallen beech limbs.

"Son of a *bitch!*"

Ash stood still. She looked around, listened again. An older fear churned in her stomach: the knowledge that this was an abandoned track, that the wildwood covers league upon league upon league of land, and that once in it, men have died both of hunger and thirst. She put the thought out of her mind.

"This isn't wildwood. We'd be trying to climb over fallen trees if it was, wouldn't we? Come on, you." She firmly patted the gelding's nose. He dipped his head in weariness, as if he had been ridden far and hard; and she could not tell, trying to spot the direction of the sun, what time of the day it might now be.

White and gold moved in the forest.

She saw the hart plainly, against a green-black glossy holly tree. His smooth flanks and rump gleamed white. The tines of his horns rose up, sharp and forked; and he swung his head around as she looked, his nostrils twitching.

Wind from me to him, she realized; and then *Sweet Green Christ!*

A gold crown encircled the hart's neck.

She saw it clear in every detail: the metal pressing into the hart's forequarters with its own weight, dinting the smooth-haired white coat.

One end of a broken golden chain dangled down from the crown. The last link tapped at the white hart's breast.

iii

AS IF THE leaves did not bear old spines grown hard, the white hart turned and sprang into the holly. The green closed behind it without trace.

Ash strode forward, gripping the reins, letting the gelding find its own footing behind her. In the minutes that it took her to climb over rough ground to the evergreen trees, she thought nothing, only stared in front of her with dumb disbelief.

At the holly, she reached out first to touch the spines—no blood—and then bent and scrutinized the ground. No droppings. A slot, that might have been a hind's track; but only one, and nothing to be read from it. So smudged, in fact, that it might have been anything, a boar's mark, even, or an old track from days ago.

She tried to push the holly branches aside.

"Shit!" She snatched her hand back. A leaf spine, penetrating the linen glove under her gauntlet, had drawn blood: it welled red into her palm as she watched.

Beyond the shell of green leaves, the black-brown branches intertwined to fill the space there so tightly, it seemed no beast could get through.

She considered tethering the gelding, covering her face with her protected hands, and letting the armor guard her as she walked through the holly. Reluctant to be left on foot, she rejected the idea, and began to lead her horse on and around the great thicket of holly trees, on in a direction that might be west, but she could not be sure.

That all food, all water, was gone with her company units presumably now somewhere toward the ford of the western river was only a minor irritation.

Christ, I have to be there! They'll go in, even if I don't arrive. Thomas and Euen will see to that. But they won't get far enough to kill the Faris. I know they won't!

It was not pride but objective knowledge: her men would fight harder, and longer, if they had Ash there fighting with them, would take on trust her assessment of how necessary winning might be.

Undergrowth began to thin out. Blackened tree stumps made her think that a fire might have blazed there, a generation ago: the forest became alders and ash trees, none of them much more than fifteen feet high. Areas of brown grass grew, clear of thorns.

The gelding plodded exhaustedly at her shoulder, picking his way with her over moss-encrusted rocks. A milky light shone down from the sky. Ash lifted her head, looking for any clue to direction. She blinked, furiously, looked away, and then up again, through the alders' gnarled bare twigs.

White dots scattered across the sky, close to the horizon. Too low to be seen properly, they tugged at Ash's memory. She thought, *Of course. Stars.*

The constellations of autumn, pale against pallor, glimmered behind the noon sky.

Visible behind the weakening sun.

"*Cristus vincit, Cristus regnit, Cristus imperad,*" she whispered.

The wood creaked around her.

The ground dropped away at her feet. She could see nothing down the slope, only the bare tops of trees, some darkly glossy and evergreen. The brown half-dead grass was slippery under her sabatons and boot soles. She mounted up again, every muscle aching, and coaxed the gelding forward and down between the trees.

Red dots dappled the earth.

From the saddle, she could see that what covered the slope—what the gelding now trod under his hooves—were rose briars. Pale green briars, soft and easily crushed. The scent of bruised vegetation filled her nostrils. And roses, red and pink petals coming loose in a shower of golden pollen, releasing their sweetness.

Some last, sheltered autumn blossoms, she thought, determinedly.

The ground flattened out as she rode toward tall rocks, jutting up between the trees. Moss covered the rocks, bright lime green and bottle-glass green. Very bright, as if the sun, faint everywhere else, shone on these rocks—but when she glanced up, she saw only the milky star-dotted sky. The gelding stopped abruptly.

A tiny stream ran away between grass-fringed banks. White and red flowers dotted the grass. The stream ran out from a dark still pool between the rocks. Its black surface rippled, as Ash watched, and she saw with no surprise that the white hart had its muzzle down, lapping at the water. The gold of its crown was so bright now that it hurt the eye.

A rough-coated greyhound trotted around the rocks from the far side.

The dog ignored the hart. Ash watched it sniff busily at the edge of the pool, in which the hart's tines reflected perfectly. A second dog, its leash mate, joined the greyhound. They cast about, with no great excitement, then trotted back the way they had come.

Ash looked back from watching them vanish. She saw that the white hart no longer drank at the pool.

A cat with tufted ears watched her. Bigger than a lymer, as big as her mastiff bitch Brifault. Shiny pebble black eyes stared into hers, unbeastlike; its black lips writhed back from sharp teeth, and it squalled.

"*Chat-loup*!"[65] Left hand to scabbard, right to sword grip; reins tucked under her thigh—and the cat turned and padded off across the flower-starred grass, vanishing behind the rocks.

She patted the gelding hard on his neck—unwilling to see any mount's flanks ripped by claws, no matter how bloody-minded a ride—and dismounted. There were no deer slots, nor cat tracks, in the springy grass. The scent of wild roses filled her nostrils, dizzying her with the smell of long-gone summer.

"Deliver us, oh Lord—" she muttered aloud; managed not to say *Godfrey, help me, what do I do?*

In the part of her that is shared, a growing tension is becoming triumph. Becoming distanced, interior, infinitesimal sound:

'SOON! TO BE FREE OF YOU—'

'—DRAW DOWN THE SUN!—'

---

[65] 'Wolf-cat.' Possibly, by the textual description, a lynx.

'—REACH HER: OUR CHOICE, OUR CHILD—'

'—DRAW ON OUR POWER . . .'

Even the voices of the Wild Machines are stifled, in her soul, to a faint and immaterial chatter.

A horn.

"*Over here!*"

Ash stood, head cocked sideways, eyes all but shut. A voice, female, coming from—down the slope, under the alder trees?

The gelding's soft white muzzle thumped into her breastplate, compressing steel and padding. She muttered, "Oof!" and grinned at the horse. The gelding's ears pricked up, and he stared down the slope.

"Okay . . . if you say so." She sprang heavily up into the saddle, using a blackened tree stump as a mounting block. The saddle received her, creaking. She turned the gelding and rode carefully down the hill, ducking alder branches with fresh green curlicues of leaves budding from their twigs. "*Haro!* A Lion!"

"A Lion yourself!" Floria del Guiz, still astride the rangy gray gelding, and with four hounds and two huntsmen behind her, rode up out of the denser wood. The woman in man's dress rode with complete carelessness, bouncing in the saddle; Ash marveled that she stayed on at all. "Did you see it? We lost the scent again!"

"Did I see what? I've seen a lot of things in this past hour," Ash said grimly. "Florian, I don't trust half of them—roses in winter, white harts, gold crowns—"

"Oh, it's a white hart, all right." Floria urged her mount forward from the conferring hunters. "We saw it. It's albino. Like that pup that Brifault whelped in Milan." Her amused smile took on a note of scepticism. "*Crowns?* And you tell *me* to lay off the local wine!"

"Look, I'm telling you—" Ash began stubbornly.

"Cobnuts!" Floria said cheerfully. "It's just a hart. We shouldn't be hunting it out of season—but there you go."

The scent of roses fading in her nostrils, Ash hesitated, made as if to speak, and realized she did not know what she had intended to say. *This hunt is not important, there are men I should be leading, men* you *know; look at the sun!*

One look at Floria's intent, lost expression dried the words in her throat. She could not even say, *I am starting to listen to the Wild Machines, I can't stop myself—*

"The hunt's scattered over five leagues!" Floria pushed her hood back from her straw-colored hair. Shrewd, she glanced at Ash. "If Thomas and Euen can't find their way back to the Visigoth camp, that's good. If they do find it, they're dead."

"If they don't find it, we're all dead. I should have managed to stay with them!"

Ash hits fist to thigh in frustration, gauntlet scraping on cuisse; a woman with slave-short silver hair, in armor, astride a pale, muddy horse. The gelding whickered in complaint. Ash gazed up through the winter-bare branches of alders, but the sky is too milky—overcast with clouds, or something else—for her to see the invisible sun.

One of the hunters, red-faced and fever-thin, bends down at the foot of the rocks, his shaggy-coated greyhounds have their muzzles down at his side. A very faint baying echoes between the trees. There is the rich smell of horse manure, cast from the two standing beasts.

"There's no way we can take out the Stone Golem," Ash said, "so we have to kill her. Sister or not, Florian. If Euen and Thomas aren't putting an assault in right now, killing her, I think we're finished."

For the first time, the surgeon's attention seemed to shift from the hunt. Her eyes narrowed against the milky light. "What happens?"

Ash suddenly smiled: sardonic. "I've never been on the receiving end of a miracle before! I don't know. If anyone knows what it was like when Gundobad did his stuff, they've been dead far too long to tell us about it!"

Floria chuckled. "Shit. And we thought *you* knew!"

Ash reached out, gripped the woman's hand, slapped her lightly on the shoulder. The two geldings stood flank by flank. Ash saw how Floria's mud-spattered face was, under leaf mold and a scrape or two—obviously at least one fall—remarkably happy.

"Whatever's going to happen, it's . . . happening. Starting," Ash urged. "I can—feel it, I guess."

Simultaneously, as she spoke, white flicked in her peripheral vision, the greyhounds bayed and darted forward, one of the huntsmen sounded the call on his horn to let the Master of Game know his couple were released; and Floria del Guiz stood up in her stirrups and bawled, "*Cy va! Let's go, boss!*"

The hart ran between alder trees, a furlong ahead. Ash looked over the furiously humping haunches of the greyhounds, sprinting toward their quarry. Floria's gelding kicked up great tufts of grass. The huntsmen ran forward.

"*Sweet Christ up a Tree, you can't go chasing bloody deer at a time like this—!*"

The pale gelding jerked at her shout. It stumbled forward into a canter, across the rough ground, shaking every tooth in her head. She saw red flash as she rode by: realized they had gone from alders to mountain ash, and the autumn branches blazed with red rowan berries. Ahead, across the burned-clear ground, a dozen other dogs streamed into view, heading for the foot of the granite crags ahead.

"Florian!"

The surgeon, bouncing in her saddle even at a trot, lifted

her arm in acknowledgment without looking around. Ash saw her trying to stick her heels into her horse's flanks.

Son of a bitch, she's going to be off, or the horse will break a leg—

The deadfalls cleared. Under the rowan trees, moss and brown grass covered embedded chunks of granite. More light shone down: autumn sunlight from a pale, overcast sky. She lifted her head long enough to see that the tree-fringed horizon was clear, no pale dots of stars, and rode on at an agonizingly careful walk, her spirits suddenly lifting.

"*Florian!*" she bawled after the Burgundian woman. "Wait for me!"

A sudden cry of hounds drowned her out. Ash rode up the slope. Long skidding marks in mud showed where one of the huntsmen had fallen on the rocks. She guided the gelding between them. More hounds: horns; and shouting from ahead, at the foot of the crag.

"They've bayed it, Ash—*shit!*"

Floria's gelding became visible between the slender trunks of mountain ash trees. A short-muzzled, prick-eared alaunt[66] leaped up, biting the horse. Ash saw Floria kicking at it with her foot. The black hound jumping, snarling. It barked wildly.

"Come and get your bloody alaunt!" Ash bellowed furiously at the huntsman running through the trees. She spurred to Floria, kicked away the hound with her steel-shod foot, and turned to speak to the surgeon and found her gone.

"I have to get to the ford—oh, *shit*!"

Ash urged the pale gelding after the rump of Floria's horse. The wind there, between the rowans, blew keenly; she felt the loss of her sallet and the lack of a hood. Her

---

[66] Variety of huntinghound.

ear tips and nose reddened. She wiped at her nostrils with the heel of her hand, breath whitening the steel of her gauntlet's cuff. Floria pushed her mount ahead, on up the slope.

The land falling away now to either side, it was possible to see that they were coming up on a great shoulder of land that pushed up out of the leagues of wildwood. Whatever fire had blazed there, a generation ago, had cleared ancient trees. Fifteen- and twenty-foot-high rowans covered the slope. Red berries smeared the rocks, underfoot, crushed by boots and by horseshoes; two or three more couple of hounds pelted past; and Ash reached back with her heels and jammed her spurs into the gelding, that and sheer force of will bringing the exhausted animal up the slope to the foot of the moss-grown granite crag.

A fine trickle of water ran down the rock face. The sun flashed back from it, in sparkling chill brilliance.

The gelding sank its head. Ash dismounted, threw the reins over a branch, and plodded on, on foot, toward the ridge where Floria had vanished. A howling of horns split the air. Far down the slope to her left, a great mass of people—a few still mounted, most on foot—streamed upward, hounds with them; red and blue cloth flashed brightly in the cold air. The liveries of Burgundy.

Ash stomped on, breath heaving, chest burning, her armor no more restrictive than in foot combat—conscious, while she plodded up the slope, of the thought *I'll feel this later!*—and was overtaken by two burly men, split hose rolled down below the knee, sprinting after the hounds.

Horns blasted her eardrums. Two mounted men in gowns and rich velvet hats spurred up the rocky slope, ducking to miss the berry-laden boughs of the rowans. She swore, under her breath; topped the rise, and found herself in the bramble, briar, and leafless whitethorn bushes at the foot of the rocks. An alaunt whined, nosing the rock, and she put her hand to her dagger as it looked around at her.

"Try it, you little bastard!" she growled, under her breath. The alaunt dropped its muzzle, nosed, and suddenly trotted busily off to the right, around the side of the rock.

A great clamor of horns broke out to the left. She hesitated, panting, found herself among two or three dozen people—huntsmen and citizens of Dijon, women with faces flushed under linen coifs, running sturdily behind the hounds. No one glanced at a dismounted knight; they tore on over rough ground, heading around the rocks to the left.

"Goddammit, *Florian!*" Ash yelled.

Another knight—the Frenchman Armand de Lannoy: she recognized his livery—clattered past her, on foot, at the trot. He swung round to call, "I swear we have unharbored a dozen harts this day! And none yet brought to bay!" He half-skidded on the wet, cold rock, recovered himself, and ran on.

"Do I give a shit?" Ash rhetorically demanded of the empty air, raising her eyes to the bitter cold sky. "Do I? Fuck, no! I never liked hunting *anyway*!"

Between one heartbeat and the next, the voice of Godfrey Maximillian sounded in her inner ear:

—But you will have another Duke, if you can.

She bit her lip in the surprise of it, and winced. Her muscles shook in anticipation. In the same beat of time, other voices drowned him out: the braided roar that is chorus, convocation, crowd:

'IT IS TOO LATE: HE WEAKENS, HE DIES—'

'IT IS TIME: IT IS ALL TIMES.'

'—IT IS THE PAST WE CHOOSE; AND WHAT IS TO COME—'

'HE DIES.'

'HE DIES!'

'EVEN NOW, HE DIES—'

"God rest him and take him," Ash gasped in a moment of small, frightened devoutness. Knees and calf muscles aching, she pushed herself into a run, no farther away from the voices in her head, but not able to stand still. She ran, boots heavily thumping the ground, armor clattering, in the wake of the alaunt: toward the right-hand side of the crag.

Dry-mouthed, the metal enclosing her making her breath come short, she pounded across the rocks; threw her hands over her face, and plunged into the whitethorn bushes ahead. The six-inch thorns scraped the backs of her gauntlets. One raked her scalp. She shoved through, pauldron first, out of the bushes.

"*Ash!*" Floria's voice called urgently and audibly over the noise of hounds.

Ash stopped, dropping her hands from in front of her face.

Both the black and the white alaunts danced in front of the rock face, on brown turf, their handler crying them on. The white hart lowered the tines of its horns. Rump against the rock, rubbed green with moss, it glared at the dogs with red-rimmed pink eyes, flanks heaving. There was no crown around its neck, no links of metal on the churned-up earth.

The hart made a darting movement, toward Ash and the whitethorn. The black alaunt ripped, slashing its hind leg above the hock. The huntsman furiously sounded his horn, rushing about behind the dogs, tripping, and sat down hard in the frozen mud.

"Kill it!" Floria yelled, from whitethorn bushes a dozen yards away. The scrawny gelding loped off down the slope. Floria, on foot, rushed from side to side with her arms outstretched, shouting. The hart gazed at her, lowered its head, thought better of it, dropped its tines and slashed one alaunt across the blunt, snarling muzzle.

"Kill it, Ash! Don't let it get away!" Floria clapped her

filthy bare hands together. The gunshot crack of her palms echoed back from the rocks. "We got to see—who's Duke—"

"Why you need a fucking hart's entrails—for an augury—" Ash automatically drew her sword. The hard grip bruised her palm, through the gauntlet's linen gloves. Both her armor and the blade had a thin film of rust coating the polished steel. She moved out from the bushes, covering the gap that would let the hart run down the slope.

The huntsman blew furiously on his horn, still sitting on his rump in the mud. Faintly, hounds and people shouting were audible, but somewhere far off: behind the crag. The white alaunt darted in and suddenly yelped, body twisting. It fell to its side, heaving ribs slashed red and open.

The white hart backed closer to the rock, scattering droppings. Head down, a forest of tines fronted it, and it began to drool from its neat, velvet-nostriled muzzle.

"Ash!" Floria begged. "*Use* the dog! We'll kill it!"

Hearing the surgeon's voice, Ash found herself thinking of it not as a beast or a hunt, but as an enemy and a field of battle. Automatically she widened her gait, moved to the opposite side of the tiny space to the black alaunt, and lifted her sword to a guard position. Eyes on the hart, she moved left as the dog went right, watched its head drop to threaten the alaunt—

Between the tiers of white horn, shining as if the sun blazed down upon it, Ash saw the figure of a man upon a Tree.

Her sword point dropped.

The alaunt whined, backing off, tail tucking under its body.

Delicately as a dancer, the white hart lifted its head and regarded Ash with calm, golden eyes. Every detail of the

Tree between its horns was clear to her: the Boar at the roots, and the Eagle in the branches.

The lips of the white hart began to move. Ash, dazed with the sudden scent of roses, thought, *He is going to speak to me*.

"Ash! Get a grip!" Floria ran toward her, across the narrow space between the whitethorn bushes. "It's getting away! Get it!"

The black alaunt threw itself forward, closed its jaws in the hindquarter of the hart, and hung on. Blood splashed the hart's white coat.

"Hold the abay!" the huntsman bellowed frantically. "The Master's not here, nor the lords!"

"We haven't *got* it at bay yet!" Floria bawled.

The dog's muzzle and jaws stained suddenly red, soaking red on black.

The hart screamed.

Its head went up and back, and it staggered onto its knees in the mud. The sharp tines flailed the air. The huntsman crawled away toward the whitethorn bushes, a yard to Ash's right, and she could not move, could not lift the sword in her hand, could not tell the yelling and baying outside from the voices in her head:

'*No!*'

Ash could not tell which she saw: a hart with muddy, bloodstained sides, and red rolling eyes, or a beast with a coat like milk, and eyes of gold. She froze.

Someone tugged her hand.

She felt it, dimly, felt someone unpeeling her fingers in her gauntlet from the grip of her sword.

The weight of the weapon left her hand. That jolted her into full alertness.

Floria del Guiz strode forward in front of her, the sword

held awkwardly in her right hand. A woman in doublet and hose, with her hood thrown back to the cold air. She circled right. Ash saw her expression: intent, frustrated, determined. Brilliant eyes, under straw gold hair: all her tall, rangy body alert, moving with old reflexes—*of course, she's from a noble Burgundian family, she will have hunted as a girl*—and as Ash opened her mouth to protest the loss of her sword, the black alaunt feinted left, and Floria stepped in.

As fast as it happens in the field of combat, Floria reached out and grabbed one of the kneeling hart's tines. The sharp bone slashed up at her arm.

"*Florian!*" Ash screamed.

The alaunt let go of the flank and closed its square jaws around the beast's hind leg. The bite severed the main tendon. The white hart's body jerked back, falling sideways.

Floria del Guiz, still holding its horns, lifted Ash's wheel-pommel sword and shoved the point in behind the hart's shoulder. She laid all her body weight into it; Ash heard her grunt. Blood sprayed, Floria thrust, the sword bit deep in behind the shoulder, and down into the heart.

Ash tried to move: could not.

All lay together in a huddle: Floria sprawled on her knees, panting; the hart with the sharp metal blade and hilt protruding from its body lying across her; the alaunt worrying the hind leg, bone cracking in the cold, quiet air.

The hart jerked once more and died.

Blood ran slowly, cooling. The hart's relaxing body let a last flux of excrement out onto the cold earth.

"Get this bloody dog off me!" Floria protested weakly, and then suddenly looked up at Ash's face, astonished. More than astonished: frightened, pained, illuminated. "What—?"

Ash was already snapping her fingers at the huntsman.

"You! On your feet. Blow the death. Get the rest of them here for the unmaking."[67]

She put her empty hands to her sword belt, stunned with the astonishment of that.

"Florian, what part of the butchering is the augury? When do we know if we've got a Duke?"

A bright flash of color blinked over the whitethorn bushes: someone's velvet hat. A second later and the rider appeared, men on foot with him; twenty or thirty Burgundian noblemen and women, and the other hunters took up the call, blowing the death until the harsh sound echoed back from the crag and rang out far and wide across the wildwood.

"We haven't got a Duke," Floria del Guiz said.

She sounded suffocated.

What alerted Ash, made everything clear to her, was a sudden internal silence—no choral voices thundering in her mind, only a bitter, bitter quiet.

Floria raised her gaze from her bloody hands, stroking the dead hart's neck. Ash saw her expression: a moment of gnosis. She had bitten her lip bloody.

"A Duchess," Floria said, "we have a Duchess."

The wind hissed in the whitethorn spines. The cold air smelled of shit, and blood, and dog, and horse. A great hush took the voices around Ash, the men and women on foot and riding falling silent, all in the space of a second. The huntsmen blowing the death fell quiet. All of them silent: chests heaving, breath blowing white into the cold air. Their flushed faces were full of amazement.

Two men-at-arms in Olivier de la Marche's livery rode their bay geldings into the narrow gap between the thorn-

[67] The ceremonial flaying and butchering of the dead beast, often done on the spot.

bushes. De la Marche himself followed. He dismounted, heavily. Men caught his reins. Ash turned her head as the Burgundian deputy of the Duke walked past her, his creased, dirty face alight.

"You," he said. "You are she."

Floria del Guiz shifted the hart's body off her knees. She stood up. The black alaunt flopped at her feet. She pushed it away from the white hart's body with the toe of her boot, and it whined, the only sound in all the stillness. She squinted at Olivier de la Marche, in the pale autumn sunlight.

Gently and formally, he said, "Whose is the making of the hart?"

Ash saw Floria rub at her eyes with bloody hands and look around at the men behind de la Marche: all the great nobles of Burgundy.

"I did it," Floria said, no force in her voice. "The making of the hart is mine."

Bewildered, Ash looked at her surgeon. The woman's woollen doublet and hose were filthy with mud, soaked with animal blood, ripped with thorns and branches; and twigs clung in her hair, coif gone missing somewhere in the wild hunt. Floria's cheeks reddened, finding herself the center of all gazes; and Ash stepped forward, businesslike, gripped her sword, twisted the blade to pull it out of the hart's body, and said under cover of that movement, "Is this trouble? You want me to get you out of here?"

"I wish you could." Floria's hand closed over her arm, bare skin against cold metal. "Ash, they're right. I made the hart. I'm Duchess."

In Ash's mind, there is no sound of the Wild Machines. She risks it, whispers under her breath, "Godfrey . . . are they there?"

—Great is the lamentation in the house of the Enemy! Great is the—

Angry voices drown him out: voices that speak as the thunderstorm does, in great cracks of rage, but she can understand none of them: they rage in the tongue used by men when Gundobad was prophet—and they are faint, as a storm is faint, over the horizon.

"Charles died," Floria said with complete certainty. "A few minutes ago. I felt it when I put the deathblow in. When I knew."

The sun, weak in autumn though it is, is a perceptible warmth now on Ash's bare face.

"Someone's Duke or Duchess," Ash breathed. "Someone is—someone's stopping them again. But I don't know why! I don't understand this!"

"I didn't know, until I killed the hart. Then—" Floria looked at Olivier de la Marche, a big man in mail and livery, the arms of Burgundy at his back. "I know now. Give me a minute, messire."

"You are she," de la Marche said, dazedly. He swung round to face the men and women crowding close. "No Duke, but a Duchess! We have a Duchess!"

The sound of their cheer ripped the breath out of Ash's body.

That it had been some kind of political trick, was her first thought; that assumption vanished in the roar of acclamation. Every face, from huntsman to peasant woman to Duke's bastards, shone with a gladness that could not be faked.

And *someone* is doing—whatever it is that Charles was doing, whatever it is that holds the Wild Machines back.

"Christ," Ash grumbled, under her breath. "This lot isn't joking. Fuck, Florian!"

"*I'm* not joking."

Ash said, "Tell me."

It was a tone of voice she had used often, over the years, requiring her surgeon to report to her, requiring her friend to tell her the thoughts of her heart; and she shivered, inside padding and armor, at the sudden thought *Will I ever talk to Florian like this again?*

Floria del Guiz looked down at her red-brown hands. She said, "What did you see? What were you hunting?"

"A hart." Ash stared at the albino body on the mud. "A white hart, crowned with gold. Sometimes Hubert's Hart.[68] Not this, not until the end."

"You hunted a myth. I made it real." Floria lifted her hands to her face and sniffed at the drying blood. She raised her eyes to Ash's face. "It was a myth, and I made it real enough for dogs to scent. I made it real enough to kill."

"And that makes you Duchess?"

"It's in the blood." The woman surgeon snuffled a laugh back, wiped her brimming eyes with her hands, and left smears of blood across her cheeks. She edged closer to Ash as she stood staring down at the hart, which none of the huntsmen approached for butchering.

More and more of the hunt staggered uphill to the thorn-sided clearing below the crag.

"It's Burgundy," Floria said, at last. "The blood of the Dukes is in all of us. However much, however little. It doesn't matter how far you travel. You can never escape it."

"Oh yeah. You're dead royal, you are."

The sarcasm brought Floria back to something of herself. She grinned at Ash, shook her head, and rapped a

---

[68] St Hubert (died AD 727) is one of the saints credited with a vision of a hart bearing a crucified Christ-figure between its horns.

knuckle on the Milanese breastplate. "I'm pure Burgundian. It seems that's what counts."

"The blood royal. So." Ash laughed, weakly, from the same overwhelming relief, and pointed a steel-covered finger at the hart's body. "That's a pretty shabby-looking miracle, for a royal miracle."

Floria's face became drawn. She spared a glance for the growing throng, mutely waiting. The wind thrummed through the whitethorn. "No. You've got it wrong. The Bugundian Dukes and Duchesses don't perform miracles. They prevent them being performed."

"Prevent—"

"I *know*, Ash. I killed the hart, and now I know."

Ash said sardonically, "Finding a hart, out of season, in a wood with no game; this *isn't* a miracle?"

Olivier de la Marche came a few steps closer to the hart. His battle-raw voice said, "No, Demoiselle-Captain, not a miracle. The true Duke of Burgundy—or, as it now seems, the true Duchess—may find the myth of our Heraldic Beast, the crowned hart, and from it bring this. Not miraculous, but mundane. A true beast, flesh and blood, as you and I."

"Leave me." Floria's voice was sharp. She gestured the Burgundian noble to go back, staring up at him with bright eyes. He momentarily bowed his head, then stepped back to the edge of the crowd and waited.

Watching him go, color caught Ash's eye. Blue and gold. A banner bobbed over the heads of the crowd.

Shamefaced, Rochester's sergeant plodded out to stand beside Ash with her personal banner. Willem Verhaecht and Adriaen Campin shouldered their way through to the front row, faces taking on identical expressions of relief as they saw her; and half the men at their backs were from Euen Huw's lance, and Thomas Rochester's.

In all her confusion, Ash was conscious of a searing relief. *No assault on the Visigoth camp, then. They're alive. Thank Christ.*

"Tom—where are the fucking Visigoths! What are *they* doing?"

Rochester rattled off: " 'Bout a bowshot back. Messenger came up. Their officers are in a right panic over something, boss—"

He broke off, still staring at the company surgeon.

Floria del Guiz knelt by the white hart. She touched the rip in its white coat.

"Blood. Meat." She held her red hands up to Ash. "What the Dukes do . . . *I* do . . . isn't a negative quality. It makes, it—preserves. It preserves what's true, what's real. Whether . . ." Floria hesitated, and her words came slowly: "Whether what's real is the golden light of the Burgundian forest, or the splendor of the court, or the bitter wind that bites the peasant's hands, feeding his pigs in winter. It is the rock upon which this world stands. What is *real*."

Ash stripped off her gauntlet and knelt beside Floria. The coat of the hart was still warm under her fingers. No heartbeat; the flow of blood from the death wound had stopped. Beyond the body, not flowers, but muddy earth. Above her, not roses, but winter thorn and rowan.

Making the miraculous mundane.

Ash said slowly, "You keep the world *as it is*."

Looking up into Floria's face, she surprised anguish.

"Burgundy has its bloodline, too. The machines bred Gundobad's child," Floria del Guiz said. "And this is an opposite. The machines want a miracle to wipe out the world, and I—I make it remain sure, certain, and solid. I keep it what it is."

Ash took Floria's cold wet hand between her own hands. She felt an immediate withdrawal that was not physical:

only Floria giving her a look that said *What happens now? Everything is different between us.*

Sweet Christ. *Duchess.*

Slowly, her eyes on Floria's face, Ash said, "They had to breed a Faris. So that they could attack Burgundy the only way it can be attacked: on the physical, military level. And when Burgundy is removed . . . then they can use the Faris. Burgundy is only the obstacle. Because 'winter will not cover all the world'—won't cover us here, not while the Duke's bloodline prevents the Faris making a miracle."

"And now there's no Duke, but there is a Duchess."

Ash felt Floria's hands trembling in hers. The hazy overcast cleared, the white autumn sun throwing the shadows of thorns sharp and clear on the mud. Five yards beyond the sprawled body of the white hart, rank upon rank of people waited patiently. The men of the Lion Company watched their commander, and their surgeon.

Floria, her eyes slitted against the sudden brilliance of the sun, said, "I do what Duke Charles did. I preserve, keep us quotidian. There'll be no Wild Machines' 'miracles'—as long as I'm alive."